NIGHT OF

DEMONS AND SAINTS

Also by Menna van Praag

The House at the End of Hope Street

The Dress Shop of Dreams

The Witches of Cambridge

The Lost Art of Letter Writing

The Patron Saint of Lost Souls

Men, Money and Chocolate

The Sisters Grimm

NIGHT

OF

DEMONS

AND

SAINTS

A NOVEL

Menna van Praag

HARPER Voyager
An Imprint of HarperCollinsPublishers

NIGHT OF DEMONS AND SAINTS. Copyright © 2022 by Menna van Praag. All rights reserved. Printed in the United States of America. No part of this book may be used or reproduced in any manner whatsoever without written permission except in the case of brief quotations embodied in critical articles and reviews. For information, address HarperCollins Publishers, 195 Broadway, New York, NY 10007.

HarperCollins books may be purchased for educational, business, or sales promotional use. For information, please email the Special Markets Department at SPsales@harpercollins.com.

Harper Voyager and design are trademarks of HarperCollins Publishers LLC.

First published in Great Britain in 2022 by Bantam Press, an imprint of Transworld Publishers

FIRST U.S. EDITION

Illustrations on pp 235 and 291 copyright © Alastair Meikle
Map copyright © Naz Ekin Yilmaz

Library of Congress Cataloging-in-Publication Data has been applied for.

ISBN 978-0-06-293250-1

22 23 24 25 26 LSC 10 9 8 7 6 5 4 3 2 1

For Vicky van Praag. Life-Coach, Therapist, Writer
(co-writer of the short stories contained within),
Mother and Dearest Friend. I don't know
how you manage to do and be all these things
with such beauty and brilliance, but you do. You
continually illuminate so many people's lives,
including my own. This world truly is a brighter
and better place because you're in it.

An Entreaty

The human heart is a tender thing.
Easily bruised and easily broken.
Rough fingers will leave their marks,
And cruel words will etch their scars.
So take care, my love, to place your heart
in only the kindest of hands.
And hold every one in your keeping
as gently as you do your own.

Goldie

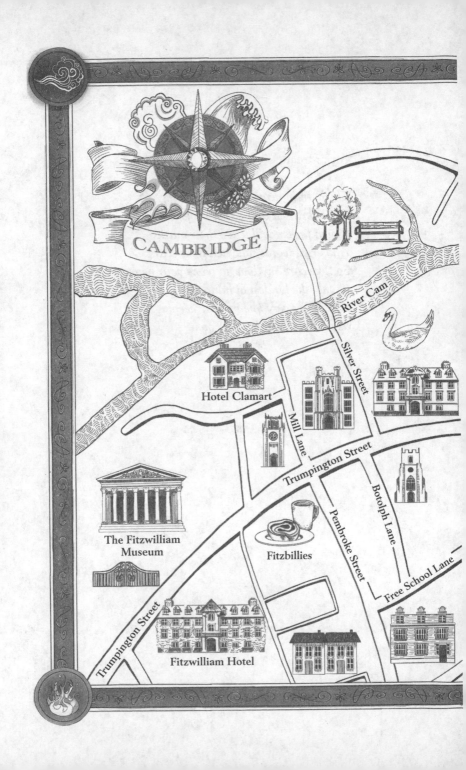

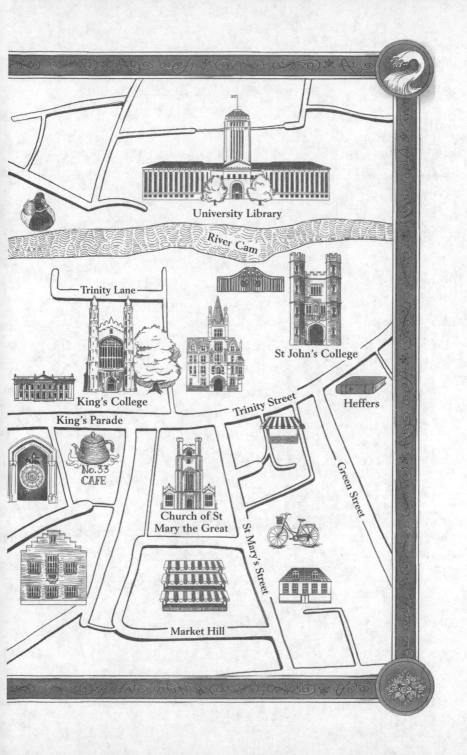

University Library

River Cam

Trinity Lane

St John's College

King's College

Trinity Street

Heffers

King's Parade

No. 33 CAFE

Green Street

Church of St Mary the Great

St Mary's Street

Market Hill

Prologue

All souls are special. Son or daughter, Grimm or not, Life touches her spirit to every one of her creations. But the conception of a daughter is a particularly mystical event, requiring certain alchemical influences. For, to conceive a being who can bear and birth life herself needs a little something . . . extra.

Every daughter is born of an element, infused with its own particular powers. Some are born of earth: fertile as soil, strong as stone, steady as the ancient oak. Others of fire: explosive as gunpowder, seductive as light, fierce as an unbound flame. Others of water: calm as a lake, relentless as a wave, unfathomable as an ocean. The Sisters Grimm are daughters of air, born of dreams and prayer, faith and imagination, bright-white wishing and black-edged desire.

There are hundreds, possibly thousands, of Sisters Grimm here on Earth and in Everwhere. You may well be one of them, though you might never know it. You think you're ordinary. You never suspect that you're stronger than you seem, braver than you feel or greater than you imagine.

THREE YEARS LATER

A Fallen Star

Once upon a time a star hung in the sky with her six sisters. She shone brightly at moonrise and slept deeply at sunrise and was happy. Then, one day, she fell to earth.

The fallen star was scared and alone, wandering lost through the wilderness, walking aimlessly through unknown places, trying to find her way home. Every night she sat beneath the twinkling sky and cried, calling out and shouting for her sisters. But the world below was chaos and noise, and her sisters could not see or hear her, and so they said nothing.

After many such nights the fallen star grew hoarse from shouting and weak from disappointment, and so she stopped shouting and began sleeping instead, just like everyone else. Having spent an eternity – or thereabouts – in the sky with her sisters, the star had never before been alone and it was a great shock. She sought solace in worldly things but every comfort was fleeting and only brought in its wake greater loneliness and heartbreak.

As the years passed the fallen star became more and more disconnected from who she had been and what she had known, until she could no longer remember her sisters or even her own name. She did her best to try and live in the world but still felt lost and alone. She tried to do the things she saw other people doing – work, marry, have children – but at the centre of it all she felt a dull grey ache in her heart and a nameless despair in her soul.

5

Finally, the fallen star decided that since she would never again feel happiness she may as well end her life, for at least then she'd know peace. So, one night, she went out into the woods to die. She wandered through the darkness, unafraid, searching for a suitable tree from which to hang herself.

When she finally found one, the star was surprised to hear snatches of chatter and laughter on the wind. Curious, she followed the sounds and came to a glade of willow trees where a group of women were gathered in a circle. They looked up at her and she back at them.

'Welcome,' one woman said. 'Please, join us.'

And so, she did. And, as the fallen star sat with the women and began to chatter and laugh with them, she felt the ache begin to lift from her heart and the despair begin to sink away from her soul.

For she had finally found, not the family she'd lost, but the one she'd never known was waiting for her: a family of other fallen stars.

20ᵗʰ October –
11 nights . . .

Goldie

'You're going!'

'I'm not.' Teddy stamps his foot. 'I'm not and you can't make me!'

'It's school, Ted.' Goldie sighs. 'You have to go, that's the law.'

She could make him, of course. With just a few words, she could draw out the tendrils of the spider plant sitting on the kitchen shelf and bind her little brother's legs, then drag him to school by his ankles. She could suspend him in mid-air, immobile and mute. She could rip every thought from his head, every memory from his mind, so he'd forget all about—

'The law?' Teddy sneers. 'And since when did you care so much about the law? You're a thief and a liar and I know what you did to Dad, so—'

'Stop it,' Goldie snaps. 'Stop it. Anything I've done has been to protect us. I've never done anything just for the sake of it.' She glances up at the clock. 'Now, you'd better go or you'll be late.'

Teddy glares at her across the kitchen table, his face so full of hate that, for a moment, she thinks he might be about to hit her. How did he grow so tall, she wonders, and so full of hate? Goldie remembers when he was skinny as a sapling, limbs so thin she worried they'd snap if she hugged him too tight, when he used to barrel into her every evening, arms flung wide, when he begged for 'just one more' bedtime story and for her to stay until he fell asleep at night.

'Go.' Goldie hopes she sounds more authoritarian than she feels. 'Now.'

Teddy hesitates a moment longer, then snatches up his bag. 'You're a bitch and I hate you!'

Goldie feels herself waver as the desire to renege, to plead for his approval, rises. 'And I'll be checking in with your teachers that you actually turned up,' she says, keeping her voice steady. 'If you bunk off with Brandon, I'll know.'

'Yeah?' he sneers. 'And if I do, what you going to do about it?'

Goldie holds her breath and slowly exhales. 'Don't test me, Teddy, okay?'

He looks at her then and laughs. He laughs as if she's the most naive, pathetic twit he's ever had the misfortune to meet. She stares at him. How *did* this happen? How did her dearest, darling Teddy turn into this insolent monster? Are all teenagers like this? She can't believe they are. Yet she knows that the blame for his behaviour is to be placed, at least in part, at her door.

'Go to your room,' Goldie snaps. 'And don't come out till you can be civil. You can tell Dr Biddulph that you're late because you were learning manners.'

'I don't have a fucking room,' he snaps back.

'Don't swear!' Goldie shouts. Curses strain in her throat and she tries to calm herself. She will not hurt him, not more than she already has. If only she could undo it all, if only it could be as it was when Teddy was a boy, when it was just the two of them and she was always here, her heart still hopeful, soft and unshattered.

'I'll swear at you all I fucking want,' he shouts back. 'Maybe if you weren't a fucking hotel cleaner, if you could get us out of this shitty flat, maybe if you weren't such a pathetic loser, I'd have some respect for you. But you are and you can't, so—'

Goldie's eyes fill. 'Please, Teddy,' she whispers. 'Don't.'

'Stop. Calling. Me. *That*,' he hisses. 'I've told you a million times, my name is Theodore.'

Goldie stares at him. He hasn't, has he? Surely she'd remember a thing like that. 'What? It's not – you're Teddy, or Ted. And neither of those are short for Theodore.'

Her brother rolls his eyes. 'I told you last month, at my exhibition. Ana was there, ask her. I reminded you three days ago at dinner, the one time you actually came home early, remember? I told you it's got class and . . .'

He talks on but Goldie's no longer listening, she's thinking to his art exhibition last month, the one Ana helped him organize at the fashion café in Finchley – what was it called? – and he'd displayed all his designs. So, why can't Goldie remember that? Why can't she remember anything about the evening at all? She tunes back in.

'If you paid any fucking attention, if you even gave a shit about me,' he's saying, 'you'd know who Ford is and why – Ana knows. At least she listens to me.'

Goldie stands up from the table, all at once full of remorse. 'Tell me again,' she says. 'Please.'

He glares back at her and again she feels the sharp slap of fury across her face. She stiffens, stepping back. His mouth is tight, cruel words waiting on his tongue. But then his blue eyes, the ones that mirror hers, the ones she could gaze into for hours when he was a baby, soften. He's about to tell.

Goldie offers him a hopeful, apologetic smile.

Teddy's fist tightens around the strap of his bag and he, now an inch taller than she, steps forward and leans closer, so there's only a breath between them.

'You're too late,' he whispers. 'You're too fucking late now.'

Then he turns and storms out of the flat, slamming the door behind him. Goldie watches him go, long after he has gone.

Later, when she's scrubbing the lavatory in room 23, and worrying about Teddy and the mystery of Ford, and thinking of how well she used to take care of her brother, when she was happy, when she was in love. She's still in love, of course, though now that's the cause of her deepest misery as it was once the cause of her greatest joy. So, surely she can be forgiven for retreating so often to the past. But as the past recedes and memories shrink and skitter away as she tries to grasp them, Goldie increasingly stumbles upon unpleasant places, remembering times she would rather forget.

Now, as she stands to flush the loo and stares down at the swirling water, she thinks of when her bastard stepfather flushed her beloved bonsai tree, the one thing she owned and adored. Her brother's goldfish had later met the same fate after her stepfather had accused it of glaring at him. Maybe she should buy her brother a new goldfish, maybe that would make him happy.

She thinks of how she was just after Leo died. And for a long time afterwards, she was often as absent as if it had only just happened, thrown back in time to relive it all. The neglect Teddy suffered and, if she's honest, still suffers at her self-absorbed hand. If not for her sisters, she can't bear to think what might have happened to him, to them both. For months, perhaps years, afterwards they took turns coming down from London with food and love and hope. She'd never noticed how *relieved* Teddy was whenever they arrived. He would fling himself into their open arms while she only shrank deeper into the sofa.

'Auntie Ana!' he'd exclaim. Or, 'Auntie Scar!' before launching into a story of what he'd done that day. 'I saw a woman wearing Louboutin Green Louis Spike Suede Sneakers at the park! But she'd paired them with yellow jeans, it was all wrong. I told her that black would've been much better and if . . .'

By this time Goldie had invariably stopped listening, though she still said: 'You did? That's great.' At the end of every anecdote, regardless of subject matter.

'If that's her style, it's okay,' Scarlet had said, ruffling his hair. 'Anyone can wear whatever they want, Ted. It doesn't matter, so long as they like it.'

'I suppose.' Teddy scrunched up his nose. 'But I still wish they wouldn't; it hurts my eyes.'

Scarlet laughed, pulling him into a hug. He'd always squirmed a little when his aunts hugged him, but the protest was nominal and he never pulled away.

'I've brought you fish for dinner,' Scarlet said. 'Sea bass.'

'Thank you,' Goldie always said, regardless of subject matter.

'We don't need fish,' Teddy protested. 'We've got six of your cinnamon buns in the freezer. That's my favourite dinner, the best ever.'

'Oh, Ted.' Scarlet planted a kiss on his head, then carried the bags to the fridge. Teddy followed like a duckling. 'But you also need to eat real food. Sis, Ana can't make it tomorrow so I've brought you extra, M&S ready meals – salmon, green beans, potatoes – you only have to heat them up, okay?'

Goldie looked up. 'Sorry?'

'The fish. The salmon, for tomorrow.'

Goldie frowned, confused. 'What fish?'

Scarlet closed the fridge. 'Why don't I stay tonight? Then at least I can make you a killer breakfast.'

As Teddy's whoops of delight echo away, Goldie returns to room 23 of the Hotel Clamart. She peers down at the swirling lavatory, at the fat, bristled brush she holds, at the radioactive yellow of her Marigold gloves. And she knows that it'd take more than a pet goldfish – or blue whale – to inspirit her brother's forgiveness.

Liyana

Do you ever think of who you were years ago and wonder what went wrong? It's something Liyana does more often than she should, given that she's not yet twenty-one. Life should be dreamy now, she thinks, shouldn't it? Yet none of the sisters are happy, none of them have been happy since they were children which, some might say, they still are.

As far as Liyana's two sisters are concerned, it's quite clear what went wrong: men. Goldie lost one and Scarlet found one. But since Liyana can't blame men for her own misery, she supposes it's her own fault.

Exactly when it – the losing of herself – happened, she isn't entirely certain. Liyana can still remember when she stood on the banks of a lagoon, naked after a swim, droplets clinging to her dark skin and springy curls, arms held up to the skies, luminous with joy and radiant with strength. The memory is blurred and dim, but it has not disappeared. Liyana remembers when she could boil water at her fingertips, when she could draw forth rain and – if she was feeling foul – thunderstorms too, the crack of lightning illuminating the skies of Everwhere, momentarily eclipsing the light of the unwavering moon. Liyana remembers when she was like Alice discovering all the magical delights of Wonderland, when she was like Lucy: daughter of Eve, Queen of Narnia. At eighteen, she'd thought that her magnificence in Everwhere would mean she would become somebody on Earth, but she is still nobody at all. A shell of herself: a river without currents, an ocean without waves, a lake without depths. A shallow puddle on the pavement, fast drying up.

'Come on, *Dagā*,' Liyana says. 'You've got to get up.' She strides across the threadbare carpet to the faux leather sofa scattered with the crumbs of half a dozen cheese crackers. 'And you've got to improve your diet, you eat nothing but biscuits.'

'Cheese biscuits,' Nya says, gaze still fixed on the flickering television. 'They've got protein.'

'Hardly.' Liyana tries to sweep crumbs from the cushions into her open palm but succeeds only in redistributing them in a greasy spray to the carpet. 'You need vegetables and fish. You've got to stop eating this shit, it'll kill you.'

She glances at the half-empty bottle of Asda chardonnay on the glass coffee table; Liyana knows it's not the first of the day. Nyasha takes a gulp of wine. 'I can think of worse ways to die.'

Liyana sighs, stooping to pinch up the crumbs. 'Oh, *Dagā*, what a thing to say. You don't want to die.'

There was a time, not so very long ago, that her quick-tongued aunt had been brimming with witty comments and a delightful font of inane information such as the calorie count of an Ottolenghi poached salmon salad or which Chelsea café served the most flavourful non-fat, half-caf latte. But it'd been years now since Nya had ventured out of Hackney to set foot in any place more hallowed than a Starbucks.

'Don't I?' Nya shifts on the sofa, reaching into her pocket

to pull out a packet of cigarettes. 'Because I can't really think of anything to live for.'

'Nya!' Liyana scrambles up off the floor to snatch the cigarettes. Her aunt pulls away but Liyana is too quick, scrunching the packet in her fist. 'You promised you'd given up.'

Nyasha shrugs. 'I started again.'

'I'm flushing these down the toilet.'

'Loo.'

Despite herself, Liyana smiles, relieved. 'You can't be so very miserable, if you're still giving me elocution lessons.'

'It's not elocution, it's . . . never mind. It doesn't matter.'

'It *does* matter,' Liyana says. 'Life matters, even if it's not the one we used to have.'

Nyasha returns her gaze to the television. 'This isn't life, it's . . . waiting for death.' She sighs. 'I honestly don't know how half the population lives like this; they ought to be euthanized.'

Liyana stares at her aunt. 'Nya!'

'Well, it's true.' Nya flicks her hand in a sweeping gesture at the room. 'What's the point of enduring all this if you don't have to? It'd be the humane thing to do.'

'You're appalling.'

'I'm honest, Ana.' Without moving her head, Nyasha lifts her eyes to her niece. 'It's all right for you. You're young and beautiful. If you wanted, you could have men falling over themselves to bed you – and wed you – you'd only have to give the nod.'

Liyana folds her arms. '*Dagā*, I've been with Koko nearly four years now, I think it's time to start accepting the fact that I'm not interested in men.'

At least, she hasn't been, not so far. But Liyana believes that sexuality is as fluid and the currents as changing as the sea. For now she is a lover of women in general and Kumiko specifically. As it was from the first moment they met; to know Kumiko was to love her. It was nothing and it was everything. The way she looked: small and slight, porcelain skin, midnight hair, dark almond eyes that seemed to take up half her face like a Manga illustration. The way she dressed: black silk, white cotton, red lipstick. The way she spoke: slow and soft, so you had to lean in to listen. The way she moved: seeming not to walk but to glide through life like a river fish. The way she was confident, certain, unlike any other teenager Liyana had ever known. And, perhaps most of all, it was the way Kumiko made Liyana feel about herself: as if she was exactly as she should be.

Ignoring Liyana's statement, Nya only shrugs and reaches for her wine glass, taking another gulp of chardonnay. Liyana strides to the television and flicks it off.

'Hey! I was watching that.'

'You've seen it a thousand times. Why don't I do a reading for you? It might cheer you up.'

'Unless you perform a miracle and pull the King of Pentacles then I doubt it,' Nya says. 'I'll get The Devil, I always do. So, you'll only hasten my descent into despair.'

Ignoring the histrionics, Liyana frowns. 'What do you mean, you always do?'

Nyasha shrugs again, as if it's of no importance.

'Have you been reading my cards?'

'Sometimes, when I've got nothing better to do.'

Liyana steadies herself. The Tarot is her sacred space, untouched, untainted by anyone's essence but her own. A surge of fury rises at her aunt's violation of her privacy. And then, as she takes a deep breath, Liyana realizes what this means. Hope. Nya would only bother consulting the cards if she believed, however infinitesimally, that there was a chance their dismal circumstances might one day change.

That night, Liyana shuffles the cards. She resists the urge to ask the question she always asks: when will success come? When will a submission of her illustrated stories be returned with a response other than the usual: *Thank you for giving us the chance to consider your work, which we thought showed great promise. However . . .* What she wants to ask, but never dares, is: will I ever be published? Or am I wasting my life trying and hoping to make manifest my longing when Fate has something else in store for me?

With a sigh, Liyana pushes aside her own doubts and fears to focus on her aunt. She's never done a reading for someone in their absence before. She doubts it'll work but thinks it worth a try. She'd snuck into her aunt's bedroom to borrow the silk Hermès scarf that Nyasha kept hidden at the bottom of her underwear drawer (and didn't think Liyana knew about) upon which she now lays the cards. She deals them out slowly, mumbling a prayer as she turns each one over: the Three of Swords, The Devil, The Tower.

Liyana gazes at them, trying to reshape their story into a happy one. But no matter how she tries to shape it, this is a prophecy of loss and despair. There is no polishing it up, no positive spin. She can only be grateful that Nyasha hasn't seen it herself. Liyana scoops up the cards and sets them aside. Then she lifts the Hermès scarf delicately in one hand, sneaks back into her aunt's bedroom and slips it into the drawer. Tiptoeing past the bed Liyana stops, leans over and kisses her sleeping aunt softly on the cheek. She would give all the magic at her fingertips to bring her aunt joy again but she knows even that wouldn't do it. All Nyasha wants is money and a man and, since Liyana has access to neither, there's little she can do. Except keep trying.

*

When her bedside clock ticks past two o'clock, Liyana surrenders to sleeplessness and reaches for the sketchbook she keeps under her pillow. Then she does what she always does when overcome by sadness – or, indeed, any emotion – she draws. Usually these are illustrations of the stories that Goldie (who doesn't yet know what else to do with them) has sent for the purpose. Tonight, Liyana rereads her sister's latest tale and wonders, again, how much autobiography it contains. As she wonders, Liyana begins scattering the pages with dozens of scribbled, howling wolves.

The Wolf Woman

It happened at night. She wished it wouldn't, she wanted to sleep. She wished it would happen in the daylight, but it could not; only when everyone was asleep, only when there was no one to see.

During the day the woman was consumed by mundanity: preparing meals, folding laundry, washing dirty plates. She paid attention; she did not shirk her duties. She took pride in doing everything properly – even if she alone noticed what had been done. She had learned this from her mother: 'This is your job and you must do it right. It will not matter to anyone else, but it should matter to you.' She had not explained why.

At night, when everyone slept, the woman ran. She shed her clothes. She felt the cool touch of moonlight on her bare skin. She ran until she fell to all fours, until her smooth brown body was spread with soft black fur. Then no one could catch her. She could have outrun a car, a train, a plane. She could have outrun Time.

Running was better than anything. More powerful, more sensual, more exquisite. Better than dancing, better than fucking, better than flight.

Sometimes she paused to glance up at the other women. Some were wolves, some cheetahs, some birds. The birds flew across the skies, over the houses and trees, their wild, jubilant cries tumbling out of the dark. The wolf woman could feel their joy, but she preferred to run. She relished the thud of her paws on the ground, not simply swooping above it all but beating past every constraint that – during the day – contained her.

She wished she could run during daylight hours. But she was too tired and anyway never had time. Demands filled every hour. Work must be done. Meals must be cooked and, once eaten, must be cleaned away. Clothes would be worn and must be washed. Beds were slept in and must be made.

She could leave, of course. She could leave the home and the husband and the children. She could leave the food and the laundry and the unmade beds. She could spend the rest of her life running. Often, she wanted to. But guilt and fear (and love) held her back.

And so the wolf woman sated herself with wishing, imagining and hoping. More than anything, she wished that she hadn't been born a woman but only a wolf. That she wasn't sliced in half, that she didn't know freedom, that she wasn't trying to live two lives having only been given one.

Scarlet

Scarlet doesn't often think on the past; why should she, when the present is so perfect? But sometimes she finds herself missing certain things: Cambridge and her grandmother's café and the days when they spent early mornings together in the hot kitchen concocting the No. 33 Café's famous cinnamon buns; Scarlet on tiptoe powdering every counter with yeast and spices and sneaking pinches of dough while her grandmother pretended not to notice. She would say she missed seeing her sisters every night, and Everwhere, and having electricity at her fingertips, but Scarlet tries not to think about those things. It's of no matter, she's happy enough without them.

For, even though the chrome sterility of her boyfriend's Bloomsbury flat hardly feels conducive to comfort cooking, Scarlet often finds herself slipping into the kitchen when she's unable to sleep to do a little midnight baking. When the scent of sugar fills the air and the grease of butter slicks her fingers and the dust of flour settles over her skin, she feels content again; almost as if she's stepped back into her grandmother's kitchen: always warm and womb-like, filled with sweet smells even if nothing was toasting in the oven, as if the walls had soaked up the scent of every bun and cake baked over the past fifty years. And after the cinnamon warmth wraps around her body and her shoulders sink into softness, then how can she resist eating a few of her creations hot from the oven with a cup or two of tea? Occasionally she'll make toast of a morning using only her heated hands, but often forgets altogether she has the power to do that.

Tonight, Scarlet isn't baking but cooking a three-course extravaganza to celebrate their anniversary, marking the day they first met: three years ago, when Ezekiel Wolfe first walked into her life. She's been to the market and bought two loins of venison, which she doesn't particularly favour, but Eli enjoys very rare, and plans to serve them with confit potatoes, braised kale and a red wine jus. This will follow a beef carpaccio and be finished off by chocolate soufflés with lime-coconut sorbet.

Scarlet's been planning the menu and preparing for weeks,

perhaps she's gone a little overboard with the decorations (having made one thousand and ninety-six origami hearts to represent each day they've known each other) but that's fine. She knows Eli will have bought her an extravagant gift, he always does, and since she doesn't have the financial means to do the same, she gives her time instead. And Scarlet has plenty of time.

It is just past eight o'clock and everything, having been timed to perfection, is almost ready. Eli is due home at half past, and Scarlet will set the carpaccio on the table just before he walks through the door. She's been scattering and hanging the hearts throughout the flat since he left for work that morning. Just picturing the look on his face when he sees it all makes her giggle, like a kid on Christmas Eve anticipating the delights of the following day.

At the last minute, Scarlet changes her clothes and puts on the dress. The silk dress she bought from Selfridges that has been limiting her usual intake of cinnamon buns in order to fit into tonight. She doesn't buy couture, for the cuts never accommodate her curves, but the dress wasn't cheap, probably equalling Goldie or Liyana's wages for the week. This fact weighs on Scarlet's conscience and she always avoids discussing finances with her sisters, though she knows they resent her anyway. She wishes she could level the playing field, but how can she when the money isn't hers?

The dress is green silk, Eli's favourite, and Scarlet lets her dark red curls slip over her shoulders, knowing that the colour complements her hair. And, even though Scarlet always feels she needs to lose at least a stone, even she feels beautiful tonight.

She sets the table with china plates and crystal glasses and slips the bottle of Boërl & Kroff Brut into the silver bucket of iced water. At eight twenty-nine she takes the beef carpaccio from the fridge, sneaking a sliver to appease the hunger scratching at her belly – she's not eaten since breakfast to ensure she can consume all three courses and still be able to breathe in the dress.

At eight thirty-five Scarlet calls Eli. And again, at eight forty-four. By five past nine she's leaving panicked messages and considering phoning round the local hospitals. She envisages him splayed broken-limbed on tarmac framed by a bloody halo, victim of an accidental but murderous hit-and-run. At last, on her twenty-sixth call, Eli picks up.

'Hey, babe, are you okay?'

'Me?' Scarlet, fear and fury colliding within her, tries not to shriek. 'Me? I'm fine. What the hell happened to you?'

'Oh, I' – the line cuts out – 'sorry, can you hear me? I had to work late. I meant to call, I just lost track of time. I'm sorry, sweetheart.' – the line cuts again – 'I won't be long.'

Scarlet glances at the kitchen clock, even though she knows the precise time – 10.28 p.m. – having been monitoring every timepiece in the flat for the past two hours.

'How long?'

'Half an hour,' Eli says. 'Not more than an hour.'

This is a joke, she thinks, an elaborate joke that'll climax in a grand and glorious surprise. Please, she thinks, please let him not have forgotten. It's all she's been talking about for days, which would mean he's been tuning her out.

'Do you know what day it is?'

Stay calm, she tells herself, don't screech, don't scream; don't scare him away.

'Um, Monday?'

'Not the day,' – her voice cracks – 'the date.'

21

He takes a moment longer. 'Er, the twentieth of October?'

'Yes. Ring any bells?'

'I . . .' He's silent, then she hears him curse under his breath. 'Shit. *Shit*. I'm sorry, Scar, I'm so sorry. We've been prepping a major opening, and a shedload of takeovers, I just . . . I remembered and then I . . .'

'Forgot.' Scarlet's eyes fill and she presses the heel of her right hand into her right eye socket, then the left, to stop the tears slipping down her cheeks. 'You forgot.'

'I did, I did and I'm sorry, but don't worry, I'll make it up to you. I'll pick up a takeaway – have you eaten – what do you want? Your choice. I'll even let you have the greasy Chinese on Dean Street.'

Scarlet takes a deep breath.

'What do you want?'

He's being kind, she thinks. Be kind.

'I don't mind. Whatever you want.'

He pauses. A penny drops. 'Oh shit,' he says. 'You didn't do something special, did you?'

Scarlet blinks, blurry eyed, at the table. A bottle of tepid champagne bobbing in melted ice, plates of nibbled beef carpaccio, forlornly empty glasses and all overhung with a disappointed burnt venison fug. 'No, nothing special.'

Eli exhales. In the background, she hears someone calling him. 'Sorry, babe, I've got to go. I'll make it up to you later, okay, I promise.'

Scarlet sits for a while in the aftermath of her failed dinner, wanting Eli to see what he missed, what he spoiled. But eventually she pulls herself up from her chair, exchanges the dress for jeans and an apron and begins the arduous process of cleaning every trace of specialness from the kitchen.

In the end, Eli returns even later than he promised,

crawling in just after midnight with tubs of cold chicken noodles, so Scarlet is able to consign every heart to the recycling bin.

Everwhere

In the sisters' absence, another has taken their place. It's easy for her, since in three years she has never left.

Bea soars through the Everwhere skies as the air beneath a raven's wing, until those moments when she has a mind to become the bird itself, to see black feathers glistening in the moonlight, to hear the shriek of her cries, to feel the rush of wind as she swoops up under the stars. When, on Earth, the clock ticks to 3.33 a.m., she visits the dreams of Grimm girls who don't yet know who they truly are or what they can truly do. And she whispers to them of what awaits . . .

It is a place, she says, her voice the breath of possibility brushing their cheeks, *a place of rustling leaves and clawing ivy, of mist and fog, of stardust and moonlight. This place never changes – the mists rise and fall, the fog rolls in and back over the rivers and lakes – but the moon never sets and the sun never rises. It's a nocturnal place lit by an unwavering moon that illuminates everything but the slithering shadows. It is an autumnal place, but with a winter's chill and hue – everything, water, stone, moss and tree, is as white as if dusted with snow. Every inch of the ancient forests, every one of the thousands of branches stretching to the starlit sky and the thousands of roots reaching out to the edge of eternity, is pale as bone.*

The entrance to this place is guarded by gates, perfectly ordinary if (often) ornate gates, that now and then – on that certain day, at that certain hour – transform into something extraordinary. And, if you've got a little Grimm blood in you, you'll be able to see the shift.

Stepping through a gate, you'll first be met by trees. They used to greet you with white leaves falling like rain, dusting a crisp confetti across your path that crunched under your feet as you began to find your way, but now the leaves no longer fall. Instead they cling to the branches, rustling their greetings, until you listen more closely and realize they're whispering their secrets to you . . .

Step carefully over the slick stones, or you may slip. Reach out to steady yourself, palm pressed to the bleached moss that blankets every bone-white trunk and branch. Perhaps you can already hear the rush of water, a vein of the endless river that twists through the trees, turns with the paths and spills now and then into lakes. The rivers and lakes are black as night, until the moon brushes her light over them and their waters ripple with pleasure in response.

You walk a while before you notice that everything around you is alive. You hear the breath of the trees in the murmur of their leaves – contented as purring cats – you feel the hum of the earth beneath the soil.

As your eyes adjust to the light you'll see the marks on rocks, crushed leaves, slips in the mud: footprints. Others have been here before and you're following in their footsteps. You wonder how many have preceded you, which paths they took, where they went and what they found. And so, you walk on . . .

As you walk, please be careful to avoid the shadows, for they are more spirited and far more dangerous than they might appear. Their predatory whispers will poison your mind and the effects will be as fast and fatal as arsenic. So please stick to the path, follow your heart and let it lead you to the others, just as they will be led to you.

Come now, Bea tells them. *Don't wait. Don't dawdle*

through your days and sleep through your nights. Don't waste what you've been given. Wake up to the fact that you're currently living only a half-life, you must discover who you truly are and what you can do. Time is passing at a clip and it will all be over before you know it.

Bea saves the most important entreaty for last; if she can't stir them out of their slumbers with pleas and cajoling, she hopes that an appeal to sisterhood might work: *there's a storm coming soon and your sisters are going to need you.*

21st October –
10 nights . . .

Liyana

Liyana takes a deep breath before sinking slowly under the water. After three years of living in a dingy council flat in Hackney, she's come to accept the mouldy walls, rat droppings in the corridors, stink of piss in the invariably broken lifts and the perpetual views of concrete high-rises, but she still resents the dismal little bathtub. Before her aunt had blown their entire fortune on gambling debts, when they'd still resided in an Islington townhouse, Liyana could fully submerge, starfish style, in their palatial bathtub and still not be touching the ceramic edges. She also had access to a rooftop pool, in which she liked to relive the glory days of her youth, pretending she still had a shot at the Olympics. Now, the only rooftop pool is the one which leaks from the neighbour's bathroom floor into their kitchen ceiling. Still, even with considerable squirming and shifting in this cramped plastic piece of shit Liyana can only completely immerse herself while assuming the foetal position.

Her shift starts in an hour. Eight until eight at the Serpentine Spa – an improvement on stacking shelves at Tesco, but only marginally. After twelve hours of enduring the condescending snobbery of the north London elite, she sometimes longs for the sympathetic silence of boxes of cornflakes and sliced white bread. While she shifts in the water, alternating between submerging knees and breasts, Liyana thinks of her aunt downstairs, slumped on the sofa, watching repeats of *The Antiques Roadshow* and lamenting the exquisite treasures she once owned. In three years, she hasn't stirred; still stuffing herself with cheese crackers and inhaling cheap chardonnay, Nyasha Chiweshe remains ensconced in her carefully curated bell jar of denial. And with the years that pass the glass thickens, so Liyana's voice – no matter how wise or well-timed her words – is never heard.

Now Liyana rises. Droplets cling to her hair and skin, unwilling to let her go. She uncurls her legs. *Shitty bath. Shitty job. Shitty life.* The dulcet tones of Fiona Bruce seep through the flimsy walls, triggering in Liyana a wave of fury that quickly gathers force. If Aunt Nya hadn't been so irresponsible, she wouldn't be in this mess. She'd be sitting in a bathtub that didn't cramp her muscles, she'd still be living in her family home, she'd be studying Fine Art at the Slade, or Illustration at Anglia Ruskin and living in Cambridge with Kumiko, instead of only seeing her every other weekend. Or, being immersed in the creative milieu, she'd have met a gallerist who wanted to exhibit her illustrations. What she wouldn't be doing is what she *is* doing: being unproductive and getting nowhere.

The furious wave subsides, drawn back by guilt, but soon swells again, undulating along the bottom of the bathtub. Water laps at the islands of Liyana's knees as she imagines slapping her aunt, while screaming loud enough to shatter the damn bell jar and finally shock Nya out of her catatonic state. Waves splash over the sides of the tiny bath as Liyana imagines seizing her aunt by her cornrows and shaking her so hard she starts to cry.

The water bubbles, so hot now that it starts to boil. With a yelp, Liyana scrambles out of the bath and slips like a seal onto the wet floor while curls of steam lift from the surface of the water. Reaching for a towel, Liyana feels a sob rising in her throat. She watches the water quickly cooling while her anger subsides – as it always does – into sorrow and she starts to cry.

'You don't think I'm a bitch?'

'Of course not,' Kumiko says. 'I think you're entirely normal. It's her job to take care of you, not the other way around. She's inverted the natural order of things and of course you resent her, it's perfectly understandable.'

'But she did take care of me, Koko; when I was a kid she did everything a mother would do. But now she's . . . I don't know.' Liyana sighs. 'She seems like she's sort of on the edge of a nervous breakdown.'

'Oh,' Kumiko says. 'That's shit.'

'Yeah, it is a bit.' A colossal understatement.

'So, what will you do?'

Liyana sighs. 'I haven't a clue.'

She closes her eyes to think on happier times, times when Nya attended every swimming competition, every class, every concert. She'd dropped Liyana at school and picked her up. She comforted Liyana every time kids threw insults or dropped thinly veiled insinuations, or outright told her to go back to Africa, though they probably couldn't find Ghana on a map. She was there when Liyana lost her first tooth and, five years later, when she ripped that ligament in her left knee, dropping her out of the Olympic race and into a depression for nearly a year. Aunt Nya sat by her bedside that summer, bringing food, brushing hair, reading fairy tales . . . She'd cast a lifebelt into the sea of despair and gradually pulled her niece back to shore. Nya had bought Liyana her first art book: *Ruskin and the Pre-Raphaelites*, encouraging her to draw and to dream. Without Nya there would be no expectation of exhibiting in the first place.

'Which train will you get on Friday?' Kumiko tactfully changes the subject. 'If you make it in time for dinner you can join me in Hall; Dr Skinner has invited me to High Table.'

'That's great,' Liyana says, and while she's happy for her girlfriend's glittering academic success, she's also (though she'd never admit it aloud) bitterly jealous. 'But I can't come this weekend after all; the bastard Justin's insisting I pull a double shift.'

When Kumiko is silent, Liyana knows she's in trouble. Kumiko conveys her greatest displeasure by saying nothing at all. After a handful of seconds, Liyana thinks she might have hung up.

'Koko?'

'He did the same thing last weekend,' she snaps. 'Can't you tell him to fuck off?'

'Would that I could, love, but he's my boss.'

'He's a jumped-up little shit.'

Liyana nodded, though Kumiko couldn't see her. 'You'll get no argument from me. Look, I've booked out the following weekend on pain of death, okay? Whatever he says, I'll be there.'

'You'd better be.'

Now Liyana is silent. We don't all have wonderfully supportive parents who fund half our exorbitant tuition and accommodation fees at St John's College, Cambridge. Some of us don't have the luxury of immersing ourselves in books all day long, of writing essays on etymology; some of us have to endure crappy jobs and even crappier managers.

'I will.'

'All right,' Kumiko says. 'Look, I'm sorry. I just miss you, okay?'

Again, Liyana nods. 'I know, I miss you too.'

With a sigh, she leans her head against her bedroom wall. In the crack between the wall and the bed she sees a large patch of damp and a spider's web housing a fat black spider. She closes her eyes to picture her girlfriend's face: skin pale as starlight, curtains of black hair that often slide shut, rendering her face a waning crescent in a midnight sky. 'I wish I was with you.'

'I wish you were too,' Kumiko says. 'Look, I've got to go. I'll call tomorrow, okay?'

But, before Liyana can answer, she's hung up.

Suppressing the urge to call her back, Liyana slides her phone under the pillow where it bumps against the sketchbook. She won't sleep tonight, she knows, for she'll be up drawing again. Perhaps she'll draw a picture for Koko and ask Goldie to write an accompanying story, an apologetic one.

Just as Liyana is sinking beneath the waves, her phone pings with a message:

I found you a new word: 'Plitter: to play about in water, to make a watery mess'. (origins: Orkney) Made me think of my favourite pluviophile.

Liyana exhales. The fear that Kumiko will leave her, will meet a beautiful nerd with whom she bonds over discussions of linguistical anthropology or some such, lingers like a stone on the riverbed. But it is all right, she tells herself; she is, at least for now, still loved.

She writes back:

I love it & I love you.

She closes her eyes and thinks on Kumiko, who knows her more intimately than anyone. Kumiko has not only touched every nook and cranny of Liyana's body but has also seen inside every nook and cranny of her mind. Kumiko knows who she really is and what sorts of magics she can do, though they rarely talk about it anymore. And, come to think of it, it's been a while since the touching too. It used to be – before Liyana was defeated by the various vagaries of life – that she made her girlfriend laugh with little tricks: conjuring fleeting rain clouds on too-hot summer days, re-heating cold cups of coffee, creating waves in swimming pools . . . In happier times Liyana had brought her powers into the bedroom, coaxing from an enraptured Koko a stream that flowed like the Everwhere rivers, and a grin as bright as the Everwhere moon.

Before Kumiko left London for Cambridge, they'd lain in each other's arms almost every night. Now it has been weeks, months, since Liyana has held an ecstatic Koko and far longer still since any rivers have flown or passionate, all-consuming kisses been shared.

Goldie

She used to be lithe as ivy and strong as oak, but three years of grieving have seen her pared down to a sapling and just as easy to snap. And she snaps all the time, over the most insignificant things. If the overprivileged hotel guests request their linen to be washed every day – have they not heard of the climate crisis? If someone jumps a queue – do they have no manners? Preachers on street corners – couldn't they try to save people's lives instead of their souls? *If you care so much*, she wants to shout, *then do something useful!* Feed the hungry, house the homeless, protect the weak . . . there is so much to do.

Goldie does what she can, tiny redresses to the massive

imbalance on the scales of social inequality. She steals frip-
peries from the rich and distributes them to the poor:
gourmet sandwiches, cashmere jumpers, stray ten-pound
notes. Sometimes the net of poverty is cast to include her
and Teddy, but only when absolutely necessary. Goldie still
steals designer clothes for her little brother now and then
but not so often as before; not because she's developed a
guilty conscience, but because he usually throws any couture peace offerings right back in her face.

Goldie waits for the day she will have recovered, forgotten, or whatever it will take for her to step out of the past
and into the present. But nothing happens, nothing changes.
Still she is steeped in loss, her breath is wet with sorrow, her
bones gnawed away by longing. Three years of unmet love
and thwarted desire has drained her blood. She's defeated,
slowly but surely dying. Sometimes her heart rages, sometimes it is quiet. But it's still shattered, it's never whole.
Sometimes her thoughts are white-hot with fury, sometimes bottomless-black with grief, sometimes grey with lost
hope. But never clear and fresh and new. Her sisters say that
time will help. *Time.* But the only thing time has done is
watch Goldie, hour by hour, being slowly whittled away.

She still writes now and then. Not the great novel she'd
once planned but small stories that sometimes burst from
her like sneezes; stories she sends to her sisters – most often
Liyana, who likes to illustrate them and tentatively suggests
they should collaborate on a publication, though yesterday
she sent one to Scarlet, since it seemed particularly apt for
her – but she bats away Liyana's suggestions and doesn't
deem the stories fit to send to anyone else. So, while there
still remains in Goldie a restless, occasionally uprising, creative urge which spills onto blank pages, the plan for the
great novel has long since been shelved.

Instead of writing into the wee hours, every night Goldie visits Everwhere. As a full-blooded Grimm, she doesn't need a gate, but travels on the coat-tails of her dreams. It's the simplest thing in her life: closing her eyes, slipping into that place between day and night, light and dark, one world and the next, the waking world and the world of reveries. It's the one thing she can do easily and well. Unlike almost everything else.

Goldie had good intentions once, of service and self-sacrifice. And, for a little while, encouraged by her sisters, she fulfilled them. But she soon grew tired, so tired, of doing things for other people. She could hardly manage to pull herself through the day without weeping, let alone be an *inspiration* to the younger generation; the effort it took was beyond her. So Goldie visits Everwhere not to see her sisters, not to educate the young or enlighten the old; she goes to only one place, the place she last saw Leo alive, the place she feels his spirit the strongest.

She can't see him, of course, can't touch him. Yet, sometimes, she's surprised by a whiff of his scent, a hint of wood, moss and sea salt on the misty air, and she inhales to breathe him in and sticks out her tongue to taste him. Most importantly of all, in Everwhere she can hear him. They don't have conversations; this afterlife is not quite so merciful as that. But now and then snatches of Leo's last words will echo through the trees, so Goldie can close her eyes and swallow his voice, can imagine that she feels his fingers slip through her hair. Occasionally, when the conditions are just right, when clouds slide over the unwavering moon, when the whispers quieten, when the breeze falls still, Goldie can trick herself that Leo still lives and is with her again. Only for a moment, the briefest of moments, but it is enough; just enough to keep her breathing until next time.

Goldie is so often living in her memories that she can recall conversations almost verbatim and images as clearly as if she'd photographed them. She can conjure scenes by closing her eyes, dipping in and out of these recollections as she might a box of chocolates. Today, she's thinking of firsts: their first words, their first kiss, the first consummation . . .

She'd been stealing a pair of blue silk socks from the French family in room 13 when she looked up to see him standing in the doorway, watching and smiling as if she was doing something incredibly wonderful, instead of slightly immoral. He stepped forward and Goldie gazed at him, anchored, still clutching the socks.

When he was only inches away, Leo stopped. Expectant, nervous, shy.

Goldie smiled: a reassurance, an invitation. Even then, she couldn't quite believe it had worked. She'd summoned him, commanded him. Just as the first time they met. Through sheer force of will she'd conjured him to her side. *Stop*, she'd thought. *Walk up the stairs, turn left. Open the door to room 13. Come in and kiss me.*

At her smiles, Leo cupped her cheeks in his hands, she tipped her head up to meet him, opened her mouth and let him in.

The first night followed not long after. She'd spent so long imagining that moment that it had felt entirely natural, normal, not at all new. As if she already knew every inch of him, as if she fit into his embrace, anticipated what he'd say next. It was so beautifully effortless, so easy.

'It's strange,' Goldie said. 'All I want to do is touch you.'

Leo smiled. 'Ditto.' He reached up to slowly draw his

finger along her face, following the shape of her eyebrows, nose, lips. 'You're a rose – no, that's too sedate, too commonplace, you're a . . . peony.'

Goldie laughed. 'I'm a daffodil.'

'Nonsense! And a rose is too tame. You're . . . cornflowers and peonies and . . . all I want to do is inhale you.'

'You're insatiable,' Goldie said, resting her cheek in his palm. 'I'd think you hadn't been with a woman in a hundred years.'

'I haven't been with you,' Leo said. 'Which is much the same thing.'

Goldie laughed. 'I bet you're with a different woman every night of the week.'

Leo smiled. 'Are you suggesting I'm something of a slut?'

'I don't think I used that particular word, did I?' Goldie said. 'A slight insinuation, perhaps. But then you're a man, aren't you, so—'

'—we wouldn't have been able to do everything we've just done if I wasn't—'

Goldie pinched his nose and he laughed. 'I meant, as a man, the more women you sleep with the more of a stud you are, as opposed to—'

'If I'd known you felt that way about promiscuity,' Leo said, 'I'd have put more effort into it before I met you.'

'Shut up.' Goldie gave him a playful nudge. 'You know what I mean.'

'But why is it strange?' Leo asked.

'What?'

'That you want to touch me. I'd have thought that was the natural thing' – he gave her a coy smile – 'in the circumstances.'

'Yeah, I guess so.' Goldie shrugged, not yet ready to tell the story of her stepfather. 'I don't know.'

'You say that a lot.'

'Do I?'

Leo nodded. 'Yeah.'

'Oh, sorry.'

'Don't be sorry,' he said. 'It's nothing to be sorry for.'

Being with him was effortless. And yet, there was much Goldie didn't know and didn't expect, most of all how it felt to be with him; a feeling she had never felt before. Not in her life, not with anyone else. It took a while to realize what it was. It felt *right*. And nothing in Goldie's life had ever felt right before. She'd always struggled to make things fit, to patch holes, ignore cracks, press mismatched puzzle pieces into place. But with Leo she didn't have to be what she didn't want to be or do what she didn't want to do. She didn't need to do anything different, anything special. Indeed, she didn't have to do anything at all. Just breathe. Just be. And that was enough.

It is unsurprising then that every day Goldie is stuck on Earth she only wants to be in Everwhere.

Scarlet

Scarlet sits in the cool of the kitchen, everything cleaned and cleared away, everything sterile and shining again. Eli is sleeping but Scarlet can't. She tried, for a while, but eventually gave up. It's a shame, because it'd be a relief to dream herself to Everwhere tonight, for perhaps her sisters will be there. She misses them.

Scarlet glances out of the window at the moon. Its silver light falls like a blanket across her legs – clad in flannel pyjamas – and she wishes she could pick it up and wrap it around her shoulders. She cradles her teacup more snugly in her lap.

Of course, Scarlet thinks, instead of sleeping she could find a gate. She's full-blooded too, so doesn't need to walk through gateways, but sometimes she likes to – the ritual is a pleasing one – though then she'd have to brave the cold and the dark, and, for a woman, walking alone on the streets of London – even Bloomsbury – is never the wiser choice. Scarlet can't recall the last time she walked into Everwhere through a gate, though she'll never forget the first time.

Bea had dared them all to do it, to leave their homes in the middle of the night and find the nearest gate. She was vague on the details of exactly how they were supposed to do this, mumbling something about intuition and 'special senses', so when eight-year-old Scarlet stepped into the street at three o'clock in the morning – having slipped out of the house while her grandmother slept – she was terrified of failing the test. But, as Scarlet walked, she discovered that, despite not knowing where she was going, she seemed to know where she was heading. So she walked on, meandering along pavements and across roads until she came to a stop twenty minutes later at the garden of Little St Mary's Church. The first gate, she knew, wasn't it and so she clambered over into the small dilapidated graveyard. Wandering along the unkempt moonlit paths – the newer gravestones shining as they caught the light, the old ones dirty grey and mottled with lichen – she reached a third gate. This one was locked and roped with ivy so thick it might not have been opened in a hundred years.

Surely, Scarlet thought, this couldn't be the one. Yet, at the same time she knew that it was. And, sure enough, at precisely 3.33 a.m., the moon (at its first quarter) shone its soft light on the gate. And, despite the rust and leafy ropes, it swung open with only a slight creak. Scarlet hesitated a moment before stepping through.

Now, for a single, surprising and strange moment Scarlet misses Bea. A flare of longing blazes briefly in her chest and then fizzles away. It's too late to call Goldie or Liyana, but Scarlet wonders what they'd say about the spoiled anniversary. She knows that Liyana doesn't think much of Eli, though Goldie's more forgiving. She thinks about the first time she'd kissed Eli, when he'd left, then, two days later, returned. Such relief and joy had sparked at her fingertips that Scarlet knew she was in trouble.

'You,' she'd said, as he'd crossed the café to reach her.

'You thought I'd kiss and run?' He'd smiled. A smile full of the promise of fire. 'What sort of cad do you think I am?'

'Oh,' – she'd met his gaze, sparks in her own eyes. 'I know exactly what kind of cad you are.'

'My, my.' Eli had laughed. 'You're a feisty one, aren't you?'

'It's the hair.' She'd held his gaze. 'But I imagine you already know that.'

'Actually . . .' Eli reached out to graze his thumb across her cheek. 'I've never had the pleasure of knowing a red-head intimately before.'

As his skin had brushed hers, Scarlet had felt a sudden and disturbing desire to have him scoop her up and lay her down upon the nearest table. Sparks had fired at her fingertips and she'd hidden her hands behind her back.

In three years she's never stopped thinking that Eli is the most beautiful man she's ever met.

Now the clouds glide past the moon and silver light shines through the window onto the tea in the cup she cradles in her hands. Scarlet stares, recalling another memory, that of moonlight caught on the surface of a lake. She had stood at the edge watching Liyana show off her tricks. Together they'd cast shifting shadows on the water, broken only by the current and the falling leaves. Scarlet had watched its eddies and swirls, as if the brook was being stirred by the hand of a water nymph. Another leaf fell. Liyana swayed and shaped it. Like a water god, she commanded it. She turned her fingers in circles until waves splashed on the riverbank.

Now, Scarlet rests a palm atop the teacup, eclipsing the moon's reflection. As her hand heats the cooling tea, she tries to remember herself back into Everwhere and takes a sip of tea. She should go back to bed and snuggle with her beloved. Instead, she stands and shuffles to the chrome counter to root about in the biscuit tins.

Gobbling bourbons from one hand, Scarlet tidies the counter with the other. A clutch of letters slides out from behind a chopping board where she must have stuffed them earlier that day. She shuffles the envelopes, ignoring the bills, then she sees a handwritten letter, her name and address in swirling inky script.

Reaching for a bread knife, she slices it open and pulls out a single page. Scarlet scans the sentences. It's not a letter but a story. And scrawled along the top, along with the title, are the words: *This one's for you, Sis, love G.*

The Good Girl

Once upon a time there was a little girl who grew up in an unhappy family. Her parents fought all the time. At first, the little girl joined in, stamping her feet and shouting whenever she was upset. Her parents punished her, shouting louder still and banishing the girl to her bedroom. Every time she was locked in the dark, the girl wept uncontrollably, fearing that her parents would never come back for her. Soon, she stopped being loud but kept silent and did what her parents wanted.

When the little girl did as her parents wanted, they were happy and praised her. And the little girl realized that it didn't matter quite so much what she wanted for herself, because what she wanted most of all was for her parents to love her. And so she was a good little girl and did as she was told.

The girl grew into a woman and soon she had a family of her own. The woman loved her husband and though he loved her too, she was scared that if she did anything to upset him he would leave her. So she did her very best to behave sweetly, dress prettily, agree with his opinions and never get angry. Because she didn't know any other way, the woman behaved in this way with everyone she met, nodding and smiling through every conversation, always careful not to disagree with or displease anyone.

Then one day the woman was shopping in the market and saw a new bakery on the corner. The baker was setting out loaves and pastries in the window, singing to herself a beautiful song. Drawn by the music and the scent of fresh yeast, the woman bought a loaf of bread, while her gaze lingered on the pastries.

'Does the smell of fresh bread not fill your heart with happiness?' the baker said.

The woman frowned, for she could not recall the last time she'd been filled with happiness. Then she quickly nodded and smiled. 'Yes, of course.'

'I'll give you a pastry,' the baker said. 'Which would be your favourite?'

'Oh no,' the woman said, shaking her head. 'That's terribly kind of you, but no I couldn't.'

The baker laughed. 'Come now, I'll share one with you. Take your pick.'

Embarrassed, the woman wanted to leave, but didn't want to be rude. 'I . . . I don't know. I'll have whatever you're having, I'm sure they're all delicious.'

'Naturally.' The baker laughed again. 'But that doesn't mean each will be equally to your taste.'

Flustered and confused, the woman mumbled her thanks, along with an excuse, and hurried away. Afterwards, she thought about what the baker had said and realized that she did not know what brought her happiness, be it pastries or anything else. She had never asked herself if she was happy, only if she was loved. She'd spent her whole life doing what others wanted and no longer knew what she wanted.

The next day she visited the baker again. For here was someone, the woman thought, who knew exactly what she wanted and who she was.

'I don't know my taste,' the woman admitted. 'I don't know anything about myself at all.'

'Not to worry, your voice has been long drowned out by the voices of others. But it's never too late to listen to your own.'

Tears filled the woman's eyes. 'But how?'

The baker considered. 'Well, it's harder to know what you do want than what you don't, so how about we start with that.' The baker stood, fetched two fresh croissants and set them on the table. 'Now, would you like tea or coffee with those?'

'Oh, I don't mind,' the woman said. 'Whatever's easiest, whatever you're having.'

The baker smiled. 'Then I'll bring you a triple espresso, the darkest and bitterest I have.'

For the first time, the woman gave a little laugh. 'All right then, Earl Grey tea please. No sugar, a splash of milk.'

The baker winked. 'Sounds perfect.'

When the tea was ready, she sat again. 'Now, tell me all the things you don't like, everything you really hate.'

The woman gripped the teacup and gazed into the tea. 'I don't know.'

'Indulge me,' the baker said. 'There's nothing so fun as a good rant.'

'Well . . .' the woman considered. 'I suppose . . . I'm not so keen when my son leaves his socks all over the house . . . or when my husband finishes my sentences and . . . I hate my boss, and accountancy is about the most tedious thing known to humanity and my mother-in-law is an absolute dragon, she thinks me beneath her beloved son, and he never defends me, sometimes it makes me furious!' She clapped her hand over her mouth. 'Oh dear, I didn't expect – I bet you think I'm frightful.'

But the baker smiled. 'No, I think you're a woman who is true and honest. I think you're a woman who knows herself. I think you're just the kind of woman I'd like to befriend.'

'Really?'

'Yes.' The baker tore off a bite of croissant. 'Now, if you stop doing the things and being with the people you hate, you'll start making space for finding the things and people you love.'

That night the woman went home to her family. Tentatively, she tried to say how she felt and what she didn't want. At first, it made no impact. She told her husband she didn't appreciate his condescension. He was incredulous. She asked her son to pick up his socks. He ignored her. Still, though she was scared, she persisted in risking the displeasure and disapproval of others. And, to her surprise, plenty of people – not only the baker – remained friends with her even when she disagreed with them, even when she said 'No'. And in these moments the woman finally knew for the first time in her life how it felt to be truly and fully loved.

When Scarlet has read the story she reads it again, and then a third time. She frowns, wondering what it is Goldie is trying to tell her. Is she supposed to be this woman who doesn't know herself, who doesn't understand who she is and is too scared to find out, terrified to know and declare her own desires? If so, then her sister is wrong. Goldie might judge Scarlet as living an empty, unfulfilled life, but what does she know? Scarlet doesn't have ambitions; she doesn't want what Goldie wants, she's perfectly happy as she is. A perfect future as she imagines it would be marriage and babies and . . . But another memory niggles. What is it?

Scarlet reaches for another biscuit and nibbles the rounded edge.

Something is out of sync, off kilter. Something's missing.

How many days has it been since she last bled?

Everwhere

Bea had not been a good person, not thoughtful or kind. She was truthful and often cruel. She loved, but she regrets how she treated those she loved. She's making up for it now, spending an eternity in service to her fellow sisters.

Come to Everwhere and you'll step into a glade, she tells them tonight, *where stones give way to a thick carpet of moss that sinks pleasantly under your feet. You step forward and the moss springs back. You stand and glance at the trees flanking this hidden space, so closely pressed together that their boughs might be entwined. You look up to see a canopy of branches and leaves so dense that the sky is no longer visible. And yet, as you squint into the darkness, all at once it becomes brighter: the shadows retreat, the sounds fall silent, the air stills. Gradually, the fog rolls back and the mists lift. The veins of the leaves glimmer silver in the moonlight.*

You notice that you feel lighter too. You begin to realize that each of your senses is sharper. You see the imprint of the shadows as they flit away, you sniff the ebbing scent of bonfire smoke, burning peat and kindling, you hear the call of a bird in the distance and you know, without knowing how, that it's a raven. The beat of its wings disturbs the air as it takes flight. You reach out to touch the nearest tree and realize that your fingertips are tracing the grooves of the bark before they've even been pressed to the trunk. You taste the dew on your tongue, though you've not opened your mouth: wet earth and salt.

You feel clear. You find that you know answers to questions you've been wondering about for weeks, solutions to problems that have been plaguing you for months. You feel calm. Well-stoked anxieties crumble and dissolve to dust. You feel content. Violent wounds soften and fade, leaving no scars inside or out. You stand and breathe the moonlit air, slowly and steadily, until you no longer know what's breath and what's air. Until you no longer feel where you end and the forest begins . . .

22nd October –
9 nights . . .

Goldie

After she's finished the washing up and wasted a little time scrubbing the chipped tiles above the sink, Goldie stands in the kitchen wondering what to do next. She glances up at the clock: 8.34, too early for bed. She thinks of Teddy, who hasn't come home for dinner and isn't answering his phone, and dearly hopes he's all right. Another uneventful evening stretches before her, yet she hasn't the energy to read a book or even watch TV. Anyway, what's the point? She might as well be unconscious. And then, as she starts to walk across the living-room carpet to slump on the sofa, she feels it rise up, like the twitch in her nose before the sneeze: a story rising to the surface.

Goldie darts to the sofa, seizes a notebook from the glass coffee table, and a pen, and starts to write . . .

The Paladin

There was once a scholar of literature who longed to be a poet. Reading poetry brought him great joy but attempting to compose it caused him great suffering. Still, it was what he wanted to do more than anything; if only he could write sentences as beautiful as those he read he would be happy. However, whenever he strayed from academic dissertations and tried to write words which veered from the rigours of the mind and into the territory of the heart, he would stumble.

The scholar wept with frustration over his furiously scribbled pages, sentence after feeble sentence obliterated as soon as it failed to reach the exquisite heights of heartfelt expression to which he aspired. One day, as he was about to tumble into an irretrievable pit of despair, the scholar asked his teacher for advice.

'Perhaps you're not a poet,' his teacher said. 'Perhaps you're a scholar and you must simply accept that. Very few people have such genius, after all, and if you were one of them, surely you would be able to write sentences of great beauty and truth.'

This statement tipped the scholar straight over the edge of the pit of despair on which he had been teetering. He stopped writing anything at all.

After descending into abject misery and wretchedness for many months, he picked himself up again and hauled himself out of the pit, leaving his disappointment – and with it his hope – behind; buried so deeply that he could no longer feel either of them.

The scholar found employment as a clerk and married a woman he loved. For a time he was, if not happy, then content with his lot.

One day, his wife was cleaning out cupboards and found the clerk's old notebooks bulging with furious scribbles and obliterated pages. She took them to her husband and asked him to explain.

He fell silent, overcome with a great melancholy, so that his wife soon regretted her question.

'I wanted to be a poet,' he whispered. 'A long time ago. But I could not write.'

'It is a difficult thing to do,' she said, moved by his sorrow. 'Yet every skill takes practice; why did you stop trying?'

'Because I believed that if I was a true poet then my words would flow.'

'Perhaps,' she replied. 'Or perhaps there is another reason.'

That night the clerk couldn't sleep and when he did he had strange, restless dreams. He dreamed of his father, who had died long ago, of his study with its locked door, of taking lessons at his knee, of gazing awestruck at the man he respected and revered so much as he spoke on every subject and could answer every question his son asked. Then here he is again, knocking at the oak door, clutching in his sticky fist a paper scrawled in childish script. His father had taken it, curious.

'It's a poem, Papa,' the boy says. 'I wrote it for you.'

His father scans the page, then hands it back. 'Give it to your mother,' he says. 'It's more her sort of thing.'

Then here the boy is a second time, with a child's fragile elasticity, presenting his father with another poem. The glance this time is barely cursory.

'Another one?'

The third visit is the final one.

'Son, you've got no gift for language,' his father says, ripping the page in exasperation. 'I do wish you'd stop embarrassing us both with these efforts.'

At this, the boy began to cry; snuffling tears that he tried to swallow even before they fell.

'No one likes a cry-baby,' his father said. 'If you can't take a little criticism you'll never get anywhere.'

The clerk woke in a sweat. His wife woke beside him and he told her his dream.

'Now I understand,' he said. 'It was not my ineptitude that stopped me, but my shame. When I put my pen to the page, I was haunted by the echo of his voice.'

His wife, who was wise and knew there was more to come, nodded and kissed him and went back to sleep.

The following night the clerk dreamed again of being a child. He stood in his father's study, only this time his father wasn't there. Instead, a creature with pointed ears and turned-up toes sat engulfed by the high-backed leather chair.

'Who are you?' the boy asked.

The creature folded his arms. 'I am your paladin.'

The boy frowned. 'What's that?'

The paladin rolled his eyes at the boy's ignorance. 'Your champion, your protector, your saviour.'

'Ah.' The boy smiled. 'You're here to protect me from my father.'

The creature clapped his tiny hands. 'Finally, he gets it.'

The boy frowned. 'You don't sound like a protector,' he said. 'You sound like him.'

'Exactly.' The paladin sat straighter. 'Now you're starting to catch on. I'm here to remind you every day of his words.'

'But why . . . why do you do that?' The boy felt his bottom lip tremble. 'If . . . if you want to protect me, why can't you be kinder about it?'

The creature looked momentarily confused. 'I'm not sure, that's the only way I know how.'

The boy considered this. 'I suppose . . . except when you do that, when you say the things my father says, it hurts.'

Now it was the paladin's turn to frown. 'No, but . . .' He trailed off, scratching a pointed ear. 'Surely it hurts more when other people say those things than when I do.'

The clerk woke, the paladin's words still echoing in his ears. At first he felt angry that his child-self had conjured up this creature to torment him privately so he could escape being tormented publicly. Then the clerk realized that although the creature had made him suffer, he had only been trying to help.

'Now I'm curious,' he whispered, so as not to wake his wife. 'To see what my words will be when I'm not listening to the echo of my father's voice in my head.'

Then, for the first time since he was a small boy, the poet sat down to write.

Goldie stares at the story for a long time after it's finished. She hadn't thought of that word – paladin – not since she'd learned it from Kumiko (that lovely fountain of lexical knowledge), and hadn't realized she'd remembered it until now. She hadn't thought about her stepfather either, not for a long time. Tears prick her eyes and this story, Goldie knows, isn't for either of her sisters nor anyone else but her; though what on earth she's supposed to do with it now she has no idea. Eventually, with a sigh, Goldie leans her head back against the sofa and closes her eyes.

Tonight, the conditions are right. Tonight, the sense of Leo's spirit will be strong. Goldie just has to wait. She sits in the glade where her lover died, her seat a tree stump overgrown with ivy, cushioned by moss. She sits with legs crossed, feet bare. She closes her eyes to conjure the unendurable image of the last time she saw him: tied to the great oak at the centre of the circle of trees, dwarfing and dominating them all. The tree he was tied to, the tree upon which he was slaughtered. Though there is no trace of that now.

It is overgrown, roped by thick vines of ivy, long tendrils that twist up the trunk, lassoing the branches, snapping off twigs and swallowing them whole. It's only been a few nights since Goldie visited, since she undid the growth, but all this has happened since. Change is so slow on Earth, so fast in Everwhere. And it feels as if the place wants to erase Leo's memory, to envelop his tomb until the tree is gone and the glade indistinguishable from any other. And so, every time she visits, Goldie must begin the uncovering again. As if she was standing beside his coffin and lifting the lid.

She takes three deep breaths and, with each exhale, the fog rolls back a little further, until she has a clearer view. She raises her arms above her head as if reaching for the moon. She presses the air, pulsing her hands together without letting them touch, until her fingers begin to twitch. Quickly, they find their own rhythm, staccato taps playing a piano sonata she can't hear or see.

After a few moments, Goldie opens her eyes to watch the ivy slowly unwind, retracting its tentacles, unwrapping each branch, slipping back into the soil until the trunk is free. Now the tree can breathe. Now Goldie can see the long lashes across the bark – flayed by her father's whip – the imprint of Leo's death.

She brings her hands into her lap again and waits. The misty air settles in droplets on her skin; she smudges them along the bridge of her left foot and thinks of Leo's spine: the constellation of scars, how she'd once stroked them so tenderly, how she'll never have the chance to touch him again.

A gust of wind whips through the glade, bringing the scent of wood sage and sea salt. Goldie inhales a deep breath and, for the first time in days, smiles. Not long now. The whispers of the leaves are falling silent. She'll hear his voice soon. In a minute or two, the clouds will slide across the moon. In the darkness she'll feel his touch and, for a few glorious minutes, she'll be able to pretend they are together again.

Goldie's heart quickens, the hairs on her arms rise and she grins, too giddy with anticipation to contain it.

She feels his voice before she hears his words – the first echo pulsing through the air. She closes her eyes.

Goldie, I—

She opens her eyes. It is not Leo's voice.

Her disappointment is so heavy and loud, such a thud in her chest, that it's a moment before she realizes whose voice it is.

'Bea?'

'Hey, Sis.' Bea's words are carried on the scent of bon-fires and charcoal. 'It's been a long time.'

It's a long breath before Goldie answers. 'Three years.'

'Do you forgive me?' Bea asks.

'Sometimes.'

The clouds glide over the moon, casting the glade into darkness. Goldie blinks away tears.

'I'm sorry I'm not him,' Bea says, hearing her sister's thoughts. 'I'm sorry he can't—'

'But why?' The tears fall. 'Why . . . why can I talk to you and not to him?'

Bea's sigh nudges the clouds past the moon and silver light fills the glade once more, casting long shadows from the trees.

'I don't know,' she admits. 'Perhaps because sisters are stronger than soldiers . . . or because this place is more hos-pitable to us than them. I don't know.'

Goldie sighs. The leaves of the great oak rustle in response. 'But . . . why are you speaking to me now?' she asks. 'It's been three years. You've never—'

'I didn't think you'd want to hear me,' Bea says. 'Not after . . . Anyway, I've never had anything to say that you'd want to hear. Until now.'

'I don't understand,' Goldie says, once Bea has explained. 'How is that possible?'

Bea's laugh is the crack of twigs underfoot. 'All you can do, all you've seen, and you still have such a limited idea of what's possible?'

'Yes, but ...' Goldie's thoughts ricochet. 'But ... resurrection? Surely that is—'

'Impossible.'

'Exactly.'

'Under every ordinary circumstance, of course. And usually it'd be beyond even your strength, but not on one very special night: on that night you'll be strong enough, skilled enough, powerful enough to do anything.'

Goldie raised her eyes to the top of the great oak tree. She wishes she could see her sister; it's too strange being given impossible information from an invisible source. While this thought is still lingering, a bird swoops down from its perch on a branch of the great oak. It settles atop a white rock close to Goldie's feet. She eyes the bird – a black raven with a single white feather on its left wing – curiously.

The raven cocks its head. 'Is this better?'

Despite herself, Goldie laughs. 'It's rather surreal, but yes, I suppose it is.'

'Very well,' the raven says. 'Then let me explain.'

'I still think you're crazy.' Goldie folds her arms across her chest and leans forward. 'But go on.'

The raven appears to shrug. 'It doesn't matter what you think, it only matters what's true.'

Goldie sniffs, though she can't deny it. 'So,' she says, still suspicious. 'So, what are you saying I should do?'

'You'll have the power to bring Leo back,' the raven says. 'On the night you turn twenty-one.'

'Why that night?'

The raven fluffs its wings like a self-important Cambridge professor donning his black gown. 'Of the 525,600 minutes in this year, there's only one that matters. It can pass in sixty quick seconds or last an eternity, depending on whether you're on Earth or in Everwhere. It's the moment of midnight, as the clocks strike twelve, as October ticks into November, as autumn wilts into winter and All Hallows' Eve becomes All Saints' Day. This minute is the moment you turn twenty-one, the moment your power will reach its zenith and anything, good or evil, will be possible.'

Goldie stares at the bird, at her knowing sister, as the final words of the speech are carried away on the misty air. And, in the silence, she imagines looking into Leo's eyes again, holding his hands, touching his lips . . . Later, she will tell herself that she thought about it, that she first asked questions about the particulars, ensuring that nothing too immoral would be involved. But, in truth, she did not.

'Well then,' the raven asks. 'What do you—?'

'Yes,' Goldie says. 'I'll do it. Whatever I have to do, I'll do it.'

Liyana

Liyana sinks down, slipping like a stone to the bottom of the pool. Languidly, she crosses her legs and closes her eyes, pretending she's sitting on sand with salt water soaking into her skin. One day, Liyana promises herself, she'll live beside a beach. She doesn't much care which beach, with water hot or cold, so long as the sea is within walking distance. Although, lately, Liyana's been wondering if Loch Leven wouldn't be the ideal place to live. Ever since spring, when they'd taken a long weekend break together to Scotland, Liyana has been entertaining fantasies of getting a job at the island hotel, a full-time position which would mean she'd have to stay on-site, if such a thing were possible. Imagine, waking early to dash along the pebbles and dive into the lake before anyone noticed you were gone. Liyana is fairly certain that public swimming in the loch isn't permitted, but that wouldn't matter since she'd prefer to go alone anyway. The allure of sneaking out very early or very late to take a clandestine swim is so strong that, when Liyana thinks on it for long enough – wherever she is and whatever she's doing – she could swear that her toes are wet and she has to glance down to check that she hasn't stepped barefoot into a puddle, even when she knows she's wearing shoes.

If Liyana didn't have Nya to look after, she'd be on a train to Scotland without a second thought. Of course, she'd miss seeing her sisters almost every day, but they could meet every night in Everywhere, so that would lighten her loneliness a good deal. Several times over the past few days, Liyana had tentatively broached the subject of relocation with her aunt, suggesting that a move up north might be beneficial for them both. However, the deft speed with which Nya shut the conversation down made it clear that, despite her beleaguered circumstances, she still wouldn't hear of leaving London. She might be living in a minuscule, mouldy flat in the rougher part of Hackney, but 'London is still the centre of everything and the only way I'm leaving is in a coffin. Even then, you'd better be sure you've nailed that lid down tight.'

Liyana lets out a slow sigh, opening her eyes to watch the string of bubbles rise to the surface and pop. She still has more than enough breath left in her lungs. If Justin doesn't interrupt her, Liyana could linger for hours. She'd come in early that morning and since the spa didn't open until eight o'clock, Liyana hoped for at least one long languid hour underwater. She needed to forget, to pretend. Pretend that Aunt Nya wasn't sinking deeper and deeper into the quicksand of depression, pretend that she hasn't had a fight with Kumiko, pretend that nothing at all is wrong.

So Liyana stays under, uncrossing her legs to glide along the bottom of the pool, trailing her fingers in patterns over the dark blue ceramic tiles. One day she'd like to have a bathroom decorated in these tiles, though they'd no doubt cost a fortune, along with a bathtub even wider and deeper than the one Aunt Nya had once owned, before she'd been bankrupted. Liyana swims lazily, imagining she has a mermaid's tail, imagining Kumiko is a mermaid too and they're floating together in Loch Leven, naked under a moonlit sky. Though they wouldn't be mermaids there but selkies, the seal folk of Irish and Scottish lore, streaming through the lake, the water slick on their oily skin, transforming into girls only upon reaching the shore.

'Liyanaaaa!'

Liyana looks up to see her supervisor, Justin, walking along the pool's edge towards her, his flip-flops splashing in the disparate shallow puddles of dispelled water. She swims towards him and, when they are level, she hoists herself out. His gaze lingers and she folds her arms over her breasts. This is the one aspect of working in water that Liyana doesn't like: being on display in her swimming costume. While she's in the pool, protected by a translucent but flickering veil, she forgets. But as soon as air touches her skin she hates it.

Justin steps forward, narrowing the distance between them, hemming Liyana in. If she steps back, she'll hit water. Eyeing him, Liyana tosses her head, scattering droplets like a shuddering poodle. Justin steps back. He's frowning, but won't display any weakness by complaining.

'How can I help you?'

'I need you to work Halloween weekend,' Justin says. 'We're throwing a costume party. Fancy dress mandatory.'

'I can't,' Liyana says. 'I'm already working this weekend. Anyway, I can't, it's my birthday, I've got a thing.'

Justin sighs. 'It's time and a half, double pay after midnight.'

Liyana thinks of her aunt, and how welcome the extra income would be, then remembers Kumiko. 'I can't.'

'Oh, come on, Ana. We need you, all hands on deck.'

Liyana shakes her head, less vigorously. 'Sorry, I can't.'

'Don't be difficult, Ana.' Justin sighs. 'Don't make me pull rank.'

Liyana takes a deep breath. She hates doing it, but she must. 'I'm . . . I'm only contracted to work one weekend a month,' she says, eyes on her bare feet. 'And I've already fulfilled my quota this month.'

She doesn't have to glance up to know he's clenching his jaw now and probably his fists. If there's one thing her supervisor hates, it's being told 'no'.

'All right, but you'd better not be late on Saturday.'

'I won't,' Liyana says. She's never been late in her life.

'And don't expect to be finishing early,' he adds. 'We're having a pool party for VIPs. I want as many staff here to schmooze as much as possible and it'll likely go on into the morning.'

'Yeah, fine,' Liyana says, swallowing a sigh. 'I'll be there.'

'Great.' He gives her another up-and-down glance. 'And wear something . . . nice, will you?'

Liyana, knowing exactly what he means by the euphemism, doesn't reply.

Scarlet

How is she going to tell him?

This was not the plan, not hers and certainly not his. They were supposed to get married first then enjoy lots of lovely time together indulging in spontaneous holidays

56

before finally having children in the vague and distant future, years later. She's not yet twenty-one. She needs to do something with her life first, before she surrenders her body, much of her time and most of her emotional equilibrium in dedicating herself to the welfare of another human being. What that something should be, Scarlet has no idea. Unlike Liyana she has no burning desire to create or achieve, she only wants to feel fulfilled, but is uncertain what will ignite that feeling. Being with Eli does it, so surely being with both him and his baby would be even better.

Scarlet hasn't slept for thinking about it. Questions, of what she should do and how, circle like planes over a city that never descend, their long trails of smoke staining the air and clouding her mind so she can't guide them down to land. She should call her sisters, she needs advice, other less fogged perspectives. But something holds Scarlet back, a sense that she knows what they would say and how they would react: it wouldn't be delighted shrieks of 'congratulations' amid jubilant embraces. And that's the only way Scarlet wants any declaration of pregnancy to be met. She cannot endure the humiliation of pity. If this is going to happen – and when the grey dawn light filters through the cracks in the curtains she's still very certain – then it will be a happy event, she'll have nothing less.

At breakfast that morning, Scarlet had said nothing. She'd kept the secret, words locked inside her mouth that tasted sweet as golden syrup so long as they remained unspoken. Once released, once heard, she didn't know how they would taste. In Eli's mouth they might become bitter as vinegar.

At dinner that evening, she said nothing. Eli was late, as was now becoming his habit. So she saved his meal – roast chicken with potatoes and green beans – wrapped in foil in the oven, and served it after ten o'clock when he finally stumbled with a sigh into the flat. Scarlet had fallen asleep on the sofa watching *The Great British Bake Off* and woke with a snap at the slam of the door.

Now she sits opposite him at the round oak table cradling a cup of peppermint tea while Eli pours his second glass of red wine and nibbles a green bean.

'You're not hungry?'

'I'm sorry.' Eli looks up, sheepish. 'I already ate.'

'Why didn't you tell me?'

'I didn't want to hurt your feelings.'

'You should've called.'

'I forgot.' He swallows the bean. 'I'm sorry.'

'It's okay.' Scarlet shrugs, wishing it was okay, wishing she didn't mind. She feels a sudden wave of fatigue, as if engulfed by a dense grey fog that's pressing on her body and trying to push her down. She sets the teacup on the table and rubs her temples.

'Are you okay?'

'I'm fine,' she says. 'Just tired.' And sad. On the coat-tails of exhaustion comes a great gust of pitch-black sadness that sweeps into her chest and settles, suppressing her breath.

Eli nods, not questioning her, poking half-heartedly at a small potato.

All at once it seems to Scarlet the worst thing of all that he's accepting her pathetic excuse, that he doesn't want to delve deeper, that he doesn't want to *see* her. All at once, she needs to be seen.

'I'm pregnant.'

The words have flown, like birds escaped from a foolishly unlocked cage, before Scarlet even quite realizes she has spoken.

Eli drops his fork. It clatters onto the plate with a sharp crack. They both stare at it, saying nothing. At last, Eli looks up.

'Are . . . are you pleased?' he asks.

Scarlet nods and, until that second, she hadn't known whether or not she was. 'I am. Are you?'

'I . . . I . . .' Eli stumbles. 'Give me a moment, I . . . it's a lot to process.'

Scarlet nods again. She twists a curl of hair around her finger while she waits for him. The contrast of red is sharp against her pale skin; she tugs until her scalp stings and her skin blushes with displacement of blood.

'I am.'

Scarlet releases the curl and it springs up. 'You are?'

Eli's face, set so seriously, breaks into a grin. 'I am.'

'Yes?' Scarlet is tentative, hardly daring to believe it. 'Really?'

'Yes!' Eli is bold, slipping off his chair and gathering her into his arms before she can take another breath. He squeezes Scarlet tight and she laughs, and he kisses her and her laugh lifts with her spirits, soaring up to follow the path of those escaped birds to the ceiling and out through the open window into the air.

'I love you, Scarlet,' Eli whispers into her neck. 'I love you, I love you, I love you . . .'

And, just when she thinks it's not possible to be any happier than this, he takes both her hands in his, looks into her eyes and says: 'Will you marry me, Scarlet Thorne?'

'I'm so happy, I can't believe I'm allowed to be this happy.'

'Well, you are.' Eli laughs. 'And I'm glad. At least, I am if it has something to do with me.'

Scarlet smiles. 'It has everything to do with you.' She's been waiting so long for this proposal; every birthday, anniversary, Christmas and Valentine's Day she's been hoping to be given a tiny box that could only contain one thing. And now, at last, it's happened. Without the ring, but that's of no matter. Not yet.

'Oh, yes?' Eli pulls Scarlet into his lap, hands sliding from her waist into her hair. 'Tell me more.'

'You don't get enough adoration already?' Scarlet says. 'I didn't think it'd been so very long since I told you how much I love you.'

'It's been at least . . .' – Eli pretends to check his watch through the thick curls of her hair – '. . . three minutes. I think it's high time you said it again.'

'Three whole minutes?' Scarlet laughs. 'That's scandalous. I'd no idea I was so neglectful.' She kisses his forehead. 'Then let me tell you that I love you.' She kisses his nose. 'Very. Very. Very.' She kisses his mouth. 'Very much.'

Eli laughs. 'That's more like it.'

Scarlet lays her head on his shoulder, her cheek resting on his cotton shirt. 'I've got the sexiest husband in all the—'

'—steady on,' Eli says. 'We're not married yet.'

'I know,' Scarlet mumbles into his neck. 'It just feels like we already are, don't you think?' She closes her eyes. 'I can't imagine feeling any more married than this, can you?'

Eli laughs. 'I haven't a clue, I've never been married before.' He reaches down to gently rub her stomach. 'Anyway, what's marriage compared to parenthood? In fact . . .'

Scarlet opens her eyes. 'What?'

Eli shrugs. 'Nothing.'

'What?' Scarlet lifts her head off his shoulder. 'What?'

'I don't know,' he says. 'It's just . . . this is more binding than gold rings and vows, don't you think?'

Scarlet sits up, pulls back. 'Don't think you can sweet-talk your way out of this, Mr Wolfe. You asked, I said yes. So now we're doing it and we're doing it properly. White dress – I don't care if it's hypocritical. Church. Flowers.

Three-tiered cake. Shrimp salad. Mr and Mrs Wolfe. Happily ever after.'

'*Mrs?*' Eli rolls his eyes. 'Really? I thought you were a feminist.'

Scarlet shrugs. She is a feminist. At least, she'd always thought so. But she wants this. She wants to be united, joined, a family in title and deed. And, if she'll lose her own identity in the process, then it's a price she's willing to pay.

'Well . . .' Scarlet is tentative now. 'Unless you'd like to be Mr Thorne.'

Eli laughs, not even dignifying this suggestion with a response.

'Or, we could double-barrel.'

'You can do as you wish, my dear.' He kisses her again. 'But I'm happy just as I am.'

Scarlet nods. For what other choice does she have? Briefly she wonders why the woman is the one expected to surrender herself for the sake of the whole? Why do so many women take their husband's surname and so few men take their wife's? A statement of inequality and disrespect, all the more galling since it's the women who bear and birth the babies; surely then they should be the ones to bestow their own names on their children, instead of the fathers with their roles limited to the moment of conception. Scarlet opens her mouth, then shuts it again, shelving this thought lest it interfere with her happiness.

Because she *is* happy, happier than she's ever been. She loves Eli and she loves their life together. Even though, despite their intimacy, there are certain things that Scarlet doesn't tell him. Like the fact that she dreams of Everwhere every night, or that she's got flames at her fingertips and can set fire to anything in an instant, or that when she presses her palm to her belly she receives a mild electric shock.

Everwhere

Tonight the raven Bea visits her sisters' dreams again, telling them the story of how those with only a little Grimm blood in them can step through the gates into Everwhere.

You don't need to know where you're going, for your instincts will lead the way. You only need to be out on the streets of your particular city in the early hours of the morning and, so long as you give yourself enough time for a little seemingly aimless meandering then you're bound to find what it is you're not sure you're looking for.

The timing is important – it must be the night of the first-quarter moon – and you must arrive at the gate before the hour and minute of 3.33 a.m. At some point you'll feel it: a shift in the air. But sure then that the next gate you see will be the one. It might not seem anything special, though usually the gates to Everwhere are ancient and ornate. Some are prestigious, others entirely ordinary. Perhaps the gate is the entrance to the British Museum or the Brooklyn Botanical Gardens, perhaps the Père Lachaise Cemetery in Paris or Kyoto University in Japan, perhaps it only opens into a private arboretum or courtyard. Wherever it is, wherever you are, the feeling will be the same and you will know it.

All you must do, at that certain minute and that certain hour, as the moon peeks out from behind the clouds to cast a silver shimmer over the curlicues of iron or finials of steel, is press your fingertips to the gate and give a little push. And it will swing open, as if it had been waiting for you.

'You're special,' Bea whispers. 'You can join us. Walk through a gate, if you wish. The experience has a pleasing sense of theatricality. But if you'd rather not, then come on the coat-tails of your dreams – set the intention before you fall asleep and it'll be done. Easy as anything.'

23rd October – 8 nights . . .

Goldie

Now it is all she can think about: bringing him back. *Is it really possible?*

Goldie thinks of all the things she'd once thought impossible: telepathy, astral projection, bringing withered plants back to life. When she was eight years old her bastard stepfather had flushed her beloved bonsai tree down the toilet. Pulling it from the water, she'd sat on the edge of the bath, cupping the wet tree – stripped of soil and leaves – in her palms. Gradually her hands grew warm then, all at once, Goldie felt a sudden jolt, as if the tree's throttled heartbeat had just twitched back to life. She had stroked every branch, every root; whispering encouragements to coax it back into the realm of the living. Three days later the first leaf sprouted, a bud of bright, insistent green. A small impossibility made possible.

So could Bea be right? Can she actually bring Leo back? Perhaps. Although, of course, resurrecting a bonsai tree is one thing, resurrecting a spirit quite another.

Tonight, she'd left Teddy sleeping – asleep, he returns to being the boy Goldie loves, kind and sweet and innocent again in his silence – and dreamed herself into Everwhere. Tonight she's hoping that her sisters don't show up; tries to banish them from her thoughts, careful not to call or inadvertently summon them. She cannot allow her sisters to interrupt when she reveals to Leo the plan. Of course, she has no idea if he'll be able to hear her, but perhaps he might.

We've only got a few nights to wait, my love, until I turn twenty-one, when I'll be capable of conjuring the necessary strength to do such an incredible thing.

For the past twenty-four hours Goldie has hardly slept but instead has spent every minute investigating – ancient texts, pagan rituals, the powers of past and present Sisters Grimm. She's been listening – to the murmurings of the Everwhere leaves, to the chatter of night creatures who speak of unknown things, to the deep wisdom and dark promises of the demons that lurk in the shadows. She's been watching: for blackbird feathers fallen across her path, for the clock to beckon her at 3.33 a.m., for all the signs that point in unseen directions and towards unimagined possibilities.

Goldie takes her time walking the path to the glade. She steps carefully over the slick stones, letting her feet sink deep into the moss, reaching out to trace her fingertips over the knots and whorls of every tree, brushing the leaves and listening to their whispers. She glances over at the silver shadow of the moon shimmering along the still river that follows alongside her path. Goldie forces herself to idle and lag, though she wants to rush, to sprint, to leap over rocks and fallen trees, flying to her destination, ignoring everything along the way. But that is not the right way to do a thing of such importance; it must be given all due reverence and gravitas. So she will walk when she wants to run, she will pay attention to every leaf when she wants to brush them away, she will breathe deeply when she can barely – for the excitement – breathe at all.

Goldie's patience is rewarded when she finally steps into the glade. Her senses are heightened, as if she could hear a leaf fall on the other side of Everwhere, as if she could hear an echo of Leo's voice before it's even quivered the air. His breath is on the mists tonight, his touch is the light of the moon.

Goldie steps slowly across the glade towards her seat, passing her hand over the tree stump, with a twist of her fingers flattening out the moss, softening it. And then she changes her mind, for beside the tree stump is a flat rock that tonight feels more fitting as a seat.

Bending down, Goldie rolls the rock over the carpet of ivy and moss, pushing it up against the trunk of Leo's tree. The gesture is perhaps a little morbid: since this bleached stone now resting on the spot where he died is effectively his gravestone. Still, Goldie doesn't mind, she only wants to get as close to him as it's possible to be.

She takes three long, deep breaths.

'I'm going to save you,' she whispers. 'In eight days, when I'm at my strongest, I will bring you back to life.'

She waits for an echo of Leo's voice on the breeze. She waits for a sign to show her that he's here, that he's listening, that, somehow, he hears her, that, somehow, he *knows*. But her hope is met with no friendly voice, no friendly sign – nothing. For one cruel moment, Goldie fears it's all for naught, that she's only fuelled by hope and imagination, that Leo really is forever gone, that she will never see him again. Then she remembers her plan and she remembers her power and she pushes aside her doubt.

'I will resurrect you,' Goldie says into the silence. 'We will be together again.'

Liyana

In the flickering fluorescent light of the hospital room, Liyana tries to blink away what she'd seen but can't. Every time she hooks a distraction for more than a moment it slips from her grasp and her eye is drawn back again: Aunt Nya slipped from the sofa onto the floor, a half-full bottle of wine on the table, the glass rolled to the carpet, the bottle of spilled pills almost hidden under her splayed arm, a bloody gash across her cheek, already swelling, where she hit the table's edge as she fell.

Liyana sits only a few feet from the bed where Nya lies sleeping, her stomach pumped, her breathing shallow, her rich dark skin mottled and blotched under the lights, her hair fuzzy and unbrushed. Liyana can't bear to look, not only for the sorrow the sight evokes but because she's embarrassed, knowing the shame Nya would feel to be on display looking like this.

Years ago, as a rich wife, Nya had spent small fortunes on facials and salons, spas and gyms. She'd been a client of Dr Suha Kersh, the Paris surgeon and Botox *artiste extraordinaire*; she'd never let anything less than cashmere or silk clothe her and wouldn't have been caught dead in public without a full face of Bobbi Brown.

Liyana wishes she could dress up her sleeping aunt, pull off the hideous pink NHS hospital nightie and slip on her silk pyjamas instead. How thin Nya has become, Liyana sees, her long body barely a bump beneath the covers. Of course, her aunt had always been very slim, in the way that most upper middle-class London wives were, but she'd never crossed the line into skeletal. How long has she looked like this, Liyana wonders, and how hadn't she noticed before?

Liyana wipes her eyes. She keeps her mouth firmly closed, but guilt still seeps through her lips every time she takes a breath. The taste is bitter, as if she's filling her lungs with burnt smoke. She wishes Kumiko was here, wishes she was gripping her hand and holding her gaze so Liyana would be more easily able to avoid looking at her aunt. Her girlfriend would provide a kindly flow of small talk to drag away Liyana's thoughts which now string themselves together like chains to flay her. Liyana knows that if she called Koko, even at two o'clock in the morning, she would come. And it's not because she doesn't want to disturb her that Liyana hesitates but for some deeper, darker reason that Liyana neither understands nor wants, in this moment, to investigate. Instead, she tries to fall asleep.

Eventually, Liyana's thoughts settle and her breath slows till a merciful sleep switches off the flickering fluorescent hospital lights, spiriting Liyana from the hospital room and into Everwhere. As she steps onto stone and moss, opening her eyes to gaze up at the friendly unwavering moon and the trees reaching towards the sky, feeling the misty air softening her parched skin, Liyana begins the search for her sisters.

When they seek each other in Everwhere they use the compass of their instincts to find the glade or clearing, the fallen tree trunk or rock upon which the other sits and waits. Tonight, Liyana follows one of the many veins of the rivers that run on and on, twisting through the trees, turning with the paths, snaking across the infinite landscape stretching to horizons never seen. As she walks, Liyana listens to the soothing rush of water, the pulse of her own blood syncing with its rhythm until her heartbeat slows and she feels a fresh sense of peace wash through her body.

It's not long before Liyana is tugged away from the river and towards a circle of willow trees. Reluctantly, she follows her instinct and leaves the water behind as she walks towards the trees. The fog hangs low and Liyana can only make out the shape of a woman standing beside a curtain of leaves that she brushes back and forth with her fingers the way Liyana would luxuriate under a waterfall.

It must be Goldie, she thinks. But as Liyana approaches, she realizes that the woman isn't either of her sisters, but a stranger.

When Liyana's a few feet away the woman turns and exclaims, 'Lili, at last!'

Liyana holds herself back from the grinning woman who, arms now outstretched, is bouncing on her toes as if about to fling herself at Liyana and never let her go. The woman is short and plump, with skin the colour of the ocean's depths and a halo of hair the colour and texture of dandelion fluff. A memory tugs at Liyana's skirts. She frowns, trying to remember.

'Who are you?'

'Oh, Lili, don't tell me you don't know your own aunt!'

Liyana thinks of Nya, her only known aunt, unconscious in the hospital bed. The one who, like everyone else, calls her 'Ana'. No one calls her 'Lili'.

'My aunt?'

'Your *other* aunt.' The stranger doesn't stop smiling. 'Your secret aunt.'

Liyana's frown deepens. 'My secret aunt?'

The woman nods, dropping her arms to her rounded sides. 'The one your mother never told you about, the one she feared would corrupt you, the one she pretended was dead.'

Liyana feels herself flailing in a current of confusion. 'Dead?'

The woman waves her hand dismissively. 'Oh, all that's water under the bridge now, my little water nymph. She forbade me to contact you, meet you here, till you turned twenty-one.' She winks. 'But what's a few days between family?'

Liyana stares at her secret aunt. 'I don't understand . . . How did you . . . ?'

'Oh, the whys are neither here nor there.' The aunt waves a hand to dismiss such questions. 'You know how your mother was, no doubt suspected I'd corrupt you with my wicked ways.' She giggles. 'But the how is easy enough, because I'm like you.'

Liyana frowns. 'You're a Grimm?'

The woman claps, as if Liyana has just performed a magic trick. 'Indeed I am, my little mermaid, indeed I am. Now, come and give your Aunt Sisi a hug!'

Liyana hangs back; then, when the woman widens her arms again, takes a tentative step forward. This is enough for her secret aunt, who rushes forward with a speed that belies her size and sweeps Liyana into a long, deep hug. At first, Liyana is stiff, her own arms at her sides, then she softens and lets out a small sigh. Now, she remembers *this*. A hug from Aunt Sisi is the softest, most spirit-lifting, soul-warming of hugs ever given by a human being. Liyana sinks in and holds on, bending her knees, shrinking herself to better snuggle into her aunt's cosy bosom. Now she's five years old again and the magical properties of the hug are seeping slowly into her body, into her blood and bones, until she is well.

'It's sweet as sugar to see you, Lili,' Aunt Sisi whispers. 'I've been waiting a long time for this moment.'

Liyana opens her mouth to speak but she's so over-whelmed with emotion that instead she kisses her aunt's neck. Her aunt giggles again, sounding, Liyana thinks, like a freshwater spring gurgling up from the ground. At last, Aunt Sisi lets Liyana go and steps back to survey her, a head-to-toe appraisal.

'Lord, how skinny you are.' Sisi exhales. 'Who's been feeding you?'

'I'm fed just fine, *Dagā*.' Liyana smiles. 'I just swim a lot – I can't eat enough to get fat.'

Sisi regards her niece as if she's never heard of such a thing. 'If you ate my food you'd get meat on your bones. Remember how I fed you waakye rice on Sundays after church? That'd sort you out soon enough, give that pretty girl-friend of yours a chunk or two more of you to hold on to.'

Liyana stares at her aunt.

'Oh, please,' – Sisi waves her hand again – 'I know who you are. I know everything about you.' She walks to a fallen tree trunk and sits, exhaling at the relief from standing, then pats the space beside her. 'You think I've not been watching you all these years? Truth be told, I probably know you better than you know yourself. Now, sit.'

Liyana steps over moss and stone to sit beside her aunt on the trunk. Sisi shuffles about, rearranging a bottom that's as large and soft as her bosom, making herself comfortable; then pulls a flask from a bag at her hip that Liyana hadn't noticed before. Her aunt unscrews the flask's cup lid then pours a few glugs of liquid into it and holds the cup out to her niece.

Liyana eyes the drink. 'What is it?'

'You think I'm trying to poison you?' Aunt Sisi laughs. 'Don't worry, it won't make you smaller. Go on, drink.'

Liyana takes a tentative sip, then another, before swallowing the rest in a single gulp. She holds out the empty cup. 'That's delicious, what's in it?'

Aunt Sisi rolls her eyes. 'You've forgotten *sobolo*?'

Liyana gives an apologetic shrug.

'I see that sister of mine not only lost her senses – we'll discuss how to sort her out later – but also went and forgot where she came from.' Sisi sighs. 'No wonder you're so skinny, Lili. She's taught you nothing.'

'That's not true,' Liyana protests, thinking of poor Nya in the hospital bed. 'She took good care of me, she just . . . she's . . . Could I have some more?' She nods to the flask. 'It's delicious.'

Aunt Sisi gives her niece a look to say she's no fool, but isn't averse to a little flattery either. 'It's hibiscus leaves,' she says, 'infused with ginger and pineapple juices. I add a little lime to mine, but don't be telling everyone that.' She pours out another glug of juice, filling the cup again.

Liyana gulps it down, then wipes her mouth with the back of her hand. 'Your secret's safe with me, *Dagā*.'

Laughing, Sisi hands over the flask. 'Go on, have it all, knock yourself out.' She shifts on the tree trunk, then glances up at the sky. A raven caws overhead. 'But enough chit-chat for now. I've got much to teach you and we don't have a lot of time.'

Liyana takes another sip of the *sobolo*. 'Time for what?'

Aunt Sisi frowns, seemingly surprised at the question. 'Why, to stop your sister, of course.'

Liyana mirrors her aunt's frown. 'Which sister?'

'The one who brings things back to life, the one who's got her mind set on resurrection.' Sisi reaches for Liyana's free hand and squeezes it tight. The clouds drift over the moon and eclipse its light. Liyana feels herself shiver. 'There's a storm coming, child, and you're the only one who can contain it.'

Scarlet

'Goldie!' Scarlet hurries across the glade towards her sister. 'I hoped I'd find you here tonight.'

Goldie's eyes open, her smile gone.

'Hey, Sis,' Scarlet says. 'I've been trying to track you down, I didn't . . . I couldn't sense if you were here or not. My radar's been all off lately. I—' she stops. 'Am I interrupting something?'

Goldie swallows her irritation and shakes her head. 'No.' She slides off the rock. 'I was just startled, that's all.'

Scarlet smiles, her face so bright with delight it almost eclipses the glimmer of doubt beneath. 'What are you up to?'

'Nothing,' Goldie says, glancing at the ground.

Scarlet lets this go, then smiles again. This time it's full shining joy, untainted by anything. Goldie stares. For a second, she's speechless.

'You're p-pregnant.'

Scarlet grins, she doesn't need to ask how her sister knows.

'B-bloody hell,' Goldie stutters. 'Th-that's . . .'

'Isn't it?' Scarlet's still grinning. 'I still can't quite believe it myself.'

'Did you p—?'

'No.' Scarlet presses her hands to her belly. 'A happy accident.'

It seems, for a moment, that the moon shines brighter then, making a halo of her hair, the curls full and fluffy, the dark red almost sunset-orange in the light. Lit from within, Goldie thinks, which, she supposes, Scarlet is.

'Bloody hell.' Goldie sighs. 'Bloody hell. I don't know what to – well, I mean, congratulations.'

A slightly awkward pause follows as Goldie wonders if she should hug her sister, then the moment passes.

'Hey, girls.'

Goldie and Scarlet turn to see Liyana striding towards them, arms swinging at her sides, almost marching, as if she's a soldier striding into battle.

'Ana!' Scarlet exclaims. 'You're here!'

'I am.' Liyana looks from Goldie to Scarlet, as if she's just disturbed a furtive little gathering. 'What's up?'

'Scarlet's—'

'Fuck!' Liyana exclaims, interrupting. 'You're pregnant! How the . . .'

Scarlet smiles. 'You didn't see this in your cards, did you?'

'No.' Liyana frowns. 'I didn't. So . . . is this a good or a bad thing?'

Scarlet mirrors her sister's frown. 'A good thing, of course.'

'Ah, well, great. *Mazel tov* and all that,' Liyana says. 'But, it's hardly "of course", is it? I mean, you're practically a teenager, you've not done – is this what you want to be more than anything, a mother?'

'Motherhood doesn't mean I can't do other things,' Scarlet says, frostily. 'This isn't the nineteen-fifties.'

'Really?' Liyana raises an eyebrow. 'I didn't realize you knew that, living like the little *hausfrau*—'

'Shut up,' Scarlet snaps. 'You're jealous because I've got a boyfriend – a fiancé – who loves me and wants us to raise a family together – something you can't do without some willing sperm and a turkey baster.'

'And thank God for that,' Liyana says. 'Thank God that I don't need to pump myself full of pills, or mess about with my sacred parts to ensure I don't fall foul of that particular catastrophe.'

Sparks flare at Scarlet's fingertips. 'Well, it's not a disaster for me. Quite the opposite, in fact, so—'

Liyana raises an eyebrow. 'You don't think you're being a little cavalier about procreating, given the state of the world; don't you think it's more than a little selfish? Having kids is just about the worst thing you can do for the environment, you know.'

Arcs of electricity snap and crackle through the air, encircling Scarlet's hands.

'Look,' Goldie says, stepping between them. 'Why don't we change the subject?'

Liyana eyes Goldie. 'To what?'

Goldie shrugs. 'I don't know. Something less contentious.'

'So you think it's fine, do you?' Liyana cracks her knuckles;

high above the air shudders with a crack of thunder. 'That she's pretending to be just like everyone else, that she's still ignoring her powers and potential. Is that how you're going to raise your daughter, eh, Scar? To be nobody, to give everything up for a man, to—'

'I met Bea,' Goldie says, more loudly than she'd intended. Liyana and Scarlet turn to her.

The thunder calms and the clouds clear. 'What?'

The electricity fizzes out. 'How?'

'I was here the other night,' Goldie says. 'And she spoke to me.'

'Really?' Liyana folds her arms and narrows her eyes, as if suggesting that Goldie might be making it up. 'What did she say?'

'Um . . .' Goldie bends to pick up a small round stone at her feet and, standing again, rubs it between finger and thumb. 'Well . . . she told me she's okay, at peace, and . . .'

'What else?' Liyana says. 'What else did she say?'

'What about Leo?' Scarlet says. 'I mean, if they're both here,' – she looks up at the inky sky and the unwavering moon – 'can she contact him?'

'No.' Goldie shakes her head, her voice heavy. 'No, and he can't contact me. It's only the dead Grimms whose spirits live on here who can do that.'

'Oh,' Scarlet says. 'That's . . . I'm sorry.'

Goldie gives a sad little nod. But, Liyana notices, doesn't meet her sister's eye.

'Is she here now?' Scarlet asks, turning this way and that as if Bea's ghost might be sitting behind her in the bough of a tree.

'I don't know,' Goldie says. 'I suppose she must be. But I don't think we can summon her, I expect she'll only come when she wants to.'

'Death hasn't made her any less stubborn then,' Liyana says. 'No surprise there.'

'No.' Goldie rubs her stone thoughtfully. 'I suppose not. But she is different. She's kinder, softer, more . . .'

Scarlet sits forward. 'How?'

And so Goldie tells them everything she can about their lost sister, omitting anything incriminating, scattering a few little lies into the tale for extra flavour. And, with that, everything else is forgotten.

Everwhere

The raven settles on a branch in the great oak tree, ruffles its feathers then cocks its head, turning a beady eye on the three women below. Bea hadn't anticipated the rising emotions and clashing opinions between them; she might need to intervene, to bind the cracks before they become crevasses. For if the three sisters aren't united on the night they turn twenty-one, when Goldie attempts the resurrection, the effects could be catastrophic. Bea can see probable futures snaking out like the rivers twisting through the land below; too many turn into rapids and torrents and ending in tempests and tsunamis.

It's just as Sisi had said: a storm is coming and cannot be stopped, but it might be contained.

24th October –
7 nights . . .

Liyana

Liyana wakes with a start. For a moment she's confused, doesn't understand where she is. She blinks into the flickering fluorescent lights, takes a breath of stale, disinfected air, wincing as she stretches out her stiff neck. Then Liyana's gaze settles on her aunt lying in the bed, shrouded in white, head tipped back on the pillow, eyes closed, arms unnaturally straight at her sides.

Liyana doesn't want to be there. She wants to be in Kumiko's bed, encircled by her arms, their limbs entwined till they've become one glorious multi-limbed creature; an immortal, untouchable goddess: Kali, Durga, Lakshmi – instead of an ineffectual girl unable to achieve anything, be it getting published, or pleasing her girlfriend or inspiring in her aunt the will to live.

Liyana glances up at the plastic clock on the wall ticking away each interminable second. Tick, tick, tick . . . Why is it, she wonders, that time becomes so sluggish after midnight? Especially the hours between two and four o'clock. When she's in Everwhere it's never the case, but always on Earth. Which is why when she's in this world Liyana hates being in a hospital, where time passes most slowly of all, infinitely preferring to spend the dwindling hours with Kumiko.

Fortunately, Liyana has plenty of thoughts to distract herself with. She thinks of her aunt Sisi, the secret that'd been kept from her all these years. She thinks of what Sisi told her she must do to stop Leo's resurrection from destabilizing the delicate symmetry of good and evil in Everwhere. 'There're demons still lurking in the shadows and darkness ready to rise up from the earth,' Aunt Sisi had said. 'An act like that is in great danger of tipping the balance, especially given the sacrifice.' Despite Liyana's questions, Sisi wouldn't be pressed on the details of this sacrifice, only muttering cryptically that 'you will know when you know'.

And then Sisi had taken her to the lake.

They had only walked for a little while, though it could've been longer, given the strange passing of time in that place, but had then come upon a small dense wood of silver birch trees unknown to her. And, beyond that, a lake larger than Liyana had ever seen, either on Earth or in Everwhere.

'My God,' she'd gasped. 'It's . . . incredible.'

While Liyana stood gazing open-mouthed, Aunt Sisi had slipped off her shoes and walked to the edge of the water. 'I've brought you here to be blessed by Mami Wata,' she said. 'Just as I did when you were a little girl.'

Still gawping at the great expanse of liquid made silver by the moonlight, Liyana kicked off her own shoes to pad barefoot across the banks of moss and stone to stand beside her aunt. 'Who's Mami Wata?'

Sisi gave a short, derisive snort. 'She's the goddess of water, of course. She bestows many things on her followers: healing, fertility, creativity, wealth . . . Any of those sound good to you?'

Liyana gave a wry smile. 'Yeah, all of them except fertility. I've no need for that.'

'So you say now, child.' Aunt Sisi peeled off her dress and dropped it at her feet. 'But one day you might change your mind.'

Liyana, a little startled by her aunt's sudden nudity, took a moment to reply. 'Did you?'

'Touché.' Aunt Sisi's laughter rippled through her ample flesh. 'You're a smart one, aren't you? And no, I did not. And I never regretted it. But then, I have you.'

'Hardly.' Liyana dipped a toe in the water, enjoying the shiver of the chill through her foot. 'You've not exactly been an active presence in my life.'

'Too true,' Sisi admitted. 'But I've always been watching.' With a nimbleness that belied her age and girth, Sisi sprang down the bank and into the lake with an effervescent splash. She turned back to her niece, grinning. 'What are you waiting for? Come on!'

With a shrug, Liyana cast off her own clothes and waded out to her aunt's side. Side by side, Liyana stood immersed to her belly, Sisi to her breasts. A sudden thrill of anticipation shuddered through Liyana, sending ripples across the stillness of the silver water. She itched to swim; she itched to dive in, to push deep under the surface till her fingers brushed the mud beneath, feet kicking to churn the lake as she glided along the murky bed. She wanted to swim till she was exhausted, till her lungs hurt, her legs ached and her skin was mottled and grey.

Liyana closed her eyes, sinking her hands into the water then pulling them slowly back and forth, encircling her legs, feeling the tremendous power of the lake drawing up through her fingertips.

'I've a gift for you.' Aunt Sisi's voice skimmed across Liyana's thoughts like a stone skimmed across a pond.

Liyana looked up. 'Sorry? I didn't – what?'

Instead of answering, Sisi reached into the depths of her bosom to extract a necklace from between her breasts. She held it out. 'Wear her around your neck.'

Reaching out to take the charm – a tiny woman sculpted of wood – Liyana clutched it tenderly in wet hands, running her fingers along the leather strap before undoing the clasp and fastening it around her neck. She held the wooden carving, caressing the woman's body, her strong, thick limbs, the curves of the serpent that curled around her waist and up her arms.

'She's your talisman – or, rather, your "taliswoman" . . .' Sisi smiled. 'She's been blessed by a vodou priestess in the waters of Lake Volta. Now you can invoke the power of Mami Wata to help you create and conjure, or you can call upon her protection, as you wish.'

Liyana nodded. She could already feel the quickening of her heart and breath, as if the little statue was a miniature moon controlling the ebb and flow of her emotions, the pulse of her blood. She began thinking of what might be possible, how perfectly she might be able to manipulate the elements, when harnessing the deity's powers. She smiled.

'Now, for the ritual.'

Liyana frowned at her aunt. 'What ritual?'

'You will submerge in the lake and I will invoke the incantation, then—'

Liyana's frown deepened. 'What incantation?'

'Oh, nothing much.' Sisi gave a little shrug. 'I'll teach it to you after—'

'But I don't speak Ewe,' Liyana said. 'My mother wouldn't let me. One day I want to learn, but I can only recall a few words, and my accent is shameful.'

'Oh, don't worry about that.' Sisi waved a wet hand in the air, dismissing the words almost as soon as they were spoken. 'Anyway, this is a language more ancient even than Ewe. It comes from before the time words were carved on

79

rocks and stories read by fire under moonlight – and you'll be able to learn it just fine. Now, stop stalling and lie down.'

'Here? Now?' Liyana held her talisman protectively. 'But she'll be soaked.'

Aunt Sisi laughed again, her shuddering body sending ripples across the water. 'She's made of wood, she'll float. Besides, she loves getting wet. Nothing pleases her more.'

'Oh,' Liyana said, submerging herself before the words had even escaped, so that 'me too' bubbled and popped on the surface above the billowing cloud of her hair, before it too disappeared. Then she rose again and spread herself like a starfish across the surface of the lake, her dark skin glimmering under the unwavering light of the moon. Mami Wata lay between Liyana's breasts looking for all the world as if she was smiling.

Aunt Sisi took a gulp of air then bent down into the water, her own fluff of white hair elongating like strands of bleached seaweed as she reached to scoop a scraping of mud from the sediment, then rose again and with her forefinger drew a small circle of dirt on Liyana's forehead.

'*Ina kiran albarka da kariya ga Mami Wata.* I invoke the blessing and protection of Mami Wata,' Aunt Sisi intoned. 'I ask the goddess to lend her strength and powers to my niece . . . *duk lokacin da ta bukaci su. Na gode* . . . I offer my blood as compensation for this gift.'

She bent down into the lake again, curved like a comma, blinking open-eyed in the clear water, searching with quick fingers before winkling a sharp-edged flint from the mud and bringing it up. Without pause, Sisi drew the stone swiftly along the heart-line of her left palm, clenching and unclenching her fist so the droplets of blood fell fast into the water.

Liyana opened her eyes and turned her head. But, if she was shocked by the pooling blood, her face didn't show it.

'*Jinin jinni na jinni, iko na iko,*' Aunt Sisi continued. '*Ina rokon kakanninsu su shiga tare da ni don neman kariya ga wannan 'yar, wannan yaro na ruwan sama, wannan' yar'uwar Grimm*. I ask the ancestors to join me, to protect this daughter, this child of the rain, this sister Grimm.'

As if summoned, all at once Liyana drew in her arms and legs and flipped her body so her feet met the bed of the lake, toes pressing into the mud; then she rose from the water, straight and tall, her halo of curls springing free, her skin shimmering as if bejewelled. She lifted her arms, reaching towards the skies, dipping her head back to grin at the heavens. Standing waist-deep in the lake, without instruction from her aunt, Liyana brought her hands together in prayer, murmuring her thanks and afterwards her blessings, as if she too had gifts and magics to dispense, as if she too was a water goddess.

Goldie

Seven nights. Seven nights until she will touch Leo again. This notion is so wildly unreal as to be beyond all imagining. Which is odd since Goldie has spent every conscious minute of the past three years trying to do exactly that, to push her memory into recasting every detail, to contort her imagination to its most creative limits to bring Leo from dust and into form again. She's become so used to these efforts that they're almost as automatic as thought or breath. And yet, now her thoughts and breath have stalled.

Bea hasn't yet revealed all the details of what must be done and, though it's only seven nights away, Goldie doesn't dare ask. Instead, she tries to immerse herself in the mundanities of life, of action, and forget. Though, of course, that is impossible. She tries to distract herself with other thoughts:

she thinks of her sister Scarlet, and how she's scornful of Goldie's job, saying she's smart and ought to do something better. It's an old fight they've been knocking back and forth like a battered tennis ball for years now. Goldie knows that Scarlet's right, in theory, but feels her sister should be more forgiving of the fact that she's been crippled by Leo's death, that for a long time she could barely be bothered to brush her hair in the morning, let alone put herself together enough to find a new job. Scarlet should know the real reason she stays at the hotel, cleaning dubious stains from strangers' bedsheets; for what better job could she find when she's not got a single qualification to her name? And it annoys Goldie that Scarlet herself hasn't done anything remotely spectacular with her own life and is hardly in a position to crow. Any idiot can get knocked up. Liyana, herself the possessor of an unspectacular job, doesn't judge Goldie on that front but she does plead now and then that they write a book, or graphic novel, together. But while Goldie enjoys – or rather, is invigorated by the writing of stories – the idea of shaping them into something proper, into a project, a publication, feels too . . . much.

Goldie's scrubbing the porcelain toilet in room 56 when her mobile rings. She fumbles in her apron pocket to answer. She doesn't recognize the number.

'Hello?'

'Miss Clayton?'

'Yes.'

'Is this the Miss Clayton who resides at 89 Cockrell Road?'

'Yes,' Goldie says, suddenly nervous. *Teddy*, she thinks. Her heart thumps, her palms prick with sweat. *Something's happened to Teddy.*

'Are you the sister of a Mister Theodore Clayton of the same address?'

'Yes, yes,' Goldie says. 'What's – is he all right?'

'No, Miss Clayton. He's just been arrested for shoplifting.'

For one long second Goldie says nothing.

'Miss Clayton?'

'Yes, I'm here. Yes, I'm coming. Where is he?'

'He's being held at Parkside Police Station. If you'd like to—'

'They're letting you off with a warning.' Goldie sits cross-legged on the concrete floor of the holding cell opposite Teddy, who sits on a metal bench staring at his scuffed trainers, saying nothing. 'Because it's your first offence.'

Teddy stays silent.

'You've got nothing to say?'

He shrugs.

'Jesus Christ, Teddy!' Goldie slaps her hand against the floor so hard it stings. He glances up. 'Do you think this is a fucking joke? This is the *police*. If you get a criminal record you'll never get a job.'

Still, Teddy says nothing. Goldie waits a moment, then pushes herself up to stand. She steps over to her brother and grabs his chin, forcing him to look up. 'Do you understand?'

He twists away.

She doesn't let go.

'Get off me.'

'It'll ruin the rest of your life,' Goldie snaps. 'Don't you get that?'

Teddy sighs and rolls his eyes. Without thinking, Goldie pulls back her hand and slaps him. He stares at her in shock. She stares back, equally shocked.

'What the fuck?' Teddy shrieks. 'You can't fucking do that. I'll report you. I'll call social services.'

Goldie feels the sting of tears. She wants to weep, to beg his forgiveness, to hold him like she did when he was a baby. But she knows she can't show any weakness now. 'Go ahead,' she says, suppressing her sobs. 'You're in the right place.'

Teddy narrows his eyes, his gaze flicking from her face to the door, trying to gauge how serious she is. Goldie stares him down. His eyes turn to the floor. Goldie exhales.

'You can't do this, Ted,' she says, soft now, consoling. 'You can't keep stealing. You'll get yourself—'

'Why not?' Teddy kicks his feet against the bench. 'Why shouldn't I?'

Goldie frowns. 'What? For all the reasons I just—'

'Yeah,' Teddy says. 'But that didn't stop you, did it?'

Goldie blinks, trying to maintain her composure while scrambling in her mind for answers, excuses, denials, or, failing all that, a defence.

'What?' He sneers. 'You think I'm an idiot? You think I don't know?'

Now Goldie is silent, staring down at her shoes.

'You can't afford my clothes or school fees – how can a hotel cleaner buy Boss trainers? And Moschino T-shirts?' Teddy folds his arms, puffing out his chest. 'You've been stealing shit since I was born.'

Still, Goldie can't speak. For what can she say? What *is* her defence? That it's okay to steal, so long as you don't get caught?

Scarlet

As a child Scarlet had always vowed that when she had a little girl of her own she would spoil her rotten, would give her everything she asked for and plenty more she didn't. As an eight-year-old, Scarlet wasn't entirely certain how to go about getting a daughter but if her own mother, who hadn't seemed to want one, had managed, then surely it couldn't be too difficult. And once Scarlet had worked out the particulars, she'd do everything to ensure that her own daughter (for she knew it'd be a girl) would grow up under a blanket of devotion, almost smothered by feeling exceedingly and excessively loved.

As a child, Scarlet had no blanket, nor even a cloth, and was forced to cling to the occasional maternal scraps, ripped tissues of almost-affection. Scarlet never understood why her mother didn't feel for her what mothers were supposed to feel, but she knew that when she was a mother she would be different. She would dote upon her daughter, nurse her, stroke the soft tufts of red hair, plump cheeks, tight curled fists . . . Scarlet would adore her daughter from the start, before she'd done anything to earn it, when all Red (as she'd be called) could do was cry.

Scarlet had often thought about how it might feel to be loved for no reason at all – without trying to twist yourself into agreeable knots, without having to give what you might not want to give, safe in the knowledge that you were loved for just being your own simple self. With her daughter, Scarlet determined to prove that unconditional love was possible, to prove that it had been her mother and not her who was flawed.

Scarlet glances across at Eli, who's sitting beside her on the sofa typing emails into his phone. It irritates Scarlet that he does this while they're watching films together; she wants him to give the film his full attention, as if he was at the cinema, as if he was at the theatre. It seems disrespectful otherwise, both to her and to the filmmakers, though

Scarlet can't quite explain *why* exactly, and so she says nothing.

'Have you thought about names?' Scarlet asks.

'Names for what?' Eli says, without glancing up.

Scarlet looks at him, head dipped over the glowing screen, wondering how it's possible that he doesn't immediately understand what she's saying, that he's not constantly thinking about it all as she is. Barely a moment passes when Scarlet doesn't flush with amazement and awe at what's happening in her body right now.

'The baby, of course.'

Now Eli looks up and Scarlet can tell, from the momentary glimmer of confusion, that he'd entirely forgotten. 'Yes, yes, sorry,' he says. 'I thought, I was just thinking of . . .' He trails off, leaving the alternative subject unnamed. 'But don't you think it's a little soon for that? I mean, we only just found out. Surely right now it's the size of a pea and anyway . . .'

'What?'

'Well . . .' Eli gives a slight shrug. 'Shouldn't we wait till it's been three months? Isn't that what most people do?'

'Yeah, I suppose.' Scarlet slumps down into the cushions. 'But it's just . . . I mean, if we don't tell anyone, then what's the harm?' She thinks of her sisters, but since they've still not met Eli, there's little chance of her getting found out.

'All right,' Eli says. 'If it makes you happy.'

Scarlet's about to object when he pulls her foot into his lap and starts rubbing her toes. When he presses his thumb into the sole of Scarlet's foot she groans.

'Oh, yes, please. Yes, right . . . there. Don't stop, don't ever stop.'

'I'm not quite sure quitting my job to become your

full-time masseur is an especially wise career move.' Eli laughs. 'But it's entirely up to you.'

'So, what do you think about names?'

Eli stops massaging and looks at her. 'You've already thought of one, haven't you?'

Scarlet gives a slight shrug.

Eli smiles. 'All right then, what is it?'

Scarlet's silent for a little while. 'Red.'

Eli considers this with a frown, while Scarlet feels her heart beating too fast.

'Red?' he says. 'Isn't it a little . . . trendy? How about something more traditional?'

'Like what?' Scarlet says, her voice sharper than she'd intended. 'Elizabeth Windsor or Prince George?'

Eli laughs. 'Not exactly. But what's wrong with . . . I don't know . . . Charlotte, Kate, Emma, Frances, Lucy—'

'Hold on,' Scarlet interrupts. 'If this is turning into a list of all the women you've slept with, you can consider all those already crossed off, okay?'

Eli looks sheepish. 'All right then, how about . . . Annabelle, that's sweet, isn't it? Then she could be Bella or Ana. Or Arabella, that's pretty.'

Scarlet shrugs. 'If you like that sort of thing.'

'You don't?'

'I don't *mind* them.' Scarlet twitches her toes, pressing them into Eli's fingers, a subtle nudge. 'They just don't mean anything to me, that's all.'

'Well, that's all very well,' Eli says. 'But while Blue might seem—'

'Red,' Scarlet says. 'Not blue, it was . . . a name, the name I wanted my mother to call me.'

Eli falls silent. 'Oh. Well, that's different. Why didn't you say—'

On the arm of the sofa his phone starts to vibrate. Eli glances at it. Hesitates. Then picks it up and stands. 'Sorry, I need to take this.'

'Don't,' Scarlet says. 'Can't you call them back?'

'I'll only be a minute,' Eli says, striding out of the room.

'No,' Scarlet mumbles, her eyes filling with tears. He won't be a minute, she knows. He never is. Eli is all business, whether calls come in late at night or early in the morning, he always answers and always sees every conversation through to the bitter end. Sometimes Scarlet catches the odd snatched sentence, sometimes she even eavesdrops and sometimes she suspects that Ezekiel Wolfe is keeping secrets. About what, she has no idea, but she wonders if he might be involved in things that aren't entirely legal. She hopes not but won't ask. But perhaps she only thinks he's keeping secrets from her because she's keeping so many from him.

Is it right, Scarlet sometimes wonders, that she tells him so little of significance about herself? Is not saying certain things the same as lying? Well, she tells him plenty of truths, just not *the* truth. Which is all right, isn't it? She is real and true with him, giving her heart fully and completely. She simply separates the two main parts of herself and presents them selectively, being her Grimm self in Everwhere with her sisters and her non-Grimm self with Eli. Scarlet isn't duplicitous, doesn't deny things, never deceives him after the fact. Of course, that's easy enough since Eli hasn't got even the vaguest notion of who Scarlet is and what she can do. And what if he did? This is a question to which Scarlet has devoted a great deal of thought. She knows he'd be astonished and possibly horrified. Which is why she still hasn't told him. Because Scarlet's terrified that if Eli knew who she really was, he wouldn't love her anymore.

Everwhere

The raven sits on her favourite branch, now and then cocking her head to turn a beady eye to the ground to check on the state of things. Below her the girls gather, waiting for her to speak, waiting for her to teach what they need to learn. Some nights only half a dozen might come, other nights over a hundred: daughters of air, earth, water and fire. For many it is the first time, others have been attending the gatherings for months, even years. For those who are new, Bea will focus solely on inspiration and motivation, teaching them the basics of their skills, demonstrating the potential of their strengths. As for those who have already mastered the fundamentals, Bea must tell them of the things they might not want to hear: now it is time to plunge into trickier topics, to reveal secrets she's been skirting around so as not to scare anyone. It's essential not to ignite in them too much fear, for there's no greater suppressor of strength and power than that. Still, Bea must speak of the shadows, must tell her sisters that Everwhere is not simply a safe haven of self-empowerment but that it contains pockets of darkness best avoided if one hopes to hold on to one's strength and sanity.

And so, Bea tells of the first time she stumbled into the dark and what might yet happen to them. She ruffles her feathers, wraps her clawed feet around the branch, then turns her beady eyes to the crowd below. Her voice is the breeze that ripples the leaves.

Everwhere is a place of enchantment and empowerment, but it contains dangers too. You must always be on your guard, aware of the warning signs. The sounds of rustling leaves or rushing water or bird calls, these are the hue of Everwhere's enchantments, but when you hear whispering in the shadows watch out.

They are soft voices, low. They are not human. Do not listen. When they say your name it'll be a hook in your mouth, pulling you on. You'll stumble forward towards the shadows then, a fish snagged on a line. Soon the hook will twist, ripping into your cheek as the words darken, taunting and mocking you, saying things you never wanted to hear, never wanted to believe to be true. Fear and despair will surge in you, coursing through your blood, clogging your heart. You'll clutch your chest as it starts to constrict, you'll gasp for breath but the air is mustard gas. Your breath will come in gasps, till it doesn't come at all.

When she's issued her warning, Bea is assaulted with a thousand questions, some shouted, some shrieked, some whispered. She asks for silence then invites each sister to raise her hand and, one by one, she answers them all. Finally, she addresses everyone:

We cannot vanquish the shadows; they're as much part of the fabric of Everwhere as the voracious ivy and the unwavering moon. But I'll teach you strength of mind so you can better resist them, should you go astray. One thing you must always remember: be ever vigilant, for the human mind is a fragile thing – always teetering on the edge of despair, always vulnerable to manipulation – so please don't think that it can't happen to you, for that is when it will.

25th October –
6 nights . . .

Liyana

Liyana feels different. Stronger, taller, more solid; as if circling within her belly is the power of a gathering wave. This difference feels visible, as if should she step into a crowded room people would turn and stare, perhaps even gasp. She still wears the carving of Mami Wata; she will not take it off.

Having woken from her dream, Liyana's sitting again beside her aunt's hospital bed. When a nurse pokes her head around the curtain, Liyana closes her eyes and pretends to be asleep. She wants to ask: *shouldn't my aunt be awake by now? Does this mean she's going to die?* But, despite her burgeoning strength, Liyana doesn't want to risk an answer she doesn't want to hear. The nurse bustles about to take Nya's blood pressure, wrapping the plastic cuff round her puny arm, pumping it up and squinting at the monitor as it emits its sharp, static beeps, before the cuff deflates and the nurse peels the rasping Velcro straps apart. Liyana resists flinching at the sound.

When the nurse bustles out again, Liyana reaches for her phone. First, she texts Kumiko:

I need you.

Then she calls Goldie.

Goldie points at the talisman hanging around Liyana's neck. 'What's that?'

Liyana's hand goes to the wooden figure, her fingers rubbing along the length of snake curled around the woman's waist and up her right arm. 'Mami Wata. Vodou goddess of the sea, oceans, rivers – water.'

'Oh,' Goldie says. 'I didn't know that – so, who's the goddess of earth?'

'I don't know. I'll ask Aunt Sisi.' Liyana gives her sister a sideways glance, then turns back to the river. On Liyana's request, they'd spirited themselves to Everwhere, since that is the right place to address matters of resurrection and has the added convenience of being far easier for them both to reach, and far faster than travelling between London and Cambridge. 'Do you fancy a swim? Or a paddle?'

Goldie shakes her head. 'No thanks.'

Liyana eyes her sister seriously. 'You really should learn to swim, you know. I can teach you.'

'Maybe,' Goldie says. 'One day.'

'By which you mean never.' Liyana shrugs her shirt over her shoulders so it slips to the ground, then tugs off her trousers and underwear, before sliding naked down the muddy riverbank and into the water. Mami Wata, hanging on the cord around Liyana's neck, seems to smile. When she's submerged her halo of hair is still buoyant above the surface as she sinks under. Goldie's heart quickens when Liyana doesn't rise, even though she knows that her sister is fine, that she's the strongest swimmer on earth, that she can hold her breath for an eternity, that she can manipulate water at her fingertips . . . Still, Goldie doesn't exhale until Liyana resurfaces.

When Liyana emerges she explodes from the water with a joyous whoop, catching Goldie's eye, fixing her with a look of such inquisitive suspicion that Goldie starts wondering what her sister suspects. Then Liyana dives again, kicking up her feet with a splash to send her gliding along the riverbed, so close that the reeds entwine her toes and the mud leaves its mark on her knees.

As Liyana swims she washes herself free of every trouble that's been smearing its dirty fingers on her porous skin, every worry that's been wrapping its tentacles around her clear blue thoughts. She opens her eyes, seeing nothing in the dark water but endless, boundless night. She cannot see Nya in her bed, cannot see Kumiko at her desk, cannot see Goldie standing on the bank; all is beautifully empty and free. As Liyana swims she is held safe by the water's soft touch, floating weightless like a babe in the womb. She cannot feel where she ends and the water begins, cannot feel her stupid human limits, for here she has no limits, here she is free.

Only when Liyana senses Goldie getting impatient, when she feels her sister's attention skimming the surface of the river like a fishing net, does Liyana finally drag herself to the surface again and tear herself away from the river. She seizes the twisting roots of a willow tree, slowly pulling herself up the embankment like a rock climber, fixing her eyes on those roots meandering through the soil, the trees' branches reaching down to dip into the current that eddies and swirls around its leaves, the water sometimes snatching a leaf away.

Liyana shakes off the water like a dog before finding her clothes again. Buttoning her shirt, Liyana sneaks glances at Goldie, contemplating whether she should be direct or subtle. She touches Mami Wata and steps forward. 'I know what you're thinking.'

Goldie glances up. 'What?'

'I said,' Liyana draws out the words, as if her sister is hard of hearing and short of sense. 'I. Know. What. You. Are. Thinking. I know what you want to do.'

Goldie studies the ground, pretending to be particularly interested in a tendril of ivy that – on her touch – slithers away through the moss and stones like a snake. 'And what am I thinking?'

Liyana says nothing, but waits for Goldie to meet her eye. She waits so long that a drift of fog starts to roll in. 'So, are you going to tell me?'

'Tell you what?'

Liyana folds her arms. 'It's going to be like that, is it?'

'Honestly,' Goldie says. 'I don't know what you're talking about.'

Liyana takes a deep breath, exhaling slowly and looking at Goldie as if she's her own wayward child who's been sneaking a little weed on the side.

Picking at another tendril of ivy, Goldie sighs and snaps off a leaf. 'How do you know?'

Liyana shrugs, folding her legs under her to sit. She thinks of what Aunt Sisi has told her, but won't mention that yet. 'I'm the telepathic one, right?'

'Perhaps,' – now Goldie eyes Liyana in turn – 'but there's something you're not telling me too.'

'You're one to talk.' Liyana reaches up to pull her fingers through the thinning fog. 'And you're not going to deflect me that easily.'

'And I suppose . . .' Goldie rips the leaf apart and twirls the split parts between finger and thumb, 'that you're going to try and stop me.'

Liyana plucks her own leaf from the ground, its anaemic veins stark against her smooth dark skin, as if she was holding her sister's hand.

'And I don't suppose . . .' Liyana unwraps her words slowly, carefully, 'that I could persuade you it's a dreadfully dangerous idea, messing with magic like that.' She reaches up to pull a ball of fog from the air and begins rolling it between her hands, as if shaping dough. 'I don't suppose there'd be any point in trying to talk sense into you.'

Goldie shakes her head.

'I thought not.' Liyana lets out a long sigh, her breath cutting and splitting the fog. 'Well then, it looks like I've got no choice but to help you.'

Slowly, purposefully, Goldie twitches her fingers, drawing shapes in the air until a vine of ivy begins to uproot itself from the soil, dragging free and rising up like a scorpion's tail. 'Help me how?'

'I don't know yet,' Liyana says. 'I'm working on it. But you can start with this . . .'

While Liyana shows her sister the incantation Aunt Sisi had taught her, she wonders if in fact Goldie is keeping a greater secret than resurrection, for the air still feels thick and fogged with hidden truths and her sister still won't meet her eye.

Goldie

Goldie sits at the kitchen counter staring down at a dead bluebottle, thinking of the time she resurrected her bonsai tree. Beside the bluebottle is a crumpled piece of paper bearing Liyana's instructions. Most importantly, the prayer to Mami Wata.

'Can't be so very different from a plant,' Goldie mumbles. 'Can it?'

Still, she feels unconvinced and regards the bluebottle dubiously. Dead. Not simply stunned or sleeping. Do they sleep? She's never seen one settle before. Always flitting from one surface to another. Goldie gives it a tentative prod with her fingernail. Up close the fly is quite strangely beautiful: the iridescent sheen on its body like blue-green silk, the wings such delicate gossamer it seems impossible they could lift the little insect into the air. But it's been so long since she's even coaxed a green shoot from the ground that Goldie wonders how easy it would be, if she even could. After another half an hour of questioning her own abilities, of spiralling down into inevitable despair, Goldie recalls her story, 'The Paladin'. What was it she'd written? It's a few moments before the words return: *'I'm curious to see what my words will be when I'm not listening to the echo of my father's voice in my head.'*

Taking a deep breath, Goldie sits a little straighter. *All right*, she thinks. *Enough self-doubt. Don't tell yourself you can't do it when you haven't even tried.*

She picks up the paper, squinting at Liyana's scrawl, and begins, tentatively, to read aloud.

'*Ina rokon albarkunku, Mami Wata*,' Goldie ventures, trying to remember the way Liyana had spoken the words. '*Rike hannuna kamar yadda na kawo wannan dan kadan daga sauran rayuwa.*'

As instructed, she imagines the bluebottle alive – buzzing from spot to spot, never settling long, never satisfied, engaged in a perpetual-motion-powered search for its own holy grail. This, at least, will be easier with Leo, since she can picture him so completely, though she'll have the extra challenge of not having his body to hold. Gingerly, Goldie picks up the dead fly between finger and thumb – mindful of the gossamer wings – and sets it in her open palm.

A clamour of disparaging thoughts flood in at the brush of the bluebottle's fine hairs on her skin: jeering declarations of impossibilities, arrogance and madness. With great effort, Goldie pushes them away. For she cannot afford to indulge them now, cannot afford to be deflated or swayed; she must allow only for the possibility of success. It is the only chance she has.

Minutes later, Goldie is so focused on the dead fly that she doesn't hear the click of the front door, doesn't hear her brother walk into the flat, doesn't feel him watching her from across the room.

'*Ina rokon albarkunku, Mami Wata*,' Goldie repeats, imagining the bluebottle flitting through the room, before cupping one hand over the other as a regenerating warmth starts to seep from her skin and into the space between, where the dead fly lies inert. '*Rike hannuna kamar yadda na kawo wannan dan kadan daga sauran rayuwa . . . Ina rokon albarkunku, Mami Wata. Rike hannuna kamar yadda na kawo wannan dan kadan daga sauran rayuwa.*'

Nothing.

Goldie chants on. She takes a peek at the bluebottle's six bent legs reaching into the air. Her words, deflated by disappointment, sink into a duller tone.

Still, nothing.

Resisting the urge to take another peek, she chants.

All at once, within the protective curl of her hands is a sudden flurry of movement, the tickle of the six whisper-thin legs spasming, the flicker of increasingly frantic wings, an incessant buzz scratching at the silence. Grinning, Goldie opens her hands to release the resurrected insect, the burst of her laughter exploding under its flight, lifting its wings so it doesn't tumble but soars like a minature jet through the kitchen. She watches it fly, feeling a surge of hope that rises with the bluebottle's flight.

*

'What was that?'

Goldie turns to see Teddy gazing at her, curious, incredulous.

'What?' Goldie echoes him, stalling. 'What was what?'

'What did you do to that fly?'

'Nothing.' Goldie shifts in her seat. 'I was just ... I caught it. I was going to squash it. I – I changed my mind and let it go.'

Teddy narrows his eyes. 'It was dead.'

Goldie frowns, as if this is absurd. 'Of course it wasn't.'

'I saw it.'

'You didn't.'

'Yes, I did.' Teddy steps forward, crossing the carpet to stand on the edge of the kitchen, toes skirting the linoleum. 'I know it was dead because I killed it this morning, with that newspaper.' He nods at the unfurled *Daily Mirror* on the counter.

'Then why did you leave it here?' Goldie says, a surge of panic snapping through her words. 'Why didn't you throw it away?'

Her brother's look shifts from intrigued to angry, glowering at Goldie as if he's just stumbled into a crime scene and, upon spotting the body prostrate on his living-room floor, has been chastised by the murderer for not taking his shoes off at the door.

He folds his arms. 'What are you even talking about?'

Goldie shrugs.

'I knew you were keeping some killer secrets from me.' Teddy drops his school bag to the linoleum with a dull thud and leans against the counter. His collar is flipped up, high around his neck. Goldie resists the urge to turn it down. 'I just didn't think it was this slick.'

Goldie sees something in her brother's eyes then, creeping into the edges of the usual furious contempt: admiration. Her teenage brother, who fails to be impressed by anything at all, is impressed with her.

'You're a witch.'

'I'm not.'

'Yes, you are,' he says, a smile breaking across his face. Goldie can't remember the last time she saw him so delighted, certainly not with her.

'N-no,' she says, hesitating. 'I'm not.'

'Then what are you?'

Goldie flicks through her duplicitous options: continuing attempts to convince him that the bluebottle wasn't really dead; invent something scientific-sounding, tell him he must be imagining things – divert the conversation into chastising him for the shoplifting or turning things in the direction of his probable truancy and possible drug use . . . But the temptation to tell him the truth, to have him be happy with her and proud of her, is suddenly quite overwhelming.

'I'm not a witch,' she says. 'I'm a Grimm.'

Scarlet

Something is wrong. Scarlet isn't at all sure exactly *what* is wrong, but the feeling sits all day in her belly like nausea, drawing her attention, pulling her away from every mundane thing in which she tries to become immersed: scrubbing the cooker, hoovering the carpets, strolling to Daylesford Organics for delicious but overpriced squid ink crackers and cheddar, while gazing longingly at forbidden blue cheeses, trundling about the house to tidy and rearrange things which have already been tidied and rearranged . . . And all the while this knowing of some unpindownable wrongness sits like a squat toad, eyes glistening above the pond weeds.

Finally, Scarlet gives up trying to ignore those bulbous, blinking eyes and decides to peer into the pitiless darkness and find out what it is. Which means she must visit Everwhere. The idea that perhaps Bea can tell her something has been niggling at Scarlet since lunchtime, when she started to hear the toad squelching in the mud, threatening to clamber out of the pond. After all, the dead, unbound by the limits of space and time, can surely see everything?

By midnight, the toad is emitting long guttural ribbits and Scarlet is so desperate to silence it that she can't wait for Eli to return home and no longer cares about the possible dangers lurking on the dark London streets. What does she have to care about anyway? Scarlet can electrocute a man at a hundred paces, if she sees fit. She has nothing to fear. And so, at half past twelve, Scarlet leaves the flat.

As she walks, she tries not to worry about where Eli might be – under a bus or in someone's bed or, most likely, creating another marketing plan to enhance the world domination of Starbucks – but just focus on the tap-tap of her steps, of her heels on the pavement. Of course, Scarlet does not need to go to a gate but tonight she wants to. She knows, though won't fully admit, that this is a ploy to delay the truth that might be revealed. For, though she's driven forward by the need to know, she's also terrified of what the consequences of this knowing might be.

The nearest gate is just around the corner, but Scarlet won't go there. She'll take herself further afield, travelling in circles, making unnecessary detours, slipping down side streets and wandering into dead-end lanes, all the while edging towards her favourite gate: on the grounds of the

British Museum. If she went directly, taking the quickest route, it'd be a twenty-minute walk, but Scarlet is infinitely adept at stretching out time, at making a thirty-minute job take three hours. She has, as a woman without purpose or employment, mastered the art of procrastination and spinning out.

And so, she walks on. As she walks, Scarlet thinks of fairy tales. Of the stories she'll one day read to her daughter. She thinks of those she loved as a little girl and those she hated. Red Riding Hood, unsurprisingly, was her favourite, Hansel and Gretel her most loathed. She couldn't bear the witch fattening Hansel or the cages and the oven's glow. The witch made her think of her grandmother, who also loved sweets and baked gingerbread but was the kindest, loveliest soul in her world. The one who saved her, the one who raised her. Scarlet wanted to keep these two people as far apart in her mind as she could. But still, the story had etched itself into her mind and she could not wipe it free.

Now, as she walks, Scarlet thinks of the captured twins as she follows her own path, marked by the glow of street-lamps, her own golden breadcrumbs in the moonlight, as she passes darkened windows and silent doors. When the clock is ticking towards half past three, Scarlet turns in the direction of her favourite gate. It stands at the entrance to a private garden close to St Pancras Church. It's locked, of course, and looks impenetrable – unless one were to clamber over the top of it – but Scarlet knows better.

And sure enough, at 3.33 a.m., moonlight illuminates the gate and Scarlet pushes it open. She steps not onto soft green grass but soft white moss, and the air is not clear but hangs heavy with fog. Scarlet isn't sure how best to call upon her deceased sister. Goldie hadn't explained; so perhaps Bea had simply come, unbidden. Possibly, as with any summoning, the elements must be properly aligned – the only problem being that Scarlet doesn't know what these elements are or how to align them. Which leaves recourse to only one thing: intuition.

Scarlet follows a well-worn path for a time then veers off the path towards a clutch of trees, stepping over stones and moss and twigs slick with lichen until she comes to a dead silver birch tree marking the centre of a clearing. Scarlet eyes the cracked branches divested of leaves, the trunk brittle and dry. And, all at once, she knows what to do. The summoning Bea would surely most appreciate is one with drama and flair.

Scarlet approaches the tree, hands outstretched, palms turned up to face the sky. Before she's reached the furthest creeping root, sparks catch at her fingertips, and before she's taken another step, two arcs of fire flare out from her hands and cut into the centre of the trunk. Instantly, the dry bark is ignited and within minutes the tree is a pillar of fire. Scarlet stands back to survey her beacon and smiles, satisfied. She looks to the sky, not sure what to expect, not sure if she's expecting anything at all.

Scarlet stands watching the fire for what feels like a long time, so long in fact that, despite the beauty of the flames and the warmth they emit, she almost turns and walks away. But just as she's thinking it was all for nothing, she hears the cry of a bird and glances up.

From the topmost branches of a nearby oak a raven drops, beating its wings so it quickly swoops up again, gliding on currents of hot air. Scarlet follows its flight until the bird alights on a branch of the burning tree.

'I . . . I . . .' Scarlet had prepared a speech but now her words are ash.

You summoned me and now you cannot speak.

Scarlet nods, her throat dry. She swallows. 'I want—'

I know what you want.

At this Scarlet is not surprised. The sisters can hear each other's thoughts in life, there's no reason they cannot do so in death.

I can tell you, but you won't want to hear it.

Scarlet considers. Should she turn back? Should she pretend not to know what she knows? Should she shut her eyes and hope for the best? Scarlet watches the fire.

'I want to know.'

Very well. The raven beats its wings, fanning the flames. *He will burn you. He will scar you. He will break your heart.*

Scarlet catches the words as they fall, each sentence a leaden anchor that drags her under, pulling her down into the soil, into the suffocating dark. And then, when it doesn't seem possible to descend any further, the raven's voice returns.

And you will not give birth to this baby.

Scarlet looks up. This cannot be.

'No, I don't—' She does not know what to say, how to bargain, to insist that this must be untrue. But she can't because, as sure as she knows herself, Scarlet knows that her sister is telling her the truth. When will it happen? When will the miscarriage strike? Scarlet wants to scream, wants to drop to her knees and howl. But she's paralysed, frozen. She presses her hands to her belly, imagining death hidden inside, gathering force, readying itself for the flush of blood, lurking unseen like a rapidly multiplying cancer. And now she must just wait for the flood upon which this cruel announcement will be borne.

'When?' Scarlet manages. 'How? I . . .'

But this is all that Bea will say.

Everwhere

'When will it happen?'

'Just after half past three.'

Goldie glances up at the darkened sky. No stars tonight, too many clouds, the moon only showing a slip of herself.

'Why do we have to wait till then?' Teddy asks.

'I don't know,' Goldie says, because she doesn't.

They stand outside the gate to the Botanical Gardens, chilly and impatient – furtive, to anyone looking on. Ten minutes ago, a police car screamed along the main road and Goldie half expected them to come screeching to a halt and arrest her brother again.

They're here because Teddy wants proof. He woke at two o'clock, demanding it. Further proof of who she is – the resurrection of bluebottles being not quite enough. Goldie spent the afternoon showing him what she can do with plants. She's coaxed fresh leaves from her bonsai tree, drawn blades of grass from the ground and wrapped them around his ankles until he, laughing, begged to be set free. By then, he no longer had doubt but still wanted to know more. When she made the mistake of telling him about the gates he wouldn't be silenced.

He won't be able to pass through, of course. She's explained that much. In a few minutes he'll be left standing alone on the pebbled entrance to the gardens, staring at the space, at the expanse of empty air in her wake. But with this conjuring trick he'll finally be certain. He'll know she's telling the truth about it all.

'It's three thirty-two,' Teddy says.

'Okay.' Goldie reaches for the gate, curling her fingers around a solid wrought-iron finial. She gives it a little shake to show her brother that it's locked, that she holds no tricks up her sleeve. In the next moment, the slip-moon seems to shine a little brighter, its brilliant light shimmering across the gate, as if the metal had all at once been brushed with quicksilver.

At that, Goldie pushes at the gate and it swings open. She glances back at her brother, grinning.

'Here we go,' she says, and steps through.

When her feet sink into soft moss, Goldie knows that Teddy will now be standing on stones, wondering where she's gone, wondering how to lock the gate to the gardens again, wondering at the sister he'd previously held in such disdain but who will now, from this moment on, be by far the most fascinating element in his otherwise prosaic life.

Goldie's about to turn back – she doesn't want to leave her brother for too long, since who knows what trouble he might get into on the streets in the early hours of the morning – when something catches her eye: a shifting in the shadows, a muted squawk.

She steps forward, tentative, not wanting to disturb or scare it, since she doesn't know how broken the bird might be. At first, it's hard to make out its shape, the lines of the body and the broken wing, since the raven is even darker than the shadows. With a flush of panic, she thinks it might be Bea, but then realizes it isn't possible since her sister's not really a raven, only manifests her spirit as one whenever she wishes. And this bird is no spectre. It's small – a baby perhaps – but as real as she is. Goldie stands over the lamely flapping shape, wondering what to do. Could she bring herself to end its misery (with the assistance of a rock) rather than let it suffer a miserable, drawn-out death? Then she pauses, as a fresh thought snatches at the tail of the departing one: *I've brought a bluebottle back to life; why not try to heal a raven's wing?* Having finally won her brother's admiration has injected Goldie with a dash of boldness. And surely healing a broken body is a commensurate skill, easier even, than resurrection. It'd certainly be a kindness, at least to try. And, if nothing else, the practice will do her good.

In one swift movement, Goldie kneels beside the frantic bird, taking hold of its body as gently as she can. Enfolding it with one hand she strokes its feathers with the other, whispering conciliations. Without closing her eyes, Goldie imagines the raven in flight, soaring above the Everwhere trees, higher and higher, before swooping down to almost alight on a fallen trunk mottled with lichen and snaked with ivy, then rising again to drift on currents of air and watch the twisting rivers and blankets of bleached moss and stone below.

'Ina rokon albarkunku, Mami Wata.' Goldie whispers the incantation she knows now by heart, as a regenerating warmth starts to seep slowly from her palms and into the raven's feathers. *'Rike hannuna kamar yadda na kawo wannan dan kadan daga sauran rayuwa . . . Ina rokon albarkunku, Mami Wata. Rike hannuna kamar yadda na kawo wannan dan kadan daga sauran rayuwa.'*

As she speaks Goldie feels the thin, fragile bones of the bird begin to mend beneath her fingers. She feels the pulse of its blood, the frantic beat of its heart. She feels the mending as surely if she were resetting the wing herself, meticulous, bone by bone.

'Rike hannuna kamar yadda na kawo wannan dan kadan daga sauran rayuwa . . . Ina rokon albarkunku, Mami Wata.'

When at last Goldie opens her hands to free the bird she's not surprised to see it flap to the ground then twice hop, both wings tucked safely in, to perch on a nearby stone. It eyes her for a moment then, all at once, with a shudder of ruffled feathers, unfolds and spreads its split black cloak and, hopping accelerated now, takes flight.

The raven is swallowed by the shadows and the only sign that it was ever there, that Goldie hadn't imagined it all, comes in a flurry of caws dropped from the inky sky.

Bea

Every night she divides her time between being with the sisters, new and old, in Everwhere and visiting the dreams of those who've never been or don't come anymore. To those held back by ignorance or fear, she tells another tale – a tale to remind them that Everwhere is their true home, it's in their blood, and to deny it is to deny themselves.

As you step outside the gates you notice the shift – deftly, Bea weaves the words into the flickering images of their unconscious minds – *It's so subtle that, at first, you hardly perceive it. But, as you begin to leave Everwhere behind, as the scent of bonfires no longer lingers on your skin, as your eyes adjust to the sharper light, feet quickening on concrete after moss, ears twitching at the close honk of a car horn and the distant bark of a dog, you notice that you feel a little duller, a little denser, a little sadder. Your head feels heavy, as if you haven't been sleeping well. Something niggles at you, as if you'd recently received bad news but can't quite recall what it was.*

As you walk deeper into the world you've always known, this place where the bricks and mortar are so familiar, the shift feels ever stronger, more acute. The contentment you had felt, the calm, the clarity, is evaporating. The touch of sadness presses on your chest until it seems to pierce your core. Steadily, you feel as if your spirit, every memory of laughter, every capacity for joy, is being sucked out of you, just as clouds leech light from the sky.

You want to turn back, want to run to the place you've left but you know you cannot. There's no going back, not until the next first-quarter moon, not until the gates open again. And so, you walk on. Until you no longer notice the dull ache of disappointment and sorrow, for now it's as much a part of you as the blood flowing in your veins. And, after a while, you forget how you once felt. And, finally, you forget that you were ever there at all.

Still, once you have been, Everwhere will never leave you. The memory, vague and fogged, will linger at the edge of your thoughts and you will not be able to shake it free. It will niggle, it will nudge, until you cannot ignore it anymore.

You start to wonder when you'll go back. Now you want to, but longing is trumped by fear. Fear of the shadows, yes, but also fear of who you are and who you might be. So you try to forget but, every time you wander past a particularly ornate gate, you wonder if – so long as you arrived on the correct night, at the correct time – it might be the one to take you back to Everwhere. You carry on past these gates, knowing you won't return on that particular night, at that precise time. Not yet. You're still too fearful of unleashing the great waves of power lying dormant inside you. And yet, the question of what might happen if you did lingers long after the gate has gone.

But you must listen to that nudge and let it lead you back. Do not hide in your fears for too long because you need to realize your true self and we need you too.

When the sisters awaken, squinting into the morning light, still inhabiting the soft, milky space between sleeping and waking, just before they stretch and yawn, the threads of those sentences tug at the edge of their minds and slowly unfurl and twist into unexpected thoughts: *you're stronger than you seem, braver than you feel, greater than you imagine . . .*

26th October – 5 nights . . .

Goldie

Goldie is no stranger to magic, of course, and what would seem extraordinary to most seems perfectly ordinary to her. But the surprise now, what feels like true magic, is the sudden miracle of her brother's forgiveness. Yesterday he couldn't stand her, yesterday he was so stewed in furious resentment he could barely string three civil words together in her presence. But now. *Now* he finds her so incredible, so fascinating, that all his teenage fury seems to have been forgotten. Now Teddy wants to spend time with her, wants to talk, wants to ask every question, wants to stay up all night visiting gates and watching Goldie disappear through them.

Tonight, since it's not a school night, she allows him to stay up until midnight and ask whatever he likes while she does her best to give honest answers, although there is, of course, a great deal she will never tell him.

When Teddy – having been dragged under significant protest to his bed – finally sleeps Goldie determines to visit Everwhere. She needs to meet Bea again, needs to learn every particular of how she will resurrect Leo. Her sister had been very blasé about the details, smoothing over facts with promises, skipping details with reassurances that everything will be fine.

Tonight, treading softly along a path of white moss, stepping lightly over stones and occasionally cracking a pale twig underfoot, Goldie knows where she's going. She can't explain how – she's long given up trying to explain the mysteries of Everwhere – but she knows that Bea awaits and that she's expecting her. Taking (seemingly) random turns along trails and around coppices and alongside winding rivers, she finally stops at a fallen trunk that lies across the water and there, on the opposite bank, is her raven sister perched atop a snapped bough, preening her wings.

You're late.

'How can I be late,' – Goldie grips hold of a broken branch and bounds up from the ground, as effortlessly as if the moss were a springboard, to stand astride the trunk – 'when we didn't have an appointment?'

The raven offers a derisive squawk.

'You expected me then?' Reaching the other bank Goldie jumps down, crosses the glade to a large stone, flat as a stool, and sits.

Of course. Swooping down from the bough, the raven alights on a nearby stone.

'I needed to ask you some things.'

I know.

Goldie's gaze snags on a tendril of ivy winding up the trunk of a nearby oak tree. She plucks a leaf and twirls it between finger and thumb. The gentle swish of the leaf slowly calms the rapid thump of her heart. 'Then you'll already know what I want to ask.'

Naturally. Her sister pecks at the stone, chipping at its edge. *And the first answer I'll give is this: you need to steel your nerves, remember what you can do and why you'll be doing it.*

'O-kay.' Goldie coaxes fresh leaves from the ivy vine, bright green tight-curled buds that unwrap at accelerated speed. 'Care to be a bit less cryptic?'

Very well. The raven dips its head as if looking down its

beak at Goldie. *It's not giving life you should be practising, but taking it away.*

Goldie stops and the remaining buds stay closed. 'What do you mean?'

Well, of course you'll need a body for Leo's spirit to enter, in order for you to fully resurrect him. There's a twinkle in the raven's eye. *Did you not realize that?*

The leaf in Goldie's hand shrivels and wilts. 'B-but, I . . .' She feels the ground shift and tilt, herself being pitched forward as the promise of being reunited with Leo is snatched away. 'But, I can't . . .'

Oh, don't go soft on me now. Bea ruffles her feathers. *Of course you can.*

Goldie shakes her head. 'I . . .' She's teetering on a precipice, reaching out for strong, solid words, words she can brandish, words she can use as pickaxes to bring her back from the edge. 'N-no, I . . .'

The raven cocks its head, pinning its sister with a disdainful gaze. *I thought you loved him.* A low, chastising caw. Bea knows she's being unfair, even cruel, but she can't help herself. She lost a love – the only man she ever loved – and wasn't able to bring him back. She would have done anything, still cannot forgive herself for what happened, and Goldie's hesitation irks her. *I thought you wanted him back.*

Goldie shakes her head. 'I-I do.'

Then why are you crying? There's no sorrow here. You want to resurrect Leo and I'm telling you how.

'B-but, n-not . . .' Goldie bends over, head between her knees, staring at the bleached moss at her feet, breath coming in gasps. 'Not like this.'

You'll do it. The raven gives a derisive cry. *If you love him as you say you do, you'll do anything.*

Liyana

The wolf whistle hits Liyana before she's even seen who fired it. Her smarmy supervisor stands behind the reception desk, grinning. She can tell from a glance that Justin is already well on his way to being wasted.

'Well, well,' he says. 'You certainly scrub up nice, don't you?'

Liyana shrugs as she reaches him. 'You told me to wear something smart.'

'What I said was "sexy"' – his eyes dawdle up and down her – 'and I'm delighted to see that you followed my instructions. To. The. Letter.'

Liyana grits her teeth. Officious prick. 'Where should I go? Upstairs?'

'Oh, no,' Justin says with a smile. 'We've brought the bar down to us. It's a pool party. Head on through.'

Great, Liyana thinks, trudging along the tiled corridor, an evening of fat, letchy VIPs and their botoxed, bulimic wives. She'll stay for two hours, maybe three, get paid and get out. It'll be tedious, enduring fumbled gropes from the husbands and condescending talk from the wives, but she'll get through it.

Music throbs behind the double doors. But – she frowns – those pounding bass notes aren't Vivaldi or Miles Davis. Trance? Techno? Certainly not what she'd expect middle-aged, middle-class VIPs of South Kensington to enjoy. Liyana pushes open the doors, then stops.

Around the edge of the swimming pool stand half a dozen young men wearing Bermuda shorts and gripping shot glasses which, upon spotting Liyana, they raise aloft. A roar of approval lifts above the thump of the synthesized drums as they down their drinks in unison. When the roar rises again Liyana turns to see Justin striding through the doors behind her.

'Woah!' he bellows, raising his arms like a ringmaster. 'Do we approve of the entertainment then, lads?'

Another roar.

Liyana grabs at Justin's arm, pulling it down. 'What's going on?' she hisses.

A chorus of excited 'Oos' and 'Ahs' ripple through the line of men.

'Well, I learned something rather interesting about you the other day.' Justin fixes her with a knowing look and a slow grin. 'I know your secret.'

Liyana frowns. 'What secret?'

He folds his arms, glancing at his audience before loudly delivering the punchline. 'A little birdy told me that you – how shall I put this? – favour the fairer sex.'

The men burst into spontaneous applause.

Liyana glowers at him. 'And how the hell is that any of your business?'

'I make it my business to be interested in the lives of all my staff,' Justin says. 'What sort of a manager would I be if I didn't care?'

'You're not a manager,' Liyana says. 'You're a supervisor, and a shit one at that.'

Laughter ripples through the six, silenced by a glare from Justin.

'I don't know what you're planning tonight.' Liyana turns back towards the doors. 'But I'm not playing it. Not today or any other day.'

'Wait.' Justin grabs hold of Liyana's arm as she passes. 'You're not going anywhere just yet.'

'Let go of me,' Liyana snaps. 'Right fucking now.'

'Oh, calm down.' Justin laughs. 'We don't want to touch; we just want to watch.'

Pulling herself free, Liyana scowls. 'What the hell are you talking about?'

'Oh, Tilly!' he calls out. 'Come on out, you're up!'

The six teenage boys turn to watch a teenage girl emerge slowly from behind a white stone pillar on the other side of the swimming pool. She's tall and slim, with blonde hair falling to her waist, wearing a string bikini. Despite herself, despite the circumstances, despite the stench of sweat, beer and chlorine, Liyana feels a stirring of attraction.

'You like her, do you?' Justin grins, releasing Liyana's arm. 'I thought you would. Come on, Til,' – he beckons her forward – 'don't be shy.'

'What are you doing to her?' Liyana says. 'You'd better not—'

'Oh, don't be so filthy.' Justin sighs. 'We haven't touched her. No, Tilly here' – he slips a protective arm over her shoulder – 'came to me for advice. Officially, she's Nick's girlfriend' – he nods towards his friends and a tall, muscular boy proudly raises his hand – 'but she confessed to me that she's a little ... bi-curious. Asked if I knew anyone she could ... experiment with.'

Liyana stares at them both. 'And you want me to – are you fucking serious?'

Justin shrugs. 'Why not? You'd be doing ol' Til here a favour and I wasn't kidding about the double pay. Better still, you won't be schmoozing with letchy VIPs, you'll be doing ... what you like to do best.'

Liyana regards him. 'And you and your buddies are proposing to watch this encounter, are you?'

'Only if you girls don't mind,' Justin says, as if it's of no consequence. 'We promise to be on our best behaviour.'

Another drunken roar rises in the wake of his words.

'You really want to do this?' Liyana turns to Tilly, who blushes and shrugs.

'Fuck.' Liyana shakes her head. 'You're fucking crazy, the lot of you.'

Liyana turns and strides towards the double doors. As she presses her hand to the glass, two pairs of hands grab her arms. Liyana lashes out, kicking and twisting, hitting one boy's shin with her heel so he cries out.

'Jesus,' Justin says, as they drag her back to him. 'Anyone would think we're trying to rape you, the bloody fuss you're making. And here we are, taking great pains not to leave a single mark on your beautiful body.'

A boy whoops and beer bottles clink in a toast.

'Sit, gather yourself,' Justin says, as Liyana is deposited on a lounge chair beside the pool. 'And calm down. It won't be any fun unless you relax.'

'Let me go,' Liyana snaps at the two boys gripping her.

They glance at Justin, who nods. They let go. Liyana tugs at her skirt, pulling it as far down her thighs as it'll go. She crosses her legs, then uncrosses and pushes them together. Tilly, ushered to the chair, perches on the edge, so an inch of air still remains between them.

'Don't be shy, girls,' Justin says. He glances at the bar. 'How about a little champagne to loosen – lighten you up.'

The boy who'd grabbed Liyana's left arm leans over and whispers in Justin's ear. Justin frowns.

'Okay, so it appears these louts have drunk all the champagne,' he says. 'How about Bud? A step down. I apologize. But the effects will be the same.'

Liyana shrugs. Tilly nods.

When she has a beer in hand, Liyana glances at the pool. 'I was just thinking . . .' She takes a swig from the bottle and splutters.

Justin looks up from his own bottle. 'Yeah?'

Liyana swallows. 'Yeah, I was, um – why don't you boys get into the pool?'

Justin frowns again. 'And why would we do that?'

Taking another gulp, as if she really couldn't give a damn either way, Liyana nods at his crotch. 'To preserve your modesty, for when things start getting . . . wetter. I know how sensitive about your tent poles you boys can be.'

Beside her, Tilly giggles.

A blush rises to Justin's cheeks. Then he shrugs, as if he too doesn't give a damn. 'Sure, why not?' He nods at his six cohorts who, mimicking his shrug in their own way, proceed to march in single file like soldiers down the steps and into the pool. Their lieutenant watches until they're all standing in a line, water lapping at their chests, sniggering and staring at the girls, then he walks slowly down the steps, beer in hand, to join them.

Liyana leans into Tilly, without touching her. 'You don't have to do this,' she mutters. 'You can just tell them all to fuck off and go home.'

'Stop being a tease,' Justin shouts. 'Give her what she wants.'

'Nick's your boyfriend, right?' Liyana whispers. 'If you say no, he won't let the others—'

'Look, it's no big deal,' Tilly hisses. 'Let's just get it over with, okay?'

Liyana looks at her, at the barely concealed fear in her wide eyes, wondering how many times Tilly has applied this logic to having sex with her boyfriend.

'Get a move on,' a boy shouts. 'My dick's shrivelling to the size of my finger in here!'

'No change there then,' another quips.

'Fuck off,' the first boy snaps, as the others explode with laughter.

'All right then.' Liyana places her palm on Tilly's cheek, generating a chorus of whoops and cheers. 'Let's just hope they don't do themselves an injury in that pool, shit-faced as they are.'

When Liyana touches her lips to Tilly's, her other hand grips the figurine of Mami Wata hanging around her neck. Slowly, a current begins to swirl beneath the boys' feet. She closes her eyes as a wave gathers. The boys, whipped as they are into a frenzy of shrieks and howls, don't notice the shift. The wave builds behind them but still none of them feel it, not until it crashes over their heads, pushing them down, the current clutching their ankles, pulling the boys under. Their thrashing and flailing is eclipsed by the deep beat of the electronic drums, so Tilly doesn't hear them. Liyana opens one eye to survey the churning pool and smiles.

Just enough to scare them, she thinks, just enough to make them think twice before going into the water again, just enough that they'll doubt the wisdom of sexual assault in the future.

When at last the water stills, one by one the boys burst to the surface, no longer shrieking with delight but spluttering in panic, no longer jeering but speechless. Justin is shaking. Nick is weeping. Liyana draws away from Tilly who gapes at the boys, open-mouthed. Liyana pulls herself up from the chair and steps to the edge of the pool.

'You all right?' She looks down at them and seven terrified faces look back up at her. 'No one drowned? That's lucky, isn't it?' She pauses. 'You might not be so lucky next time.'

Then she turns and walks away, slowly, steadily, forcing herself not to run.

Scarlet

'What's going on?'

'What do you mean?' Scarlet asks.

Eli sets down his wine glass. 'Why do you keep staring at me?'

Scarlet studies the pierced carrot on the end of her fork. 'I'm not staring at you.'

'Not now you're not. But you certainly were. You've been sneaking strange looks at me all day.' Eli slices through a boiled, buttered potato and pops half in his mouth. 'As if you think you've seen me somewhere before but aren't quite sure where.'

Scarlet stabs her own potato and swallows it whole. Followed by a forkful of peas. She gulps a few times, then starts coughing.

'Are you all right?' Eli frowns. 'Drink some water.'

Scarlet waves him away. She tries to say 'I'm fine' but finds she can't quite catch her breath to speak. In one movement Eli pushes his chair from the table, darts to her side and is smacking the heel of his hand between her shoulder blades, before Scarlet even realizes she's choking.

Seconds later Scarlet has, in a heart-pounding mess of saliva and stomach acid, regurgitated the peas onto her plate, watching them spit through the air in seeming slow motion as she grips the table edge and burns the imprints of her fingertips into the wood. For those few seconds Scarlet's thoughts courted death, for those few seconds she saw the darkness closing in, for those few seconds she felt the chasm of eternal solitude open at her feet.

Snotty tears running down her cheeks, Scarlet grips Eli's arm like a life-rope, as if Ezekiel Wolfe is the only thing standing between her and eternal damnation.

'Y-you saved my life,' Scarlet splutters, as soon as she has breath enough to speak. 'I-I . . .'

'Don't be silly.' Eli laughs, though the sound is too shrill. 'You're fine, you were fine. Nothing to worry about.' He squeezes Scarlet's shoulders.

'Wait, don't—'

But Eli is patting her on the back before she can stop him letting go, returning to his chair just as she's reaching out to try and catch his fingers with her own. On the slipstream of this small rejection another thought comes: could the few seconds without oxygen have hurt *her*? Scarlet presses a palm to her belly, checking. She waits, willing herself to feel a spark of electricity, a single volt.

'No need to let this go to waste,' Eli says, taking a forkful of peas, nodding at Scarlet's plate. 'Come on, old girl. Jump back on the horse and all that.'

Not hearing him, she waits. And then, thank God, she feels it. Their singular method of communication: a tiny electric shock. Scarlet exhales.

'Oh, Scar, don't be such a scaredy cat. Eat up.'

Slowly, Scarlet eases herself back into the chair. She glances down at her plate, wiping her cheeks with the back of her hand, sniffing up her snot, dabbing her fingers under her eyes to erase inevitable smudges of mascara. Won't he ask after the baby? Has he even thought of her? Scarlet wants to say something, to admonish him. But her need for Eli right now is overwhelming, her fingers twitch with it, and it's all she can do not to run to him, lay her head in his lap and cry. So, she says nothing.

Scarlet can't eat after that. She pushes potatoes, peas,

fillet of wild salmon around the bone china plate in an attempt to feign gluttony, but it's no good. As Eli eats, Scarlet's racing heart starts to settle, her blood-red fear begins to fade, her fierce grip on her fork slowly loosens. By the time Eli brings his knife and fork together, Scarlet's spine is straighter, her breath stronger, her sense of self gradually returning.

'I heard something,' she says.

'Oh?' Eli leans back in his chair, lifting his wine glass to his lips.

He saved you, Scarlet thinks. *He loves you*. Don't mess with that. 'About you.'

'Okay,' he says. 'So, are you going to tell me what it is, or am I going to guess?'

Scarlet takes a deep breath. 'Are you having an affair?'

Eli frowns, then laughs. The explosion of sound is deep and low and real, heaping sand on the flames of Scarlet's anxiety. 'Am I – what a ridiculous question,' he says, still laughing. 'Whatever made you ask that? No wonder you've been giving me the evil eye all day, if that's what you've been thinking. Bloody hell, Scar, you are a silly goose.'

'"Silly goose"?' Scarlet smiles. 'That's a new one. And I know it's silly. I just, I just . . .'

'What?' Eli sits forward. 'What have you been thinking?'

Scarlet shrugs. 'I don't know, I . . .'

Eli opens his arms. 'Come here.'

Scarlet shakes her head, embarrassed, ashamed. She bites her lip, casts her gaze to the carpet. Eli shifts his chair back, spreads his legs, pats his left knee.

'Come now,' he says, as if she's a naughty schoolgirl. 'Don't make me come and get you. You won't like the consequences.'

Scarlet smiles. She knows what follows this: deep, wet

kisses that last all night. Head down to hide her smile, Scarlet stands and walks over to sit on Eli's knee.

That night, as Scarlet lies beside a snoring, sated Eli, she realizes that he never actually answered the question.

Everwhere

The raven sits on its favourite branch, cocking its head every few minutes to turn a beady eye to the ground. When the girl steps tentatively into the glade the raven swoops down from the oak tree and glides to the ground.

What's your name? The raven settles on a fallen trunk a few feet from the girl, noting that she barely flinches at the shock of the intrusion. She is perhaps eleven, short and plump, with curls of blonde hair to her shoulders – reminding Bea of Goldie.

'Gaia,' says the girl.

The raven gives a quick nod of approval.

'It means . . .' The girl looks to her toes, momentarily self-conscious. 'I'm named after the Greek Goddess of the Earth.'

Oh? The raven feigns surprise, as if this is news to her. *Well, that's perfect.*

Gaia twists a blonde curl around her finger. 'What do you mean?'

Bea feels her spirits lift and, if it were possible for ravens to smile, she would be smiling now. This is always her favourite part.

You're not dreaming – her voice is the crack of twigs beneath Gaia's feet – *You've come here because you're a Sister Grimm, because you can do special things and I'm going to teach you what those things are.*

'Oh.' Gaia brightens, then looks nervous. 'But, are you sure? I mean, I'm not very good at maths and I never get As – none of my teachers think I'm special.'

The raven gives a dismissive flick of its head. *There's much more to life than school. By the time I've finished teaching you what you can do, you probably won't bother going back to school.*

The girl frowns. 'But I think I have to. My mum says it's the law.'

The raven emits a cackle and a caw. *I suppose so; but what I'll teach you will be far more important than anything you'll ever learn in school.*

Now Gaia cocks her head in a way that mirrors the bird, so they are observing each other curiously.

'What'll you teach me?'

The raven draws up one leg and taps three times as it speaks, as if counting off on its claws. *How to coax seedlings from the ground, how to bring dead plants back to life, how to animate them as you wish ...*

'Really?' Gaia stares at the bird, eyes wide.

Yes. The raven ruffles her feathers. *And that's just for starters.*

Gaia grins and claps. So they sit together late into the Everwhere night, twining vines of ivy into plaits, teasing stuttering new shoots from the trunks of dead trees and trying to inch the blankets of bleached moss further across the stone-scattered ground.

It's not as if he's a man, Bea had said. *You'd be killing a soldier, a fallen star – you've done that before, you can do it again.*

'Just because he's not a man,' Goldie had said, finally finding her voice, 'doesn't mean it's not murder.'

Oh, pish. He'd kill you if he had half the chance. He'll

122

probably have killed many of your sisters before you; consider it retribution.

'There aren't any soldiers in Everwhere anymore,' Goldie said. 'We're no longer fighting that war.'

I've seen a few strays now and then, the sort who don't need a reason, who just do it for fun – surely that's the kind of soldier who's better off dead. You'd be doing your sisters a service, protecting them.

Goldie had frowned. 'But none have been hurt, have they?'

No. The raven cast out its wings, then drew them back in. *Not yet.*

Goldie had felt shamed then, that she didn't know rogue soldiers still roamed Everwhere; she should have been protecting her sisters, she should have been teaching them, but she was so absorbed by her own life and her own loss, that she hadn't even given it a second thought.

27th October – 4 nights . . .

Goldie

Goldie yanks sweaty, stained sheets from the beds, replacing them with crisp, clean ones, tucking in tight hospital corners. She kneels on marble floors and scrubs porcelain toilet bowls. She dusts the same shelves she dusted yesterday, polishes the same mirrors. She's on autopilot today, without even the heart to steal anything, for all she can think about is what she must do: kill one man to bring back another. Can she do it? Can she commit murder?

Goldie pauses for a few minutes in room 13, spying a clutch of silk socks (all in Teddy's size and his favourite colour: teal) but doesn't reach for them. And when she finds a cornucopia of sparkling nail polishes scattered across the floor of room 17, she doesn't pocket a single one. She's been sapped of all desire, all will to interact with this world gone; she wants to do nothing beyond what she absolutely must. And every moment she's haunted by echoes of the words Bea spoke last night.

Wrapped around the words are memories of Leo, her discovery of who he was and what he had done. He was a soldier, sent to fight her, to kill her if she wasn't strong enough to prove her worth. He hadn't chosen the war, had been manipulated into thinking Goldie and her kind were the enemy, but still he would've fought her if he hadn't loved her first.

Once, when Wilhelm Grimm lived, hundreds of soldiers, those fallen stars, had patrolled the paths of bleached moss and fallen leaves hunting for Sisters Grimm – every month on the night of the moon's first quarter, stepping through gates at 3.33 a.m. from Earth and into Everwhere. Now only a few rogue soldiers remain, but still Goldie knows she will only ever kill in an act of defence. Anything else would be murder.

Still, she wonders now, is it different if you extinguish the life of someone who's bringing (or intending to bring) great harm to others? Might that not be a benevolent act concealed within a malevolent one? If, in killing one, you saved many, would that not be a good thing? No one, after all, could argue with the notion of travelling back in time to kill Hitler and those of his ilk.

'But then am I only justifying myself?' Goldie says to herself as she smooths the sheets across the king-sized bed in room 14. Oh, how she longs to lie down and take a nap, to forget all this awfulness and sink into temporary oblivion. 'After all, I wouldn't be thinking it at all, if not to satisfy my own selfish ends.'

With a sigh, Goldie steps away from the bed and sinks down to the floor. *Am I a dreadfully selfish person, wanting to bring the love of my life back? I used not to be – what's happened? I dropped out of school to take care of Teddy, I raised him, I gave him everything, did all I could to make him happy. And now* . . . She drops her head onto her knees and cries.

Goldie's tears are stopped by the tug of a story at the edge of her thoughts. And, although she has neither the energy nor the will to write, still she does as she's bid and drags herself from the floor, wipes her eyes and nose, and scurries to the desk in the corner of the room, snatches up the pad of hotel paper and starts to write. The words unfurl across the page as quickly as if she's taking dictation:

Worthless/Priceless

There was once a king who had everything he could wish for: wealth beyond all imagining, lands that stretched to every horizon and victory on every battlefield. There was only one thing missing: an heir.

One day, at last his queen was blessed with a child and the king was overjoyed. However, when the child was born it was not an heir but a girl. The king was distraught that he'd not got what he'd wished for and the queen was distraught for having displeased the king. And for their misery they blamed their baby girl.

As the princess grew, she learned from her parents' every word and gesture that she was not as she should be. The sad princess wondered what had gone wrong, what had she done to repel the king and queen and destroy their love? She did not know and so she searched. Perhaps she was not pretty enough, or clever enough, or good enough or sweet enough or kind enough or . . . Perhaps it was none of these things, or perhaps it was all of them. The princess did not know and so she tried, she tried everything to change herself and win her parents' love.

But nothing worked. Whatever she did, however hard she tried, still her parents did not love her. The princess did not stop trying, twisting herself into different representations of rightness, attempting to be winning in every way to compensate for whatever it was she was not. Finally, she realized that her failure meant she was worthless and could do only one thing: slink into the shadows and hope to be forgotten.

One day, the princess was married to a prince, a man her father had chosen, a man she didn't love. Still, she was relieved to leave her parents, thinking that she might be happier, even in an unhappy marriage, since she no longer had to try and win her parents' love. Now she could move on and be whoever she wanted to be.

Sadly, the princess soon realized that she was wrong. For whenever she tried to do anything or be anything, she felt inadequate and unable. She felt wrong, she felt worthless. Just as she had as a child. Nothing had changed.

One day her husband found her sitting in the garden weeping.

'What's wrong?' he asked.

'I don't know,' she cried. 'I just . . . I can't do anything. I try and I fail. I'm useless.'

'No you're not,' her husband said. And he took her hand and promised that he would help.

The prince was true to his word and encouraged the princess in every endeavour until, at last, she was the most accomplished, brilliant and adored woman in seven kingdoms. Word of her great success reached the king and queen and, their curiosity piqued, they invited the princess home to visit. Overjoyed and buoyed by hope, the princess went. However, she quickly discovered that her parents' feelings had not changed, they still didn't love her. She was still wrong; she still wasn't enough. She returned to her husband in tears.

'Whatever I do,' she cried, 'however I am, it'll never be right, it'll never be enough for them to love me.'

'You don't need to be a better person,' the prince said. 'Nothing you do will make you any better than you already are.'

The princess pondered this, but it did not lift her sorrow.

'You did nothing wrong,' he said. 'The only mistake you made was thinking it was you, not them, who was wrong.'

The princess pondered this too, but she did not believe him.

'Being unwanted is not the baby's fault,' he said. 'A baby cannot purposefully do anything to make itself more or less pleasing or wanted. That choice lies with the parents, not the child. It's very sad but many children are unwanted, and there is nothing they can do to change that. No matter how good they are, how nice, how pretty, how sweet, how clever, how successful . . .' He paused. 'Indeed, some of the most sparkling people in this world were unwanted and felt worthless, so spent their lives trying to change that.'

'How do you know all this?' the princess asked.

The prince gave her a shy shrug and smiled. 'Personal experience,' he said.

'So why do we do it?' she asked. 'If it's really not our fault, then why do we blame ourselves?'

'Because . . .' He trailed off, contemplating the best way to explain. 'Because we cannot blame our parents. If we believed it was their fault then we'd also believe that the situation was irreparable, because we can't control them. It's the same with our gods; they must be infallible and we must be flawed, since then we always have the chance to change ourselves, to appease them, to invoke their love and protection with our right behaviour. It's the same with parents; we believe that because it feels safer and gives us hope.'

'I suppose so,' the princess conceded. 'At least, miserable though it was, all those years of believing if I changed, if I found the magic recipe I'd win their love, then at least I could keep on hoping that one day it might work, that one day they might love me back.'

'Yes,' the prince said, softly wiping the princess's tears with his thumb. 'The death of hope is the saddest of all things and something we will endure almost any pain to avoid feeling.'

'So . . .' the princess sniffed. 'So how did you survive it?'

'I was lucky,' the prince said. 'One day I realized that it wasn't my fault that my parents didn't love me, and there was nothing I could do to change that or to please them. So instead, I set about loving myself.'

The princess sighed. 'Oh, I wish I could do that too.'

'But you can,' said the prince. 'I know, it's not easy, but you can. It starts with . . . realizing that you've turned on yourself, that you've believed in the judgements of others and made their opinions and feelings your own.'

The princess sighed, for she did not know if she could love herself. But at least, this time, she knew that he spoke the truth. And she knew that was the first step. If she accepted her parents' valuation, if she believed herself to be worthless, she would never be happy. For all people need love, and inside our own hearts is where the greatest love is to be found.

Reading what she's written, Goldie wonders who this story is for. Could it be for her? Perhaps. But she senses that it's for someone else.

That evening Goldie sits opposite her brother, eating the hotel's lunch special out of a foil takeaway carton.

'This is good,' Teddy says. 'Give the new chef my compliments. The sauce has just the right amount of chilli.'

Goldie nods, though she's not really listening. She's eaten half the dish but tasted none of it. 'Ted . . .'

He looks up. 'Yeah?'

129

'I . . .' She takes a deep breath and sets down her fork. 'I need to tell you something. It's important.'

'Okay.' He doesn't set down his own fork but holds it above the carton, hovering.

'And I need you to listen.'

Teddy shrugs – the perpetual shrug of the teenage boy – and fidgets with the hem of his back-to-front T-shirt. 'All right then, I am.'

'Okay . . .' Goldie picks up her fork, then puts it down again. Teddy waits patiently for her to speak. The aura of awe with which he's regarded his sister ever since he saw her stepping into Everwhere has hardly abated. It's not something she wants to discourage, since it's a definite improvement on the disdain and disgust with which he'd been viewing her for the past few years, though she does occasionally find it slightly disconcerting, especially when she catches him fixing her with a curious frown – as if trying to burrow inside her thoughts. Tonight, though, she's hoping it'll stand her in good stead. 'Okay . . .'

When she doesn't continue, Teddy gives her a quizzical look. 'Go on then.'

Goldie nods. 'Yes, yes, all right. Well . . . in a few days I'm . . . I'm planning on doing something that should be fine, it's not as risky as – well, anyway, I'm guessing everything will be fine but . . . if something goes wrong – which I'm sure it won't – if I . . . I've put things in place so you'll be taken care of.'

Teddy stares at her.

Goldie sits forward in her chair. 'Do you—?'

'What the hell do you mean?' Teddy is still staring when realization dawns. 'You mean, if you *die*?'

'No, of course not.' Goldie presses her hands together.

130

'That's to say, I mean – look, don't worry. It'll be fine, I'm sure it'll be fine. I just need to—'

'Stop saying that,' Teddy snaps. '"It'll be fine, it'll be fine." What if it's not? Then you won't be able to do fucking anything about it, will you?'

'Ted,' Goldie says. 'Please.'

'What?' Teddy pushes away from the table so he's standing over her. Goldie notices that he's growing out of his trousers again. 'If you're dead then you won't be able to stop me swearing, will you? I'll be able to say any fucking thing I want then, won't I? I—'

'Ted, please' – she reaches out to him across the table – 'please, sit down.'

'I can tell everyone in the fucking world to go fuck themselves!' He's shouting now, tears slipping down his cheeks. 'And you won't be able to do a fucking thing about it! Will you?'

Goldie pulls herself up from her chair and stumbles towards her brother as he backs away, finally catching him in her arms. He pushes her off, but she's stronger and holds him until he stops swearing, until he stops fighting, until he presses his face into her neck and starts to sob into her shoulder, mumbling tear-soaked words in a waterlogged voice, murmuring limp curses into her cotton-wet skin.

'Don't worry.' Goldie strokes his hair, holding him tight. 'It's okay, it'll be okay . . .'

When Teddy pulls away he looks up at her with puffy eyes. 'Don't do anything,' he begs, in his soggy voice. 'Promise you won't.'

Goldie meets his gaze and touches his cheek, smearing tears with her fingertips, trying to dry him off, trying to smudge away her guilt.

'Promise,' he begs again.

'I . . .'

'Please.'

Goldie looks at her little brother, the baby she's raised, the boy she's loved more than anything in the world since the moment he was born. And she does. She would die for Teddy, in a heartbeat. And if anyone hurt him, she'd kill them. And, if he died, Goldie would want to die too. She loves him – if it were possible to measure such a thing – even more than Leo. But – and here love dovetails into obsession – but she doesn't need her brother like she needs her lover.

'I – I promise,' Goldie says. 'Okay. I promise.'

Teddy's sodden face lights up. 'Really?'

Goldie nods.

'Cross your heart and hope to die?'

She nods again. 'Cross my heart and hope to die.'

Teddy grins and squeezes her tight, then leans up to kiss her cheek. Not long ago he'd have had to stand on tiptoes, Goldie thinks, but not anymore. She feels his love and relief surge through her like released breath and thinks she's never hated herself as much as she does right now.

Liyana

When Liyana returns to the hospital this morning she's still shaking. Last night she'd taken a taxi from the Serpentine Spa back to the flat – unwilling to walk the streets alone, despite the expense of the fare – but even the sight of the taxi driver had scared her, the thought that he could lock the doors and trap her inside the car. She'd called Kumiko, who hadn't answered, then texted her again:

I really need you now. Please. xxx

As she lay in bed, wishing she could visit Nya, wishing she could hold Kumiko, Liyana slowly resigned herself to sleeplessness, because she couldn't bear to close her eyes and risk seeing Justin's face, or any of the boys, or even Tilly. She knew then that she would never go back; what she'll do for work now she has no idea, though she can't afford to dally.

It was a shame she couldn't sleep, for she could have visited Everwhere and Aunt Sisi, who might have hugged her until she stopped shaking, then inspired her with confidence until she was strong and herself again. Tomorrow. Liyana promised herself, she would find Sisi tomorrow.

Now Liyana sits at Nya's bedside, texting Kumiko again – having received no reply last night – and glancing up at her aunt every few minutes to check for signs of life. While Goldie is formulating a plan to resurrect Leo, Liyana is creating her own plan to strengthen Nya's tenuous grip on living and bring her fully back to life. Liyana is studying her aunt from the corner of her eye when the paper curtain, which she's pulled around the bed for privacy, twitches. She glances up, expecting the intrusion of a kindly nurse and hoping it's not the rather arrogant ward doctor, but instead is faced with the familiar swish of long black hair, which parts to reveal the most beautiful face she's ever seen: large red lips and big black eyes wide with kindness and love.

Liyana's heart surges and, after a moment's shocked pause, she leaps up from her chair to half skid, half slip across the vinyl tile floor and fall into Kumiko's arms. For a long time they hold each other; Liyana cries and though Kumiko is silent her embrace is tender and tight. When they finally part, Kumiko reaches up to wipe Liyana's eyes.

'Oh, Ana.' Slowly, she kisses Liyana's wet cheeks, each in turn.

For a moment Liyana is still, absorbing the warmth of

her girlfriend's touch, then she breaks into a grin. 'Koko, I can't believe you're ...' Liyana kisses Kumiko's lips, her cheeks, her neck, her hair. 'How did you escape, how did you ... ? I'm so sorry I let you down before, I'm sorry I've been so rubbish, I've missed you so much, I ...' Then she grabs Kumiko again, squeezing her so tight that Kumiko emits a small squeal. 'I can't believe it's really you, I can't believe you're really here!'

When at last Liyana lets Kumiko go, she steps back. 'You said you needed me, so I came.'

Later that evening, with Kumiko snoring softly beside her, Liyana thinks of her aunt Nya, of healing and resurrection, of the possibilities of reigniting the spirit of someone still alive. She fingers the little carving hanging around her neck. She hasn't removed her talisman, even at night, since fastening the clasp for the first time.

In Liyana's lap lies a book bestowed upon her by Aunt Sisi: *Binding the Bones: how to imbue life into inanimate matter*. Over the last few days Liyana has made several attempts at reading it, though the words always seem to slip away. Tonight, perhaps because she has Kumiko to anchor her, it is slowly, slowly starting to make sense. Now Liyana revisits every sentence of the first chapter until she has fully understood, fully imbibed each paragraph. Though, of course, she thinks as she closes the book and sits back into soft pillows, knowledge is of little use until it has been put into practice.

Liyana strokes her hand over the leather cover, circling her fingers around the title, whispering encouraging words of invocation and invitation. *Give me a chance*, she thinks, *give me the chance to see if I can do what you promise is possible.* She gazes at the book a while, listening to Kumiko's breathing, then presses it to her chest and glances about the room, wondering. After several long, empty minutes Liyana sets *Binding the Bones* down on her bedside table and notices a shadow on the windowsill. She leans closer to peer at it: a dead dusty black moth with orange spots dotted across its folded wings. Liyana prods it with a tentative finger. Definitely dead.

Mumbling a quick prayer under her breath, Liyana scoops up the little body and holds it, lying sideways, cupped in her hands. *Goldie should be doing this, not me*, she thinks. *She's a daughter of earth, she can give life. I can only take it away.* But as she gazes down at the moth she recalls a story Goldie told her once of how she'd imbued a dead bonsai tree with new life. Liyana focuses on the memory. What had she said? What had she done? Focus, Goldie had said; she'd focused on the warm rhythm of her veins compared to the cold stillness of the little tree and transferred that spark of aliveness across the void.

Now Liyana closes her eyes to concentrate on that and, after a while, starts to feel it: the chasm between life and death and what might be required to cross it. She pictures the moth as it must have been not long ago, beating its wings against windows, bumping into lightbulbs, clinging to musty curtain folds to hide from the sun. As these thoughts multiply, Liyana feels the cocoon of her hands grow warmer and she begins to mumble words from the book: words of birth, growth and life, words that reach across the void, until the gap between death and life is no longer so very great at all.

'*Ina rokon albarkunku, Mami Wata*,' Liyana murmurs. '*Rike hannuna kamar yadda na kawo wannan dan kadan daga sauran rayuwa.*'

And then, all at once, Liyana feels a shift, a jolt, a spark; as if the faint thump-thump of the moth's faded heartbeat is twitching back to life. She pictures the moth flying. She mumbles the words. She feels the heat of her hands. And finally, when the gap is almost closed, Liyana opens her cupped hands to peer down at the tiny creature. Astonished, she watches as its antennae quiver and its wings flicker and its four remaining legs spasm. The moth is reaching for life and Liyana reaches back.

'*Ina rokon albarkunku, Mami Wata,*' she intones, louder now. '*Riƙe hannuna kamar yadda na ƙawo wannan dan kadan daga sauran rayuwa.*'

Liyana bends her head, purses her lips, and blows a gentle breath beneath its feathery wings. Two of the moth's legs find purchase on one of Liyana's fingers and it flips itself over in her palm so it's upright once more. Then suddenly it lifts and takes flight, gliding on Liyana's breath, flitting haphazardly across the unlit room, lifting and falling, until it regains its own strength and is flying off into the darkness; then it's gone, a shadow and a memory once more.

Long after the moth has disappeared, Liyana gazes out into the dark, grinning.

Liyana falls asleep for a while and, spiriting herself into Everwhere in the hopes of finding Aunt Sisi and sharing her triumph, is disappointed not to find her. Just past midnight, Liyana is woken by the ring of her phone. Rubbing her eyes and squinting into the illuminated dark, she glances at Kumiko still sleeping beside her, wondering who could be calling, then clumsily gropes for the luminous phone on her bedside table. No Caller ID. *The hospital.* How the hell could she have forgotten?

With a lurch in her stomach, Liyana picks up.

'Hello, Miss Chiweshe?'

'Yes, but don't tell me that she's—'

'Don't worry, Miss Chiweshe, everything is all right. I'm calling to say that your aunt has just regained consciousness.'

Scarlet

When Scarlet wakes, Eli is sleeping. She can't see his face, only the wall of his back, the mess of his hair. He's turned away, curled around a pillow, as if he's protecting secrets. What is he thinking, she speculates, what is he dreaming of? If only it were possible to carve into someone's mind and view every thought, every idea, every desire. If only it were possible to know, unequivocally, if a person was lying. No need for interrogation or lie detectors or supposition. To just *know*. How gloriously reassuring that would be. Scarlet knows with her sisters, of course, but has no such certainty when it comes to Eli.

Scarlet glances at his bedside table, at the lamp and the phone beside it, the screen a dark, polished mirror, revealing nothing. She glances at his briefcase propped up against the oak leg of the leather armchair in the corner of the room. She thinks of her sisters. *Get it over and done with*, Liyana would say. *Then stop obsessing, get some sleep.* Goldie would shake her head. *He's your fiancé, your baby's father. Trust him; leave him alone and let him be.* If her grandmother was still alive she'd probably add an admonishing note on pre-marital pregnancy, but that's by the by.

Scarlet lets her gaze linger on the briefcase, then drift to his jacket and shirt draped over the back of the chair, to his jeans in a crumpled heap on the carpet – their passage to the laundry basket derailed by a phone call. She should trust him. Her grandmother's reassuring, reasoning voice returns. *Once you sow the seed of suspicion, Scarlet, it'll spread into everything and you'll never uproot it. It'll be the blight on your relationship, the weeds that will choke your roses.* Esme Thorne loved a gardening metaphor. She'd also had a long, happy marriage. She was sensible, experienced, wise. Scarlet should listen to her, she should—

Oh, fuck it.

She reaches, slowly, carefully, over Eli's body, elongating her fingers to stretch for his phone. Nearly, nearly. Scarlet pincers the phone between finger and thumb, holding her breath until she's dropped it into her lap. She taps in the password and begins searching.

Forty sweaty, panicked minutes later, she's found nothing. Hundreds of tedious work emails. Texts concerning orders for paper coffee cups. Graphs charting the extra costs of ecological packaging. No suspicious names. No affectionate messages. No deleted histories. Nothing.

Scarlet exhales. Everything is fine. He's not doing anything wrong. He's not cheating, lying or betraying her. Her heartbeat slows. She should consider herself lucky, count her blessings and leave it alone. She should go back to sleep. Though, Scarlet thinks, there is still the small matter of the briefcase.

She pulls back the covers and slips out of bed. In ten carpeted steps she's standing over the chair and sliding her right hand into each of his pockets. In the jacket she finds a receipt for a grande iced latte and a cinnamon bun. *Starbucks.* Scarlet makes the sign of the cross. It's bad enough that he works for them, that he put her out of business, but that he still consumes their tainted produce feels like a betrayal one step beyond. And a cinnamon bun? She makes the best cinnamon buns in Britain, arguably the free world. And here he is eating someone else's sub-standard produce. She shudders. This is a smaller betrayal, but a betrayal nonetheless.

Scarlet sighs. Her grandmother, as usual, was right. No

good can come from snooping. Still, she's come this far; surely it'd be careless not to finish the job? She turns out the pockets of his trousers, front and back. Nothing. She checks his shirt. Empty. *Stop now, sweetheart, no damage done.* Scarlet bends her legs to kneel on the soft white carpet. Glancing back at the bed, she clicks free the brass clasp and opens the briefcase. Quickly, Scarlet scans every line of every page.

Moonlight shifts behind the curtains, casting its milky glow into the room. Scarlet glances up at the clock on the wall: 4.38 a.m. An hour later, she's discovered nothing, except Starbucks' plans for global domination. What is it with these locust-like companies – why can't they be satisfied with their silly levels of success, why must they be intent on annihilating all competition? Scarlet sighs, thinking of the melting ice caps and global emissions, suddenly overcome with sadness at the state of the world. Why is she bringing a child into this? Aren't eight billion struggling, suffering souls enough?

Scarlet's about to click the briefcase closed again when she notices a zip. A pocket, a pouch, hidden and full. Heart accelerating, she pulls until the teeth of the zip release to reveal a small square turquoise box. Carefully, Scarlet lifts it out. Upon the box are printed the words *Tiffany & Co.* The box opens with a snap that causes Scarlet, in her heightened state, to start. She glances at the bed – still he sleeps – then back to the box. A silver bracelet sits on a soft, cream leather cushion.

Scarlet lifts the charm bracelet from the box and sets it in her palm. A tiny silver rabbit. A teacup. A playing card – the queen of hearts. A key. A miniature bottle engraved with the words 'drink me'. *Alice in Wonderland.* The details are so precisely rendered, the chain so delicate, the craftsmanship infused with as much enchantment as the story itself. Gossamer lace and spiders' webs, moonlight and ice. It is exquisite.

Scarlet's eyes cloud with tears. How can he be giving this gift to a woman? How can he betray her so cruelly, so completely? She had perhaps expected phone calls, dirty text messages, receipts for hotels and flowers. Generic, clichéd things. Not something so personal, so beautiful, so unique. Not evidence of true feelings, of deep affection, of love. Tears slip down her cheeks and the bracelet becomes blurred. She is tumbling down the rabbit hole into the dark.

Scarlet stuffs her free fingers back into the hidden pouch. The pain is an insatiable plague, it needs to feed, it demands fresh evidence, fresh humiliation, fresh pain. Scarlet's fingers find a square of paper, a note. She snatches it out, wiping her eyes. An envelope with a tiny, thick card inside. No name on the front. She extracts the note and squints at it. A scrawled line in blue ink. Eli's handwriting. She wipes her eyes again.

Scarlet, thank you for giving me everything. Eli x

Scarlet blinks and reads it again. She lets out a blurt of laughter, clamps her hand to her mouth. Giggling. Relief floods her body. He loves her. He loves her after all. Whoever the raven was talking about, it wasn't Eli. It is all right. *Everything is all right.*

Slipping the bracelet back into its hiding place, Scarlet turns away, silently chastising herself for being so suspicious. She's pulling herself up from her aching knees when a shaft of moonlight slips through the curtains and falls across the carpet, casting a spotlight on the back pocket of Eli's crumpled jeans. And there, between the denim folds and cotton stitching, is a glinting metallic edge. It's nothing, she thinks, as she stands. Then, Scarlet feels an internal tug. She stops and, in the silence, hears the whisper of intuition, the tap-tap of a hunch.

Scarlet reaches tentatively into Eli's pocket and pulls out another phone.

Liyana

When Liyana arrives, Nya is sitting up in bed. It's only when she sees this, when she feels tears fill her eyes and breath catch in her throat, that Liyana realizes she'd feared she would never see her aunt alive again.

Pretending it's nothing out of the ordinary, that it's not the middle of the night in a hospital ward, Liyana slips into the chair beside Nya's bed, sliding off her shoes, crossing her legs. She wishes her other aunt was here to share the burden but since she cannot find Sisi, cannot ask her to come, Liyana must do this alone. 'Hello, stranger.'

Nya doesn't meet her niece's eye but offers a weak smile. The silence between them is as sharp and bright as the fluorescent hospital lights. Liyana hears the mechanical beep-beep of a heart monitor, the incoherent ramblings of a woman in another bed, the false cheer of a nurse changing a catheter. Liyana wishes they were back in the private room, away from everyone else. But that would mean her aunt was still unconscious, still on the brink of death.

'How are you?' Liyana asks, regretting the question as soon as it's escaped. 'I mean, does it hurt? I mean . . .'

'I'm fine.' Nya picks at the edge of the lime-green hospital blanket. 'Just tired, that's all.'

How can you be tired? Liyana wants to ask. *You've been asleep for five days.* She presses her fingers into the balls of her bare feet. 'So, um . . .'

In the wake of her words, the flickering silence returns; abrasive and alarming as a scream. Liyana digs her nails into her skin. She needs everything to be all right again, she needs laughter and silly, meaningless chatter, she needs lightness and softness and not a care in the world. She needs to set down her fear and be happy again. But then, Liyana thinks, how long has it been since she's had that? It feels like a lifetime.

'So, um,' Liyana ventures. 'What happens next?'

Nya pulls a loose thread from the blanket and rolls it between finger and thumb. Liyana watches, wondering if her aunt is still listening or if she's slipped down inside herself again.

'I'm coming home.' Nya drops the thread to the floor, watching it fall. 'In the morning, when they've processed the paperwork.'

'What?' Liyana grips her toes, feels the panic rising again. 'Are you sure?'

She hadn't – in so far as she's had a chance to contemplate the immediate future – foreseen this eventuality. She'd imagined psychiatric hospitals and therapists and medication and doctors, lots and lots of doctors.

'Are you sure?' Liyana persists. And, when Nya doesn't reply, 'Don't you need to get well again first?'

'They've assessed me,' Nya says, in a low monotone, as if Liyana hasn't spoken. 'I can go home.'

'Go home?' Liyana releases her feet to grip the edge of her chair. 'But, but you . . . you need help.'

Nya nods. 'I've told them I'll get help.'

Feeling panic dragging her under like a current, Liyana suddenly stands, pushing back her chair, wincing as it squeaks on the plastic floor. 'I'm just . . . I need . . . the toilet.'

When Nya doesn't correct her, doesn't insist she say 'loo' instead, doesn't even seem to notice the degradation of language, Liyana feels herself flailing in the water, being pulled under. Struggling to catch her breath, she yanks the paper curtain aside and rushes out of the ward and into the corridor. Forcing herself not to run, Liyana scampers from bay to bay, seeking an available nurse. Instead, sitting behind a desk and barricaded by telephones and computer screens, she finds a doctor writing in a folder of notes. Liyana exhales.

When she's been waiting a full minute – which feels like a full hour – for the doctor to look up and see her, Liyana coughs. Then again.

'Oh.' The doctor looks up. 'I'm sorry, I didn't see you there.'

'Yes, I . . . Sorry to bother you' – Liyana glances at the ID card hanging around the doctor's neck – 'Dr Patel, but I, I need, if possible, to talk to you about one of your patients.'

Dr Patel closes the folder and sits up. 'Yes, of course. But please, call me Natasha.'

Liyana frowns. In the past week of encountering doctors, she'd noticed this disconcerting habit of offering their first names, with the intention, she supposes, of putting patients and relatives at their ease by dispensing with formality and hierarchy, but she doesn't like it. She wants the weight and solidity of 'doctor', like an anchor in a storm, it imbues her with confidence and trust that they actually know what they're talking about.

'Okay . . . Natasha. Well, I, um, I just wanted to talk to you about my aunt, Nya Chiweshe.' When Dr Natasha's face remains blank, Liyana adds, 'In bay four.'

'Ah, yes, of course.' Recognition sparks in her eyes. 'She's made an excellent recovery. We're delighted by her progress.'

'Yes, well, about that . . .' Liyana scrambles for the right words. 'You see, here's the thing . . . she might have made an excellent physical recovery, but she's *not* all right, I mean, I've known her virtually all my life and she's . . . well, she's not been all right for a very long time . . .'

As she trails off from her ineffectual speech, Liyana

expects the doctor to dismiss her, to usher her away with excuses, to belittle and override her concerns with medical jargon. She's surprised then that the doctor says nothing but continues to listen, considering Liyana's words long after she's stopped speaking.

'Yes,' Dr Natasha says. 'I understand. And I share your concerns. Indeed, if it were up to me, I would keep your aunt in a little longer for further assessment and then would recommend she check herself into a clinic.'

'Yes, exactly.' Liyana brightens. 'That's what should happen. So, can't you make her do that?'

The doctor's pretty face furrows and she gives a single, regretful shake of her head. 'I'm afraid we can't force your aunt to do anything. She's been assessed by the clinical psychiatrist as having the mental capacity to make her own decisions. And so' – she fixes her soft, sorrowful gaze to meet Liyana's own – 'we have to respect and honour your aunt's decisions, however . . . misguided we might consider them to be.'

'Oh,' Liyana says, crestfallen. 'Oh, I see.'

Eight hours later, when they leave the hospital together, Liyana takes Nya's hand so she doesn't slip on the slick, wet pavement. And she feels, as they shuffle along the pavement to the waiting taxi, as if she's now responsible for an unexploded bomb, and she alone is responsible for ensuring that it does not detonate.

That night Liyana sleeps fitfully again and, whenever she's spirited to Everwhere she wakes before she has a chance to search properly for her aunt Sisi. Frustration and longing build until she wakes Kumiko, sleeping deeply beside her, and they talk about Liyana's fears for Nya and the secrets Goldie might be keeping and the state of Scarlet's relationship, until milky morning sunlight begins to brighten the dull room.

Goldie

It is decided. She will do it. She must do it. If not she will shrivel and die, then what will become of Teddy, and her sisters? If I do this, Goldie vows, *if* I take a soldier's (a murderer's) life to get Leo back, then I – we – will dedicate our lives to doing good in the world. I will give my time – and my healed heart – to aiding all the Sisters Grimm. I'll join Bea in Everwhere every night and teach them. I will do what I always promised to do, what I always intended to do: visit Everwhere every night, find our remaining sisters and show them who they are and what they can do.

Goldie will teach them how powerful they can be, show them that they are bound by nothing, not even the laws of gravity, only the limits of their own imagination. She will watch them ignite sticks and create waves and make tendrils of ivy dance. She will remind them, over and over again, of their limitless potential, so they won't forget. For, even though they'll no longer have to fight for their lives in a gladiatorial battle, the potential danger of the stray soldiers remains, and there will still be many battles in their lives which will require great strength. She will warn them of what's to come in their teenage years, she will offer to tattoo their wrists with a symbol of their own particular power: a flame, a drop of water, a feather, a leaf; and underneath inscribe these words: *Fortius quam videris, fortius quam cogitas, et sapientior credas*: *You are stronger than you seem, braver than you feel, wiser than you believe.*

Goldie will tell them to seek the other Grimms, their sisters scattered throughout the world; she will tell them to spread the word, to talk of hidden magic, of whispers that speak of unknown things, of signs that point in unseen directions to unimagined possibilities. This is what she will do.

28th October –
3 nights . . .

Goldie

Welcome back, Sis. I've been waiting for you.

Goldie looks up to see the raven swoop down through the trees, parting the fog with the broad sweep of her wings. Goldie steps back.

Walk with me.

Goldie follows her raven sister who glides on a current of air, now and then brushing Goldie's shoulder with her wing-tip. They accompany each other a while along the mossy stone paths, occasional white leaves drifting down from branches – token offerings from friendly trees – until they come to a hilltop with a valley below cupping a river.

I've arranged something – the raven settles on the lowest branch of a silver birch – *to assist you on your mission.*

'Oh?' Goldie stops walking and glances up nervously. 'What—'

Just wait. The raven caws. *He's on his way.*

Goldie holds her breath, scanning the valley. Has her sister summoned a soldier? – her stomach drops – surely, she's not expecting . . . ? Goldie watches the stream that runs through the valley, its waters shimmering under the silver light of the unwavering moon, the eddy and swirl of the current flicking up droplets like tiny silver fish. As she's watching the water, he appears: a stag, his antlers bone white in the moonlight, cresting the opposite hill, parting the fog like curtains of smoke, as he lopes down towards the river and bends his long neck to drink.

Someone gave me a similar lesson once. The raven ruffles her wings. *And now I'm giving it to you.*

But Goldie is so fixed on the stag that she doesn't register her sister's words. 'I . . . I've never seen,' she whispers. 'I've never . . . I didn't know they were so . . . magnificent.' This word feels inadequate, but in her befuddled state it's the only one she can find. 'Majestic' follows soon after, but it too falls short.

At Goldie's words the stag raises his head from the river to look straight at her, ears twitching, large brown eyes unblinking. Goldie watches, feeling the distance between them fall away, so she might be standing beside him, her hand pressed to his flank, the muscles taut, flickering beneath the smooth, thick coat. The sensation is so vivid, so sharp that Goldie senses the heat of his skin under her palm, the deep, soft fur of his back through her fingertips. She wants to reach up, to have him nuzzle her with his dark, wet snout; she wants to bury her face in his neck and breathe him in.

'Thank you,' Goldie mumbles. 'I love—'

But the raven caws. *He's not for you to love, he's for you to kill.*

'What?' Goldie looks to her sister, eyes wide with shock. 'Why? No, I can't—'

You eat steak, don't you? Bea interrupts. *And what—*

'I don't,' Goldie interrupts. 'I haven't for years.'

How virtuous; and anyway what would you get in exchange for death, apart from extra iron in your blood and a succulent taste on your tongue? In killing the stag you'll not only be preparing yourself for killing a man, you'll also be imbued with his life force: his strength, his stamina, his stature, his dominance and power – and for what you're planning to do you'll need all the strength you can possibly—

'No.' Goldie shakes her head. 'I can't. It wouldn't be, it wouldn't—'

The raven swoops down from the branch to alight on Goldie's shoulder. She flinches.

You can't have it all, Sis. Bea's voice is the rippling current of the river. *You can't remain good, and still get what you want, it doesn't work that way. Resurrecting the dead means stepping into the dark.*

Goldie is silent. She feels the weight of the bird on her shoulder as if it's a boulder pushing her into the ground.

'I can't,' she says again.

You must do this, or let go of Leo. Bea's words shudder through her. *The choice is yours.*

Heat flushes across Goldie's chest and she shudders, her head heavy and full of fog, as if experiencing a sudden onset of flu. Guilt pricks behind her eyes, drawing tears, because she knows that, no matter how wrong it might be, she will always choose Leo.

'But' – Goldie hears her words as if she's eavesdropping on someone else – 'how?'

I recommend the spears of the hawthorn tree. At this, the raven lifts from Goldie's shoulder and rises into the air. At this disturbance, the stag, who'd returned to drinking from the river, looks up again, ears twitching.

Goldie follows the trajectory of the raven's flight until it settles on the branch of a hawthorn tree. Her gaze falls upon its lethal spikes. About to ask how it's possible to extract the thorns and turn them into arrows, Goldie realizes that she knows what to do. Still, she hesitates. *After this, I'll dedicate my life to doing good,* she thinks, *I'll dedicate myself to making amends for this act and the act to come.*

When the raven caws, flapping its wings and causing the stag to startle again, Goldie takes a deep breath and focuses on a single branch. With one twitch of her fingers she strips it of every thorn, quickly and easily, as if her fingernails are knives. The thorns hover in the air, and Goldie gestures again, pinching together forefinger and thumb, bringing the twelve thorns into a line. Then the thorns fuse, tip to tip, into an arrow.

Quickly, before she can change her mind, she lets the arrow fly. Numbly, she watches it pierce the stag's heart, feels the thud of his body falling to the ground, the tremors echoing under her feet, and she senses the slow, aching flow of his life force as it seeps from his veins and floods into her own.

A moment later, Goldie drops to her knees, face hidden in her hands, and weeps.

Liyana

'Don't go.'

'Oh, Ana, I've got to.' Kumiko gives Liyana one more long, lingering kiss, before slipping out of bed. 'I don't want to, but I must. Skinner's lectures aren't optional.'

Liyana sighs.

'Should I say goodbye to your aunt?' Kumiko yanks on her jeans. 'I don't want to be rude.'

'No, no, it's fine,' Liyana says, sitting up in bed. 'She's in her room and . . . Anyway, she doesn't even know you're here.'

'All right.' Pulling her jumper over her head, Kumiko steps back towards the bed. 'Look, I've been thinking . . .'

'Yeah?' Liyana feels a quick flash of panic. 'What?'

'It's nothing bad.' Kumiko laughs. 'I think it might help your aunt. And you too, actually.'

Liyana frowns.

'You should ask Goldie to write her a particular story – one to motivate and invigorate her – that you could illustrate. It might inspire her back into life.'

Liyana lies back on the pillows. 'That's very sweet, Koko, but Aunt Nya favours gifts that prioritize cost over thought. Whenever I brought pictures home from school, they'd be stuck on the fridge for a few weeks before disappearing. A pair of Louboutins, on the other hand, would be cherished forever.'

'Ana!' Kumiko laughs again. 'You're not twelve anymore. You could create something to help her heal.'

'I don't know . . .' Liyana pulls her knees to her chest. 'I can try, but I think she's beyond the reach of stories now. She needs doctors and drugs.'

'Yes, but if she won't do that then . . .' Kumiko shrugs. 'What else can you do? She needs to get her confidence back, her joy in life.'

'Joy in life?' Liyana raises an incredulous eyebrow. 'Goldie's stories are beautiful, but I don't think Shakespeare resurrected could do *that*. Desire to get out of bed would be good progress.' Liyana sighs. 'She used to be so . . . brazen, so pushy, so – she used to piss me off all the time,' – she smiles – 'always coming up with madcap schemes, wrapping the world, and half the men in it, around her little finger.' She drops her chin to her knees. 'Now what wouldn't I give for her to get up off her arse and start bossing me about again.'

Kumiko sits on the bed and slips her arm over Liyana's shoulders. 'Then perhaps Goldie's story could remind Nya of who she used to be, of who she's forgotten she is.'

Liyana reaches up to seize hold of her girlfriend's hand. 'Don't go.'

'I don't want to, but I must.' Kumiko places a soft kiss

on Liyana's cheek. 'And while you're at it – helping your aunt to remember herself – you might start remembering yourself too.'

Liyana frowns. 'I haven't forgotten myself.'

'Not yet perhaps, but that's where you're heading if you don't keep creating, if you don't give yourself a sense of purpose.'

In the wake of Kumiko's departure Liyana stares at the wall. The room is much emptier without her girlfriend in it, much quieter, and her life much lonelier. Liyana sniffs, wiping her nose on her sleeve. She thinks about what Kumiko has said. Is it true? She hasn't lost her creativity, has she? Why, only a few days ago she illustrated Goldie's story of the Wolf Woman. It's been a while, though, since she's drawn anything of significance and even longer since she's worked on her graphic novels. So perhaps she has forgotten.

Life has for so long been nothing more than the dull ache of disappointments. And, after a while, getting out her sketchbook has just felt like too much effort. She often skips a day, then another; until it fades to a few thin squiggles seemingly done by someone she's never met.

Liyana had thought she didn't mind too much. No, that was a lie. She knew she minded a great deal but had tamped down those feelings so well that they rarely rose up anymore. Certainly she thought about it from time to time, but only fleetingly and never with great sorrow. Only when she felt the sting of rejection – after sending her work to an agent, publisher or magazine – did the disappointment flare again, burning bright until Liyana extinguished it by submerging herself in water so long that her skin was pruned and her ears clogged and her thoughts smooth as the sand washed by the waves. Then she no longer felt the itch to return to the page, as a true artist surely would. She only felt numb.

Now Liyana's gaze settles on the closed sketchbook propped up beside her desk and gradually feels herself begin to emerge from a fog she hadn't even realized she'd been wandering through. The image of the bright, blank page beckons like a first kiss. And, as Liyana imagines pressing her pencil to the page again, she feels the thrill of hope and expectation that always used to accompany the start of something new.

Liyana pulls back the bedcovers and walks across the room. She lifts the sketchbook and sets it upon the desktop, then sits down at the desk. Slowly, she opens to a new page and picks up a pencil. At first, she holds back from marking the unblemished leaf, not wanting to ruin it with inadequate renderings. Then she touches the figurine of Mami Wata at her neck and brings the deity's head to her lips. A surge of strength rises through her body as if she'd just injected herself with adrenaline.

Taking a deep breath, then another, Liyana touches lead to paper. And as she draws, as she lets her fingers find their way, as they begin to swoop and rise, conducting an orchestra of lines and curves, Liyana feels that she too is rising and swooping, that she too is being conducted, that she is both the creator of the symphony and every note being played.

Kumiko was right, she *had* forgotten. She'd forgotten what she loved, how deeply she loved it and why. And in doing so, Liyana had forgotten who she used to be, who she is still.

That night, Liyana returns to her Tarot cards. She shuffles and shuffles, reluctant to ask the question, scared to see the answer. She prolongs the preliminaries, postponing the inevitable, cutting and slicing the deck, using her left hand and then her right, until finally she surrenders and begins to deal the cards out onto the bed. Liyana cannot bear to ask about her aunt – there are some things it's best not to know – and is too scared to ask about Goldie, so asks instead about herself: *Will my illustrations ever be exhibited? Will anyone ever buy them?*

It's a question Liyana returns to often, like an itch she can't stop scratching, made all the more insistent by the fact that she's never given fully clear and satisfactory answers. Tonight Liyana chooses the Pentagram Spread and selects the cards.

The first card is reversed – The Emperor: a black-eyed man holds a staff and a marionette, antlers sprout from his head, jackals flank the pedestal upon which he stands. *Abuse of power, obsession, self-sabotage.* The Five of Cups appears next: a sorrowful girl walks through a desert, two cups floating above her, three tipped over at her feet. *Disappointment, sadness, conflict.* The third card dealt is the Four of Pentacles. A pixie girl sits in the uppermost spiny branches of a towering winter tree; she clutches a large coin to her chest, three others are balanced precariously on her lap. *Greed, selfishness, possession.* Then, just as Liyana had feared, comes the Nine of Swords: a terrified woman hides from a terrible ghoul. Six swords point towards the creature, the other three are pressed against her chest. *Fear, nightmares, agony of mind.* After that, and even worse, is The Tower: a grey wind blows, a tall stone tower crumbles beside a naked tree, a man and woman tumble to their deaths from its windows. *Sudden collapse, reversal in fortune, defeat.* The fifth and final card is the Three of Swords: a girl sits on a stone holding her heart in her hands; the swords pierce her heart and blood drips from their tips. *Heartbreak, isolation, devastation.*

Liyana stares at the spread. It cannot be a reading for her career, it simply cannot. Unless she's set to become not only the greatest failure ever to court recognition, but an aspiring artist who's also a megalomaniac psychopath. Liyana frowns. Surely not? Then, as she gazes more intently at the cards, the story they are trying to tell starts to become clear. Slowly, as if she's beginning to understand a few words of a foreign language, Liyana realizes what she's looking at: a reading not for her, but for Goldie. And, all at once, Liyana sees the full scope of her sister's plan, that it doesn't simply involve resurrection but murder too.

Scarlet

'I'm sorry. I'm so very, very sorry.'

Scarlet looks at Eli, his red eyes and crumpled face, his pleading expression. They have been circling this topic: her interrogation, his final confession and subsequent abject grovelling, for nearly twelve hours. In truth, though Scarlet cannot ever again believe a single word that leaves his mouth, she cannot deny that she has never seen him look so broken, so undone.

He's crying, and he never cries. Not when England lost to Croatia in the World Cup, when he'd truly believed they'd finally make it to the finals. Not the first time he was fired. Not when his mother died. Ezekiel Wolfe is not an emitter of emotion. He's stoic. A nineteenth-century version of manhood. And yet, here he's unravelling before her.

'I love you, I love you, I . . .' Eli breaks off, pressing his face into his palms, shaking his head, as if unable to believe he's actually done what he's done. 'I can't – if you leave me, I don't think, I don't know . . . I can't.'

'If you loved me,' Scarlet says, 'you wouldn't have done it.'

They're still in bed, Scarlet having confronted Eli with the phone an hour after she'd found it, replete with filthy text messages and dozens of calls to 'V'. The seemingly endless words of recrimination and atonement have unfurled and encircled them like a lasso that's tied them to the mattress.

Scarlet feels herself strangely more stable now, as she watches Eli crumble. It's so unexpected, this reversal of roles, that it imbues her with sudden strength. As if, only for a moment, she is the heartbreaker and he the heartbroken.

'No,' he pleads. 'No, no, that's not—'

'It is.'

Intractable silence spreads thinly between them.

'I loved *you*.' Scarlet folds her arms to hide the sparks igniting her fingertips. 'Which is why *I* didn't go about carelessly fucking every man I met. If I hadn't, I might have. You see?'

Eli sighs. 'That's not . . . You can't compare. It's different for men. It's—'

'Oh, don't be so pathetic,' Scarlet snaps. 'Don't insult me with that bullshit about biology. You can't hide behind your dick. You've got a brain too, haven't you? One quite capable of overriding your carnal urges.'

'Look.' Eli sat up. 'It's not like that. It's not quite so dreadful as you're . . . Okay, here's the thing: all men are unfaithful in their mind. They all want to cheat. And those that don't are just afraid of being caught, of losing what they've got.'

'And that didn't worry you?' Scarlet clutches herself tight, as if afraid she too might unravel. 'You didn't care about losing me . . . losing us?' Her hands go to her womb. Protective. Defiant. 'You don't care about losing your own daughter?'

'No.' Eli sits forward, reaching out to her. 'No, that's not what I – I'm not going to lose you. We're going to fix this. I'm going to – tell me what I have to do to fix this.'

'Fix it?' Scarlet shrinks back from him. '*Fix* it? How can – is that why you did this so easily? Because you were so sure of getting me back?' She swallows, wipes her nose on her sleeve. 'You think that you can fuck around and, if you're unlucky enough to get caught, then, what? You just have to figure out how to make it better, how to make it up to me? Is that what you think?'

'No.' Eli pulls a hand through his hair. She's never seen him looking so unkempt, so rumpled and unbrushed. 'No, of course not. But I will. I'll do whatever you want. Whatever you ask.'

Scarlet glowers at him. She is defiant, renewed, emboldened. She's Cleopatra facing Caesar. She will subject him to such pain. Suffering such as he's never known. She pulls away, looking up at him, eyes glassy with hate.

'Destroy the phone.'

'Done.'

'Tell that woman you'll never speak to – never set eyes on her again.'

'Yes, of course.' Eli nods vigorously, though he can't meet her gaze.

Scarlet narrows her eyes. 'What?'

'Well, I . . .'

'*What?*'

'Well,' – Eli looks at Scarlet as if he wishes all the flames of Hell would incinerate him – 'she works for me.'

'Then fire her,' Scarlet says, surprised by how defiant she feels. 'Or fire yourself. Get another job. I don't care.'

'All right,' Eli says, softly. 'All right.'

'Give me the passwords to all your accounts. Phone. Email. Bank.'

'Absolutely.'

What else, Scarlet thinks, what else to test him, to prove his love? It takes only a moment for inspiration to strike.

'Have a pre-nup drawn up,' she says. 'If we divorce, I get this flat.' His grandmother's flat, worth perhaps £2.4 million. 'And half your trust fund.'

Eli nods. 'Done.'

Scarlet narrows her eyes again. She'd expected at least a slight hesitation, but not a flicker.

'You can have the Jag too,' Eli offers. 'And the Degas sketch.'

'The sketch?' Scarlet frowns. His prize possession. The thing he cherishes – and Eli has plenty of things he cherishes – above all others. And he'd offered it himself. She didn't even have to ask. Hope rises, desire. His offer is a lifeline flung out, a chance of saving what was lost. Scarlet feels her body shifting towards him.

No. The quiet voice speaks up. The whisper of intuition. *He'll burn you.* That tug, gentle but firm. *He'll scar you.* The tap-tap. *He will break your heart.*

'Please,' Eli pleads. 'Anything you want. It's all yours. I promise.'

'No,' Scarlet mumbles, thrown by the voice. 'No, I can't.'

'Please,' Eli begs. 'Please, please.'

'No.' Scarlet shakes her head. 'No.'

The words unfurl and the lasso tightens.

'But, I, I love you.' Tears spring again to his eyes, startling them both, and she knows that it's true, he does. In his own twisted way, Ezekiel Wolfe loves her.

He reaches out again and touches her arm. This time, she doesn't pull away. Then, all at once, he draws her into a hug, tight against his chest.

'Please,' Eli begs. 'Please, I promise. I promise I'll never—'

Scarlet starts to sob, shaking her head. 'No,' she mumbles. 'I can't, I can't ever . . .'

'You can.' Eli's breath is hot in the curls of her hair. 'You can. I promise, I—'

Scarlet looks up at him. 'Don't promise,' she says. 'Swear.'

'Yes, of course.' Suddenly the grief darkening Eli's face gives way to gratitude, relief. And, despite herself, Scarlet is touched by just how grateful he looks. She holds his gaze, his eyes still soft with sorrow. And Scarlet understands that Bea was wrong. Eli loves her.

'I swear,' he says. 'I swear I will never hurt you again.'

When at last she falls asleep, drained and exhausted, Scarlet dreams. She dreams of holding her baby girl. She dreams of birthing the baby, on a flood of tears and blood, with Goldie and Liyana at her side. The three of them breathing together, with such strength and force that they bear the baby through the birth canal and bring it into the world on their singular breath. She dreams of raising her daughter alone, struggling through those first nocturnal years, offering to sacrifice sleep and sanity until she's hollow and empty and must bury anger and sorrow beneath love. She dreams of the days when Red will be able to love her back in a real and equal sense, when they will talk as adults and friends. She dreams of how, despite everything, she will love this little girl more than anything or anyone else in her life.

Scarlet smiles as she dreams, and cries. For, at the centre of it all, is an absence. Where there should be a father standing next to the mother, an oak tree beside the willow, is only air. She will hold one of her daughter's hands, but who will hold the other? How will Red grow up to feel secure enough to fling herself feet first into life, to love with abandon, to live without looking for a safety net? Will two aunts be adequate compensation? Will a tribe of sisters make up for the missing father?

She dreams of her own childhood, her own absent father, of the emptiness especially acute on birthdays and Christmas but never gone even during dull, ordinary times. She'd always wondered where he was, what he was doing, why he had left and why he had never returned. Sometimes she'd blamed her mother for his absence, sometimes herself, but rarely her father. And she'd always felt unstable, unsafe, with only one parent to depend on. What, she'd feared, would happen to her if something happened to her mother?

When Scarlet wakes she knows she's done the right thing. Even though the sorrow at his betrayal has not softened, has not been soothed by sleep or the passing of a little time, she knows that her pain is not the most important thing. She will be a mother and this will be her first sacrifice for her daughter: a shattered heart.

Liyana

Before falling asleep amid her Tarot spread, Liyana wishes she could give Goldie her heart's desire, but by a process that precludes murder. Not that she cares such a great deal about taking the life of a soldier – once a fallen star and who, as a man, is no better than a serial killer – rather, she fears that something might go dreadfully wrong and Goldie will die.

Liyana wakes in Everwhere, lying face down in a patch of bleached moss. Pulling herself up from the ground she waits a while, breathing in the misty air, refreshing her lungs and drawing strength into her body. When she's feeling reinvigorated, Liyana walks along a path of stones until her way is blocked by a fallen oak. Climbing up to stand atop the trunk, Liyana dips back her head, reaches her arms towards the unwavering moon and begins to coax cracks of lightning and rumbles of thunder from the sky. Soon she's summoning torrents of rain, great deluges of water sluicing through the trees, running in rivulets off the leaves to drench the mossy soil with ever-expanding puddles.

When Aunt Sisi walks along the path and reaches the fallen tree, the clouds clear from the sky. Confused, Liyana wipes the rain from her face, blinks several times, then looks about.

'*Dagā*!' She drops her arms to her sides. 'Where did you – I didn't see you.'

Sisi folds her arms across her plump bosom and turns her round, delighted face up to her niece. 'It's lovely to see you too, Lili. You're looking well.'

'Thanks, I'm feeling much better after that.' Liyana jumps down, landing in a mossy puddle which responds with a satisfying squelch. She's already dry, the remnants of the rainstorm having run off her skin and evaporated from her clothes as if she's a swan shaking off water. 'Where have you been? I keep hoping, I thought you'd come back before—'

'I wanted to come, Lili,' her aunt interrupts. 'Of course I did. But I had to let you alone a little while to find your own way. Strength can't grow with too much mollycoddling, you know. A teacher must find the right balance of support and stepping back.'

'So,' Liyana asks. 'Where have you been?'

'What do you mean?' Sisi laughs. 'I'm here, Lili, I'm always here.'

'But, you've not been . . .' Liyana frowns. 'You're not often here.' She sighs. 'I've been missing you.'

'Oh, sweetheart.' Sisi scoops up Liyana's hands in her

own. 'I wish I could be here every night that you are, but I can't.'

'Why not?'

'Well, the truth is . . . it's not . . .' Sisi hesitates. 'The choice is not really mine to make.'

Liyana's frown deepens. 'What do you mean?'

With one more squeeze, Aunt Sisi lets go of Liyana's hands and shrugs. 'It all depends on the phases of the moon and the positioning of the stars.'

'What?' Liyana regards her aunt, who now seems to be shimmering in the moonlight. 'I thought you were – I thought you could meet me in Everwhere whenever you wished.'

Sisi shakes her head. And all at once Liyana realizes that she can see right through Sisi to the willow tree behind her. 'Oh! But how . . . ? Are you . . . you're . . .'

'Alive and dead are such binary concepts, don't you think?' Sisi's deep laugh fills the air. 'Given that the essence of life – Qi, Jing, Prana, Nyama, Shakti – is immutable, the spark of life is never extinguished; it simply transmutes itself into something else.'

'But . . .' Liyana leans back against the tree trunk, feeling her spirits sinking like rainwater into the soil. 'I was hoping . . .' She takes a deep breath, blinking back tears. 'I was hoping to visit you in Ghana and stay with you and, I don't know . . . let you fatten me up. I was hoping you'd come to London, to visit us and . . . help me look after Nya.'

'Oh, Lili.' Sisi's voice sinks down with Liyana's spirits. 'I'm so sorry you're having to deal with that alone. I wish with all my heart I could be there to bear that burden with you. But—' She brightens. 'We don't need to let a little thing like death stand in the way of me being with you. In fact, we can kill two ravens with one rock.'

Liyana squints at her aunt, who's now returned to a more substantial form. 'How?'

'Well . . .' Sisi folds her arms across her ample bosom. 'There are many ways of contacting the corporeally challenged from the comfort of your kitchen, but my favourite is by way of a cup of tea and Nkatie cake.'

Liyana begins peeling a strip of stray bark from the trunk. 'What's Nkatie cake?'

'I'll explain that later,' Sisi says. 'But now we need to talk about Goldie and how you're going to save her.'

29th October –
2 nights . . .

Everwhere

Goldie wasn't certain that she'd return to Everwhere tonight. She'd barely been able to make it through the day without crying or breaking something, since her hands have hardly stopped shaking. It's taken all her strength to hold her composure, avoiding encounters with hotel guests or staff and leaving a tenner for Teddy with a note telling him to get a takeaway. For, while the banker in room 26 neither noticed nor cared about the emotional state of the girl cleaning his room, her increasingly sensitive and attentive brother would sense Goldie's sorrow at ten paces. And she cannot bear to tell him what she's done.

It's guilt that trembles through her fingers, guilt that hurries her heart, guilt that rushes blood through her veins. Never would Goldie have considered herself to be this selfish. She's kind to the environment, always recycles, sticks to a (mostly) vegan diet, signs petitions and attends protest marches. She's spent most of her life in service to her little brother, giving up her freedom, her education, her time, to raise a boy she didn't birth. She never thought herself capable of cold-blooded killing. An innocent animal has died so that she could practise the skills and soak up the strength that she'll need to kill a soldier. A *man*. All so that she can be reunited with the love of her life.

Goldie knows that she should stop, knows she should stay on the side of the good and true, knows she should surrender to a lifetime of longing and loneliness, to a world without Leo.

She's managed it for three years, after all, so how hard would another sixty or seventy be? Impossible. If she doesn't commit murder, the only other option is suicide. But then she couldn't abandon Teddy.

Goldie has left him sleeping to return to Everwhere tonight. She doesn't want to see Bea, doesn't want to remember the killing, but needs to bury the stag. She'd left him in the glade, his body broken, his corpse exposed to the elements, a cruel ending for such a majestic animal – a cruel ending for any creature.

Goldie doesn't have to think, doesn't need to remember the way; she wanders along paths and past streams and around scatterings of stones and fallen trees with her eyes cast carelessly down to the ground or up to the sky to fix her gaze on the moon and try to forget. Finally arriving at the crest of the hill, Goldie hesitates. She doesn't have to look to see the fallen stag, she doubts she'll ever be able to blink the image away.

Silence falls as Goldie walks down into the valley. In a cowardly move, which she later regrets, Goldie lifts her hands to coax tendrils of ivy from an ancient oak tree which grows close to the riverbank. Slowly, they tear away from the bark to slither along the ground and wrap their protective leaves around the stag's flanks until the body is shrouded.

When she reaches his side, Goldie can barely see through her tears, though she feels shame every time one slides to the end of her nose. What right does she have to cry? More shamefully still, she cannot bring herself to touch him. Instead she stops a few feet from the body and sits, then splays her fingers and pushes them down into the soil. At Goldie's touch the ground begins to tremble, as if struck by a sudden earthquake, and cracks snap along the forest floor, ripping dank, jagged chasms into the soil and opening a pit around the corpse.

A moment later the body is gone, the soil closed over, and the blanket of moss is stitching itself together to once more spread evenly across the ground. Goldie squeezes her eyes shut and when she opens them again all evidence of death and murder is gone. Her heart lifts a little, and she thinks of Leo.

'I'm going to save you,' Goldie whispers. 'On All Hallows Eve, when my magic is strongest, I'll bring you back.'

She waits, as she always does, for the echo of Leo's voice on the wind. She waits for a sign to show not simply that he's there but that he's listening and somehow he hears her, and somehow, he knows. But tonight Goldie's wish is answered only with silence.

For one cruel moment, she fears it's all for nothing; that she's only been fuelled by hope and imagination these past three years, that her lover is forever gone, that she will never see him again. Goldie closes her eyes to see Leo's face. He's sitting on the edge of the bed, turning to look at her, his eyes soft, his gaze laced with love and desire. A twist of longing wraps like a vine of ivy around Goldie's neck and constricts her throat, tightening and choking out the little breath she has left. A fog of loss descends.

'I will resurrect you,' Goldie whispers at last. 'We will be together again.'

Liyana and Scarlet find Goldie still on her knees beside the stag's unmarked grave. Sensing the weight of her sorrow, not having the words to lift it and knowing that sometimes silence is best, they sit down beside her.

Beneath the unwavering moon and the starlight and the rustling leaves, they sit on the mossy ground, three points of a triangle. Scarlet begins setting twigs alight, then blows them out, Liyana juggles dense balls of fog and, after a while, Goldie starts to coax tight curled shoots from the earth, the saplings of fresh silver birch trees. The mists roll in to hang heavy in the air and soften the silence.

'We know everything now. We know that you're planning on killing a soldier.'

Goldie looks up, shaken from her reverie, unsure which of her sisters has spoken.

'I saw it in the cards,' Liyana says. 'I called Scarlet, and we've come to—'

'You've come to stop me.'

'No,' Liyana says. 'Not stop you but protect you; offer you an alternative.'

Goldie plucks a weed from the soil. She doesn't look up.

'I'm learning the art of resurrection,' Liyana continues. 'I've been taking lessons from Aunt Sisi and she believes that, together, we can bring Leo back in a much . . .'

'Safer way,' Scarlet finishes. 'Unless – unless you'd be willing to consider the safest way of all: not doing it.'

Goldie shoots her sister a furious, incredulous look.

'All right, all right.' Scarlet holds up her hands. 'It was only a thought.'

'So,' Goldie turns to Liyana. 'What are you proposing?'

'It still sounds dangerous.' Goldie presses her hands together, looking to Liyana who's just finished explaining Sisi's plan. 'And not at all certain to work.'

Liyana drags a finger through the fog, drawing circles. 'It's better than the alternative. At least this way you can avoid murder.'

'It still sounds insane to me.' Scarlet ignites another twig. 'But if we must, we must.'

166

Goldie gives her a grateful smile. 'Thank you, I know it's not . . . ideal.'

'To say the least.' Scarlet shrugs. 'But you'd do the same for me.'

Goldie nods. 'If Eli dies, I promise I'll be the first in line to help bring him back.'

Scarlet sighs. 'Right now, I'm not entirely sure I'd want you to.'

'What?' Liyana raises an eyebrow. 'Trouble in paradise?'

'Shut up.' Sparks flare at Scarlet's fingertips. One lands, like an errant ember from a fire, on Liyana's knee, singeing a hole in her jeans. 'No, everything's fine. I'm just . . .'

'Damn.' Liyana spits on the smouldering fabric, patting out the burn. 'These are my favourite – you did that on purpose.'

'Sorry.' Scarlet flashes her an innocent smile. 'It was an unfortunate accident.'

'Please, stop,' Goldie says. 'We'll need to be united for this to work. We need our combined force to be mightier than Death, for goodness' sake. We can't mess around.'

Scarlet and Liyana look at her, momentarily distracted from their feud.

'Please,' Goldie begs. 'I need you both to do this. And, if you won't help me do it this way, I'll go it alone and do it the other way.'

At this, she feels their mutual anger ebb, rolling back with the fog that folds like a fallen soufflé and sinks down into the soil.

'All right,' Scarlet says. 'If Ana can manage not to undermine my relationship for two days, then I'll keep my sparks to myself.'

'Okay.' Liyana drops the three balls of fog which instantly evaporate. 'I promise I won't mention what a colossal mistake I think—'

'Ana!'

'Okay, okay,' Liyana says, as a crack of thunder sounds in the distance. 'I'll keep my mouth shut.'

'That'd be a miracle,' Scarlet huffs. 'You couldn't last—'

'Scar,' Goldie warns. 'Stop it, both of you.'

Liyana and Scarlet fold their arms, both glower at Goldie.

With a sigh, Goldie reaches into her pocket and pulls out a peace offering. 'I wrote this' – she hands Liyana a crumpled page scrawled with lines of cursive script – 'I think it's for you.'

Taking it, Liyana starts to read.

'No, not now,' Goldie says. 'Later. When you're home.'

'Okay.' Liyana nods. 'Thank you.'

Scarlet gives Goldie a piteous look. 'Nothing for me?'

'Oh, please,' Goldie says. 'You know I'm not playing favourites, I don't decide what to write or who to write it for. The stories come to me and then, at some point, I figure out who to give them to.'

Scarlet retorts with a begrudging sniff.

'Don't worry' – Goldie pats her sister's knee – 'it won't be long before one arrives for you.'

Scarlet raises a disbelieving eyebrow but says nothing. The sisters fall back into silence again and the fog rolls in.

They follow the meandering curves of a river, with Liyana casting longing looks at the water, and Goldie staying on the far side from the bank and Scarlet in the middle. They walk the paths of stone and moss without speaking, brushing through the curtains of willow trees, stepping over decaying trunks blanketed with lichen and choked in vines of ivy. The only sounds are the rush of the river water, the ravens' cries which drop from the moonlit sky and the wings of bats that pitch and roll above their heads.

'Are you sure you're okay?' Goldie looks at Scarlet. 'Because, despite all Ana's taunting, you know we'd do anything for you, don't you?'

Scarlet stops walking to lean against the trunk of a silver birch tree, as if too exhausted to go on. Watching the river, she follows shards of mirrored moonlight dart across the rippling water, absently snapping a twig from a branch and dropping it into the current.

'Did you ever play Poohsticks?' She doesn't look up.

'Of course.' Goldie steps over the stones to stand tentatively at the edge of the river beside her. The fog has rolled in again and she can't see the path. 'Doesn't everyone?'

Scarlet snaps off another twig and drops it into the stream. At the splash, Goldie peers into the water. She still can't understand Liyana's attraction to something so potentially dangerous; never would she want to set foot in the sea. Hearing Liyana approaching behind them, Goldie reaches for Scarlet's hand, wanting to draw her back from wherever she's retreated inside herself, but instead she loses her footing on the slick moss and slips, falling back and smacking her skull on the roots of the silver birch, sliding down the muddy bank and into the water.

As Goldie sinks the last thing she hears is Scarlet's cry, then she's dragged under by the quickening currents. All she hears now is the rush of water, the muffled slosh-slosh, the pulse of her blood. All she sees, before darkness envelops her, is a liquescent view of the fog hanging low over the river. Time quickens and slows. Goldie wonders if her sisters are calm, expecting her to emerge unscathed any second, or if they're panicked and screaming.

To her surprise, Goldie *is* calm. Even as she starts swallowing water, she's calm. *I should have learned to swim*, she thinks. *I'll rise before I'm swept too far*, she thinks. *Or I'll sink down into*

Leo's embrace. If it's not suicide, she's got no reason to feel guilty. Her sisters will look after Teddy. He's got grit. He'll be okay. But then she thinks: it *is* suicide, if I don't fight it. She begins, half-heartedly, to thrash her legs, but the current is still lashed tight around her ankles, tugging her down. She kicks harder, reaching for the surface, her hands clutching only liquid dark.

When all the fight has left her, Goldie closes her eyes and lets herself sink. It's all right now, she's allowed. It was an accident. It's not her fault. But then she thinks: was it? She's been wanting to die for so long. She's been waiting, hoping, begging for that gift. Perhaps she cast a spell, perhaps this is the culmination of all that longing. *It doesn't matter*, she thinks. *No one will ever know but me.*

Goldie smiles, gulping a fresh, final rush of water into her lungs.

I'm coming, Leo. I won't be long.

And then she's rising. Up, up, up. Breaking through the water, out of the dark and into the silvery light. Convulsing, coughing, great racking coughs that burn her trachea and wrench at her chest as if long-fingered ribs are slashing into her organs and ripping her asunder. Goldie splutters and spits and chokes, as half the river expels itself from her lungs, leaving her panting and blinking, eyes stinging, until at last she stills and squints at the shapes of her sisters' faces hovering above her, edges blurred by the fog.

She peers at them; before she's doubled over by a fresh bout of hacking that folds her in half, until she's clutching her sides and moaning and gasping for breath, eyes tight shut. Goldie gulps at her sisters, her mouth reaching for words but finding none. Why is she here? The moss is soft and wet beneath her body, a few rogue stones pressing hard into her skin. Where is Leo?

She mouths words and, on the fourth attempt, manages to expel them. 'Where's Leo?'

Liyana and Scarlet frown through the fog.

'What?' Scarlet asks, pressing her face closer. 'What is it? You're gabbling.'

Liyana grabs Goldie's arm, fingers digging into flesh. 'Why the hell' – she's shrieking – 'why the hell didn't you learn to swim?'

30th October –
1 night . . .

Goldie

After regaining enough strength to return home, Goldie crawls into bed with Teddy and hugs him tight. To her surprise, he doesn't squirm away but, once she's unwrapped her arms, lets her lie beside him. Goldie's body aches as if she's just been beaten, her throat raw from hacking up water, so she places her hands on her chest to heal herself, to soothe her bruised muscles and sore bones, to inject herself with fresh energy and strength, to restore her former levels of power – a small resurrection of sorts. Blinking up at the swirls of plaster across the ceiling Goldie wishes they were the clouds of Everwhere and the ugly oval lightshade the unwavering moon, that she was lying on a blanket of bleached moss listening to the rustling of leaves and the raven's calls, instead of Teddy's shallow breaths. Lying beside him only exacerbates the thick, sticky guilt that coats her tongue and settles over her heart like the crush of a rock, guilt for having been so willing to die, to abandon her brother so readily, to discard him so easily.

'I'm sorry,' she mumbles into Teddy's warm neck. 'I've been so miserably selfish, I should've made more effort, I should've tried to snap out of it and live for you and take better care of you, I'm so, so . . .' Tears slip down her cheeks and a sob rises in her throat, swallowing her words. *If I could go back in time and do it again, be a better parent to you, I would. I only wish I could, but I can only . . . I won't do it again, I promise to be a better person and to take care of you*

*and stop thinking only of myself, of my own miseries and my
own desires.*

Responding with a sleepy groan, Teddy turns to bury his
face into Goldie's hair and squish his skinny, hard body
against her softer one. At that, Goldie only cries harder,
shaking with the effort of smothering her sobs from fear of
waking him, unfurling a string of promises that she will not,
under any condition, ever leave him.

Liyana

Aunt Nya still hasn't left her room. Liyana has tried dragging her out of bed to slump on the sofa instead, thinking it
would provide a slightly less depressing location to pass the
time and that shuffling across the hallway into the living
room at least suggests an attempt, albeit nominal, to get on
with your day, to live your life. Not getting out of bed at all,
Liyana thinks, is tantamount to giving up. To spend the rest
of one's life asleep, one might as well be dead.

When Liyana brings her aunt a tray of tea and toast for
breakfast (as she did every day for lunch and dinner too,
though each was discarded with barely a sip or a bite taken)
she slips the handwritten page of Goldie's story, 'Worthless/
Priceless', under the plate. She hopes it'll pique Nya's curiosity enough for her to pick it up and read. Whether or not
it will help reignite Nya's heart and reawaken within her
the desire to live, is another matter. Liyana's hopes are not
high.

Two hours later, when Liyana tiptoes back into her aunt's
room to retrieve the tray, the story is gone, the tea drunk
and the toast eaten. She stares at the empty plate and cup.
She has seen rivers rerouted, rain coaxed from the sky,

moths resurrected, but now, met with this most simple and commonplace of sights, Liyana is almost unable to believe what she's seeing.

Scarlet

Scarlet and Eli sit at the dinner table. Tonight, he was home before seven. A small miracle. Scarlet pokes at the salmon – overcooked and untouched – and stares down at her plate. Eli pours his third glass of wine. He proffers the bottle.

'Do you want some?'

'No, thank you.'

Eli sets the bottle on the table.

'Had you forgotten I'm not drinking?'

'What? No.' Eli chews and swallows. 'Of course not. But you are allowed some, you know. You don't have to be so militant about it.'

Scarlet says nothing. *I'm just being careful*, she thinks. Silence stretches between them like a sulky child. Scarlet can't imagine them, one day, having their own sulky child. How will these multiplying cells transform into a small human being? It seems impossible.

Eli looks up. 'Are you all right?'

'I'm fine.'

'You don't seem fine.'

Scarlet gives a slight shrug. 'I will be.'

Eli sets down his fork. 'You know, this isn't going to work if you don't trust me.'

Scarlet feigns interest in her potatoes. 'I know.'

Eli reaches for her hand across the table. She doesn't reach back but manages not to flinch when he touches her. 'So, do you?'

'What?'

'Trust me?'

Scarlet hesitates. 'Yes.'

Eli squeezes her hand. 'That sounds' – she hears the smile in his voice, the attempted levity – 'more like a question than an answer.'

Scarlet fixes her eyes on their hands. How long since she's seen those little showers of sparks when they touched? Finally, she looks up.

'I want to trust you,' she says. 'I will . . . But it's only been a few days. I just, I – I'm doing my best.'

'I know you are.' Eli lifts her hand to his mouth and kisses it, softly. Scarlet closes her eyes. 'And I'm . . .' – he searches for the word – 'monumentally grateful that you're giving me another chance. I only wish everything could be back to normal again.'

Then perhaps you shouldn't have fucked another woman.

'That's not my fault,' she says.

'Oh, God, I know that.' Eli shakes his head. 'I wasn't saying, I wasn't suggesting . . . And, believe me, I'm going to spend the rest of our lives making it up to you. I'm just . . . I'm looking forward to having again what we had before.'

He kisses her fingertips and Scarlet watches him. Will we ever have that? she wonders. Is it possible that it'll be the *same* again? Will I ever stop wanting to check his phone? Will I ever completely trust that he's alone on his business trips? Will I always have a niggling whisper of doubt? In this moment, Scarlet can't imagine that forgiveness is achievable, much less forgetting. How *does* one forget? How does she stop imagining their sex? The kissing. The dirty talk. The pillow talk. What *did* he say to her? *I love fucking you. I want to slide my . . .* And did Eli say to *her* what he says to her?

Scarlet shakes her head, dislodging the words, for the thought of this is almost too much to bear – the only thing worse being talk of love. Eli maintains, adamantly, that it was 'just sex'. Though isn't that the foulest phrase in the English language? 'Just sex.' Inconsequential enough to be instantly discardable, but not *so* insignificant that he could resist it, not *so* irrelevant that he could have simply chosen to do something else instead. Watch a football match. Drink a pint. Read a book. No, not quite so 'just sex' as that.

'Are you all right?'

Scarlet looks up. 'Sorry?'

'I was asking if you were okay,' Eli says. 'You didn't hear me.'

'Sorry,' Scarlet says again. 'I was . . .'

She could talk about it. She could ask him again for details, for reassurance, for promises. But this ceaseless, hideous carousel of words and images and tears that never stops, never reaches a new, longed-for destination, is so agonizing and so *exhausting*. The questions are painful to ask and the answers painful to hear and never, never does the asking or the hearing undo or repair or lead anywhere but back to pain. Unremitting, relentless pain . . .

'I, I . . .' Scarlet begins again. 'I'm fine.'

Goldie

Pushing the hoover across the plush cream carpet in room 27, Goldie glances longingly at the bed. She's so tired after not sleeping last night – exacerbated by weeks of very little sleep – that she can barely stand straight. In all the years she's been cleaning hotel rooms she's never once even sat, let alone lain down on a bed. It's too risky, and both the chance of getting caught and the subsequent price to be paid too high. But exhaustion has softened the edges of both reason and fear. *What can it hurt*, Goldie thinks, *if I only stop for a moment?*

Goldie stands in a glade. The willow trees flanking this hidden space are so closely pressed together that their boughs entwine into a canopy of branches and leaves so dense that the sky is no longer visible. It takes a few moments for Goldie to become accustomed to the dark and a few more moments for her to realize that she's back in Everwhere, which means she must have fallen asleep on that hotel bed. *Dammit.* She's about to wake herself and return when she sees something at her feet: a small body. Goldie bends her knees to crouch beside the creature: a fox, its body broken as if it has been snapped in half. Wondering what to do, she places a hand on its flank: still warm.

'What are you doing?'

Goldie looks up to see Liyana emerging through a curtain of willow leaves, striding towards her. Quickly, Goldie withdraws her hand from the fox and stands.

'I didn't kill him. I wasn't—'

Liyana frowns. 'I didn't say you had. Why would you think I would?'

Goldie shakes her head. 'Nothing. I just, I found him here and I thought . . .'

'What?'

'Well, I just arrived and he was here and I thought—'

'That you should practise,' Liyana finishes her sister's sentence. Now she too is standing over the fox, gazing down at the curl of fur and bone.

Goldie nods, relieved. 'Yes, exactly. We don't have long, and what if it doesn't work, what if—'

'It will.'

177

'Yes,' Goldie persists. 'But if it doesn't, we've only got till tomorrow night—'

'I know. And it's fine,' Liyana says. 'Stop worrying.'

'It's not fine,' Goldie says, her voice starting to rise. 'It's fine for *you*. You've got the love of your life with you, every day. And if she's not with you, you can phone her. You have no idea what it's like for me – three years without a word or a touch or . . .' Tears roll down Goldie's cheeks and drop onto the fox's body. 'That's nine . . . over a thousand, that's . . . too many days. And every one of them like a year. Do you know? Do you have any idea what that's like?'

Liyana shakes her head, having the decency to look a little shamed.

'No,' Goldie says, calming slightly. 'And now I have a chance – one chance – to get him back. So, forgive me if I'm panicking.'

'It should be in the water.' Liyana reaches into her shirt to extract the talisman of Mami Wata. 'We'll harness the greatest power there.'

'This is only a practice,' Goldie says, casting an anxious glance towards the river. 'We can do everything properly tomorrow.'

'We shouldn't do it at all,' Liyana mutters. 'It's too dangerous. Look what happened last night.'

At her words, Goldie lets out a small sob and sinks to her knees.

'All right, all right.' Liyana kneels down beside her. 'I'm not saying – let's try it like this, let's do it together.' Mumbling an incantation, Liyana kisses Mami Wata's tiny wooden head. Behind her, a line of willow trees shiver, scattering leaves over the sisters and the small corpse. Liyana closes her eyes and bows her head, rhythmically rubbing the carving and continuing to murmur the inaudible invocation.

Following her sister's lead, Goldie closes her eyes, bows her head and chants her own invented, intuitive prayer – a call for assistance and a blessing. She looks up to see Liyana stretch out her hands across the fox – now shrouded in leaves – head still bowed. Goldie takes her sister's hands.

'*Ina rokon albarkunku, Mami Wata* . . .' Liyana intones softly at first, then louder and louder so her voice fills the glade. '*Rike hannuna kamar yadda na kawo wannan dan kadan daga sauran rayuwa.*' She pauses, inviting Goldie to join in. '*Ina rokon albarkunku, Mami Wata,*' they chant together. '*Rike hannuna kamar yadda na kawo wannan dan kadan daga sauran rayuwa.*'

Still chanting, Goldie imagines the fox, its yellow eyes blinking, its soft russet fur dappled with white spots like splashes of sunshine. She pictures the fox alive – bounding over fallen trunks, its paws a dash across stones and rocks, body taut as wire, ears flicking at the faraway crack of a twig. Liyana releases one of her sister's hands to brush the leaves from the fox's body, then she presses both palms to the fox's breast, while Goldie follows suit and cups its heavy head. They begin the recitation again.

A rush of warmth seeps from them and quickly, more rapidly than has ever happened when they've healed anything alone, the fox's whole body begins to heat up.

'*Ina rokon albarkunku, Mami Wata,*' Goldie echoes Liyana, pressing her hands tight around the fox's skull as the reanimating heat seeps from her skin and into the dead animal. '*Rike hannuna kamar yadda na kawo wannan dan kadan daga sauran rayuwa* . . .'

'*Ina rokon albarkunku, Mami Wata,*' Liyana incants. '*Rike hannuna kamar yadda na kawo wannan dan kadan daga sauran rayuwa.'*

Then, they feel it. The quiver of an ear, the sudden twitch of rigid legs. Liyana looks up to meet Goldie's gaze and, still chanting, they grin at each other. A convulsion jerks through the fox from nose to paws and then in one sudden, swift movement it's up, shaking off the remainder of its leafy shroud, staring at the sisters for a split second with its keen yellow eyes before leaping away, darting across the stones and disappearing through the curtains of leaves.

'Not so much as a thank you,' Liyana says, gaping. 'How rude.'

'Kids nowadays,' Goldie says. 'So ungrateful.'

They grin at each other like ecstatic fools; their laughter – buoyed by relief and hope – peals in the fox's wake and rises up and up, high above the trees. On a hidden branch the raven regards her sisters below with a proud, beady eye.

None of them see the cracks starting to snap along the trunks of every tree in the glade, marking them like lightning strikes. None of them feel the building tremors shuddering deep beneath the network of roots and the moss-covered ground.

Liyana

Sitting on her bed she shuffles the cards. Again, again, and once more for luck. As the cards slice into each other, shifting from Liyana's right hand to her left, one snaps out of the pack and falls. She bends over the edge of her bed and reaches to the floor to pick it up: The Devil.

Liyana cuts it back into the pack and continues shuffling. But, whenever she glances down, The Devil has come to the front. She slices him into the deck, again and again. Still hoping. The buoyant joy she'd felt in Everwhere has faded and now she's scared.

'Tell me about tomorrow night,' she whispers. 'Tell me that it's going to work.'

Liyana holds her breath for one final shuffle, then deals out five cards onto her duvet. He is the first to appear, followed by the Three of Swords, The Lovers – reversed, The Magician and The Tower. Their pictures are intricate, bright against the white sheet.

The Devil: a man and woman are chained together by their ankles; the woman is dressed in a flamboyant costume, the man naked, with green skin and red eyes, hair slicked into horns, feet shaped into hooves. The woman has turned her face away but he is looking at her, as if he wants something that she doesn't want to give. *Greed, temptation, obsessions and addictions.* The Three of Swords: a girl sits on a stone holding her own heart in her hands, the swords pierce her heart, blood dripping from their tips. *Heartbreak, isolation, devastation.* The Lovers (reversed): an amorous couple embrace on a flying carpet of hearts that soars over the top of an illuminated city. *Deception, separation, loss.* The Magician: a golden-cloaked woman holds a shining wand to the sky, an owl flies above, fairies and sprites dance at her feet. *Infinite possibilities, power, determination, action.* And, just as Liyana had feared, The Tower: a grey wind blows through a crumbling stone tower, a man and woman fall to their deaths from its windows. *Sudden collapse, reversal in fortune, defeat.*

Liyana searches for patterns in the cards, for connections in their meanings, for hope where there is none. Gradually the elements blend, creating the unique interpretations that come with every dealing of the cards. When the reading is complete, when there is nothing more to see, no hope to be found, still Liyana waits. The identity of The Devil still isn't clear but this much is certain: Goldie won't get what she wants. Exactly what *will* happen, Liyana does not know. But she is sure of one thing, that great suffering will be wrought upon all.

31st October – Tonight

Goldie

Teddy brings her breakfast in bed. Wonky triangles of burnt toast with cold butter slathered too thickly and strawberry jam slathered too thinly, along with a tepid cup of milky tea.

'Happy Birthday,' he says, grinning with the pride of a chef who's just cooked a three-course supper culminating in a perfectly risen soufflé.

'Thanks, Ted.' Goldie takes a tentative sip of the tea. 'This is very unexpected and very kind.'

'You're welcome.' Teddy's grin widens. 'And I got you something too.'

'You did?' Goldie says, trying not to sound nervous.

'Don't worry, I didn't steal it!' Teddy laughs. 'But I couldn't buy it, so I drew it.'

'You did?' Goldie smiles, pleased that he's drawing again, having so loved it when he was younger, and touched that he's bothered to do anything at all. 'Show me.'

Teddy scurries across the living room to dip behind the screens surrounding his bed. He returns a moment later, arms behind his back.

Goldie sits up. 'This is exciting.'

Grinning, Teddy hands her a piece of paper. 'It's —'

'Everwhere,' Goldie finishes. She doesn't need him to tell her, for it is the most exquisite rendering and he has captured it all: the unwavering moon, the meandering rivers, the misty air, the fog-shrouded trees, the leaves, every stone, shadow, branch and bird. 'But . . . how do you know?'

He shrugs, but the gesture does not hide his delight. 'You told me.'

'Yes, but . . .' Goldie grips the picture as if it's a newborn baby she's scared she might drop. 'This isn't just how it looks, it's how it feels. It's . . . astonishing.'

'Then I'm an artist *and* a chef,' Teddy says with a beaming smile. 'Not bad for one day. I can make you a birthday dinner tonight too, if you like.'

With great care, Goldie sets the picture down beside her and returns to the breakfast, nibbling a triangle of toast from the inside out. She takes a deep breath. 'It's lovely of you to offer, Ted, but I was thinking we might get a take-away. Your choice – anything you like.'

Her brother frowns. 'But it's your birthday, it should be up to you.'

Goldie smiles at him, thinking yet again how much she loves him. She feels a surge of fear at the thought of tonight and what's to come. But she reminds herself of the fox and how easy and effortless it all was; it'll be far harder with Leo, she thinks, when we don't even have a body to house his spirit – but she'll have Liyana and Scarlet too, and their powers will be at their zenith; together they can do anything. *It's okay,* Goldie tells herself, *it's okay, don't worry, everything will be okay.*

Scarlet

Scarlet lies awake beside a snoring Eli, trying to ignore the siren call of the silent phone on his bedside table. He has been so kind to her today, taking the day off work to treat her to lunch at Core, where they had the £165 tasting menu and Scarlet ate the most delicious dessert – a deconstructed Malteser extravaganza – that had ever passed her lips. He'd given her the charm bracelet, wrapped in silk and kisses, and been as tender and kind as when they'd first fallen in love. Eli had, all in all, made every effort to facilitate forgiveness.

She squeezes her eyes shut, willing herself to sleep. She should be able to sleep; she's never felt so tired. Exhaustion has pulled at her all day, as if she's dragging a leaden anchor along with every step she takes. Growing a human is no small matter, Scarlet has realized.

She tries to forget her sister's remarks, to ignore the insistent tap-tap of doubt, like a sceptical woodpecker on her shoulder. When will it go away? How long must she wait to feel halfway normal again? And, worse still, is it possible that she will *never* feel normal again?

She opens one eye to glare at Eli. How can *he* sleep? As if he's done nothing wrong, has no guilt, no shame, no worries, no discordant reality to drag him from the delicious, hushed darkness of sleep into the blazing, harsh light of waking. How can he shut off all thought, memory and care?

Deep down Scarlet knows, in this battle of wills between her suspicious and trusting selves, who must win. Indeed, the victory has already been declared. It only waits to be admitted, to be announced. It only remains to be seen how many bitter nights Scarlet will drag herself through before she again prises the lid from Pandora's box.

What are you waiting for? The woodpecker tap-taps with Liyana's voice. *You've buried your mother and grandmother, you shoot flames from your fingertips, you could roast a man alive if you so choose. You are a warrior, a witch, a wonder-woman. And you're too afraid to pick up a phone.*

The seconds tick by. The taunts echo through her thoughts. The clouds shift behind the curtains and moonlight filters into the room.

At last, Scarlet leans over her snoring fiancé and picks up the phone.

'But, why?' Scarlet is sobbing now. 'W-why did you promise? Why did you swear? Why?! If you knew—'

Now she's the one unravelling, she's the one coming undone. How could she have been so stupid? So naive? How could she have fallen so far? Liyana was right. Once upon a time Scarlet was a Sister Grimm. Once she'd won every fight she'd fought. Once she had commanded the elements, once she had channelled great arcs of fire from her fingertips. And now. Look at her now. Destroyed by a single idiot, self-entitled human being.

'Why did you do it?' Scarlet wipes her eyes over and over again, wishing she could stop crying. 'Why?'

'Because . . .' Eli mumbles. He sits on the bed, teetering on the edge, hands clasped. She stands on the carpet, far enough away to be beyond his reach. 'Because I didn't want to lose you.'

'So . . . you lied.' Her heart is beating so hard and fast she fears she might be having an attack. She presses her hands to her chest, worrying about the rush of panic through her bloodstream. But surely it can't affect such an infinitesimal foetus just yet.

Eli is silent. It's not a question and he doesn't try to answer it, doesn't attempt to defend himself against this righteous charge. 'I'm so sorry I hurt you,' he says. 'I didn't mean you to find out – I'm sorry you found out, I mean, no, I'm sorry you—'

Scarlet stares at him, incredulous. 'You're sorry I found out?' she repeats, indignation all at once enveloping sorrow. 'You're. Sorry. I. Found. Out?!'

'No, no, wait.' Eli sits up, scrambling for words. 'No, no, that's not . . . You're not, that's not what I—'

'Hold on.' Scarlet stops him. 'I'm not sure I – let me get this right.' She starts to pace the room, walking up and down the carpet beside the bed. 'So, you're not sorry that you did it? You're not sorry that you continued to see – to fuck – a woman you promised you'd never, *ever* go anywhere near again? You're not sorry about the filthy emails – no texts, right, because you're not a fucking idiot – just dozens of truly disgusting emails buried in a "Starbucks" folder you didn't think I'd have the sense to check? No? None of that? You're just sorry you got caught?!'

'No, no, no . . .' Eli reaches out for her, but Scarlet pulls back. 'Yes, of course I am. Of course. I'm an absolute total scumbag, I know this. And I, I . . . I don't know, I don't know . . .' Eli sighs. 'Please, tell me what to say, what to do to make this right and I will. I will. I'll do anything you want. All right? Please, please just tell me what to do.'

'All right?' Scarlet says, stretching out the word. 'All right?' She stares at him. 'You know . . . I read an article once, about domestic abuse – that sanitized term used for arseholes who beat their wives. Beat them, rape them. Did you know that marital rape was legal until 1991? Nineteen fucking ninety-one. That was in the article too.' Scarlet speaks in a slow, steady voice, as if explaining something simple to a small child. In fury, she has finally found her footing. No more tears. 'And there was this woman in it, this amazing woman, the sort who can turn suffering into wisdom, right? And—'

'That's all very awful,' Eli says. 'But what's any of that got to do with us? Is this a lecture about how all men are shits? Because, if it is I—'

'If you had the decency not to interrupt me,' Scarlet

snaps, 'then you'd find out, wouldn't you? And, for the record, no I don't think all men are shits – your sins aren't mitigated by your biology – so, as I was saying, what this woman said was: "Hit me once, shame on you. Hit me twice, shame on me." You see?'

Eli frowns. 'Not exactly, no.'

'No?' Scarlet says. 'I didn't think that was a particularly complex point I was making. Cheat on me once, Eli, shame on you. Cheat on me twice, shame on me.' She narrows her eyes. 'Get it now?'

'Hold on, hold on,' Eli says, again reaching out for Scarlet's hand. She snatches it away. 'Wait, you can't equate wife-beating to – who said that's the same thing? Who said I would—?'

'You,' Scarlet says. 'You did.'

Eli shakes his head. 'No, no I didn't.'

'Oh, yes you did. "All men want to cheat and the ones who don't are only afraid of getting caught." Isn't that what you said? Please, if I'm misquoting you . . .' Scarlet pauses and, when Eli says nothing, 'So, you will do it again. And again. And again.'

'I will not!' Eli shouts. 'I'm not an animal, I'm capable of discretion and self-restraint. If being with you means that I can never touch another woman for the rest of my life, then I won't.'

Scarlet glowers at him, this man she once loved, once trusted, so deeply. How could she once have thought him the most handsome man she'd ever met? Now she shakes her head. 'You disgust me.'

'I know . . .' Eli takes a deep breath. 'I know that I've done, that I've acted . . .' He searches for the right words. 'Appallingly. Without thought or care, with . . . presumption, entitlement, disregard. And I fully understand – I take full responsibility for everything I've done and I absolutely swear that—'

'No.' Scarlet shakes her head. 'No.'

And this time it is clear, to them both, that she means it. A look passes across Eli's face that Scarlet has never seen before. He's a small boy again, stripped of all assurance, all self-possession. He is, at last, bruised and broken and she is the only one who can save him.

'Please.' Eli shifts off the bed and drops to his knees, wincing at the crack of bone on carpet. 'Please.'

Scarlet says nothing.

'This can't . . .' he says. 'You can't end it like this. Please, I – don't, I just don't . . .'

Scarlet gazes down at him; still she doesn't speak.

Eli looks back up at her, his eyes pleading and brimming over with tears.

'I didn't end it,' Scarlet says. 'You did.'

And then she turns and walks away.

Everwhere

Liyana watches Goldie from the corner of her eye. They stand in the glade where three years ago they fought their demonic father and won, but Leo was lost and Bea too and Goldie was never the same again.

Liyana glances at the great oak tree in the corner of the glade, away from the river, its trunk still scarred as if struck by lightning. 'Are you—?'

'Don't worry,' Goldie says, trying to still her trembling hands. 'I'm fine.'

'We should wait.' Liyana makes a last attempt to halt the runaway train. 'The cards warned me that—'

'We can't wait,' Goldie interrupts, her voice high with

panic. 'It's tonight or never. Tonight we're stronger than we'll ever be again. We can't risk waiting, we can't miss the chance.' Goldie regards her sister with wide, tear-brimmed eyes. 'Please, Ana.'

Reluctantly, Liyana nods. Scarlet, who stands beside her, says nothing.

Standing on the riverbank, avoiding the glimmer of the water, Goldie peels her T-shirt over her head. 'Please, can we get started?'

Liyana nods again and Goldie notices that she won't meet her eye and wonders again at the secrets she might be keeping. Still, she won't ask; she's so close to the chance of getting Leo back now that she won't delay a moment longer.

'You should be able to swim,' Liyana says. 'What if . . . ?'

'It's not like last time.' Goldie drapes her T-shirt over a long, flat stone. 'That was unexpected, this time we're prepared. Anyway, you can control the river, and Scar's here too, so we'll be fine.'

Liyana and Scarlet glance at each other, and Scarlet nods. For a moment Goldie wonders why her second sister looks so sad and she's about to ask what's wrong when her first sister interrupts.

'All right,' Liyana says, decisive now. 'Let's begin before the fog rolls in.'

'All right.' Goldie starts undoing her jeans, trembling fingers slipping and fumbling with the buttons. 'Let's get on, shall we?' Losing her balance as she yanks off the rest of her clothes – only saved from falling by Liyana's proffered stabilizing arm – Goldie takes a deep breath as she stares down at the water. Her heart quickens and her lungs constrict, as if remembering the night before last. 'It's okay,' she mutters. 'Don't worry, it's going to be okay.'

Goldie glances up to see a raven settle on the branch of

an oak tree overhanging the river. Bea flaps her wings and all three sisters gaze up at her. The raven's caw ripples through the air, causing each sister to shiver with a shot of possibility and power, of hope and belief that all will be well.

Discarding their own clothes in turn, Liyana and Scarlet step forward to stand beside their sister. Goldie glances back at the three piles of clothes: unnatural, incongruous fabric hills among the moss and stone. Then she looks to her naked sisters, their skin shining and silky in the moonlight – one black pearl, one white.

They walk down to the edge of the riverbank, pushing aside a curtain of willow leaves, their bare feet seeking moss instead of stone as they creep down towards the water's edge. Goldie's eyes flick up and down from the river to the ground and back again, watchful of every careful step, this time determined not to slip on the mud. Under her vigilant gaze, the roots of the trees remain inert, waiting. While Goldie takes the steep descent slowly, Liyana simply leaps straight from the riverbank into the river, sinking deep into the flow before bobbing up again. Scarlet is next, taking two swift steps from land to water. Goldie, despite all her defiant words, is last, still clutching the bending branch of a willow tree as she eases herself in.

'It's safe,' Liyana says, fingers spreading across the surface like the legs of a water-boatman. 'It's still.'

Sure enough, Goldie sees the currents slow and slacken their grip under Liyana's touch, as if the whole river is relaxing. Moments later, massaged by Liyana's fingertips, the water is as listless as Goldie's heart is animated, beating double-time in her chest.

Then Liyana reaches up to unfasten her necklace, cupping the carving of Mami Wata between her hands, giving it a quick kiss before plunging it deep into the water. She glances up at the sky, then at the whispering leaves of the willow trees, and knows that Sisi is watching and wishing them well and cheering them on.

'Mami Wata,' Liyana begins. 'I invite you to soak up all the strength from all the waters of Everwhere.' She pauses, before beginning the chant. *'Ina kiran ku, Mami Wata, don yada ikon daga dukkan ruwa a duk Everwhere kuma kunshe da shi.* When you contain it within yourself, we humbly ask that you pass it on to us . . .'

Liyana is still mumbling her incantation when a shock-wave bolts through the water, pitching Goldie and Scarlet forward, but they right themselves in time to avoid sinking and then pull themselves through the river to stand beside Liyana, who lifts Mami Wata from the water and places her around Goldie's neck, fastening the clasp, then taking her sister's hands.

'Scarlet will hold you,' Liyana says. 'And I will bless you when you go under, okay? You'll be safe.'

Goldie hesitates. 'Go under? Is that – do we have to?'

Liyana nods. 'You must be fully immersed in the water, or it won't work.'

Goldie takes a deep breath. She thinks of Teddy, how she must keep her promise to him, then Leo. 'Okay.' Tentatively, she leans backwards until her hair brushes the water.

'It's okay.' Scarlet holds Goldie's head as she lies down. 'I've got you.'

Spreading out her body like a starfish, Goldie is anchored in one spot as the currents slowly begin to churn again and Liyana speaks the words of a spell which Goldie, with water thrumming in her ears, can't make out. As she watches Liyana's lips move time slows and stretches, swirling and idling with the currents, twisting and curling until Goldie cannot tell if she has been immersed for a minute or an hour or the entire night. When at last – scooped up by both her sisters – Goldie rises again, she feels it: the elemental force surging through her veins, as if her blood is swirling in unison with all the waters of Everwhere – every lake, every river, every ocean – the strength of a hundred thousand tonnes swelling in her body, ready to be released. Now she contains the power of earth and water both.

Liyana and Scarlet help to draw Goldie through the river until she steps up onto the bank. But, while she allows their support, she no longer needs it. Now she is a queen and they are her retinue. She is Gaia and Amphitrite, goddesses of the earth and sea; her sisters are nymphs. Now Goldie knows what to do, now she can do anything.

She hears an echo in the glade, words dropped from above: *'You are a Grimm unparalleled, powerful as any ever known. Tonight you are omnipotent, tonight you are invincible.'*

As Goldie strides across the glade to reach the place where Leo died she remembers that night: the light extinguished in his eyes, when he knew what was coming. An almighty ripping, as if an ancient oak was being torn asunder, hundreds of thorns torn from hundreds of roses, rising into the air, gathering like swarms of bees, a clutch of arrows aimed at his heart. She ran through the rose bushes, over the stones, the moss; she ran as the thorns flew but she did not reach him before he was impaled; she watched him crucified. A great crack of lightning split the sky, striking the trunk of the tree, flaying its bark and detonating Leo from the centre of his chest, scattering his dust to the four corners of the glade, leaving a glimmering white scar twisting from the roots to the crown of the tree.

When she reaches the scarred tree, Goldie drops to her knees and pushes her fingers into the soil, scooping up handfuls, lifting and letting it drop like a murky waterfall. Then she reaches up and presses her dirty palms to the scar.

'Are you ready?' Liyana stands behind her, beside Scarlet.

Goldie nods, but doesn't turn to look at them, not yet.

Liyana and Scarlet press their hands against Goldie's back, palms to shoulder blades, then step forward so they flank the tree. Goldie touches the tiny figure of Mami Wata hanging between her breasts, rubbing the snake that twists up her body, kissing her head three times.

Then the sisters take hands.

'*Ina rokon albarkunku, Mami Wata,*' Liyana begins. '*Rike hannuna kamar yadda na kawo wannan dan kadan daga sauran rayuwa.*'

'*Ina rokon albarkunku, Mami Wata,*' Scarlet joins in. '*Rike hannuna kamar . . .*'

Their voices rise into the air, sweeping up through the leaves, words wrapping around branches before lifting into the cloud-streaked moonlit sky. Goldie closes her eyes and remembers Leo. Not his death, but his life. In the greatest detail her memory will allow, she scans his body, the galaxy of scars along his spine, 268 moons and stars. The way he looked at her when they made love, his tenderness and vulnerability, as if his heart was an open wound in his chest. How her held her, how he cherished her.

'*Ina rokon albarkunku, Mami Wata,*' she whispers. '*Rike hannuna kamar yadda na kawo wannan dan kadan daga sauran rayuwa.*'

Around Goldie's neck Mami Wata glows like an ember until she begins to scorch Goldie's skin. Goldie clenches her jaw to contain the pain but does not open her eyes. The memory of Leo is so vivid now, so clear, so true that she can feel his touch, taste his kiss, hear his voice.

'Leo.'

My love.

'You've come back to me.'

You've brought me back.

Goldie opens her eyes and there he is.

He stands where the tree had been. Goldie's sisters have gone. The glade has gone. They are alone in a place that is only earth and sky. The mists have sunk into the damp soil, the fog has rolled back, the clouds have smothered the moon, so all is dark. And yet, Goldie can still see him. They see each other as if they're lit from within – as if their souls are two rising suns. They stand together, luminous, naked. Nothing separating them but their skins. And then, all at once, not even that. He's inside her and she inside him. Finally, this total absorption, this mutual deliquescence Goldie has always longed for, always wished were possible. They are two liquids poured into a glass, swirling together until each is indistinguishable. They are particles of air, reduced to their essence, to the eleven atoms essential for life. They connect and recombine, fusing again into the molecules of a single being.

'Are we—?'

Yes.

'Is it—?'

Yes.

Again, time slows and stretches, sliding sideways, rising and sinking; and they are merged for eternity or a single second, or both.

There is silence, a cessation of everything. Then time is kicked into motion again. Quickly the dark fades and Goldie begins to hear other sounds – the chanting of her sisters' voices – and see other things – the tree towering behind her, the vines of ivy wrapping around its trunk, the leaves falling from its shivering boughs – until she realizes that now she is no longer inside him and he no longer inside her.

A preternatural scream rises from the soil and descends from the sky. It pierces Goldie with the force of a hundred thousand amps, shuddering through her body and under her feet like the sudden shifting of the earth's tectonic plates, reverberating through the air like close thunder.

Then all is silent again and Goldie is still.

She knows what's happened. She doesn't need to see her sisters' faces or feel the absence of their dropped hands and their static shock. She knows that Leo has gone.

The soil swallows the echoes of Goldie's scream and the aftershock settles, the agitation absorbed into the fresh still air like a billowing sail slowly deflating upon losing the wind. All is again as it was. The mists descend, the fog rolls in. The unwavering moon illuminates the moss and stone below. The raven's cries drop from the midnight sky.

Everwhere has returned to itself.

And yet ... Something essential *has* changed. Leo is here. As he always was, in spirit, but more than that. He's closer. He's tangible. As if Goldie could reach out and—

She extends her arms, fingertips twitching until her nails scrape the bark of the flayed tree. Shuffling forward on her knees, she caresses the scar, the mark of Leo's death, the engraving on his headstone. She traces its edges, as she once traced the length of his spine.

As Goldie watches fresh marks begin to appear on the smooth wood, symbols she'd stroked so many times three years before: a constellation of crescent moons and tiny stars that spread like a scattering of kisses along the long, winding scar. Goldie's eyes fill and before her sight blurs she presses her palms to the tree, reaching her arms around the trunk to hold him.

'You're here.'

I am.

Goldie

Still naked, she sits in the branches of the tree. *Leo*. It does not feel as he felt, of course. The scratch of wood cannot mimic the soft touch of his skin. But it is all she has and it is more than she's had in so long, more than she ever thought she'd have again, and it is enough.

'You're here,' Goldie says. 'You're really here.'

She has already said this a hundred times but cannot stop.

I am.

Goldie laces her fingers between two protruding twigs. 'You've been here always, haven't you?'

Yes, but not like this.

Her eyes fill. 'I'd forgotten the sound of your voice.'

The warmth of Goldie's hand seeps into the wood and is met by the life of the tree. Her skin responds, heating up as if she's holding Leo's hand. Goldie smiles. A tear rolls down her cheek and she wipes it away with the back of her free hand.

Of course, you haven't heard it in three years. He pauses. *I've heard yours almost every night.*

'You could hear me?' Goldie sits up, uncurling herself from the trunk. 'All this time?'

No, not at first. It took a while before I began to . . . coalesce, before I could think again or feel.

'But you couldn't speak?'

No.

'I'm sorry it didn't work, I meant to . . .' Goldie's vision starts to swim, fearing his answer. She takes hold of a branch again, gripping tight. 'But are you still glad I brought you back?'

Of course, my love. Of course I am.

197

Does he hesitate? Does his voice falter? Goldie can't tell. She presses her ear to the oak tree's trunk. His voice is soft now, emanating from a knot in the bark just above the tip of the elongated scar. She sits high in the branches. Her sisters sit below, at the roots. Now and then snatches of their conversation float up, lone words snagging on sprigs of leaves.

Far below Goldie sees the fog start to roll in again, pulling its gauzy shroud over moss and stone. A slight wind whips up, trembling the boughs. Goldie closes her eyes and imagines that the breeze is Leo's breath on her lips. She doesn't know what to say now. She's been waiting for this moment for so many years and now it's finally here, she doesn't know what to do.

She wants to weep and grasp the tree so tightly and kiss it so hard that it pricks her lips with splinters; yet she's struck with a strange shyness, as if she's courting Leo anew. All the things she's wanted to say she can't remember anymore and, in the aftermath of his resurrection, she's almost speechless. But it doesn't matter; she has the rest of her life to recall the past and enjoy the present and look to the future. It's only then that Goldie realizes the great unexpected boon in Leo's unexpected topiarian transformation: he cannot die. How has it taken her so long to realize this? If he had been resurrected as a mortal, then she'd have always risked losing him again. But now they will truly be together for the rest of their lives. And that, surely, is – almost – sufficient compensation for everything they have lost.

Leo

He's no longer free. He's no longer synapses firing and molecules sparking, no longer pinballing at random and at will through the infinite skies of Everwhere. Now he's made solid, aware of his limits and reach. He's a bird trapped in a cage; a prisoner sentenced to solitary confinement for a thousand lifetimes. Now the benign oblivion through which he'd soared has shrunk and his clipped wings beat against wooden bars. Now his tranquillity has been replaced by blind, claustrophobic panic.

Of course, Leo can tell Goldie none of this. He feels her vibrant joy, her voluminous relief. She is so grateful to have him back, so relieved that the resurrection did not fail; not completely. She wanted the moon; she got the stars and that is more than enough.

And so, Leo will stay with his spirit locked within the tree and he will pretend that all is well, that he too is joyous (for he is) and content (though he's not) to stay for as long as Goldie is alive to visit him. He will save his anguish for the hours when Goldie is gone. Of course – though she does not realize this yet – when she finally dies, when her soul seeps into the Everwhere soil and her spirit is engulfed by the mists and fog, he will remain. There will be no escape for him, no release. He is trapped to suffer the eternal torture of immortal life.

But he will not ask her to release him, for that would break her heart all over again.

Everwhere

When Goldie finally steps down from the branches of Leo's surrogate arms she takes her sisters' hands as they help her to the ground. She sees Liyana's relief and returns her smile. But when she meets Scarlet's gaze, Goldie's surprised to see her eyes shift colour to pitch black as a moonless sky. Then, just as quickly, they are dark brown again.

Goldie blinks, thinking perhaps she imagined it. It has

been an extraordinary night, after all. So she hugs them both and kisses Leo's trunk and bids him goodbye – till tomorrow – and forgets.

None of them notice the shadows that lurk behind the leaves of the willow trees, slinking back into the dark as the sisters walk past.

1st November

Everwhere

Bea picks up the waifs and strays, the wanderers, the sisters that come to Everwhere looking for a little direction in their lives, a shot of inspiration or the mending of a broken heart ... Of course she reveals to them their elemental powers, if such revelations need to be made, but sometimes worldly problems must be met with worldly solutions. It's in situations such as these that Bea often finds herself at a loss. Teaching a sister how to fly is one thing; teaching her how to find the courage to leave a dreadful job or an abusive relationship is quite another.

In life, Bea didn't have the disposition or inclination for wise advice, and death hasn't much changed her. If only her sisters weren't so embroiled in the challenges of their own lives, they might be able to assist. But that's why the dead make the best counsel, because they've finally relinquished that eternal curse of the living: expectation and desire. And because they have all the time in the world.

Now, Bea perches on a branch and watches the sisters gathering below.

In the nooks and crannies, the restless shadow creatures whisper and coax, hopeful of snaring a straggler who hasn't been warned.

Scarlet

'I hate him,' Scarlet sobs. 'I – I f-fucking hate him.'

'I know,' Goldie whispers. 'So do we. He's vile.'

'It's okay.' Liyana strokes Scarlet's hair. 'We're here, we're not leaving you.'

'I wish you'd told us before,' Goldie says, for perhaps the dozenth time. 'I can't believe you were holding all this in while helping me.' She kisses the top of Scarlet's head. 'You poor, sweet, lovely creature.'

Scarlet is curled up in a ball on a bed of moss between her sisters. They'd been about to return from Everwhere when Scarlet started to cry and confessed everything, so they'd stayed to hold and comfort her.

'I couldn't,' Scarlet says. 'I ...' Trailing off, her words morph into a long, keening cry that fills the air and shakes the leaves of nearby willow trees. She's pinballing now between sudden exclamations and quiet weeping. Her sisters prefer the first; anger is surely better than sorrow, they think. Goldie knows that eventually both will soften (if never fully evaporate) though, of course, she can't suggest that while her sister sits in its core, the white-hot centre of shock and grief.

In time she will grow numb but not yet, not for a long while. For now, there's nothing much they can say or do except hold her: gently because she's bruised, and firmly because they must grip her edges so that she doesn't slip away into a place where she cannot be reached. Goldie still vividly remembers how it was after Leo died: thoughts steeped in darkness, mind and heart swallowed by despair. She lay in bed for weeks, months, weeping and wanting to die, desperate not to feel the pain that burned through every part of her. Nothing brought comfort, nothing could soften that scorching pain. A single thought circled like a vulture over a corpse, incessant, insistent: *Leo is dead and gone and there is nothing more to be done.*

'We're here,' Goldie repeats Liyana's words. 'You're not alone. We're here.'

In response, a high wail pitches into the air, a ribbon of pain that brushes the tops of the trees then drifts down to encircle their throats. Goldie feels Liyana stiffen beside her. She, the only one who's been spared such grief, is shocked by the sensation.

They hold Scarlet, until the fight inside her begins at last to flag – the way Teddy would finally go limp after a prolonged tantrum as a toddler – and she stills.

An hour later, when she wakes, Scarlet looks from one to the other of her sisters, still sitting beside her on the mossy ground, still stroking her hair, still resting loving hands on her body – though perhaps they too have nodded off once or twice.

'I'm sick of crying,' Scarlet mutters. 'I'm sick of the misery. I just want to forget for a few minutes, pretend I'm okay. Can you tell me something silly?'

It's too soon, Goldie knows – Scarlet will lapse back into sorrow soon enough – but for now Goldie will seize the opportunity to tug Scarlet back from the precipice, to coax the flicker of a smile, a momentary cessation of tears.

'Let me kill him,' she whispers. 'Maim him at the very least.'

'We'll slice off his dick with a carving knife,' Liyana says. 'Or a very blunt pair of shears.'

'Tell us how you want him to suffer,' Goldie says. 'Instruct us. We'll do whatever you want. Consider us your henchmen, your . . .'

'Your word is our command,' Liyana finishes. 'We live to serve.'

Scarlet looks up, dragging the backs of her hands across her eyes. Wiping her nose on her sleeve. Sniffing.

'A smile?' Goldie says.

'A teeny tiny one?' Liyana says.

Scarlet looks at them both, unblinking. So, they try again, saying all the silly things that come to mind. Anything to try and bring their sister back, if only for a few moments. Long enough to show her light and hope, even in this dark. They joke, they tease, they jest. They tell stories. They talk and talk until they run out of words, of breath.

Neither of them says: 'I told you so.'

On her fifteenth birthday, Scarlet ate a mushroom. And, like Alice before her, it made her shrink. She went to the woods with friends after school, telling her grandmother that she was doing research for an unspecified geography project.

In the gang of five girls, Karmilla Khatri was the leader, the one who instigated all adventures: shoplifting lipsticks in John Lewis, giving up gluten, testing the lemon-water-only diet, experimenting with psychedelic substances. She had an older brother who, naturally, blazed a trail of bread-crumbs on this particular path. And Vivaan Khatri had, he alleged one day, discovered a patch of magic mushrooms in the woods at Byron's Pool – a fact he let slip to his sister while he was flying.

'One side will make you high,' he'd slurred. 'The other side will make you low.'

Karmilla had pressed him for more detailed instruction but, given his state of mind, he'd not been able to provide any. Scarlet hadn't been nervous, since, like a good many of Karmilla's other adventures, it would probably come to nothing. Going gluten-free had lasted less than a week and the lemon-water diet barely twelve hours. So, when confronted with the mushroom, assuming it was the sort her grandmother added to the breakfast special at the No. 33 Café, she took a bite. Fortunately for Scarlet, it wasn't a

Death Cap. Unfortunately, it was the sort that made her smaller.

The darkness into which Scarlet sank that summer evening was unlike anything she'd experienced before. She tumbled into a rabbit hole and kept tumbling. Falling past shrieking monarchs and playing cards with spears and chatty rabbits, down and down, past dead mothers and troubled grandmothers, down and down, past fires and falling leaves and sisters, down and down until she'd lost any tenuous grip on reality versus nightmare.

Six hours later, she landed. It had taken Scarlet days to fully emerge from that darkness and its echoes had howled at the edges of her life for weeks, months after. She had never touched, let alone tasted, uncertain substances again. And she'd never again experienced that screaming descent into madness. Until now.

Liyana

Liyana is confused. The Tarot cards had predicted havoc and suffering, Aunt Sisi had spoken of a storm coming and yet . . . nothing. All had gone well. They had brought Leo back – after a fashion – and no one had been killed, hurt or even mildly injured.

She lies awake now, worrying. Beside her, Kumiko sleeps. She'd been waiting in Liyana's bed, a magnificent surprise when Liyana had finally returned home.

'You came.'

'Of course I did.' Kumiko smiled her midnight smile, teeth white as the moon, hair black as the night. 'It's your birthday. Twenty-one, not to be overlooked.'

Liyana leaned in and kissed her. 'I didn't think I'd see you till the weekend.'

'I know,' Kumiko said, wrapping one of Liyana's curls round her finger. 'I wanted to surprise you.'

Liyana grinned, kissing her girlfriend again. 'Best. Surprise. Ever.'

'You missed me.'

'More than anything.'

Kumiko sat up, slipping her T-shirt up over her arms and sliding back down into the bed. Liyana snuggled in, resting her head between Kumiko's breasts. Kumiko stroked Liyana's hair. Liyana's breath caught in her throat; then she let out a long, thin sigh.

'It's okay, my love,' Kumiko whispered. 'Whatever it is, it'll be okay.'

'I don't know, there's so much . . .' Liyana closed her eyes, pressing herself closer. 'Goldie is happy now, but Scarlet is miserable and I think Nya is . . . I don't know how to help her; I don't know if anyone can.'

Kumiko reached for Liyana's hand, interlacing their fingers. 'I loved a girl once who was always sad – I never knew why, or even if there was a why – and nothing I did lifted her sadness, even though I tried everything . . . I read books about depression and I told her about all the therapies that might help, and I probably would've kept on and on doing it, but one day she told me to stop and said: "Please stop trying to change me, I'm not going to change." And so I did. Some people you can't save, no matter how hard you try.'

Liyana took a deep breath, then let out another long sigh. 'You're not the first person to tell me that. But she's my . . . to all intents and purposes she's my mother.'

'I know.' Kumiko leaned down and kissed Liyana again. 'And I'm sorry, my love, I know it's not what you want to hear – and perhaps I'm wrong, I hope I'm wrong . . .'

Liyana let herself be kissed. 'I just . . . I don't want to . . .'

Her eyes filled with tears. She swallowed. 'I don't want to be alone.'

'Oh, darling.' Kumiko clasped Liyana's fingers, drew them to her mouth and kissed each one in turn. 'You will never be alone.'

And now Kumiko sleeps and Liyana, still worrying, wishes she could.

Goldie

Tonight, she returns to Everwhere as soon as she falls asleep. She knew she would, she didn't even have to will it. She doesn't even have to walk the paths or cross the glade but materializes directly in the boughs of his tree. Straight into Leo's arms.

Now she sinks into his hold, enveloped by his voice.

Tell me about your life.

'Don't you already know? Can't you see it?'

No. I can only see you in Everwhere.

'Oh,' Goldie says. 'But you can hear my thoughts here, can't you?'

Yes, but I love your voice, I like to hear you speak.

Goldie smiles, reaching for a twig and rubbing its tip between finger and thumb, as if she's stroking the ears of a cat. 'Can you feel that?'

Yes.

'Is it nice?'

Very.

She hears the smile in his voice.

'Of all the things I imagined for my future, I never thought that one day I'd be making love to a tree,' Goldie says, trying to sound light, upbeat; as if she doesn't mind at all. 'Life takes unexpected turns, doesn't it?'

Leo's silent but for the breeze rustling his branches.

Why are you changing the subject? Tell me about your life. Your sisters – Scarlet – your brother. Share your troubles with me.

Goldie sighs. 'I don't want to talk about sad things, not when you're here, not when, for the first time in a very long time, I'm happy.'

But tell me, I might be able to make it better.

'You do,' Goldie says. 'Just being here.'

Leo waits, saying nothing. An old trick of his, to smoke her out with silence.

Leo

He is impotent, in every sense. He's trapped in a dungeon of wood and enchantment, while she is free, though she doesn't want to be. He cannot hold her, not truly, can only give her comfort and, albeit illusory and transient, safety in the boughs of his awkward arms. But these skeleton branches won't shelter her from wind or rain, won't bear fruit or nuts to feed her, nor do they even provide a particularly pleasant place to rest. Once Leo was her lover, her companion, her teacher. Now he can only be her friend. And quite an ineffectual one at that.

Goldie can talk of love and, certainly, he loves her. More than anything. Indeed, the word is hardly adequate for how he feels. Yet, he cannot demonstrate these emotions, cannot make his passions manifest. He is Cyrano, but worse, because his Roxanne knows him, wants him, risked her life to have him; and yet he cannot embrace her. Surely the devil himself could not have designed a greater torture?

Liyana

When at last she falls asleep, Liyana doesn't return to Everwhere, as she wishes, but instead dreams of Ghana and Aunt Sisi. They sit side by side on a jetty at the edge of Lake Volta, dangling their bare feet in the water.

'I've missed you.' Liyana leans her head on her aunt's shoulder. 'I've really missed you.'

Sisi reaches up to cradle her niece's cheek. 'I know you're hurting, darling, but I'm so proud of what you did last night.'

Liyana sighs. 'It hardly went according to plan.'

'But you did your best,' Sisi says. 'And even the three of you at the height of your powers aren't strong enough to change fate.'

Liyana kicks a foot in the water, thinking of Nya. A fish nibbles at the big toe of her other foot. 'I wish I was.'

'Oh, child.' Sisi sighs. 'We all wish that.'

Knowing what her aunt is going to say next, Liyana peers into the lake, pretending to be caught by the sight of little fishes. With her right hand she clutches the figurine of Mami Wata at her neck.

'Don't get your hopes up, Lili,' Sisi says. 'Some people can't be saved, no matter how hard you try.'

'But . . .' Liyana thinks of the story, of the empty plate and cup. 'But, maybe . . .'

Aunt Sisi tucks her hand under Liyana's chin and lifts her head so their eyes meet. 'You can only save people who want to be saved. And sometimes, they don't; sometimes you must let go.'

2nd November

Liyana

Liyana wakes from a nightmare. She was floating on a life raft alone in the ocean, waves crashing over the raft, salt spray stinging her eyes, wind fierce and rain harsh against her skin. She was naked, flayed as if she'd been whipped, wounds open and bleeding. Then the raft, all at once, was stitched of spiderwebs and the white leaves of Everwhere were floating among the thundering waves while lightning split the skies. Liyana should have been in her element, should have leapt from the raft with a warrior's cry, should have taunted the ocean and seized command of the storm, ridden the waves and plunged into the water, let Poseidon think he'd claimed her, before emerging, indefatigable and victorious, from the depths.

She should have embraced her element with relish, but instead she'd clung to the disintegrating raft and wept.

Awake now, Liyana sits up in her bed. Beside her, Kumiko still sleeps, cheek pressed down into the pillow, hair fanned out like a widow's veil. Slowly, gently, Liyana draws back the veil to reveal her girlfriend's face. She gazes a while, breathing in her familiar beauty, the comfort of her presence, holding her fast like an anchor. She toys with the idea of waking Kumiko, of curling into her arms and pretending, for as long as possible, that all is right with the world. But she knows that it is not. She knows this as surely as she knows anything, and it is no use hiding from the fact.

So Liyana slips out of bed, pulls on jeans and a T-shirt

then creeps down the hallway to Nya's room. She lifts her hand to knock but knows, even as she does so, that it will go unheard. Liyana feels her heart pounding in her chest, reverberating against her ribs, shuddering through her body; her stomach churns and she swallows down the bile that rises in her mouth. Liyana is seized by the urge to scream for Kumiko, for she knows, even before pushing open the door, what she will find inside. But she doesn't call out, she can't. This is something she must meet alone.

When Liyana at last walks into Nya's bedroom, she's not surprised by the sight, but the muted shock doesn't lessen the sharpness of the pain. The scene is almost the same as before: the fallen pills splashed across the carpet, scattered from Nya's left hand – her arm cast out from the bed, as if reaching for someone. But this time her head is snapped back and open-mouthed, her chin and cheeks slick with vomit. Liyana doesn't need to step closer to know that she is too late. It is over, done. There will be no need for hospitals or doctors or stomach-pumps this time.

Beside the bed on a low table sits the empty bottle of wine, a glass and a white sheet of paper. Despite her sorrow, Liyana feels a strange gladness that her aunt's last act was the purchase of her favourite wine, an expensive chardonnay which she must have dragged herself out of bed and shuffled to the wine merchants on Clairmont Street to buy. A final pleasure, a final gesture of kindness.

'Oh, Nya.' Liyana's sight blurs as she crosses the room, but she can clearly see – as if through another sense altogether – that her aunt has left only her body behind, that her soul is long since gone. It has, of course, been leaving in increments for weeks now and this is the final departure.

Wiping her eyes, Liyana picks up the paper. Upon it is

the story Goldie wrote, her handwriting sloping across the page in tight, close lines. The paper is creased, as if it's been folded and unfolded many times; some of the words are smudged. Liyana turns it over. On the back, where once the page was blank, are more words, this time in Nya's hand.

My dearest Ana,

I'm sorry. Please, never blame yourself. It couldn't be changed. You gave me every joy, every day – knowing you was the best and biggest gift of my life – and if it was possible to live for another person, I would have lived for you. Please remember, death is only a tragedy for the living – not for the dead.

Infinite & eternal love,
Your Dagā xxx

It's not until Kumiko is at her side, gripping her shoulders, pulling her back, sobs smearing incomprehensible chatter, that Liyana realizes she is bent over the table, howling.

Goldie

'I want to be here always,' Goldie says. 'I want to sit in your branches until skin fuses to wood and we grow together into a single being of human and tree – do you think that's bio-logically possible?'

No – his voice is light with amusement – *sadly, I do not.*

'But maybe here, in Everwhere, don't you think?' Goldie says. 'The physical laws are far more lenient here than on Earth, after all.'

Yes. But, even then, I don't think you can affect them by sheer force of will.

Goldie smiles. 'You underestimate my will.'

A breeze of laughter blows through Leo's branches.

'Can you see me?' Goldie asks. 'Or only feel me?'

He is silent. And when he speaks, his voice is heavy and dark as soil. *No, I can only hear you and feel the weight of you in my branches.*

'Oh,' Goldie says, wondering why this bothers her so. She sighs. 'I know I shouldn't, but I do wish I could see you again, as you were before.'

A murmur of melancholy rustles through Leo's leaves. *There's a good deal we could wish for, the wishing of which would only make us miserable. Let's try then to enjoy, to be grateful for what we have.*

'Yes, I suppose you're right.'

I hope so. His voice is lighter now. *It'd be a shame indeed if I hadn't picked up a little wisdom in the past few thousand years.*

'Right,' Goldie says. 'I sometimes forget that you weren't human once.'

I forget it too. First a star, then a man, now a tree. He pauses. *An odd, unconventional evolution.*

Silence rests between them.

'I'm sorry,' Goldie blurts out, her voice quivering. 'I – I didn't mean for it to happen like this, I . . . I messed up and I'm so—'

Stop. Don't say that, not ever.

Goldie takes a deep breath. She wraps her little finger around a twig.

Okay?

Goldie's silent.

Okay?

'Okay,' she says, after a moment. Though she's only being half-truthful since, while she can agree not to speak

213

again of her guilt and regret to him, she knows she'll never stop speaking of it to herself.

Hold me.

Goldie uncurls her finger from the twig and turns to hug Leo's trunk, as close and tight as she can, for as long as she can, until her arms ache.

You can't spend every minute of every night here.

Goldie feels her stomach drop, as if she's falling. 'You don't want me to?'

What a question! Laughter shakes the boughs. Goldie grips the branch she's sitting on. *I only worry about your life imploding – how will you stay awake?*

'Life?' Goldie relaxes her grip. 'This is my life. Here. With you. Anyway, you know I hardly ever sleep.' She smiles. 'It's one of my superpowers.'

One of your many; but you still have to work, take care of your brother and—

'I know, I know, don't worry. Teddy's happier than I've ever seen him, and better behaved than any teenage boy in the history of the world, thanks to the threat of imaginary curses. And all he talks about is Everwhere and wishing I could teach him to bring bluebottles back to life ... he's lovely to Scarlet too – even brought her a slice of inedible toast this morning – so stop worrying, I can visit you and still take care of everything else.'

Oh, I know you can. A leaf brushes affectionately across Goldie's cheek. *Don't forget, I've seen what you can do – virtually anything you put your brilliant mind and mighty hands to – it's more what you will, or rather won't, do that worries me. Like get enough rest and food and ...*

'All right, all right,' Goldie huffs, since she knows he's not wrong. She does have a tendency towards impracticality, doing what she wants instead of what she needs and to hell with the rest. 'I'll take care, okay?'

Thank you. So ... Two of Leo's long branches wrap around Goldie's chest like arms, hugging her as he used to do, sneaking up to catch her by surprise, scooping her off her feet so she yelped with delight. *Why don't you try to take a little nap right now?*

Goldie says nothing but presses herself into him. The way they hold each other, both entirely different and essentially similar to before, makes her think of how half-lived their life will be. She will be emotionally fulfilled in Everwhere and physically enduring on Earth. She will never stop wanting to be here and only duty, practicality and necessity will return her to the other life. With the exception of two sisters and one brother, she'll know no other affection, no physical love. She won't have marriage and family and all the attendant sorrows and joys. No children. But Goldie can reconcile herself to this, for she's always known, ever since she came to Everwhere for the first time, that she wouldn't have an ordinary life.

She'd hoped, of course, that it would be closer to normal than this. But then, when she feels bitter that she'll never again look into Leo's eyes, never feel the touch of his hand to her cheek, his lips to hers – as other lovers do – she reminds herself that what she has now – immortal, illimitable love – is far more than what she's lost. So, she is more blessed than she is cursed.

Leo

He feels her imprint long after she's gone. The impression of her hands, her arms, her heart, is so strong as to be almost a scar. Like the scars that'd branded his body when he was a man. Before that, as a star, Leo had shifted slowly across the sky, never feeling trapped, not once in ten thousand years. Or listless. And hardly ever lonely. The views alone had been entertainment and consolation enough. He had easily passed centuries gazing around his own particular galaxy. Saturn was one of the planets he'd shone down upon and its sixty-two major moons had absorbed his attention for decades, to say nothing of the rings, which over the years had swallowed hundreds of moonlets in great galloping clouds of dust. Mars had delighted him too; and on Earth the antics of humans had provided unending amusement.

Now, Leo is static. Immutable and immovable, he can barely see five miles in any direction and the landscapes are hardly compelling. He watches herds of deer canter through forests, leaping over fallen trunks and twisting rivers. He shakes his boughs when ravens perch, ridding himself of their scratching claws and sharp, curious beaks. Winds blow leaves which settle on him in drifts and flurries, until he shakes them off. And then, all too often, the fog rolls in so, for long stretches, he can see nothing at all.

When Goldie is not with him, Leo longs to die; longs to be pure, boundless energy again. He longs to be synapses firing and molecules sparking, pinballing through the infinite skies of Everwhere. He longs to be free. It's only when Goldie visits that his longing abates. Then he doesn't care whether he's man or star or tree. But when she leaves, as she always must and always will, he is bereft.

For now, at least, his loneliness is lightened by the constant anticipation of her return. But Leo is all too aware that, in sixty years or so – depending whether Grimms live much longer than mortals – he'll no longer be afforded even that singular comfort.

Scarlet

Scarlet stares at her computer screen, blinking back tears. She'd 'borrowed' Eli's car early that morning and broken the speed limit all the way to Cambridge. Crashing out on Goldie's sofa for several hours, Scarlet had finally dragged herself out of the flat, thinking a little fresh air might buoy her spirits, and that a little company – a café full of chattering people who won't bother her – might stop her from feeling like the loneliest person in the world. Besides, Scarlet knew that if she kept staring at the walls of the tiny flat that soon seemed to be closing in, she'd feel like she was being buried alive.

However, now that she's out in company – everyone gossiping and laughing – Scarlet only feels lonelier and more miserable than before. She sits in Fitzbillies, sick from an over-consumption of Chelsea buns and accompanying hot chocolates. Having told herself that this compulsive gobbling of baked goods was simply answering the call of pregnancy cravings, Scarlet is now forced, in the nauseous aftermath, to admit that she had in fact been gobbling to appease misery.

She's always done this, since she was a little girl. One of the perils, perhaps, of growing up in a café. It accounts for the little Buddha belly she's always scorned, although admittedly less so since becoming pregnant. Which leads Scarlet to awkward contemplations about whether she finds fat (where it supposedly shouldn't be) intrinsically repulsive or whether, and more likely, she's actually absorbed societal judgements stating that a belly containing a baby is beautiful, but a belly simply harbouring an excess of Chelsea buns is ugly. She recalls a picture of an exquisitely naked Demi Moore heavily pregnant on the cover of a magazine.

She recalls similarly corpulent but censorious pictures of celebrities having 'let themselves go'.

Scarlet sighs. She doesn't enjoy introverted speculation, particularly when it verges on the intellectual. It reminds her of the A-levels she didn't take, of the university she didn't attend, about which Scarlet is even more ashamed than of her perpetually chubby belly.

The computer screen blinks. Feeling she should employ her time productively and, having exhausted pregnancy forums until she'd scared herself half to death, Scarlet is seeking employment. But, the opportunities, most of which she is decidedly under-qualified for, taunt her. Why hadn't she gone back to college? When she'd moved in with Eli, when she hadn't had to worry about money anymore, why hadn't she finally taken the opportunity to start studying for her A-levels? Because she'd been embarrassed and ashamed. Because it was easier to pretend she didn't mind being kept by her boyfriend. Because it was easier to get pregnant. *Fuck.*

Scarlet reaches for a remaining crumb of Chelsea bun and nibbles the sticky dough, the syrup sweet on her tongue. This is the first time Scarlet has admitted the fact to herself and she feels the guilt slipping through her bloodstream with the sugar. Scarlet pushes away the plate and gives her belly an apologetic pat, hoping that the foetus won't be able to sense her ambivalence.

Suddenly abandoning her laptop, Scarlet rises and steps over to the counter.

'What can I get you?' The girl behind the counter, sporting a sleeveless top and intricately beautiful tattoos inked from shoulders to wrists, smiles. 'Another bun?'

Scarlet catches sight of the tray of fresh sticky buns and feels her stomach lurch. 'Thank you, um, no. They were

delicious, but I've . . . Well, I was wondering . . . I don't sup-
pose you know if they're looking for staff?'

Liyana

Liyana has never met the neighbours, but they come; knocking on doors, pulled out of their ordinary lives by the unholy
screams. They make phone calls and cups of (untouched)
tea and rummage in the cupboards for biscuits and urge
Liyana to have a nibble; they speak to officials and help with
the filling out of reports; they introduce themselves – some
tentative and mumbling, others intrusive and vigorous, one
including an offer of overnight stay – though Liyana forgets
all the names the moment they're spoken and only wishes
they would leave.

When everyone has at last – with a great deal of awkward shuffling and blundering condolences – vacated the
flat, and Nya's body has been discreetly and respectfully
removed, Liyana lies curled on the sofa with her head in
Kumiko's lap.

'I, I keep thinking she's still here . . .' Liyana turns her
head, looking up to meet Kumiko's gaze. 'I think that if I go
into her room she'll be there, still waiting for me.'

Kumiko cups Liyana's cheek in her palm. 'I think she *is*
here and she'll be here for a long while. I don't think the
spirit leaves straight away – they say that energy can't disappear, can't die like the body . . . I'm sure you'll feel her with
you, if you try, if you focus . . .'

Liyana thinks of Bea. 'I hope so.'

Kumiko strokes Liyana's hair. 'The night my grandmother
died . . . I was awake, I couldn't sleep, I just lay on my bed and
cried and cried . . . and then, at three o'clock in the morning,
I suddenly felt her – the sense of her was so strong she might

as well have just knocked on my bedroom door and walked in. When I closed my eyes it felt exactly as if she was sitting beside me. I talked to her for hours, it was extraordinary, I never forgot it. It happens again, every now and then. Sometimes I still talk to her and I believe she can hear me.'

Liyana sighs. 'What'll happen now?'

'I don't know.' Kumiko takes Liyana's hand. 'I don't know, my love. But you're not alone. I'm here and I'm not going anywhere.'

Liyana presses her head into Kumiko's hand, feeling her solidity, the surety of her presence. Apart from her girlfriend, everything else in the flat feels insubstantial, transient, as if it might all – at a moment's notice – turn to vapour and smoke. But Kumiko is all that matters, she is here and she is rock while everything else is air.

Silence wraps round them. Kumiko never stops stroking Liyana's hair, never lets go of her hand. Liyana doesn't sleep, but drifts between memory and imagination, remembering Nya when they lived in Islington, when her aunt still laughed and made jokes and chatted about nothing in particular, when she got out of bed in the morning and loved to leave the house; when she gambled, when she still believed life to be full of glorious possibilities. Liyana imagines them curled in bed together reading a story, she snuggled into the crook of Nya's arm, a deeply affectionate moment they very rarely shared in real life. Nya had never been demonstrative in her love and, though Liyana understood, she never stopped craving it, never stopped hoping for an elusive hug. Now Liyana feels a sudden and desolate pang of longing for the impossible. While Nya was alive, so was hope, now both are gone.

'When it's all over,' Liyana says, 'I want to come with you.'

'To Cambridge?'

'Yes, I can't bear to be here without her. I can't live in this place alone, and every time I walk past her bedroom door . . .'

'Of course you can come,' Kumiko says. 'We'll find a place to rent and – but don't worry about any of that, I'll start looking and I'll sort it all out. It'll be . . .'

Liyana nods, though she's drifting off into her imagination again and is no longer really listening. She feels, though her senses are largely numb, that perhaps she should go to Cambridge sooner, that she should see her sisters, that something is wrong, secrets are being kept and dangers gathering themselves into an advancing storm. She thinks of her aunt Sisi, thinks of what she'd said about Nkatie cake and contacting the dead and thinks of Nya.

Liyana closes her eyes again and sighs. But these are not things she can deal with right now. No matter how urgent, they will have to wait.

Everwhere

Tonight Scarlet is alone; and then she's not. Her raven sister swoops down and settles on a branch a few feet above her. Scarlet, sitting on a rock beneath, looks up. She lets out a long breath and finds she does not have the energy to speak. She thinks of the tiny cluster of expanding cells in her womb and wonders how much worse it'll get. She thinks, for the first time, of the impending birth. The raven squawks.

I warned you. You didn't listen.

Scarlet frowns. 'That was you?'

Bea ruffles her feathers. *Even without the omniscient sight of the dead, I could have told you that man was trouble.*

Scarlet sinks her head to her lap. 'You and everyone else. Seems like I was the only one dumb enough not to see Eli

Wolfe for who he really was.' She lets out another long, deep sigh. 'And what am I meant to do now?'

I know what I'd do.

'Yeah, I bet you do.' Carnage and mayhem, Scarlet thinks, though she would never sink so low as that. She'll maintain the moral high ground, she will rise above the urge for revenge, she will—

But as she's having these thoughts a fresh breeze blows, spinning the weathervane in a different direction, dispersing notions of compromise and conciliation into the winds. And, in the dark, unseen, Scarlet's eyes turn the colour of the midnight sky.

3rd November

Goldie

Everything is white. She's staring into a lightbulb, a field of snow, a Tupperware sky. Shadows start to take shape and now Goldie sees that she's standing in a white garden: trees, plants, birds, butterflies, all is white ... A white cat stalks through white grass, picking his paws amidst daisies and dandelions, before disappearing into a clutch of cow parsley. Albino blackbirds trill from white birch trees, their song floating on a breeze that carries white bumblebees to and from white roses. Hundreds of flowers are sprinkled through the garden, fat and heavy, on every stalk and stem.

As Goldie watches the garden begins to expand in every direction, reaching out far and wide till all she can see are millions of roses, their scent so strong and sweet that she can taste sugar on her tongue.

She's had this dream many times before, many years ago. She knows what to do next. With a single twitch of her fingers she draws a dozen daisies from the white grasses, clipping their stalks with a quick snap. They lift up to hover patiently in the air. Goldie presses forefinger to thumb and the daisies gather into a suspended circle. She clicks her fingers and slowly, surely, they thread together until they create a floral crown which settles upon her head.

It suits you.

Goldie looks up to see her raven sister alight on a rose bush, her talons splayed to avoid the thorns, her black feathers stark against the white.

'Thank you.' Goldie scrutinizes her sister. 'Is this – did you do this?'

Do what?

'The dream.'

The raven ruffles its feathers, dipping its beak under its wing. *Perhaps.*

'Why?' Goldie takes the crown from her head. 'Why didn't you just find me in Everwhere?'

Bea regards Goldie with glinting black eyes. *Because you're never alone.*

'So?' Goldie feels herself starting to itch. 'Why does that matter?'

Bea hops down from the rose bush to settle in the white grasses at Goldie's feet.

Goldie steps back. 'What is it?'

I need to tell you something you don't want to hear.

Now Goldie feels a twist in her stomach; she wants to leave, wants to wake, wants to run. She'd rather tear through the white roses, torn at by thorns, scratched till her skin's shredded into ribbons that stream behind her as she runs and runs and never looks back.

Sometimes it's a sister's duty to say that the thing she most fears to be true, is.

Goldie shakes her head.

Yes.

'No, no you're wrong.'

And yet, you know what I'm going to say.

'I don't.' Goldie starts to walk away. 'I don't, I . . .'

You cannot trap him like this, you must let him go.

Goldie presses her hands over her ears and starts to run, but it's too late now.

Leo

Are you all right? You're quiet tonight.

She nods.

Goldie?

'Oh,' she says, remembering that he can't see her. 'Sorry, yes, I'm fine.'

You're not. You've hardly said a word. Usually you can't shut up.

'Gee, thanks.'

Laughter shakes his boughs. *And I love it, that's why I'm asking. I miss my chatty little thief.*

'Is that how you think of me?' Goldie frowns. 'That's the first descriptive word that comes to mind? Thief?'

Of course not. It was only one word. I have many that come to mind when I think of you: unparalleled, outstanding, astonishing, breath-taking, spectacular, phenomenal . . .

Goldie smiles, momentarily forgetting her fear. 'Go on.'

I think of you as a warrior, a witch, a . . .

'All right, you may stop now,' she says, still smiling. 'I'm placated.'

I'm glad. Now, instead of trying to distract me with a fight, tell me what's wrong.

Goldie's silent. 'I can't tell you,' she says, at last. 'Because it will change everything.'

It sounds as if it already has.

Goldie inhales, holding her breath for what she hopes is an eternity. 'I know you're not happy,' she whispers. 'I know you want to be free.'

Now he's silent.

Who told you that?

'My sister.'

Which sister?

225

'Bea.'

Another laugh shakes the boughs. *That's ridiculous. What does she know of my heart?*

And, if Goldie didn't know him so well, if she couldn't trace the lines of every remembered smile, decipher the meaning of every sigh, the subtext beneath every word, she might believe him.

Scarlet

It's only been days but to Scarlet it feels like weeks, months, years. So long has she been steeped in sorrow, it's as though she's never breathed anything else but the bleak misty airs of January. All her life.

How is it possible, she wonders, to be so completely and so quickly changed? What's happened to the girl she once was? So independent, so strong. Scared too, of course, but still whole. And now her heart's been cracked and her character crippled. Her spirit's been broken by betrayal and is forever changed; she'll never again be able to love in that unlimited, unbounded way: full of faith and innocent of pain. She will always hold one hand over her heart, a protection and a defence.

'Well, you were right,' Scarlet says. 'I should have listened; I suppose I'd have saved myself a lifetime of pain.'

She sits under a willow tree in Everwhere, between the exposed roots, leaning against the trunk, sheltering behind the respectful curtain of its leaves. She needs its solidity today, not the great uncertain expanse of moss and stone. Scarlet needs something to cling to, in case her broken spirit suddenly crumbles and she finds she cannot pick herself up again. She waits now, half-expecting her sister's retort. But none comes. The glade is quiet, except for the murmuration of blackbirds above, and the faraway roar of the wind.

'Tell me,' Scarlet says, after a while. 'Tell me what to do now.'

She listens, but no answer comes. No voice. No sound.

'Is this some sort of "life lesson"?' Scarlet says, making air quotes around the words, though no one is there to witness her. 'Are you telling me I need to find this out for myself? Or are you giving me the silent treatment? Are you still saying you told me so?'

When still no response comes, Scarlet curses. Her breath is tight in her chest. A sigh rises in her throat that she slowly, deliberately exhales. 'You're going to leave me all alone in this then, are you?' Her left foot starts up an agitated tapping. 'My fiancé left me, now my sister too.' Scarlet cracks each of her knuckles one by one.

And then, she stops.

Enough. In that word, in that decision, the world shifts on its axis.

She's had enough. Enough of asking others for the answers, enough of looking for advice and direction and solace. All at once, Scarlet feels very calm. Her sorrow has ebbed and, in its place, has risen rage. Now she sits up, spine straight as an arrow. She doesn't need the tree to hold her up. She will not beggar herself for love, she will not belittle her worth. Her value is not depreciated by the actions of one man. Despite everything, Scarlet is essentially unchanged. That is the truth. She closes her eyes.

In the silence the answer comes. And when it does it comes not from Bea but in Scarlet's own voice: *He did not break your heart. No one can do that but you.*

It takes one long, eternal moment for that truth to sink in and when it finally does Scarlet realizes that her sister had been wrong when she'd said: *'He will burn you. He will scar you. He will break your heart.'* Right about the man, wrong about the consequences. For, now Scarlet understands that such a thing is not possible. A man can act as foully as he likes, but he cannot harm what is not his. And her heart, along with her spirit and soul, is hers alone.

So, you may think yourself broken, but you are not. You can lose yourself only by your own actions, not by anyone else's. The enemy may spit and taunt, may do his damnedest to make you feel worthless, but if you never believe him, if you hold fast to your own truth then you know what you're worth. Even in battle, no matter how bloody and bruised you are, if you retain your will you are not broken. Even in defeat, even in impending death, if you do not surrender yourself you remain victorious.

Scarlet stands. Her spirit stirs. A spark fires. A flame is lit.

Slowly, purposefully, Scarlet smiles: she is a Sister Grimm once more.

Scarlet now hates Eli more than she ever imagined it possible to hate anyone. She doesn't care about the affairs, doesn't give a fuck who he's fucked. Only that he gave her the greatest joy then snatched it away. Ripped it up, ruptured their life, tore away their baby's future, burned it all to hell. For that, she will never forgive him.

Burn him back. A whispering rises from the hush of the shadows, like the murmuration of blackbirds above. *Burn him back.*

Scarlet cocks her head to listen. Unseen, her eyes flash as black as the raven's.

Shatter his heart.

Rupture his spleen.

Split him apart.

Scarlet listens.

At her fingertips, sparks illuminate the dark.

Scarlet sits on a cold rock, far from the glade where her sisters gather. She is steeped in shadows and fog, cloaked in black and white. For the first time in a long while, she thinks of her father. At least he, demonic though he was, never betrayed her. Never pretended to be one thing when he was another. He displayed his darkness for all to see and, even then, he loved her, wanted her. Ezekiel Wolfe did the worst of all things. He tricked her.

Burn him, the whispers in the shadows say. *Shatter his heart. Rupture his spleen. Split him apart.*

Scarlet listens. Now it's not only sparks at her fingertips illuminating the dark but great flashes of fire.

'I will.'

4th November

Goldie

Tonight when Goldie falls asleep she doesn't travel straight to Everwhere but drifts for a while in her dreams. When she finds herself standing again in the white garden, she's not surprised. She's staring into the lightbulb, stepping through a field of snow, gazing up at a Tupperware sky; the white cat stalks through the white grass and the albino blackbirds cast their songs from the topmost branches of the white willow trees. And again, as Goldie watches, the roses rise, sprouting from the soil, their tiny shoots thickening, new stalks and stems reaching up until the buds lengthen and bloom and, within minutes, thousands of flowers are scattered through the garden filling the air with their cloying, syrupy scent.

Goldie isn't surprised when her raven sister alights on a nearby rose bush, her black feathers stark against the white.

'You're back.'

The raven ruffles her feathers. *And you sound so pleased to see me.*

'I know what you're going to say.' Goldie folds her arms. 'You don't have to keep saying it.'

You don't know everything. There's a great deal you don't know.

'Oh?' Goldie braces herself. She cannot absorb any more bad news. She cannot have any more newly reclaimed joy stolen away. 'Well, I don't want to hear it. I've heard enough.'

You cannot wait. If you don't free Leo soon he'll be trapped forever.

Goldie says nothing but begins walking through the flowers, pushing past the clusters of petals and leaves, picking up her pace, thorns scratching her skin as she starts to run. But Bea's words reach her as clearly as if she hadn't moved an inch.

Every day, every hour that passes you risk never being able to release him. His spirit is already solidifying; if left too long his molecules will fuse to the tree and not even you and your sisters together will be able to free him . . .

Bea's words continue to unfurl and since it's no use running from the words, to block them out Goldie stands amid the roses and screams.

When she wakes, Goldie wipes tears from her cheeks, trying to slow her breath and pounding heart, but she can do nothing to rein in her racing thoughts. She glances at the clock: 1.31 a.m. If Bea is right, Goldie knows that she must let Leo go. If she truly loved him, surely she would. She can't let Leo suffer simply because it makes her happy to be with him. And how can she be happy, knowing that he is not?

Recently, Goldie heard a horrifying account of human trafficking – of Serbian women brought to London to service British men in brothels – and the detail that'd upset her the most was this: the clients had taken to rating these services and one had complained that the woman had continually wept while he was fucking her. Quite apart from the immorality of participating in enslaved prostitution, what had horrified Goldie most of all was that any person could have continued seeking their own gratification in the face of it causing such suffering. Surely the only humane response would have been to stop and make every endeavour to ensure the girl's release.

Goldie does not quite equate herself with this man; she is not a kidnapper nor a rapist. After all Leo loves her; the two scenarios are poles apart. And yet ... Goldie resurrected Leo against his will – at least, without his consultation or consent – and has now trapped him, bound him, eternally rooted him and will not willingly release him. Is her drive to satisfy her own desires so very different from the brutal inhumanity of that man? She, at least, can tell herself she's acting out of love, but then love is not love that does not protect the happiness of the beloved. That is warped love, bastardized love, that is obsession.

And yet, despite finally admitting this to herself, still Goldie can't let Leo go. Not now, not yet. It's too soon, far too soon. They've barely had a handful of hours together. She needs more time.

Liyana

Since her frantic heart still won't let her sleep, Liyana decides that drawing might distract from her grief. She finds a story Goldie had sent a few weeks earlier and, rereading the tale now, she wonders if it too might have been written for Nya. As she begins to illustrate it, with every scribble Liyana tries to pull herself away from the sorrow that sits like a black hole in her life sucking every thought, every action, into its bleak centre. And, sure enough, her pencil – as if enchanted – will only sketch the curve of Nya's nose, the high sweep of her brow, her full lips, her wild but tamed hair. Eventually, Liyana pulls her bewitched pen back to the page to bring memories of her beloved aunt into an illustration of Goldie's story.

The Seal-Girl

Once there was a seal-girl who lived all her days in the ocean. And she was happy, happier than any other creature in the world, on the land or in the sea. The seal-girl delighted in diving for fish, torpedoing through the water, thrilling at the chase, the silken glide, the snap and gulp of the fish caught. She loved to play in the shadows, to tumble and roll in the seaweed, to pretend herself caught before slipping free. She relished the warmth of the sun on her skin as she basked on sea rocks, feeling the hours slipping by like the clouds across the sky and watching the waves lapping at the rocks. The seal-girl was truly content; she wanted nothing else than the life that she had.

One day, the seal-girl heard a warning from the elders, who had first founded the pod, who'd kept them all safe, finding the most fecund fishing waters and steering them clear of the most treacherous currents.

'There is one thing you've not done that you must never do,' they told the seal-girl. 'You must never go onto land. You must never take off your seal-skin and dance upon the beach.'

'Why would I ever want to do that?' the seal-girl asked.

'One day you will want to,' was all they said. 'But you must not.'

Years passed and the seal-girl thought nothing more of the warning, for she was entirely happy to stay in the ocean and never go to land.

Until, one day, while she was swimming in the shallows, while she was tumbling and rolling with the seaweed, she spotted a boy walking on the beach. And, all at once, the longing hit her. She wanted to leave the sea and visit the land. Just as the elders had foretold. Not for long. But just long enough.

Waiting until she was quite alone, until the other sea folk had drifted off to sleep on rocks or dive for fish in the depths, the seal-girl swam to the beach. She slipped out of her seal-skin and walked along the sand towards the boy.

Now, the elders, not thinking they needed to go into such details since they expected her to heed their warning, hadn't told her to keep hold of her skin, for if she lost it she'd never again be able to return to the sea.

And so, the seal-girl forgot her seal-skin for a while. She danced on the sand in the moonlight with a boy she'd only just met but already loved. She closed her eyes, delighting in the soft touch of the salt breeze on her underskin, the caress of the breeze on her belly, the kiss of the sand on her toes. Soon, the seal-girl was so dizzy with delight that she didn't see the snatch of a hand in the moonlight and the stealing of her skin into the shadows.

When at last she was ready to return to the sea, the seal-girl found that she could not. She sat on the rocks and wept, her tears falling into the ocean as she mourned the loss of the life she'd loved so much.

The boy who'd stolen her skin tried to wipe away her tears, tried to persuade her to return home with him, promising to be a good husband and bless her with many babes. But the seal-girl would not go. She simply sat at the edge of the water and wept. She wept until she had no more tears left to weep, until she was as dry as the grass upon which the boy sat, watching her.

The seal-girl gazed out to sea for hours, days, weeks. And from sunrise to sunset the boy watched her. Every day he asked the same question: 'Will you come with me and be my wife?'

When the seal-girl finally realized that she could never return to the sea, she said yes. They lived together for many years. Not happily, but not unhappily. They

had many babes, just as the boy had promised. And, though the seal-girl loved her husband and nurtured her children, on the nights when the moon was new, she left their house on the hill and went down to the edge of the ocean and gazed out at the water and wept.

One night, when all her babes were full grown, the seal-woman bid her sleeping husband goodbye and walked to the sea. She sat on the rocks and thought of all that she'd gained and lost, of the life she should've had but missed: the silken glide with the tides, the thrill of the chase, the infinite embrace of the ocean . . .

Again, the seal-woman wept and, this time, she did not stop. She wept until she had shed her second skin, she wept until she had washed away all that was solid, she wept until she was nothing but tears, she wept until she was only water, until she was once more tumbling and rolling and slipping between the waves of her beloved sea.

When the drawing is done Liyana sighs a deep, melancholic sigh. In the wave of sadness that envelops her, she thinks of both her aunts, the one full of sorrow and the one full of joy, and all at once decides that now is the time to try making the cake that can supposedly contact the dead. Wondering whether or not the kitchen cupboards contain a bag of peanuts, Liyana stands. And then, about to step forward, she stills, for at the edge of her sight is a flicker: a warning. She waits for it to reveal itself and, when it doesn't, she reaches for the Tarot cards and starts to shuffle. But before she's even dealt them out onto the desk Liyana hears her sister's voice as loud and clear as if Scarlet were whispering into her ear: *I'm going to shatter his heart and rupture his spleen. I'm going to split him apart.*

Liyana pushes her chair back, grabs her jacket and sets out to find Ezekiel Wolfe.

Scarlet

Standing in a queue snaking through Fitzbillies, Scarlet imagines leaning over the counter to dip her finger in the still-bubbling syrup of the Chelsea bun tray and licking the drips of piping hot sugar. *Delicious*. Nibbling her thumbnail, she waits to be served. Scarlet is impatient. The desire to incinerate Ezekiel Wolfe builds and burns inside her, until she can't stand still for the heat that flushes her body, as if she is pulsing with fire instead of blood. As the minutes pass and the desire grows, Scarlet reasons that there's little point in waiting. Who, after all, is Ezekiel Wolfe? She doesn't need to be especially strong; she could lay waste to him in her sleep. Not that she's sleeping lately, not with dragon's breath for blood. She perspires through the night, great rivulets of sweat that steams off her hot skin, turning Goldie's living room into a sauna.

Scarlet knows that she'll continue to suffer and that her suffering will only worsen, until she expels the flames burning inside her. And so Scarlet abandons the queue, turns and walks out of the door, striding down Trumpington Street in the direction of the train station.

'I've come to collect my things.'

Eli steps back from the door, his eyes soft, his smile gentle. 'Come in.'

Scarlet strides along the hallway, into the living room and flops down on the sofa.

'Please.' Eli follows after her. 'Make yourself comfortable.'

'Thanks, but I don't need an invitation.' Scarlet plumps a silk cushion. 'I bought this sofa.'

Eli stands before her on the carpet. She can see him wrestling with what he knows he shouldn't say, but then his eyes glaze and he surrenders to his baser nature. 'You picked it, I paid for it.'

'True,' Scarlet says. 'Is that why you thought you could treat me like a hooker, because you paid for everything?'

Eli's smile disappears. 'That's hardly fair.'

'Isn't it?' Scarlet sits back on the sofa. 'Then, what's your excuse?'

Eli sighs. 'Please, not this again. Haven't we been over and over this ad nauseam? You're a saint. I'm a bastard. I think we all know that by now. Raking over it all again isn't going to get us anywhere—'

'A bastard, really?' Scarlet frowns. 'You don't think you're letting yourself off a little lightly? I think a better description of you might be lying, scheming, self-entitled, misogynistic – and did I mention lying? – privileged Etonian wanker.'

'Misogynistic? I hardly think . . . Look.' Eli slips his hands into his pockets. 'I'm not denying anything. I've confessed. I've apologized. I've begged your forgiveness and you've refused. So here we are.'

'Apologized?' Scarlet feels an unwelcome surge of sorrow like a rush of nausea, momentarily eclipsing her seething rage. 'I've not heard a word from you since I left. I hoped . . . In the circumstances I thought you'd be calling constantly, sending obscene amounts of overpriced chocolates and bouquets. But, no. Not a single word. Not a biscuit, not a daisy. I, I' – Scarlet pinches the bridge of her nose and blinks back tears – 'after nearly three years together and not even a fucking text.'

'Oh, come on, Scar,' Eli says. 'You can hardly blame me for that. You made it pretty clear how you felt. Forgive me for thinking that any approaches I made would be as welcome as a bout of the clap.'

'But that's the point,' Scarlet says. 'You send roses, I shred them. You send chocolates and I – well, I eat them, but then I burn the boxes and curse your name.' She rubs her eyes. 'But the point is, you fucking *try*. You don't do nothing. If, if you do nothing then it's . . . over.'

Eli sighs again, a sigh of deep resignation. 'But it *is* over, isn't it?'

Looking at him now, registering the sadness in his eyes and voice, Scarlet is suddenly overcome with regret. Regret that she loved him, regret that she lost him. Regret, most of all, that she lost herself because of him. She feels her heart soften.

'Eli . . .'

'Scar . . .' Just before he meets her gaze, with those soft eyes, Eli glances at his phone.

In that moment, she knows. Her eyes darken, the heat in her blood rises. 'You haven't called because you've been too busy fucking.'

He glances at the floor, but he can't hide his blush.

'Christ, I'm such an idiot.' Scarlet exhales. 'There I was, imagining you slumped on the sofa all sorry . . . and there you were, living it up in my absence, screwing everyone in London – are they as gullible as me? Do they believe your lies?'

'I don't have to lie.' Now, with a flash of defiance on his face, he looks up. 'Not all women hold such conventional views on fidelity.'

'You mean they pretend they don't care if you sleep around?'

'Jesus, Scar, don't be so puritanical.'

'Puritanical?' she snaps. 'You know, I wish you'd been a

little clearer on your views and values before – you might have saved yourself shit loads of child support.' Scarlet stands, any remaining whisper of sorrow gone.

She steps towards him. Frowning, he steps back.

'Now,' Scarlet says. 'Why don't *you* sit?'

'What? No.'

Scarlet steps closer. 'Sit.'

Eli shakes his head, seeming suddenly quite discombobulated. 'I don't want to.'

'Too bad.' Scarlet takes one more step forward so that, in avoiding her, Eli falls back into a chair, legs splayed. 'Anyway, it might do you good, not getting what you want. Character building – didn't they teach you that at Eton?'

'Look,' – Eli holds out his hands as Scarlet leans over him – 'I think you should leave. I – I promise I'll post your things.'

Scarlet smiles, eyes flashing. 'Oh, but I came all this way, I can't just leave empty handed.'

Eli pulls himself up out of the chair. 'I – I . . .'

'Not so fast.' Scarlet pushes him back down. 'Don't you want to say goodbye to your daughter, before I go?'

Eli frowns. 'What do – I told you, I'll pay my share, I'll do my bit.'

Scarlet shakes her head. Fire-blood pulses through her veins, she feels its heat rise in her chest. 'I don't think you will, and I've decided that when I have a daughter, she'll be fathered by a man with less . . .' – she casts a wary eye over him – 'odious origins.'

'Wait, you're having an abortion? But you can't, not without discussing—'

'Oh, but I can,' Scarlet says and, though she'd had no intention of doing so, now that the possibility is spoken it holds a certain appeal: freedom, a fresh start. 'I can do

whatever I want. You have no say over me or my body anymore. So, do you want a moment to say goodbye, before I
incinerate it, before I incinerate you?'

Eli stares at her, eyes wide. 'What the fuck?'

'Oh, did I not mention that?' Scarlet grins. 'Well, perhaps my introduction was a little misleading. When I said
I'd come to collect my things, what I meant was I've come
to cremate my things – given the death of our relationship,
it seems only fitting – and I thought I may as well cremate
you along with them. Since you were the cause of that
death. What do you think?'

Again, Eli tries to stand. Scarlet pushes him down.

'Wait,' he snaps. 'This isn't funny.'

'It's not a joke.' Scarlet shrugs. 'Though, I suppose that
depends on your perspective. It might be for me. But I don't
think you'll find death by fire particularly funny.' She cocks
her head to one side, considering. 'I hear it hurts.'

'What the hell's wrong with you?' Eli shouts. 'Have you
lost your fucking mind?'

'I don't think so,' Scarlet says. 'I had. I'd lost my mind and
heart to you. But I'm happy to report that now I've got my
mind back, my spirit too and, most importantly,' – Scarlet
lifts her hands up to the ceiling – 'my *fire*.'

Sparks ignite at her fingertips, gathering in clusters like
sparklers, pulsing rhythmically, building into pillars that
lengthen and thicken until they are arching in a bridge
between her outstretched hands.

Eli stares at her, utterly terrified. He stands and, this
time, she lets him. He stumbles back, reaching out behind
him for the wall. Scarlet steps towards him.

'So, any last words?' Scarlet watches the electric arc spit
and spark, for a moment mesmerized. 'Come on, I've not
got all day.'

'You're mad.' Eli gropes the wall as if searching for a hidden door. 'You're fucking insane.'

'Oh, I know.' Scarlet grins. 'And, let me tell you, it feels glorious! Now, snap, snap. I haven't got forever. And if I had, I certainly wouldn't waste it with you.'

Clutching the wall, Eli inches towards the door. Scarlet narrows her eyes and snaps an arc of electricity at the door. Eli jumps back.

'Oh, no you don't, little boy.' Scarlet laughs. 'Don't you listen? I told you I'd regained my mind. I'm not your dinky little idiot anymore.'

Eli gazes pitifully at the door, then looks back at Scarlet and falls to his knees. 'Please, Scar, don't do this, I'm begging you.'

A rogue spark lands on his leg, blazing a hole in his jeans.

'Oh, fuck!' he cries, smacking it out. 'Please, please stop this!'

'And, if I do, will you promise not to betray any more women?'

Above them, the blackened ceiling begins to burn. And Eli, seeing flames spreading as if the paint had been thinned with petrol, starts to cry.

'Yes, of course,' he whimpers, burying his head in his hands. 'Of course, of course I do. But please, please ...' – tears roll down his cheeks – 'please don't kill me.'

Scarlet claps, causing fireworks. Sparks explode between them.

'Oh, it's a little too late for that, don't you think?'

As the electricity arcs into his chest, Eli screams. As it sears his skin, flames fly up the walls, across the ceiling, and smoke rises from the floor. Scarlet thinks of the fog rolling in over Everwhere, she thinks of the whispering shadows and the promises they make. As she watches him burn, her eyes are dark as a moonless sky. Then, a glimmer of light—

'All right, you pathetic creature,' Scarlet spits. 'I'll let you live if it matters so much to you. But, tell anyone I did this and I'll come back and kill you.'

She claps again and, all at once, the electricity dies and Eli falls back, heart still beating, skin scarred. Across his chest are branded the words: *I will break your heart.* A warning for every woman who ever dares to love him. The flames sink back down and the billowing smoke, carrying the acrid scent of charred flesh, thins. Scarlet walks slowly towards the door. She does not look back.

Emerging from the building and into the night, Scarlet strides down the stone steps, reaching the pavement just as Liyana is running across the road – car horns honking – to meet her.

'Hey, Sis,' Scarlet says, not stopping. 'You've got perfect timing. It's still smouldering in there, so' – she throws the final words over her shoulder – 'you might want to make it rain.'

5th November

Liyana finds Goldie sitting in Leo's branches. She calls up and waves. Goldie glances down with a guilty look, gripping the bough alongside her as if Liyana might be about to snap the branch in half and wrench it from her grasp.

'I thought I'd find you here.'

'What's that supposed to mean?'

Liyana frowns. 'Nothing, why – you're always here, aren't you?'

Goldie says nothing.

'Can you come down?' Liyana pleads. 'We need to talk about Scarlet.'

Goldie leans back against Leo's trunk. 'Can we talk tomorrow?'

'No, I'm sorry, it needs to be now.'

'But I don't understand . . .' Goldie sinks to the ground at Leo's roots. 'How could she . . . ? And why didn't she – why didn't I know? And how—'

'I heard her thoughts,' Liyana says. 'And I saw it in the cards.'

'I thought she was okay, I thought she was getting better . . .' Goldie drops her head to her knees. 'I should've known.'

'Don't,' Liyana says. 'There's no point in all that now. We've just got to help her.'

Goldie sighs. 'But I just . . . I don't understand, why

244

didn't she talk to us, why didn't she tell us what she wanted to do? We could have helped, we could have—'

'Stopped her,' Liyana interrupts. 'There's your answer. People talk about things they want to do because they're not doing them. I mean, suicides don't share their plans, do they? If you're actually going to do a thing, you don't talk about it, you just do it.'

'Oh, Ana.' Goldie lifts her head and looks up. 'Your aunt.'

Liyana nods. 'We can't . . . not now, we've got to focus on Scarlet.'

'Yes, of course. But what can we do? She committed arson, she nearly committed murder. She'll be locked away for the rest of her life.'

'They'll have to suspect her first,' Liyana says. 'And I'm guessing she didn't leave many fingerprints.'

Goldie sighs again. 'Where is she now?'

'I don't know. I couldn't chase her; I was too busy trying to put out the bloody fire.'

Scarlet's entrance is heralded by the rustling of leaves, a drawing back of the fog, a lifting of the mists and a splitting of the clouds for the moon to cast her spotlight to the stony ground. Liyana and Goldie watch their sister striding out of the fog.

'Here I am.'

She is exactly the same but entirely different: radiant, luminous, incandescent; as if lit from within. She is straighter, taller, stronger than before, her lustrous hair a darker red. Her presence is grander, her impact greater. The fog falls away, but her imprint remains. Still gawping, now Goldie and Liyana see what the fog had first obscured – that Scarlet doesn't walk but glides, hovering a few inches above the ground.

It's only when Scarlet is standing before her that Goldie

realizes she hadn't been imagining things on the night of the conjuring: her glittering eyes are pitch black. She stares at her sister, more beautiful than any human being she's ever seen: audacious, fearless, resplendent.

Scarlet smiles. 'Miss me?'

'What ...' Goldie loses her train of thought. 'What ... what has happened to you?'

Scarlet's smile widens into a grin. 'What *hasn't* happened to me?' She lifts her arms towards the unwavering moon. 'I am all things. There's nothing I haven't done, nothing I couldn't do. I am a Sister Grimm supreme.'

'You say that like it's a good thing,' Liyana snaps. 'You nearly killed a man.'

'I nearly killed a cockroach.' Scarlet shrugs, dropping her hands. 'And I'd do it again. Perhaps I'll make that my profession – since I'm seeking a job – I could be a modern-day superhero exterminating odious males for the good of womankind – what do you think?'

Goldie and Liyana say nothing.

'I'll need a costume, of course,' Scarlet carries on, regardless. 'Something spectacular. I rather fancy a cape. Dark red, to match my hair. No cowardly mask though; if I do a deed I want the acclaim.'

'Stop it, Scar,' Goldie interrupts. 'Do you understand what you've done?'

'I was there, wasn't I?' Scarlet raises her eyes to the heavens. 'And it wasn't on a silly whim. It was planned and, I may say, executed to perfection.'

'Wait' – Goldie stares at her, incredulous – 'you admit to it? You won't even try to ...'

'And why shouldn't I?' Scarlet grins. 'Weren't you listening? If I do the deed, I want the acclaim. Wouldn't you feel the same?'

Goldie and Liyana exchange incredulous glances.

'So, you're going to confess?' Liyana says. 'You're going to hand yourself in?'

Scarlet's laugh shakes the boughs of every tree, rumbling through the ground and shivering every root. 'And why should I do that? If I'm incarcerated then I'm no use to anyone.'

'Then what will you do?' Goldie stares at her sister. 'If you're not going to run. How do you think you'll get away with it?'

As if considering this, Scarlet breaks into a beatific smile. 'Oh, don't you worry about that.'

Goldie presses her feet into the soil, in her anxiety trying to grip the ground, as little shoots begin to sprout, twining up between her toes. 'I don't understand . . .'

'Oh!' Liyana exclaims, putting her hands to her mouth. 'Oh, no.'

Goldie turns to her. 'What?'

But Liyana doesn't take her eyes off Scarlet. 'The cards, I saw it . . . The Devil . . . a malevolent spirit, the shadows . . .'

Pride illuminates Scarlet's radiant face.

Goldie looks from sister to sister. 'What the hell is going on?'

'When . . . when we resurrected Leo,' Liyana says. 'We released you.'

For a moment Goldie doesn't understand; then she recalls that spite and vengeance wait in the shadows; dark spirits that linger on – a malignant mark left by Everwhere's vanquished creator. Slowly, Scarlet starts to applaud. 'Well done, sister. I was starting to wonder if either of you was ever going to get there . . .'

'But I don't – but, how?' Goldie says. 'How did that happen?'

The unwavering moon illuminates Scarlet as if she's standing beneath a theatre spotlight, the fog swirls about her like smoke. Goldie and Liyana watch their sister begin to stride in slow, considered circles of contemplation. As she walks, her fingers spark. When Scarlet stops before the tree and reaches out to stroke the smooth bark, caressing the constellation of tiny crescent moons and stars scarred along the trunk, Goldie steps forward.

'Don't touch him.' She still doesn't understand what's happened to her sister, but can feel malevolence perfuming the air. 'Or . . .'

'I could burn you, if you like.' Scarlet presses her cheek to the trunk and whispers to Leo, as if Goldie hadn't spoken a word. 'I could put you out of your misery. Just say the word . . .'

Leo's branches quiver, as if a breeze has blown through them, though the air is still. *Do what you wish with me, but don't hurt her.*

'Oh, yes!' The deep rumble of Scarlet's laugh shudders through the trees and shakes the ground. 'But this would be by far the best way to hurt her, don't you think? Watching you burn to the ground would be more painful than any death I could conjure?'

Goldie's propelled forward but Liyana grabs hold of her and pulls her back. Goldie's scream entwines with Leo's twisted branches. In response, a raven caws.

'Oh, you're both so ridiculous,' Scarlet snaps. 'And I won't burn him, though God knows he deserves it, if only for being so insufferably gallant.'

'Stop!' Goldie shouts. 'Stop!'

Another ecstatic smile spreads across Scarlet's beautiful face as she turns to her sister. It's unnerving, still, how radiant she looks, though why the paradox of beauty and evil coexisting should be such a hard one to accept, Goldie isn't certain. She searches Scarlet's black eyes for a glimmer of affection or sisterly affiliation, but sees nothing except the glint of her own reflection.

'It would be a mistake not to fear me,' Scarlet says. 'I could, if I wished, burn you alive before you noticed me lift a finger to do it.'

'You can try.' At Liyana's words rain clouds gather above, so dense and thick it feels as if the sky is descending as darkness closes in. With a great crack of thunder, the clouds are ripped open to tip torrents of water down upon them all.

The shadow sister laughs, its lightning cackle splitting open Scarlet's mouth. 'Oh, that's too vain – really! You think I'm here just to kill the two of you and' – she nods in Leo's direction – 'the tree. No, your deaths will be an incidental pleasure; but it's the burning of Everwhere itself that I'm here for. Total detonation. Annihilation. Obliteration.'

Impossible. With a single word Liyana and Goldie share the same thought, but their shock – and fear – renders them silent. The rain ceases.

'Oh, you might think so,' Scarlet says. 'But you'd be wrong. This place' – she casts her hands open in a faux embrace – 'is not indestructible. Of course, the shadows alone cannot manage it, which is why I decided to join forces with your darling sister.'

'B-but,' Goldie stutters. 'Then surely you'll annihilate yourself too, whatever the hell you are.'

Their shadow sister draws a sigh up from the bowels of the earth. 'Ah, yes . . . It certainly will be a holocaust.' A grin contorts her exquisite face. 'No survivors, neither the living nor the dead.'

'But why?' Liyana echoes Goldie. 'Why would you do that if you won't survive to see it?'

Scarlet frowns, slowly shaking her head, as if Liyana is the greatest of fools. On the pale skin of her neck and hands the veins begin to throb, her blood now an inky black.

'My goodness, you disappoint me, my dear. Ignorance I can forgive, but not naivety. Any conqueror worth his salt would sacrifice himself for his cause. Does not every suicide bomber do the same? And what of soldiers who fight despite knowing they're outnumbered? To commit murder while contriving one's own survival is cowardice. To die for the cause is heroic; the greatest of honourable acts.'

Goldie and Liyana stare at the creature open-mouthed, incredulity having struck them dumb, horror having crushed their hearts. Neither know how to answer, how to stand, how to face or respond to such vile, iniquitous feelings. Without turning each reaches for the other's hand, their fingers lacing together, Liyana pulling Goldie back from the edge, Goldie anchoring Liyana to the ground.

But, what now?

I don't know.

Liyana glances at Goldie, an idea having struck her. *Mami Wata?*

Goldie nods.

'Ah, yes!' The shadow laughs and Scarlet applauds. 'What a fun little plan! I do so love an exorcism – it's all quite erotic, don't you find? Being delved into like that.'

Goldie's eyes go to Liyana, who looks blankly back. They cannot share their thoughts here without being overheard, cannot formulate more elaborate secret plans. So what choice do they have but to try this one?

'Let's get on then, time is ticking and I've got things to

do, worlds to destroy.' The shadow-Scarlet opens its arms wide and walks backwards, stopping just short of Leo's trunk. 'Be careful now,' it says. 'I don't want to end up trapped in a tree – it'd be most unfortunate and I'd be forced to punish you most elaborately.'

It grins again, polluting Scarlet's poor face, and Goldie hopes that the shadow is wrong to dismiss them so lightly, that its monstrous hubris might be its downfall. History, after all, is strewn with the corpses of those who believed themselves invincible. Teddy had told her their stories and, to soothe herself, she recites them silently now: Caligula, Caesar, Attila . . . as if those mad, terrible ghosts can reduce their foe or build their ranks. *The Battle of Morgarten* – Teddy's voice echoes in Goldie's ear – *1,500 Swiss soldiers beat an Austrian army of 8,000. The Battle of Salamis* . . .

Without waiting, Liyana begins to mutter, incanting her spell.

'Hold her tight!' Goldie shouts to Leo, hoping he'll move faster than Scarlet.

Instantly, Leo's two lowest, thickest branches reach out to wrap around Scarlet's waist, pulling her fast and tight against his trunk. In the same moment, Goldie wrenches thick ropes of ivy from the soil, to bind Scarlet's arms and legs, fixing her to the tree.

'My, my.' The shadow surveys its shackles. 'This is cosy, isn't it? This is—'

'*Mami Wata*,' Liyana cuts it off. '*Mami Wata muna rokonka don* . . .'

For a split second the shadow rises from Scarlet's body, so she's enveloped by a thick dark mist, and for a moment they see her face again – as it was before – until the shadow sinks back into her flesh.

Buoyed by hope, Goldie joins Liyana's incantation and

together they chant: '*Mami Wata muna roƙonka don taima-kawa wajen raba wadannan rayuka biyu. Muna roƙon ku don taimakawa wajen fitar da magungunan, a sake dawo da mazaunin jiki zuwa jikinta da kuma kawar da duk masu fadar.*'

'A parasite, am I?' Scarlet's lips are as inky as her eyes. 'Couldn't you have come up with a more fitting metaphor? An incubus, perhaps. Or succubus. The latter evokes the blood sucker, don't you—' It's interrupted by a sudden scream that slaps against the air as Scarlet's face contorts into a paroxysm of pain. Goldie gapes at her twisting, writhing sister.

'Don't,' Liyana shouts. 'Don't stop!'

'*Muna roƙon ku don taimakawa wajen fitar da magungunan . . .*'

Scarlet's scream pierces the sisters, pushing them back with the sheer force of the sound. They stare at her, horrified – Can she survive this? Can she emerge unscathed? – but do not pause in their chant. '*Mami Wata muna roƙonka don taimakawa wajen raba wadannan rayuka biyu—*'

There's a sudden shift in the scream, as if Scarlet is convulsing not with pain but pleasure: sighing, moaning, shivering with great waves of delight. Then, she's laughing. *It* is laughing, a deep tremendous rumble that shakes through Leo so violently it snaps twigs from branches, raining his pieces down upon the sisters like a pestilence. Then it is giggling, as if caught by something mildly amusing, as if appreciating a mediocre joke.

'I don't . . .' Liyana trails off. 'What's—'

'It's mocking us,' Goldie says. 'We did nothing.'

'Oh, my dears.' The shadow smiles. 'Don't be like that; sulking is so unbecoming. Anyway, you ought to be proud of your efforts. For a first-time exorcism it wasn't too bad, I felt a definite twinge or two. I'm sure, if you'd had a few more days of chanting in you, extraction would have been truly imminent.'

'Fuck,' Liyana spits. 'Fuck. Fuck. Fuck.'

'Now, now, my dear.' Its voice is taut as a wire, ready to snap. 'Let's not get carried away.'

'Or what'll you do to me?' Liyana shouts. 'I can't imagine what's worse than being burned alive!'

That malicious grin again. 'Then you've a poor imagination.'

Liyana opens her mouth but, as she does so, she falls to the ground. Goldie stares, horrified, as Liyana starts to scream, pressing her hands to her temples, tearing at her hair, her face contorting into a mask of such terror that Goldie is paralysed, transfixed.

'No! Nya, no! Don't!' Liyana's scream cracks through the air like lightning. 'Koko, Koko, stop!' Liyana scratches her face, drawing rivulets of blood down her cheeks. 'Please, no, no, *no*!'

At the sight of her sister's torture, Goldie is seized by such rage that all fear and care go by the board. She reaches out towards Scarlet, her shadow sister, hands outstretched; instantly, vines of ivy lace around the creature's throat, tightening so fast that it's being throttled before it's even aware of what's being done. Goldie pulls the vines tighter, ever tighter. As the blood drains from Scarlet's face, her head falls forward as if snapped at the neck—

Unable to continue, Goldie drops her hands to her sides and the vines go slack.

Slowly, Scarlet lifts her head, opens her mouth, clicks her jaw from side to side. 'Ouch.' She fixes large, black eyes on Goldie. 'For someone so intelligent, I'm surprised you didn't realize that sooner.'

Goldie drops to her knees, defeated. But, at least, Liyana is silent now.

'What a conundrum.' Its laughter prickles like static through the glade. 'How to kill me without hurting me: seems like an unsolvable puzzle, wouldn't you say?'

On the ground, Liyana moans. Darting over to Liyana's side, Goldie rests her hands on her sister's cheeks so the blood draws in and the scratches begin to seal up.

'We can't risk damaging this pretty one now, can we?' The shadow's grin slices through Scarlet's cheeks, as if it'd just slit them open with a knife. 'And, just in case you were thinking of sacrificing your lovely sister . . . you should know that extinguishing her body won't extinguish my spirit. It'll take far more than that. So, my dears, if you can't exorcize me and you can't extinguish me – what do you propose to do?'

In Leo's branches, a raven caws. Once, twice, thrice.

A second later black wings swoop down, beating the air now filled with the cries of screeching birds. For a moment the sky is darker than it's ever been, any glimmer of moonlight blocked by the clouds of ravens. Hundreds, thousands of outstretched talons and pointed beaks. And, before she hears Leo's plea in her mind, Goldie is pulling Liyana up, dragging her away, stumbling as he begs: *Run to the shadows, hide!*

Liyana gasps as they run, but doesn't have breath to ask, just as Goldie doesn't have breath to answer; dashing over moss and stone, through curtains of leaves, past fallen trunks, over rocks, towards the darkness. But, before they tumble into the gloom, Liyana pulls back.

'No' – she tugs at Goldie's hand – 'we can't.'

This is the darkness they've been advised since girlhood

to avoid and they know too well the impossibility of resisting the poison of spite and vengeance – they only have to see Scarlet to know the dangers of possession. A few seconds of listening to the whispers will send them mad, render them mute, strip them of every strength and skill they ever had.

'Trust me.' – Goldie pulls at her sister – 'Please.'

They're barely an inch from the shadows, their feet almost encroaching on the inky, slick, slithering darkness. Together they step into the undergrowth.

'How will we survive this?' Liyana feels the shadows clawing at her, their touch stickier than she'd imagined. It's like walking into treacle, except that the shadows slip off like oils from their skin as they walk.

'I don't know,' Goldie admits. 'But Leo wouldn't endanger us. Bea must have a plan.'

'I fucking hope so,' Liyana mutters. For she can already hear the rising chorus, the insidious words wanting to burrow into their brains, twisting and wrenching, undoing everything they've ever believed to be right and true, until they're malevolent, then demonic . . .

'I think she'll—' Interrupting herself, Goldie screams and scrambles back.

All at once the creatures have surrounded them, elongated fingers reaching out, twisted, sunken faces fixing the sisters with hollow eyes, their rattling bones beating out the clarion call of their invitation to madness, destruction and despair.

Liyana and Goldie run.

They run on and on through the dark, turning, darting, slipping, only just evading the clawing grip of the shadows. Time slips sideways again, stretching and folding, rising and falling, so they might have been engulfed by the under-growth a few swift minutes or a dozen sluggish hours.

Out, now.

At Bea's words, Liyana seizes Goldie's hand and pulls her on.

Left.

Right.

Onwards.

Yes!

Following Bea's instructions they run towards the dim light. Finally emerging, bodies streaked with dirt and filth, but minds mercifully untouched, Liyana and Goldie collapse to the ground, gasping for breath, pressing their faces into the moss, gripping vines of snaking ivy, holding tight to the earth, weeping with fear and shock and relief.

Far away a raven's call.

They're here.

They stream like salmon, fiercely determined to reach their destination, accelerated roots twisting through the soil, pressing ever forward. Hundreds of sisters rushing, leaping, flying towards the arena, called to the place they must meet. Liyana and Goldie slip into the throng, carried on waves of nervous excitement, chatter undulating through the ever-shifting group, purposeful, terrified, fervent . . .

When they reach the glade silence falls like a blanket dropped.

Their shadow sister stands at Leo's trunk, absently burn-ing fresh scars into the wood, elaborate patterns of concentric circles, as if she's stubbing out packets of discarded cigar-ettes. Goldie's screams cut a path through the swarm of women and girls, and she hurtles forward, before arms grab hold of her and pull her back.

Wait. It must be done as one, together. You cannot defeat it alone.

The shadow turns to the crowd, its malicious grin breaking across Scarlet's face, hands clasped as if in celebration.

'Well, I certainly didn't expect such a marvellous turnout,' it exclaims with faux joy. 'Whatever have I done to deserve such a warm welcome? I feel like a queen at her coronation!'

'We're not here to greet you,' Goldie spits. 'We're here to vanquish you!'

'To separate you,' Liyana mutters, 'from our sister.'

At this, a cheer rises from the crowd and, for the first time in a very long while, Goldie is lifted by a sense of camaraderie and belonging. She glances to Liyana, who nods as they take hands. Above, Bea circles the gathering.

All of you join hands. Unite your strength, double it, triple it, magnify it beyond all measure!

Instantly, every sister takes the hand of the sister beside her: sisters of fire, earth, air and water unite to control the elements at their fingertips. Sparks fill the air, cracks of lightning pierce the sky, roots undulate under the earth and gathering winds whip through the glade.

'So it's going to be like that, is it?' Sparks flare at Scarlet's fingertips. 'Well, if you want a massacre instead of a coronation, then it's a massacre you'll get!'

Flames ignite at Scarlet's feet, rising to encircle her. Goldie and all daughters of earth lift their hands as a copse of oak trees start to shake, ripping their roots from the soil – like monstrous white spiders escaping premature burial – and begin to stagger forward, an army of grotesques sending tremors through the ground with every step. The sisters of air draw the strength of the winds to channel a fierce rain to extinguish Scarlet's fire and, though it's replenished over and again, the flames never have a chance to rise.

Instead, Scarlet releases flaming arcs from her upturned palms which meet the mirrored arcs of fire from her sisters; the blazing collisions exploding with such force that the leaves of every tree in the glade ignite like tinder, raining down in hot ash to scorch the sisters below. Under the assault, dozens of sisters start to stumble and fall. On the ground they writhe and clutch their temples, heads thrown back, mouths open like howling wolves.

'What's happening?' Liyana shouts. 'What's going on?'

She's met only with blank, terrified stares as more sisters fall. Goldie, separated from Liyana, wants to run to Leo, to take refuge in his branches, to make certain he's not burning, but she looks to the sky for Bea.

'Help!' she shrieks. 'What's wrong with them? What's—'

Then Goldie falls. A thick grey fog fills her mind; her limbs feel heavy as lead; poisoned thoughts gather in strength and begin to spiral, dragging her into a maelstrom of despair . . . She cannot go on, only wants to die.

Stop! Another voice pierces the dark, a glimmer in the fog. *Expel all thought from your mind, don't listen to the shadows, don't doubt your strength!*

While fires rage and the ground shakes, a few sisters begin to pull themselves up and stand again. Goldie seizes hold of a static tree root and clutches it tight. Bea's voice pushes through the shadows, a bright trumpet over screaming violins: *You are magnificent, glorious, powerful beyond all measure! Now, pick yourself up and fight!*

As Goldie's struggling to drag herself from the ground, she sees Liyana standing above her, reaching out to pull her up. The moment she's upright, Goldie's pushed from the path of a ball of fire which crashes instead into moss and stone, flames rising and flaring until Liyana spreads her fingers, extinguishing them. Then she, joined by every sister of water still standing, turns to the moon and howls to the sound of great rolls of thunder rumbling across the sky. Seconds later, the clouds open to douse the glade in torrential rain.

The shadow-Scarlet circles her hands, lobbing fireballs at the trees. But the rain is too heavy and each is extinguished in a gasp of smoke. She throws again and again and again; crashing arcs of fire blaze from her hands, flashing into the air, only to be snuffed out.

Goldie looks to Leo, to the army surrounding her. Grabbing three sisters of earth, she forms a hasty circle, channelling their collective energies towards Leo. A moment later, his roots are pulling up from the soil and he begins creeping away from the glade towards the safety of the river. Whatever happens tonight, Goldie cannot – will not – watch him burn.

The sisters of earth, all now standing, raise a chant which draws the remaining trees together, clustering around Scarlet, trapping the thick billowing smoke within their canopy of branches. Inky veins ripple under her skin close to rupturing and, in its impotent rage, the shadow sets itself alight. Now Scarlet is a towering pillar of fire, flames licking and spitting, rising above the trees.

'Hold on, Scar, hold on!' Goldie shouts, calling to all the sisters of earth, who raise their arms, slinging ropes of ivy to knot tight around the tree trunks, binding them as they bow down and close their canopy of rain-soaked branches over the fire. The rain thickens and the winds whip and wrap around the trees, goading, teasing, taunting . . .

The explosion is tremendous. Nuclear. An apocalypse of fire. In a single shockwave of flame, the trees are obliterated and the earth cleft, opening a gigantic chasm that pulls everything it can grasp within. Every sister runs or flies from the rapidly expanding black hole, their screams swallowed by the thunderous cascade of descending soil and stone, of upwrenched roots and tumbling trees.

Until, at last, all is silent.

Slowly, every sister pulls herself up; shaking and trembling, soaked with rain and tears, blood and dirt, hoarse from screaming and mute with shock, they stand and survey what they've done.

Scarlet's cry is soft, so soft that they don't hear but only sense her. At once, every sister crowds around the edge of the crater and peers into the carnage of rocks and trees, limbs and soil. Quickly, Goldie, along with every other remaining sister of earth, plaits undulating vines of ivy into a rope and drops it into the darkness.

'Take the rope,' Goldie shouts down. 'It's safe.'

And when they feel a tugging weight, they slowly lift her up.

Emerging from the gloom, Scarlet is emaciated, stripped and raw; as if she's undergone torture, ripped from the moorings of sanity, heart still beating but barely alive.

She's pulled into Liyana and Goldie's arms, where she's held in an impenetrable embrace and gently, gradually healed: broken bones knitted together, wounds soothed and sealed, scars smoothed out . . . And as her body re-joins so, tentatively, does her mind. Now and then twitches flicker across Scarlet's face, like static on a TV screen; now and then she cries out; sometimes she screams. Until, at last, she is silent and calm.

While Goldie and Liyana tend Scarlet, other sisters work to heal and save the lives of those among them who can be saved. When all that is done, the sisters of earth join to close the chasm and flatten the ground, binding a tight blanket of moss to lay over the land, a fresh sheet of skin on the surface of Everwhere, covering a grave for the few sisters who were lost in the fight. A long time passes before the sisters begin to disperse, wandering off in twos and threes, not needing to speak or say their goodbyes, knowing they will soon return to see one another again, for they are bound together now.

When Scarlet is finally able to sit up, flanked by Liyana and Goldie, they all see the thin line of blood trickling down Scarlet's leg. They stare, breath held, until Scarlet lets out a deep sigh and begins to cry. Her sisters take her hands and whisper their solaces. But to their surprise – and hers – these are tears not of grief but relief.

In Leo's branches, the raven perches, waiting.

Goldie

Goldie presses herself into Leo's trunk, clinging to him as she did the first time, as if it's been a full century since she last saw him. She doesn't need to speak – which is fortunate, since she can't form sentences – for he can hear her thoughts and feel her pulse.

When Goldie finds the strength and the will, she climbs into Leo's lower boughs and sits while he wraps smaller branches around her body.

It's okay, it's over now.

Goldie nods.

I love you.

Goldie nods again. 'I . . .' She tries to echo his words but finds that she still cannot speak.

I didn't know I could walk and, I must say, I prefer a riverside view.

He is trying to make her smile but this she cannot do either.

Silence stretches between them and when at last Goldie makes her declaration it is so quiet she hopes the words might be lost to the wind. 'I – I'm going to let you go.'

What? I don't—

'I know you're unhappy,' Goldie whispers. 'I know you'd rather be free.'

I'm not, of course I'm not. I'm happy. I love you.

'Oh, Leo, my dearest one, I know you do.' Goldie rests her head on his branches. 'But you're trapped here and I won't live forever – I've been selfish. So very—'

No. He interrupts her with such force that he shudders. *No! I, I, I need to stay with you.*

Goldie hesitates. If he had only said want instead of need, she might have wavered.

'It's okay.' A sob rises and she swallows it down. 'I'll be okay.'

I don't believe you. You're saying that so that I'll leave you. But I know what happened before, I know what my death did to you. I won't let it happen again.

'I promise,' Goldie says. 'After this, I'll go back and I'll live and do all the things—'

I don't want you just to live, I want you to be happy.

'And how can I be happy' – Goldie blinks away tears – 'knowing that you are not?'

A sigh trembles his branches. *I am happy. I'm happy whenever you're here with me.*

'And when I'm not?' Goldie shakes her head, still trying to rid herself of the gathering tears. 'You'll be here forever; for centuries after I die. And if I don't release you soon, you'll be trapped in this tree for eternity.'

Not eternity.

'No,' Goldie admits. 'But long enough; until the sun finally implodes and this universe collapses, and Earth and Everwhere are folded into nothingness. Then you'll finally be free.'

And, since he can't deny it, Leo is silent.

'You'll be with me for sixty years or so,' Goldie says. 'Then you'll be trapped for a hundred lifetimes.'

An exchange I'll gladly make.

'You say that because you love me, but I won't let you suffer like that.'

But I won't be able to speak to you, not as Bea does, you won't hear my voice.

'You'll be here,' Goldie says, gathering her strength. 'I'll hear you.'

Not words . . .

'I know.' Goldie presses a palm to his trunk. 'But I'll remember everything we've ever said to each other, every word.'

Or touch. We'll never again . . .

Goldie hears the crack in his voice as he falters. And she can't answer this, can't convince him that she's fine knowing that she will never again feel his touch.

Silence stretches between them once more until Leo realizes that Goldie won't be the first to speak, won't say anything until he gives his consent.

All right. But, wait. Wait until the last moment; let me hold you until then.

Goldie nods. So she sits in his branches and lets him hold her and holds him as the hours pass, until she knows she must not wait any longer, until she knows it is time.

Then she steps down from his branches.

I love you.

'I love you.'

'Goodbye' is what comes next. She waits for him to say it, but he does not.

Goldie opens her mouth but finds that she cannot either; her throat is choked with tears, her eyes are fogged with them. She longs to touch him once more, one last time, but she doesn't. If she did, she might never let go. Instead she looks at him, breathes him in, loves him.

Then, at last, she lets Leo go.

It is easy to release him. She needs no words, no incantation; a mercy since she still cannot speak. All she must do is twist and untwist her fingers, set her intention and focus. Until gradually the scars on the tree begin to shift and undulate and pulse with life. The circles uncurl and stretch to acquire the aspect of a bright white snake, scales etched with a mosaic of crescent moons and stars. With a flick of its tail, the snake slithers from the tree and into the soil: Leo's soul seeping back into the ground.

Goldie brings her hands together, so close she cannot see a sliver of moonlight between them. Then, slowly, she pulls her hands apart. As she does so, the oak tree starts to crack and split, the trunk opening to reveal a bright light within. The tree's branches are splintering until, with a single burst, they scatter into a thousand fragments, like petals blown on the breeze. Finally, the roots tear up from the soil, thick knotted fingers clawing from their grave to pull the tree asunder.

The released light is so bright, so sharp – as if the sun had suddenly burst into Everwhere – that for a moment Goldie is blinded. She cannot see Leo's spirit lifting into the skies, ascending to sit among the stars. When she blinks, the light has gone.

'I – I love you,' she whispers.

But still she cannot say goodbye.

6th November

Goldie

Goldie doesn't know how long it was before she finally left, before she finally walked away. It felt like a year, a decade. She went, slowed by reluctance and regret, trudging across bleached moss and stone, along winding rivers, under willow trees, arms wrapped around her ribs, gripping herself tight to contain the emptiness, the feeling that she'd been hollowed out. And, when at last Goldie spirited herself back to Earth, she left her imprint on the air. And she knew that her most essential part would stay behind; that her heart would always remain in Everwhere.

Liyana

It had taken a long time for Liyana to stop shaking: like a gazelle having escaped a lion, her limbs trembled until finally she was still. Kumiko had stayed on – though it'd meant a missed supervision and late essay, thus incurring the not insignificant wrath of Dr Skinner – and held her through the remainder of the night, whispering soothing words, stroking her shaking body.

In the morning, when at last Liyana slept, albeit fitfully, Kumiko rose and went shopping for mangos and strawberries and grapes. On her return she prepared a breakfast of homemade granola, yoghurt and sliced fruit, then slipped back into bed with a copy of Bede's *Ecclesiastical History* and waited for Liyana to wake.

*

'You're still here,' Liyana says, before she even opens her eyes.

Kumiko closes her book. 'Of course, what did you think?'

'I think . . .' Liyana smiles a sleepy smile. 'I think I can't wait till I wake up with you every day.'

Kumiko bends to kiss her. 'Are you hungry? I've made breakfast' – she glances at her watch – 'or rather, lunch.'

'You're an angel.'

'Are you . . .' Kumiko places a hand softly on Liyana's cheek. 'Are you okay? I don't know what happened last night, but you've been in a pretty bad state since. I've never seen you like that before. It was pretty scary.'

Liyana closes her eyes and slowly exhales as if blowing smoke. 'It was, I . . .'

'Don't,' Kumiko interrupts. 'You don't need to tell me anything, not till you're ready.'

So they sit together a while without speaking, Liyana nibbling slices of strawberry and Kumiko reading, but every now and then casting a watchful eye on her beloved.

Eventually, Liyana sets her bowl on the floor and snuggles down into the bed. 'Do you have a pencil handy?' She looks up at her girlfriend. 'And paper?'

Kumiko regards her over the top of her book. 'I've got pen and paper, will that do?'

Liyana nods. 'I was dreaming of a story; I need to write it down.' She speaks absently, as if the words aren't entirely her own. 'I think it's one of Goldie's, I think . . . it must have come to her and she meant to write it but couldn't yet . . . so it stayed in her thoughts and I heard it . . .'

When Liyana trails off Kumiko has to hold herself back from asking again what happened last night, since now she's worried about Goldie too. 'Okay,' she says, sliding out of bed and setting the *Ecclesiastical History* on the bedside

266

table in place of the notepad and pen, which she hands to Liyana. Then, on second thought, she passes her the book as well. 'Use this to lean on, and when you've finished perhaps you'd read it to me.'

The Tap-Tap

Once upon a time there was a girl who grew up under an assault of instruction. Everyone told her what to do. Her teachers told her what subjects to study, her friends told her what to wear and how to behave, her parents told her what career to follow, who to marry, how to live her life.

As the girl grew a fog formed around her, created by the breath of everyone who spoke, squealed or shouted these instructions. The fog soon became so thick that she couldn't see beyond or inside it. The fog muffled her heart and clouded her mind so that her own instruction was lost.

Sometimes the girl felt a stirring inside, as if her thudding heart was a finger tapping against her ribs trying to get her attention. It was a soft tap and only felt at awkward times, so she paid it no heed. Instead the girl listened to the loudest voices, those of her father and mother: the first insisting she be sensible, the second insisting she be safe.

As a woman, she married the first sensible man who asked. And, despite the tap-tap on her wedding day strumming so violently on her ribs that it nearly caused her to faint, still the woman managed to smile and say, 'I will'. She applied for a series of safe jobs and accepted the first she was offered, although her hand was shaking as the tap-tap echoed in her chest like a cacophony of screams.

The woman went to work every day and came home every night, and gradually the tap-tap grew fainter and fainter until, one day, she could hear it no more.

For many years the woman lived like that, trudging through the fog, never knowing in which direction she was heading; but still she kept walking. She went to bed with her husband and ate meals with him, though they had little to say. She had children and raised them. She was promoted. She ran marathons, not because she enjoyed them but to stay healthy. She went on camping holidays. She attended PTA meetings. She did all the things she was supposed to do. When her children sometimes asked what they should do in certain situations the woman could only tell them what she had been told: be sensible, stay safe.

One night, the woman dreamed that she was playing hide-and-seek with her daughters. She crawled under the bed, hid in the dark and listened to them calling her name, until their cries became shrieks and suddenly she was trapped in a box underground, scratching at the wood. She cried out, but she was buried deep beneath the earth and no one heard her screams.

The dream was so terrifying that when she woke the woman could not get out of bed, could only cower beneath the covers. She stayed that way for days, then weeks. Eventually, her husband called the doctor and when the doctor saw the woman she knew what was wrong.

'You're suffering from a sickness which I cannot cure,' she said.

'What is it?' The woman gripped the sheets. 'What's wrong with me?'

The doctor folded her arms. 'You're being plagued by a demon,' she said.

The woman stared at her, horrified.

'Do not worry.' The doctor raised a hand. 'The situation isn't as desperate as it sounds. I cannot cure you, but you can be cured.'

The woman exhaled and the doctor sat back. 'Let me tell you a story my *yiayiá* once told me which will explain your malaise. Many years ago, when the gods inhabited Mount Olympus, Hera, wife of Zeus, was bored waiting for her husband to return home from his latest affair, so one day she decided to beget a companion to comfort and entertain her. She pricked her finger, letting a drop of golden blood fall to the ground, then, adding her spittle, she breathed it into life. From this pure essence of life-force grew a creature which Hera named the "lumini". The lumini, it turned out, was endowed with the special gift of being able to create anything out of nothing, including itself. This kept Hera entertained yet it also meant that soon thousands of lumini were fluttering all over Mount Olympus. After a while the lumini grew bored and begged Hera to let them go down to earth and use their powers of creation on a new canvas. Eventually Hera consented, enabling the lumini to enter the spirit of a newborn baby at the moment of its first breath. As the baby grew the lumini acted as a guiding light to steer the individual towards its unique source of sheer delight.

'Now, if the individual follows the lumini's guidance then both are happy but, if the individual ignores the lumini and listens instead to the directions of others, and begins to veer off course, then the lumini grows discontent. If the individual ignores the lumini for too long, the lumini becomes angry and increasingly malevolent until finally it transforms into a demon and turns to berating the one it came to nurture, tormenting them until the end of their days.'

The woman slumped back, for now she understood why she felt such despair.

'But there's hope,' the doctor said. 'For a lumini can always return to its original form. If you start listening, then your lumini will start directing you again.'

The woman's eyes widened. 'But how?'

The doctor smiled. 'Well, you can't reignite your lumini from underneath your bedsheets. You must go out into the world, discover some of the infinite possibilities, so it can nudge—'

'But where should I go?' the woman interrupted, slightly panicked. 'What should I do?'

'I don't think it matters where you begin; if you're going in the wrong direction then the lumini can nudge you in the right direction. You only have to begin, to start exploring. The lumini are playful creatures; they like music and dancing, good food, nature, animals, children ... those are good places to start awakening them. But what a lumini loves above all is learning; that's the quickest way to discover the direction to the source of your own particular delight. It might direct you towards being a gardener, a doctor, a dancer, a poet, a painter, a sculptor, a teacher, a nurse ... You'll have to wait and see.'

For several moments the woman sat deep in thought.

Then, all at once, she threw off the covers, slipped out of bed and strode across the room. Since it would take some time to find her way she no longer wanted to waste more of it waiting.

The story flows out so fast that Liyana's fingers can't keep pace with her thoughts and the page, when she's done, is a scribbled mess. Slowly, she reads it over and when she's finished Liyana reads it to Kumiko.

'It's sad,' Kumiko says. 'Sad, but happy too. Do you think it's meant for someone?'

'I'm not sure.' Liyana folds the paper in half. 'Yes. Scarlet, I think.'

Kumiko nods, again resisting the urge to ask what happened last night. 'You could come back to Cambridge with me tomorrow and give it to her. If she's still staying with Goldie.'

'Yes,' Liyana says, her voice distant again. 'I should go. She'll need some looking after; they both will.'

Kumiko regards her. 'And who will look after you?'

Liyana shrugs. 'I'm fine.'

'You can stay with me.'

'Are you sure?'

'Of course.'

'But I don't want to be—'

Kumiko touches her hand to Liyana's cheek and leans forward until their noses touch. 'The last thing you'd ever be to me is a burden.'

Liyana smiles. 'All right then; as you wish.'

Kumiko kisses her, whispering, 'I love you too.'

Scarlet

She sleeps. For a night and a day Scarlet sleeps and dreams. She dreams to forget the past, to forgive what she's done, to accept what happened and understand that it was not her fault. She dreams to unsee some of the things she has seen and un-feel some of the things she has felt. She dreams to separate fully from the shadows and warm herself by the light of her own internal fire. She dreams to reclaim the parts of herself she'd lost and cleanse the parts of herself that were corrupted. She dreams to unbind from what has been so that she may breathe fully again. Until, second by sleepy second, creeping minute by eternal hour, Scarlet is very gradually, very carefully pieced back together.

When at last Scarlet wakes, she is her essential self again and also someone entirely new.

12th November

Goldie

For a full seven days after that night, Goldie sleeps as if she's been drugged: the desperate crash of the insomniac for whom waking is a reluctant drag from the depths of the luscious dark and into the cruel squinting light. And who, upon waking, feels as sluggish as if they'd never slept at all. As the days and nights pass, slowly, reluctantly, Goldie becomes aware – though whether it's a dream or reality she's not certain – that Teddy sits at her bedside, holding her hand, wiping her brow, whispering kindnesses and consolations and entreaties: *Please, speak to me. Please open your eyes, sit up. Please, come back . . .*

At the end of the week, though Goldie has still barely left her bed, she nibbles occasionally on slices of slightly burnt cold toast slathered with far too much butter and starts to talk to her brother. He, thankfully, had long since called the hotel to tell them she had the flu. She lets him hold her hand and gives him a weak smile whenever he meets her eye.

Whenever Goldie sleeps she dreams of Leo, though, without him there, she doesn't return to Everwhere. She decides she never will.

Liyana

'You don't like it?'
   'What? No, yes, of course I do.'
   'But . . .'

'I'm crying,' Scarlet says, 'because the story is so sad and because . . .' She wipes her eyes. 'Because I might have lived my whole life ignoring that tap-tap . . .'

Liyana reaches across the table to take her sister's hand. They're sitting at a corner table in Fitzbillies, two cold coffee cups and two untouched Chelsea buns on the table between them. 'You wouldn't,' Liyana says. 'We wouldn't have let you.'

Scarlet sniffs and shrugs. 'Maybe you couldn't have stopped me. I mean, you tried to tell me about him, and . . .' Her gaze falls to her stomach.

'When's the appointment?'

'Ten past two.'

Liyana lets go of Scarlet's hand but leans forward, dropping her voice to a whisper. 'Are you sure you don't want me to come with you?'

Scarlet shakes her head. 'I'll be okay, it's just to confirm the . . . state of things. I'm pretty sure it'll happen naturally; I won't have to go to hospital for a sweep or anything like that.'

'That's good,' Liyana says, thinking that she'd rather not see the inside of a hospital again if she can possibly help it. 'That's really good.'

'It's a relief.'

'You're not sad?'

'No.' Scarlet picks a sticky raisin from the Chelsea bun. 'I mean, not much. Sometimes I think I should be sad, you know? But that's just guilt, not—'

'You've got nothing to feel guilty for,' Liyana cuts her off. 'Nothing at all. If anything, it's people who keep procreating who should feel guilty. The last thing this imploding world needs is an ever-expanding population.'

Scarlet chews the raisin. 'Yes, yes, I suppose you're right.'

She falls silent. 'Goldie should publish those stories or something. And' – she nods at the intricate drawings curving along the margins of the page – 'you should illustrate them.'

The blurt of Liyana's bitter laughter turns the heads of several customers. She coughs and pretends to take a sip of cold coffee.

'You say that like it's easy,' Liyana mutters. 'Koko's always on at us to do the same, but I've looked into it and the market for short stories is pitiful, especially illustrated ones. And, before you ask, the demand for graphic novels isn't much better.'

Scarlet considers this. 'So, why don't you publish them yourself? I mean, Goldie could write and you could draw and then get them printed and sell them yourselves.'

'It'd be very expensive.'

'So, find another job and fund it.'

'No one would buy them.'

'How do you know?'

Liyana is silent. The truth is, though she's loath to admit it, she's scared. Scared of failure, of embarrassment, of humiliation. Of publicly trying something and failing.

'I disagree. It's not a failure, it's a first step. And – even if you didn't sell a single one – it's only humiliating if you think it so,' Scarlet says. 'Personally, I'd call it brave.'

Liyana gives Scarlet a wry smile. 'You read my mind.'

'I don't have to be psychic to do that.' Scarlet smiles back. 'I'm your sister, I know what you're thinking.'

Scarlet

'Well, I have good news.' Behind her desk, the doctor leans forward. 'The trauma you suffered did not rupture the sac, nor did it tear the placenta from the wall of the womb, which is always the fear in these cases. So, all being well, I see every probability that you'll be able to carry the foetus to term.'

Scarlet picks at a loose thread in her skirt, not looking up, waiting for the doctor's words to settle.

'I'm sorry. Is that not what you wanted to hear?'

Scarlet looks up. 'No, I – it's just not what I was expecting . . . I thought . . . when I bled, I just assumed that meant . . .'

'Early bleeding is not uncommon.' The doctor's face is impassive. 'It doesn't necessarily mean that the pregnancy has terminated.'

Silent, Scarlet plucks again at the thread. 'And if . . .'

The doctor glances at her computer screen. 'Yes?'

'If . . . if that was what I wanted,' Scarlet says, still not looking up. 'How might . . . what would I need to do?'

The doctor nods. 'Well, you're only at – what did we say . . . ?' She glances back to the screen. 'Less than ten weeks. So, it'll be a fairly simple procedure, local anaesthetic . . . You may experience some pain, a little excessive bleeding afterwards, but it shouldn't be any worse than a heavy period and won't last long. Nothing that a few Ibuprofen and a few days in bed won't cure.'

Scarlet considers this. She's grateful for the doctor's response, for the talk of simplicity and speed, for the very normalness of the thing. And Scarlet wants to feel normal again: light, unencumbered, unburdened. She's not ready for this gargantuan event. She wants to be young and carefree a while longer, wants to start living the life she's missed out on these past three years. She wants to do something for herself – the precious, singular self she has neglected for so long – to go back to college and cultivate her mind and ignite her spirit, to feel inspired and excited again.

Scarlet realizes, as she's thinking, that the doctor is speaking again. She blinks, returning her gaze to the doctor's face.

'Would you like me to schedule the procedure?'

Scarlet thinks, momentarily, of Eli and the potential of a baby; a baby she'd once thought she wanted so much. How easily the heart can trick the mind.

'Or . . .' The doctor remains impassive. 'Would you like more time to think about it?'

Would she? Scarlet wonders. Perhaps she should – wouldn't that be the sensible thing? But no, it would be a pretence. Scarlet knows what she wants, she has no doubts.

Walking out of the doctor's surgery and into the waiting room, Scarlet glances at a woman cradling a newborn baby. The mother's arms cocoon her daughter, but – and Scarlet wouldn't have noticed this before – her face is slack, her glazed eyes staring into the distance with a look of absolute exhaustion, edged with despair. Perhaps one day, Scarlet thinks, but not for a long while yet. And so she walks on, relief surging in her chest, along with a tentative sense of something approaching happiness.

Everwhere

Tonight, a dozen sisters gather. Excited nervous chatter rises and falls between them, talk of recent momentous events shaping the back and forth of every sentence. Finally drifting into silence, memories fading and conversation exhausted, they form a circle and wait.

When the clouds part and the unwavering moon illuminates the glade, the raven Bea settles on the branch of a silver birch.

Gaia is the first to speak. 'Will Goldie join us?'

I hope so.

'When?'

Give her time.

'What about Liyana and Scarlet?'

Soon. Bea swoops down to the ground. *Soon, I hope.*

13th November

Liyana

Liyana has risen at six a.m. – a time when she can be certain that the students in Kumiko's hall of residence (since none are rowers) won't disturb her in the shared kitchen – to tip a teacup filled with caster sugar into a saucepan. She switches on the stove then reaches for a long wooden spoon and stirs the sugar. As she stirs, Liyana hears the echo of Aunt Sisi's voice: *Slowly at first; as it melts, faster. Don't let it burn.* When the sugar becomes syrup, Liyana snatches the bag of peanuts with one hand and tips the contents into the saucepan. A few nuts spill and drop to the floor like a scattering of hailstones.

Quick. Stir like crazy. Faster now, faster.

Speeding up, Liyana thwacks the spoon against the sides of the pan, imagining she hears Sisi's chuckle: *All right, child, you've punished it enough now.*

She lifts the pan off the heat, scrapes the sticky syrupy peanut mixture into the tray, and pats it down with the spoon. When that's done, she peers suspiciously into the tray.

'Are you sure, Aunt Sisi?' Liyana asks, though she knows she won't get an answer. 'It doesn't look much like a cake.'

With a shrug, she sets the kettle to boil, retrieves the tea-cup, wipes it out, and drops a teabag – Earl Grey – into the cup. Aunt Sisi had advised that the type of tea didn't matter, but Liyana decided that a smarter sort of tea was surely bet-ter. She opens the freezer, removes a single sprig of mint from the sealed plastic bag and sets it atop the teabag. When

Liyana pours boiling water into the cup, a sharp, fresh scent rises, transporting her instantly back to her dream of Ghana and Lake Volta when a kitchen counter had, in that strange mutating way of dreams, materialized on the bank of the lake where Sisi had shown her what to do.

Don't hesitate too long or the cake will harden before you're able to cut it.

'Damn!' After scrabbling about for a knife in the drawer, Liyana slices quickly into the tray of Nkatie cake and puts three pieces onto a china plate. She carries the tea and cake to the tiny kitchen table, pulls out a chair and sits. Then she picks the mint leaf from the murky water, puts it in her mouth and chews.

Surveying the pieces of cake, Liyana chooses the largest and takes a big bite, swallowing quickly as she recalls her aunt's instructions: *The dead can't eat Nkatie cake, no matter how much they want to, so you must do it for them.*

Finishing the slice, Liyana fixes her attention on the tea-cup and the rising twist of steam. '*Ina godiya da albarka ga Mami Wata, kuna iya inganta sadarwa a yau,*' she mutters, and, deciding that it might be best to say it twice for luck, repeats: '*Ina godiya da albarka ga Mami Wata. Kuna iya inganta sadarwa a yau.*'

Then, just as Aunt Sisi had done in the dream, Liyana sits back in the chair and folds her arms, keeping her gaze fixed on the cup. When the steam doesn't take any shape but its own, Liyana reaches for a second piece of Nkatie cake and chews thoughtfully, hopefully. She holds the image of her aunt in her mind, mumbling a wish and a prayer.

Nothing.

'Please,' Liyana mutters. 'Please, I miss you.'

Nothing.

'*Please.*'

When another coil of steam rises from the cup, much to her astonishment Liyana finds that she can understand its form, can fathom signs in the shapes, as if the steam were a flag and she well versed in semaphore.

Liyana grins. '*Sannu, Dagā.*'

In response, a single spider's thread of steam reaches up as if wishing to touch the strip of fluorescent lighting.

'It's good to see you too,' Liyana says, still shocked and delighted. 'Sort of.'

The thread rises further, now stretching from cup to ceiling. It hangs in the air, lengthening, thickening, before collapsing back into the cup.

'Are you truly okay, Nya?'

Two spirals of steam lift slowly from the cup; pulling apart then weaving together like embracing snakes.

'You're not suffering anymore?'

The spirals evaporate and for a moment the air is still, the puddle of tea calm. Then a puff of steam lifts like a cloud and hovers in the air.

Liyana sighs. 'I don't understand.'

For a few minutes the air is once more clear and the steam from the tea takes no shape. Not knowing what else to do, Liyana takes the third piece of Nkatie cake and – since she's slightly nauseous now from ingesting so much sugar – nibbles at it tentatively, waiting. She fears that her aunt has disappeared, has ended the conversation as she often used to do in life, conveying her disapproval through disconnection. But, just as Liyana thinks the tea must now be cold, just as she's about to discard the rest of the sticky cake and push her chair from the table, another spider's thread of steam rises, then sinks to the table and reaches out to wrap itself around Liyana's left wrist like a bracelet.

In life, Nya Chiweshe rarely hugged her niece – Liyana

could count the number of times on the fingers of one hand – so the rare sensation of sinking into her aunt's arms, the solidity of safety and comfort, is still strong in her memory. And now, at the warm touch of the steam, she feels it again. Exactly as it had been.

I'm proud of you, my dearest daughter, so very proud.

Tears fill Liyana's eyes. Never had Nya used those words: Liyana had always been 'niece' and the aunt had never vocalized her pride, no matter how high Liyana's achievements.

'Thank you . . . *Dagā*.' Liyana watches as the bracelet of steam slowly thins and evaporates and with it the sensation of being held. She flicks her attention back to the teacup, in case Nya might say something else. She waits and hopes.

But now it is nothing more than a cold cup of tea.

Goldie

It's Teddy who opens the door.

'How is she?' Liyana asks.

'Better,' Teddy says. 'But I still can't get her off the sofa.'

Liyana thinks of her aunt. 'Don't worry.' She gives him an encouraging smile. 'The sofa is okay; the sofa is much better than the bed.'

'Yeah, I guess.' Teddy shrugs. 'Except that the sofa is her bed.'

'Right, of course.' Liyana curses silently to herself. 'I forgot.'

'Anyway, come in. Maybe you can drag her outside or something.' Teddy sighs. 'She says she's never going back to Everwhere.'

Liyana perches on the edge of the sofa, still wearing her coat, bag at her feet. She peers at her sister, who's pressed into the corner, legs drawn up to her chin, half hidden by a duvet.

'Are you eating?'

Goldie says nothing.

'You've lost weight,' Liyana says. 'You're skinny and pale.'

Teddy, who's standing in the kitchen beside the boiling kettle, raises his voice. 'She hardly eats anything.'

'It's fine,' Goldie mutters. 'I just, I don't feel well.'

'You must eat something,' Liyana says. 'I'll go out and get you some Chelsea buns.'

Goldie frowns.

'Or perhaps you can come with me? Scarlet's doing a trial shift in Fitzbillies today,' Liyana says. 'We could pop in and say hello.'

Goldie says nothing.

'All right then . . .' Liyana crosses and uncrosses her legs, then coughs. She glances over at Teddy. 'Is it hot in here, or is it just me?' Peeling off her coat and jumper, Liyana wipes her sleeve across her brow. 'Okay, well, I'll get the buns myself then, in a bit. But also, I brought you this.'

Dipping into her bag, Liyana draws out a folder and, opening it, pulls out a picture she places on Goldie's knees.

'I drew it for you. I thought perhaps you could write a story to go with it.'

'I don't write the stories like that.' Goldie's voice is heavy, dull. 'I don't create them, they come already created.'

'I know,' Liyana says. 'But maybe . . . Maybe you could, if you tried.'

Goldie says nothing, but doesn't take her gaze from the picture.

Scarlet

'Take two Chelsea buns to table six.'

Scarlet nods. 'I've just done it.'

'A latte and a flat white to table three.'

'I've done that too.'

'Two hot chocolates for—'

'Table thirteen,' Scarlet finishes. 'Done.'

'Wow.' The pretty girl with the elaborate and exquisite tattoos covering most of her visible skin, who Scarlet now knows to be Cat, regards Scarlet with awe. 'You're the best. Most trial shifts are a nightmare of burnt coffees, dropped cakes and forgotten orders, but you're a natural.'

Scarlet gives Cat a modest smile. 'Thank you.'

In her ten-minute 'cigarette' break, Scarlet stands in the courtyard scrolling through her phone. The scent of smoke still lingers in the air, the aftermath of Cat's Marlboro Lights, triggering the memory of Eli's screams. Shaking herself free from the violent, discordant sounds, Scarlet refocuses on the screen.

The air is chill and, at only half past three in the afternoon, nearly dark. Scarlet hates November. Autumn has shrivelled into winter, overcast and damp; the dusting of crisp sunset leaves on every pavement has become sodden under the constant mizzling rain, squelching underfoot, and night seems to swallow the day before it's truly begun.

Scarlet thinks, as she does virtually every November day, of Herman Melville who, in one particular passage from *Moby-Dick*, seemed to voice her feelings about the loss of autumn and the onset of winter better than anyone: *Whenever I find myself growing grim about the mouth; whenever it is a damp, drizzly November in my soul; whenever I find myself*

*involuntarily pausing before coffin warehouses, and bringing up
the rear of every funeral I meet; and especially whenever my
hypos get such an upper hand of me, that it requires a strong
moral principle to prevent me from deliberately stepping into
the street, and methodically knocking people's hats off—then, I
account it high time to get to sea as soon as I can.*

She smiles, for that passage always makes her smile, and
thinks of knocking off people's hats, supposing they still wore
them. She pauses to wonder if a smudge of the shadow still
marks her, but she thinks not, since – the odd mischievous
urge aside – Scarlet feels more herself than she has in years.
She has finally reclaimed the heart she'd foolishly given into
Eli's keeping; she will soon reclaim her body and in September
will reclaim her mind.

The notion of returning to college Scarlet finds both terrifying and elating. She'll be several years older than the other
students, and has no idea anymore how to write an essay or
pass an exam, and the likelihood of miserably failing everything is high. But the idea of learning again, of stimulating her
brain with new information, of discussing politics, of trying to
solve chemical equations, of critiquing *War and Peace*, fills
Scarlet with such excitement that she can hardly bear to wait
for the next ten months to pass and for it all to start.

When the timer beeps, Scarlet tucks her phone back in
her pocket, presses a heated hand to her chest to feel the
responsive swell of her heart, and walks back into Fitzbillies.

14th November

Goldie

She wakes sharply at 3.33 a.m. She's not groggy, not murky
with being wrenched from sleep too soon, but as bright and
awake as if she's just enjoyed a delicious ten hours of deep,
dark slumber. Sitting up, pulling aside her duvet, Goldie
sees Liyana's picture on the coffee table and, beside it, a
notebook and pencil.

For a long while she does not move, nor does she look
away. And then, at last, she picks up the notebook and
presses the pencil to the blank leaf. She cannot feel a story
demanding to be told, cannot hear the shouting of its sentences in her mind, the insistent pull of the pencil across the
page. Even so, Goldie gazes at the picture and begins to
write. She doesn't know what she's doing or where she's
going and yet, rather to her surprise, she does not find that
scary, but exciting.

The Boy Frozen in Ice

Once upon a time there was a little boy who lived happily with his mother and father until, one fearful winter
when he was eight years old, his father caught a sickness
and died. His mother, consumed by grief, no longer spoke
and only wandered the house at night like a ghost. The
little boy tried to talk to his mother but she could not
hear him. He tried to hug her but she could not hold
him. At his father's funeral the boy started to cry and,
when he could not stop, the priest sat beside him.

285

'No more of that,' he said. 'You must be brave, you're the man of the house now; your mother needs you to be strong.'

Sniffing, the little boy wiped his nose on his sleeve and nodded. He didn't entirely understand what the priest meant but he knew it was important and he must do it if he was to save his mother.

That night, though he tried to be strong, the boy couldn't stop his tears. Fearful of disturbing his mother, the boy left his bed and his house and went to hide in the woods. There he knelt and wept. The air was so cold that his tears became ice and fell to the ground like frozen rain. The boy cried so loud and long that he woke the witch of the woods, who had been sleeping in the crook of a nearby tree. At first the witch was angry, but when she heard the boy's story she took pity on him.

'I cannot bring your father back,' the witch said. 'For no magic can do that. But I can take away your pain.'

'Yes, please,' the boy begged.

'It will come with a price,' she warned.

'Please,' the boy said. 'I will pay it.' He did not ask what it was, nor did he care. He would pay any price not to feel this pain.

'Very well,' the witch said. And she cast her spell.

All at once, the boy felt his tears dry up and his heart, which had been raw and breaking, stop beating, becoming as frozen as the ground beneath his feet. His mind grew shrouded in a fog like the mists of the early morning, and he started to forget.

'Tonight your despair will be buried deep,' the witch said. 'And when you wake you'll be as strong and sturdy as an ancient oak tree.'

'Thank you,' the boy whispered. 'You have saved my life.'

'I have suspended your life,' the witch said. 'For while you will no longer feel sorrow, you'll also no longer feel joy – for they cannot exist alone. And no person, not even yourself, will be able anymore to touch your heart, or know your mind.'

The boy nodded, though in truth he barely heard the witch's warning, for already the merciful ice had spread and he was now as cold as the winter air.

Years passed and the boy grew. He took care of his mother and worked hard and became a wealthy man respected by all who knew him. He met many women but loved none. He lived alone with no companion except the dull ache of loneliness he carried with him everywhere he went. When at last his mother died he did not cry.

One day, quite by accident, the boy – grey-haired now and older than his father had ever been – was walking through the woods behind his house. He stumbled upon the witch sitting in the crook of her favourite tree, but, though she was unmarked by the years, he did not recognize her.

'How are you?' she asked.

'I'm fine,' he said, walking on.

'Are you certain?'

He was silent.

'I thought not,' the witch said. 'So, would you like to know happiness again, if it means you will also know sorrow?'

She watched while he, who had never really known happiness and could not remember sorrow, considered this question. He was strong, he thought, and clever. He could stand anything an old woman threw at him. Finally, he nodded.

'Very well then,' the witch said. 'I shall undo my spell.'

He waited.

'First I must warn you,' she said. 'The pain will be very great, but you can bear it. You might fear it will destroy you, but it will not.'

Starting to sweat, though it was a cool spring day, he feigned a shrug.

And so the witch thawed the ice from the boy's heart and cleared the fog from his mind. The pain came like a crack of lightning, felling the boy as an axe fells a tree. He dropped to his knees and howled like a maimed wolf. The boy shrieked with the despair that flooded his heart and the memories that swept into his mind; he wept and wept, begging the witch to take away the pain.

The witch did not answer but took him in her arms – though he was far bigger than she – and held him tight. 'Remember,' she said. 'It will not destroy you. It's only if you feel it that it will pass and you will finally be at peace. That is what will save you.'

And so the boy stayed. For hours, days, weeks, he lay curled in the witch's lap and wept. He wept so loud and long that spring flowers grew at his feet. Until, finally, one day he stopped. He lifted his head, wiped his eyes and gave a tentative smile. It was the first true smile since his father had died. When he found his feet and stood, he took his first faltering steps as a man, a man whose heart, having felt its sorrow, could now be filled with joy.

After a great deal of scribbling, much crossing out and a lot of rewriting, Goldie is done. And when she's read it once more she's in no doubt who this story is for.

15th November

Goldie

After showing her sister the story, Goldie is quiet for a long time, so long that Liyana starts to think she might have fallen asleep. Her chin rests on her knees, her eyes are closed. Still, Liyana waits.

'I . . .' Goldie lifts her head. 'I just don't want to say goodbye. And if I never go back I . . . I can pretend he's still there.'

'Oh, sweetheart.' Liyana slips an arm over her sister's shoulders. 'You don't have to say goodbye, you never have to say goodbye.' Softly, she strokes the curls of blonde hair. 'But . . . but I think you do need, one day, to return to this world and . . . live again.'

Goldie sighs.

'I'm not preaching,' Liyana says. 'I know I could do more of that myself. But I was thinking that perhaps . . .'

Goldie looks up. 'What?'

'Perhaps you could read your stories to our sisters.'

Goldie turns to Liyana, frowning. 'In Everwhere?'

'Yes.' Liyana drops her hand. 'Of course I'd come with you, Scarlet too. I think . . .' Liyana twists her fingers together in her lap. 'I think we should go back and join them again; we could be useful, we could be part of something . . . meaningful.'

On her left knee Goldie traces the lines of the red chequered pattern of her pyjamas. 'I don't think I'd be of any use to anyone right now.'

289

Liyana reaches for Goldie's hand. 'You underestimate yourself.'

Goldie shakes her head.

'Please.'

'I can't.'

'You can.'

'I can't.'

'You don't know that.' Liyana squeezes her sister's hand. 'Not until you try.'

Liyana

When Goldie falls asleep, Liyana picks up her story again and starts to draw . . .

The Return

Goldie is so slight, so sensitive, so raw – all nerve endings and open wounds – that everything is felt exceedingly acutely, as if seeing it all through a microscope, as if hearing it all through a megaphone. The snap of a twig underfoot is a crack of thunder. The beat of a raven's wing the gust of a gale, the blood rushing through her veins the roar of river rapids over rocks.

For a moment, Goldie stops walking.

A new noise. One she doesn't recognize. She cocks her head and closes her eyes to better hear it: thump-thump, thump-thump. She frowns. Her own heart is slow and loud: the dull thud-thud of a bass drum. This beat is fast and soft: the tap-tap of a snare drum. Just like—

But, no, it's impossible.

The beat of Goldie's heart quickens, speeding until the two drums are beating as one. She remembers then how they had stood together: nothing separating them, he inside her and she inside him, two liquids poured into a single glass, merging into a single being.

So – Goldie hardly dares hope – can it really be possible?

At that, she hears her sisters' laughter. Liyana's is the splash of sudden rainfall, Scarlet's the crackle of burning branches, Bea's the wind that whips through the leaves.

When are you going to start believing in the impossible, sister?

Goldie smiles.

You know what I tell them.

'Who?'

Our younger sisters.

'What?'

Listen to the whispers that speak of unknown things. Look for the signs that point in unseen directions to unimagined possibilities . . .

Goldie places her hand over her womb.

She waits.

Tap-tap, tap-tap.

A delighted, astonished grin spreads slowly across her face.

It has his heartbeat.

The Storyteller

Everwhere

It takes weeks for Goldie to find the necessary courage – even then she turns back several times – and it's only with the cajoling of Liyana and Scarlet, along with the judicious prodding of sharp twigs, that Goldie finally arrives at the glade where her sisters have gathered.

There are nearly a hundred women and girls sitting in concentric rows in a horseshoe around a squat sawn-off tree trunk upon which a raven is perched. When Goldie enters the glade, pushing through curtains of willow leaves and stepping onto a cushioned carpet of moss, every sister falls silent and the raven hops from the trunk onto a nearby stone.

Oh, the fuss! Anyone would think we'd suggested you do a strip tease, not read a story.

In response, Goldie mutters inaudible curses and, with a heavy air of resentment, she sits. After a few moments of calming her rapid heartbeat and wiping her brow, Goldie pulls a crumpled piece of paper from her pocket. Then, without once looking up into the crowd, she begins to read . . .

The Forbidden Forest

There once was a woman who had long hoped in vain for a child. Then, one day, she gave birth to a baby girl. When she held the girl in her arms, she wished that the child would suffer no pain for as long as she lived; such was the mother's fierce love for her child that the wish became an enchantment. A protective charm fell over the cottage and so long as the girl didn't stray beyond the gate at the end of the garden, she would be safe.

The little girl, having a mother who doted upon her and nothing else to vex her, passed her days in perfect contentment. She sat in the warmth of the hearth while the bread baked, picked posies of wildflowers and fell asleep every night curled in her mother's arms. The years passed and the older she grew the further the girl strayed from her mother's knee and the more she wanted to discover what lay outside the gate.

'You must stay here,' her mother said. 'Stay here and you will always be happy.'

For years the girl obeyed her mother, until she began to grow restless.

'I want to explore the world,' she said. 'I want to go into the forest.'

'No,' her mother said. 'Here you are safe; the forest is full of dangers.'

And so, not wanting to upset her mother or risk her life, the girl stayed. But she began to notice that her contentment was now edged with loneliness and longing. So, every night while her mother slept, the girl crept to the bottom of the garden and gazed out at the village, to the fields and the forest, and wondered what adventures might be found within them. She longed to open the gate and step beyond it, but every night she returned to the safety of her mother's arms.

One night, there was an old woman standing on the other side of the gate. 'What ails you, child?' she asked.

'I want to venture from this house,' the girl said. 'But I'm feared of the dangers and I don't want to lose my safety here and my happiness.'

The old woman shook her head. 'You do not have true safety here, nor true happiness. You are under a protective spell. It is only if you brave the forest and learn what lies within that you will know true happiness.'

The girl shook with fear, yet she also knew that if she passed the rest of her days without ever stepping beyond the garden, she would have lived only half a life. With great trepidation, she opened the gate.

When they reached the edge of the forest, the old woman readied herself to depart.

'Are you not coming with me?' the girl asked. 'I cannot go into the forest alone.'

'I have been through the forest many times,' the old woman said. 'I do not need to return; and you do not need me with you.' She bent down to the ground and picked up a small, smooth black stone. 'Take this with you in my stead.'

'Is it enchanted?' The girl took the stone. 'Will it protect me?'

'No, it is just a stone. But it will serve to remind you that nothing in the forest has the strength to destroy you,' the old woman said. 'You are stronger than everything you will encounter within.'

And so the girl bid the old woman goodbye and thanked her and, with the stone clutched tight in her fist, stepped into the darkness of the forest. Once inside, the girl wondered what she had feared, for the forest soon expanded into pretty glades full of wildflowers and clutches of white mushrooms that glistened in the moonlight.

Then she came upon a clearing at the centre of which lay a lake. The moonlight shimmered silver on the surface and, as it was a warm summer night, the girl decided to take a dip in the cool water. Removing her clothes, but keeping hold of the stone, she splashed headfirst into the pool. After a few moments, the girl felt a deep melancholy rise up within her and she started to cry. She wept and wept and, when she thought she had no more tears, still she wept. She feared that she would never stop crying, that she would dissolve into the water and disappear. She tried to swim to the bank, but water reeds wrapped around her ankles, pulling her down, while waves crashed over her head. Feeling herself to be drowning, the girl flailed. But as her throat filled with water, she remembered what the old woman had said and clutched the stone tight.

It cannot destroy me, she thought. I am stronger than this sorrow.

Slowly, the reeds unwrapped themselves from her ankles and she was free. As the girl swam to the shore she wept the last of her tears, the water holding and containing her until she reached the bank. The girl noticed, as she dressed, that she now felt as if she'd been purified, flushed clean of every feeling, leaving an infinite expanse of tranquillity.

Next, the girl came to a glade circled by ancient willow trees containing a roaring fire. When she saw the fire, she ran. But no matter where she ran or what direction she took, she always came back to the glade, until she realized that she would have to walk through it or else remain in the forest for the rest of her days. She noticed then that the trees themselves weren't ablaze; though the flames licked their trunks, engulfed their branches, the wood didn't scorch or blacken. And so the girl walked into the glade of fire and stood at the centre of its flames. As the fire ravaged her, the girl felt a murderous roar rise within her chest and feared she was about to be consumed. But she, like the stone, did not burn.

It cannot destroy me, she thought. I am stronger than this rage.

As the girl walked on she felt as if a small fire was still banked down inside her, dormant until it needed to rise again, rendering her luminous as if lit from within.

The final glade was smaller than the others; the girl had to squeeze through tight-threaded boughs and thorned bushes to pass through. Inside, the trees were pressed so close that their canopy of leaves blocked out all the light of the moon. The girl felt the crush of the trees closing in, thin-fingered branches reaching out to snatch at her hair, tear at her clothes, scratching at her skin, until they started to wrap around her body and squeeze out her breath. She clutched her stone.

It cannot destroy me, she thought. I am stronger than this fear.

With her last breath the girl exhaled a scream so loud that it cracked like lightning, splintering every branch and setting her free. Leaving the glade behind, the girl felt that every lurking shadow, real and imagined, had been swept away and she blinked in the light.

When the girl walked out into the fields the moon had faded behind the rising sun. When she glanced back, she knew that when she returned to the forest, the tears wouldn't drown her, the fires wouldn't consume her and fear wouldn't engulf her. A field of wildflowers stretched before her and the girl felt that she could reach into the sky, lift the sun like a cup and swallow its light.

She had endured the forest and she had survived.

After every sister has at last dispersed, Goldie remains in the glade with the raven perched on a nearby stone.

You see, not as bad as you thought.

Goldie shrugs.

Indeed, if I didn't know you better, I'd say you even started to enjoy it – right there towards the end – just a little bit.

'All right.' Goldie eyes her sister. 'Don't be so smug. No one likes a smartarse.'

It's fortunate then that I don't care what anyone thinks of me.

'So you say.' On her knee, Goldie smooths out the crumpled paper. 'But I reckon you're less impenetrable than you claim.'

Perhaps. The raven ruffles its feathers. *So, will you do it again soon?*

Goldie gives her sister a reluctant smile. 'Perhaps.'

What will you write next?

Goldie shrugs again. 'I don't know, I was thinking of trying a poem . . .'

Then I will leave you to it.

As her sister lifts from the stone and into the air, Goldie pulls a pencil out of her pocket and begins to write a poem for all her Sisters Grimm. For, even though their blood is special and their bodies are strong, she knows that their hearts are as fragile as anyone's. When that is done, Goldie begins another story, this one as a reminder for Scarlet and to warn other sisters against succumbing to a similar fate . . .

Bluebeard

Once Upon a Time there was a beautiful blue-skinned girl. Every man in the kingdom wanted to marry her. When she was ready to take a husband, she consulted the wise woman who lived in the forest.

'There are two types of husbands,' the witch told her. 'Those who are sure and settled, and those who are always running and will never settle. Be certain that you know the difference between the two.'

'And how will I know?'

'You will feel it,' the old woman said. 'All men make promises, but when you're with ones who'll keep them you'll know it. The company of a man on the run is a lonely sort of shelter, seemingly strong as any other but unstable at its centre and soon to be snatched away by the winds.'

'But, what if . . . ?' The girl worried that she would not be able to tell the difference between the two types of husbands. 'How can I be certain?'

'When you know the truth of yourself,' the witch said, 'then will you know the hidden truth of another. You will feel those who are like you and those who are not.'

'And how do I do that?' the girl asked. 'How do I know myself?'

'Ah.' The witch smiled. 'Well that takes courage. You must be willing to sit in silence, to cultivate stillness and solitude. You must be willing to meet yourself and most people are too scared of what they'll find to do that. Be brave and you will be rewarded with the most valuable knowledge of all, that upon which all else will be determined.'

The blue-skinned girl listened to the old woman and nodded. She was not at all sure she knew the truth of herself, nor that she had the courage to find out, but still she wanted to marry. She tried to wait, to sit with herself in silence and cultivate solitude, but she soon grew impatient. And instead she devised another test to determine the worthiness of prospective husbands.

So, the blue-skinned girl tested each suitor for strength, agility and prowess, until at last, itching with impatience, she made her choice. He was handsome – with a full beard of a glorious blue that perfectly

300

complemented her skin – and kind and seemed as settled as any man might be. She told her suitor that she required only one thing from him: fidelity. He must never love, never speak to, never set eyes on another woman. Her suitor, certain that the blue-skinned girl was the most beautiful in any kingdom, readily agreed. Pleased, the blue-skinned girl set about giving her husband everything he could ever want to make him happy. She kept his bed warm and his belly full. Her husband was happy, surely the happiest man in any kingdom. He had everything his heart had ever desired: love and riches.

But, as time passed, he grew restless. He started to think that, though he'd never seen them, perhaps there were in the world more beautiful girls with even lovelier eyes and even bluer skin. He wondered, he itched with wondering, until he could do nothing but try to discover the truth. And so, one night, he crept out to find out for himself.

The husband searched and searched, knowing he had to be back before dawn, lest his lovely wife discover his betrayal. And yet, those few hours would not give him time to see all the girls in all the kingdoms asleep in their beds. As the sun started to lighten the sky, the husband wavered. He must go back, or his wife would know and he would be caught. And yet, he could not.

Three weeks passed until he at last returned.

His wife was waiting for him.

'Well,' she said. 'Did you find her?'

'Who?' he said, as he dismounted his horse.

'A woman more beautiful than I,' she said.

He tried to deny it. He tried to claim that he'd been fighting dragons and waging wars. But, under the glare of her gaze, he could not. Instead, he shook his head.

'No,' he said. 'I did not.'

The blue-skinned girl nodded. 'I told you that you would not.'

He stepped towards her. 'Now I am ready to come home,' he said. 'Now I know the truth.'

'No,' she said. 'You cannot. You have broken your vow and now you are banished.'

He begged. He pleaded words of love and remorse, words that brought the sun from behind the clouds and coaxed the flowers to bloom in the gardens. When he finally fell silent, the blue-skinned girl thought a moment, then shook her head.

'Leave,' she commanded. 'Go and spend the rest of your life seeking that which you will never find.'

After that, the blue-skinned girl became patient. She began to cultivate the life of stillness, silence and solitude that the witch had recommended. Years passed as she began to uncover the multitude of truths hidden inside herself and as she did so, she discovered that she now knew as soon as she sat down with another whether they'd had the courage to meet themselves too or whether they were still running.

The blue-skinned girl befriended the first sort. As for the second, she let them run. And then she returned to being with herself, which was, she had discovered, the very best place to be.

The End

Acknowledgements

This novel being a sequel necessitates me thanking all the same people again – to which, having gushed so effusively at the end of the first book, and not wanting to embarrass anyone with an excess of feeling, this time I will offer my thanks in a terribly British and understated way. Thusly, deepest thanks (again) to the following: Simon Taylor, Beci Kelly, Tom Hill, Lilly Cox (for the first time), Elizabeth Dobson and Vivien Thompson. Also, Frances Rutherford and Ed Wilson. Extra thanks to Viv for holding everything till the 11th hour and to all those on social media who jumped in to help out with the Latin! – Laurie (agent extraordinaire) and her genius cousin Lily, Paige, Janelle, Anita, Dave, Alan, Siren. And especially Victoria Jones.

Extra thanks to Alastair Meikle for the phenomenal illustrations and to Naz Ekin Yilmaz for the marvellous map. And to the real-life Cat for bringing me endless hot chocolates and Chelsea buns.

Continual thanks, as always, to those dear friends who do what us writers need and appreciate so much: ask after the latest novel, offer to read early drafts, read and say nice things about the published book, attend launches and events, and buy extra copies (unexpected and probably unwanted) for their own friends. I notice all this and am always deeply touched and grateful for it. Thank you, you all have my heart: Virginie (for listening and loving so deeply), Al Jago (for excessive kindness), Ash (keeper of the flame), Emily (especially this time for reading and encouraging when I needed it most), Ova (for asking so often and caring so much), Ruth (my baking fairy), Sarah W (for so generously promoting), Anita (for always making me laugh), Natalie (loveliest student and now friend), Steve (for that day in the café and many subsequent ones), Natasha (hope you like your cameo), Tanya and Ella (family and friends both), Katrin (beautiful art and beautiful smile), Naz and Laurence (who've both taught me so much), Kelly Jo (for foisting SO many copies of my books on the unsuspecting), Amanda (my fellow witch), Alice R (I love and miss our bookish chats), Dave (for all the doughnuts), Jo (for asking for the next book and, of course, the cakes), Amy (for being there and looking fabulous), Clara (I miss your cake deliveries and you), Ella (artist extraordinaire), Rachel (for kind and encouraging words), Emma (I look forward to our next slice of cherry pie), Steve (for all the postcards), Gemma and Thierry (for never missing an event), Alex G (so glad MM&C brought you into my life), Helen (for always staying in touch and reading every book), Miriam (ditto), Al P (double ditto), Lizzie (another sticky bun soon please), Roopali (your last note touched me), Kristina (travelled far but never forgotten), Barn (always late but always there), Vin (for the visits and excellent recs) and Tony (I know these ones aren't for you, but you've not given up on me). You've all been, and continue to be, generous, lovely and amazing. Thank you!

And, of course, to my beautiful and brilliant family, who do all of the above and more, without whom my life would be so much smaller and dimmer: Artur, Oscar and Raffy, Mum and Dad, Jack and Mattie, Idilia, Christine, Fatima and Manuel.

About the Author

Menna van Praag has lived in Cambridge all her life, except when she was studying at Oxford University. She is the author of seven novels including the acclaimed *The Sisters Grimm*.

Books By
Menna van Praag

"Van Praag braids mystery, magic, and a vicious hunt for power into a dark, delicious story of four estranged, supernatural sisters."

—*Publishers Weekly*

Night *of* Demons *and* Saints

All Hallows' Eve meets All Saints' Day in critically acclaimed author Menna van Praag's mesmerizing second book featuring the Sisters Grimm—a dark, contemporary fantasy that skillfully blends love, obsession, and dark magic.

The Sisters Grimm

The critically acclaimed author of *The House at the End of Hope Street* combines love, mystery, and magic with her first foray into bewitching fantasy with a dark edge evocative of V.E. Schwab and Neil Gaiman.

DISCOVER MORE AUTHORS, EXCLUSIVE OFFERS, AND MORE AT HC.COM.
HarperCollins*Publishers*

HARPER Voyager
An Imprint of HarperCollinsPublishers